Circles

Doris Mortman

BANTAM BOOKS
Toronto • New York • London • Sydney

CIRCLES

A Bantam Book / June 1984

ISBN 0-553-23983-X

Published simultaneously in the United States
and Canada

Bantam Books are published by Bantam Books, Inc. Its
trademark, consisting of the words "Bantam Books"
and the portrayal of a rooster, is Registered in U.S.
Patent and Trademark Office and in other countries.
Marca Registrada. Bantam Books, Inc., 666 Fifth Avenue, New York, New York 10103.

PRINTED IN THE UNITED STATES OF AMERICA

H   0 9 8 7 6 5 4 3 2 1

TO DAVID,
WHO FILLS MY LIFE
WITH LAUGHTER & LOVE

WITH GRATEFUL THANKS to: my friend Phil Liebowitz, my agent Peter Lampack, and my editor Linda Grey. Without them, this book might have remained an unfulfilled dream. Special thanks to my children, Lisa and Alex, for their unconditional enthusiasm and support.

One

Jennifer Cranshaw's office resembled a Broadway rehearsal hall. Long-limbed models were everywhere: slouched against walls, sitting cross-legged on the floor, doing exercises in the corner, or lounging in the doorway drinking coffee from Styrofoam cups. All attention was centered on Jennifer, who was patiently instructing a tall redhead in denim overalls and a T-shirt.

Jennifer removed her burgundy mohair jacket and dropped it on the nearest chair. Placing her left hand on the gentle curve of her hip, she shifted her weight, lowered her right shoulder, assumed a theatrical pose, and threw back her head. Then, with the grace of a dancer, she glided across the floor, her slender legs peeking through a slit in her skirt. Her trim body swayed provocatively, moving in time to an imaginary beat, her mauve silk blouse rippling as she walked. When she had reached her desk and resumed her normal posture, she was greeted by a spurt of enthusiastic applause.

It was three days before the *Jolie* party—a grand celebration of the magazine's fortieth anniversary—and Jennifer was making her final selections for the fashion show she was staging as part of the evening's festivities. Her present concern was Coral Trent. The young model was obviously nervous. After explaining once again the movement she had just demonstrated, Jennifer left Coral in the care of *Jolie*'s models' editor so she could zero in on the others. She switched on a disco tape and, directing each woman with hand signals, indicated stops and turns and do-it-agains with long, expressive fingers.

In a few days, twelve hundred people would descend on Cloud 9, New York's famous see-and-be-seen disco, to honor the magazine. As promotion director, Jennifer was in charge of monitoring every detail from the spectacular fashion retrospective, to coordinating guest lists, hiring entertainment, supervising menus, and insuring ample press coverage. As other projects piled up on her desk, temporarily ignored, she tried to balance her anxiety with her genuine anticipation of the event. Jennifer took pride in the fact that she had never missed a deadline. She was determined to maintain that record.

Three leggy blondes strode across the room in time to the music, hoping to attract her attention with the hip gyrations and bumpy dance steps of the fifties. Jennifer encouraged them to continue while she located her countdown sheet and scanned it for last-minute chores.

"Meet with caterer: 3 P.M." She jotted "hors d'oeuvres" next to his name, reminding herself to check on the current price of caviar. Brad Helms, *Jolie*'s publisher, had insisted on caviar and champagne, but with an already overstretched promotion budget and a worrisome decline in ad revenues, Jennifer had decided to exercise caution first and worry about Brad later.

"Call florist!!" Jennifer motioned for the three young hopefuls to take a break, signaling for a round-faced brunette named Uta to settle herself in Jennifer's large bergère desk chair as she dialed Vincent Matteo, the floral darling of the Park Avenue set and the man she had commissioned, with a small amount of trepidation, to do the flower arrangements for the party.

Mimi Holden, Jennifer's secretary, arrived carrying a wicker tray stocked with an assortment of eyelashes and black eye pencils. Tucking the phone in the crook of her neck, Jennifer took a tweezers and gripped a stiff eyelash between the metal tips. Like a well-trained operating room nurse, Mimi slapped a small tube of adhesive into Jennifer's free hand, watching carefully as Jennifer spread a wiggly white line on the edge of the lash, then slid it onto the model's eyelid, centering it, gently pressing it to the soft skin, fitting it to the natural lash line.

While she waited for Vincent, she cautioned herself against impatience. Her initial encounter with the florist had been just shy of combative. She suggested and he demanded. She mentioned price. He dismissed it. She wanted a contract. He preferred the honor system. Jennifer had prevailed, but it had required delicate handling to effect a tentative friendship.

She had the second eyelash trapped in the tweezers when his high-pitched voice attacked her ear.

"Jennifer Cranshaw?"

"Yes, the very same." She spread the gooey white paste along the fringe and wiped the excess off with her finger. "From *Jolie* magazine. You're doing a job for us this Thursday?"

"Jennifer. Of course. Forgive me. I'm glad you called. I don't know how to tell you this, but the big glass beakers for the lilies are out."

The second lash was in place. Jennifer stood back, squinting to be sure they were even, and counted to ten.

"Out? Why?" She selected a pitch black kohl pencil from the tray.

"Because they're tacky."

"Tacky? A month ago they were *the* most outrageous things you'd ever seen."

"I had a dream."

"You had a *what?*" Jennifer paused for a second to absorb what he had said, and then continued drawing thick black lines in a semicircle beneath Uta's lids.

"A dream, darling. I saw lilies in baskets. There they were, floating before me. Bunches and bunches of fabulous lilies in the most marvelous baskets. The colors were simply divine, and the effect, well, my dear, it was nothing short of drop dead! I knew then that the beakers were wrong, wrong, wrong."

"Did you?" Her voice reverberated with controlled anger.

"Glass is, well, too obvious. Baskets are warm. Subtle. Sort of cozy, don't you think?"

"Vincent, this is not a picnic. This is an elegant evening hosted by a major fashion magazine."

She could hear him sniveling.

"Vincent, are you listening to me?"

"You're treating me like a child, Jennifer."

"You're whining like a child," she said, struggling to keep the phone steady while she applied the lower lashes. "We agreed on huge glass beakers overflowing with prize lilies, and that's what I want."

"But I don't like it anymore."

"But I do!" Jennifer took a deep breath, standing back

to admire her handiwork and restraining an urge to shout at the man on the other end of the phone. "I know you're trying to give us the best job possible, and I appreciate the fact that you've explored other avenues, but your first instinct was lilies under glass. It was brilliant! Why tamper with genius?"

After a few minutes' deliberation, Vincent agreed. "Glass beakers it shall be."

Mimi responded to the frustrated look on Jennifer's face with a sympathetic laugh.

"That man will be the death of me. If his work weren't so extraordinary, I'd kick him out on his diamond-studded ear!"

"You pays your money and you takes your choice," Mimi said, replacing the cap on the eyelash adhesive.

Jennifer nodded and continued to experiment with a short, asymmetrical wig she had placed on Uta's head.

"Voilà!" She helped the model to her feet and presented her dramatically to everyone in the room.

The girl had been magically transformed into an exact duplicate of Peggy Moffett, the doll-faced model with the Sassoon hairdo who had helped rocket Rudi Gernreich to fame during the late sixties. As Mimi watched Jennifer lead the young woman over to the window where Hilary West, the models' editor, was auditioning newcomers, she marveled at Jennifer's unbridled energy. She was gesturing excitedly, making large sweeps with her arms, pausing only to readjust the wig. The sun was getting stronger, and Mimi noticed the way the light played with Jennifer, spotlighting her own brightness. Jennifer's hair was a flurry of titian waves, brown kissed with coppery strands that glinted in the sun with a reddish henna'd glow.

Even now, Mimi thought, with all that was going on, Jennifer appeared to tower over everyone else by comparison. A dynamo in a petite package, Jennifer had the fervor of a top-ten coach. Where her penchant for excellence intimidated others, it inspired Mimi. They had only worked together for two years, but Mimi considered Jennifer a friend and an idol. If anyone could pull off this circus on Thursday night, Jennifer Sheldon Cranshaw could. What's more, Mimi knew she would do it with tremendous style!

Jennifer returned to her desk and eased herself into the wide-bottomed chair, trying to avoid the sharp twinge stinging her lower back. Mimi handed her a cup of coffee and then some advertising proofs. Jennifer studied the ads, and marked her corrections in the margins.

"When you drop these off in the Art Department," she said, checking her countdown sheet again, "would you ask Patrick Graham to come in? I think I need help."

As Mimi headed for the door, a photographer and his assistant weaved their way toward Jennifer.

"Albert, you're so late, I was sure you had found a better job." There was more tease than temper in her voice.

"What could be better than working for you?" Albert handed his camera bags to his assistant. "But enough chitchat. How about a few snaps of the eminent Mrs. Cranshaw at work?"

"You have enough of me," Jennifer said. "Concentrate on the staff, the models, and whatever editors you can find. Also, make sure you get a couple of shots of my secretary. That poor girl has run herself ragged, and I'd like to see her get some recognition."

Albert grabbed his Nikon, spoke to his assistant in Italian, and then went to work. As Jennifer looked on, the two men stalked the room, shutters clicking. Only one of the cameras was loaded, and even Jennifer didn't know who was holding the loaded camera. Every once in a while, they switched and then switched back again. That way, they eliminated posing and posturing, framing people in natural, unaffected pictures. It was, she supposed, what made Albert's work so magical.

"What can I do?" Patrick Graham, *Jolie's* art director, had taken a seat near Jennifer, a cigarette dangling from his mouth.

"You can play Bert Parks. I'm having trouble choosing the last few models, and I've decided to take advantage of your outstanding judgment."

Pat screwed his boyish face into a skeptical grimace. "How many models do you need, and what are you looking for?"

"Seven and lots of expression. No blank faces or limp bodies. I booked all the big names months ago. Yasmine, Brinkley, Chin, Cleveland, Iman, and I don't even remember who else. But I need thirty altogether. These girls are from the runway agencies. Strictly shows. No magazine experience and no TV. They're good, but I want the best of the lot."

"Isn't Hilary handling this?"

"She is, but it's a big job, time is running out, and I'd feel better if you'd help."

"Your every wish is my command." Pat put out his cigarette and went to the opposite end of the room where Hilary stood surrounded by eager mannequins.

"Jennifer?" The photographer was coming toward her. "Your secretary seems to be a bit camera shy. She refuses to have her picture taken. I can't understand it, since she is one foxy-looking lady, but Giancarlo and I have wasted two rolls of film on the back of her head already. What gives?"

Jennifer looked for Mimi, but she was nowhere to be found.

"I don't know. I told her we might use some of these shots for a feature in an upcoming *Jolie*. I thought she'd get a kick out of having her parents see her in the magazine. If she's uptight, though, let it go. You'll catch her at the party."

Albert saluted and went back to work. Jennifer picked up the morning newspapers and began to check for press coverage on the party. She found a small blurb in *Women's Wear Daily*, circled it with a red grease pencil, and turned to *Fashion Report*.

FR was the Gideon of ladies' fashion, the indispensable trade paper for the nation's fourth largest industry. Manufacturers of everything from thread to furs looked to the *Report* for design trends, market swings, buying patterns, technical innovations, and inside information on their competitors. Retailers scoured the pages for sources producing merchandise that might prove appealing to their clientele. Designers sought inspiration as well as recognition for their current lines. Display directors searched for unique ways of decorating windows and interiors. And everyone read the fiscal reports. No one, whether chain store or specialty shop, couture designer or schlock house, could afford not to read it.

Usually, Jennifer studied the paper thoroughly, but today she flipped immediately to the gossip section. She scanned a few articles, hoping to catch a plug for the party. It disturbed her that there wasn't one. Just as she was making a note to call her contact at the *Report* and request something in the next edition, her phone rang.

"Mrs. Cranshaw? This is Mr. Helms's secretary. He'd like you to come to his office immediately."

The other woman's voice was grave and insistent. Something was seriously wrong. Brad rarely called unscheduled meetings, and he wasn't the type to invent a crisis.

"I'll be right there!" Jennifer practically ran out of her office.

Two

I f Bradford Adamson Helms had been born into a less prestigious family, he probably would have been a much happier man. Helmses, however, always knew what was required of them. They wintered in Palm Beach, summered in Southampton, and never had less than a full paragraph in *Who's Who*. By comparison to his illustrious clan, Brad Helms appeared ordinary. He had graduated from Dartmouth. A brief apprenticeship at the family bank had ended with Helms Senior declaring Brad unsuited for the world of finance. Brad did not disagree. Although gifted with a keen mind, it didn't take him long to discover that his movie-star good looks and his charm were his best assets. They had won him the publisher's seat at *Jolie*. And Ivy Calder.

In retrospect, Brad supposed that what he had felt for Ivy in the beginning was love. After all, she had been debutante of the year, sought after by every eligible young man, heartily approved of by his parents. At the time, it appeared to be the perfect match. Too soon, he found that his beautiful bride was carved from ice. For ten years he had endured her frigidity. Five years ago, he had begun to seek alternatives. He was discreet, taking great pains not to entangle himself in sticky affairs, but not discreet enough.

Now, Ivy was suing him for divorce, threatening to splash his adulterous behavior all over the newspapers. She was determined to extract from him everything she could. Brad didn't mind the monetary demands. His bank account could more than support her greed, but she had obtained a court order restricting him from seeing their children. On advice of counsel, Brad had been leading an exemplary, albeit celibate, existence, willing to do anything to prove himself a worthy father. He knew his situation was tenuous. Simple revenge was not enough for Ivy. She was watching every move he made, looking for that one slip that would assure her a total victory.

Brad's eyes wandered about his office. It was palatial, lined on two sides with generous expanses of window, picture-framing a glorious view of upper Lexington Avenue. At his request, the two inside walls had been paneled with natural cedar planking, recreating the wooded ambience of a luxurious Vermont ski lodge. Despite its size, the room was splendidly snug. Long, mahogany leather couches provided the major seating areas, the dark brown color repeated in a plush, umber, wall-to-wall carpet. The chairs he had selected stood on cylindrical ash stumps, the backs and bottoms upholstered in stretched antelope skins. Over one couch, a collection of animal horns formed a three-dimensional collage, with sharply tipped spikes and spirals reaching out over the heads of visitors. On the opposite wall hung an enormous Navaho rug.

As he studied his surroundings, a chill seeped into his body. Was it possible for Ivy to take this from him too?

"They're here, Mr. Helms."

Brad's secretary, Clara, stood at the door, waiting for a nod from her boss before allowing anyone in. At his signal, she stepped aside. Jennifer entered first, followed by Gwendolyn Stuart, the editor-in-chief, and Terk Conlon, *Jolie*'s sales director.

"Where's Brooke Wheeler?" Brad asked.

"Miss Wheeler is out ill today," Clara said, closing the door behind her.

"What's the emergency?" Gwen Stuart had positioned

herself directly in front of Brad's desk, sunglasses anchored on top of short dark hair. She had just returned from Paris and was resplendent in total Sonia Rykiel, from the soft, dove-gray sweater poufed at the shoulders to the narrow knit skirt slit to the knee. "And why isn't the executive editor here? Or the fashion editor, for that matter?"

"Because I have made a very important decision, and right now, I don't care to discuss it with anyone other than top-level personnel." Brad's tone negated further questioning.

Terk and Jennifer settled into chairs alongside Gwen, who tapped her fingers on her purse, her eyebrows arched in anticipation.

"I'd like to read a little item from this morning's edition of *Fashion Report*," Brad said, holding the newspaper in his hands as if gripping a hymnal.

'Mag in the bag. The rumor mills are working overtime on the story about the unknown money man interested in a young woman. Young woman's magazine, that is. The story goes that he's hot to get into the rag mag game. Is FP going to give him the business? Or vice-versa?'

He put the paper down and tried to assess reaction. Gwen continued to tap her fingers. Terk remained expressionless. Only Jennifer registered any emotion. She appeared shocked, looking first at Brad and then to her own copy of *Fashion Report*. There it was, a short paragraph taunting her from the bottom of the very page she had been reading. "FP" stood for Fellows Publications, parent company of *Jolie*. She understood immediately why Brad had called an emergency meeting.

"According to this," Brad continued, "a young woman's magazine is up for grabs. A friend of mine at *FR* fed me this tip a few days ago, but he couldn't confirm or deny anything. No one in the corporate sector here seemed to know anything about it, and if they do, they're not saying. What we do know is that our numbers are grim and anything's possible."

"Maybe they're talking about *Allure*," Terk Conlon said.

"Doubtful." Brad shook his head. *Allure* was the other young women's magazine under the Fellows flag. "Their readership figures currently outpace us by several millions. Our circulation plus pass-alongs adds up to slightly less than four million readers. They're at a solid six and climbing. We both belong to the same parent, but they're making money and we're not. It's not too farfetched to imagine one of us becoming an orphan."

"I don't see how we can stop the Fellows family from selling," Conlon said. "And maybe new management would be a good thing."

"I don't happen to agree with you on either point." Brad's dislike of Terk crept into his voice. "If there's a sale, it could mean a total reorganization of the staff—and I wouldn't like to see that happen." *Because I'd be the first to go,* he thought ruefully. "But I think we *can* stop it," Brad continued. "If a drop in sales is the problem, and I believe that it is, we have to counterattack with a plan that will give us an instant, dramatic boost. I've devised such a plan. Instead of doing our regular April issue featuring active sportswear, we're going to dedicate the entire issue to Hawaii."

"That's the most absurd thing I've ever heard!" Gwen reacted instantly. "I don't care if we're being auctioned off on public television, dedicating an issue to one state is boring enough, but Hawaii makes no sense whatsoever!"

Jennifer's gut reaction had been much the same as Gwen's, but it wasn't Jennifer's habit to dismiss anything until it had been thoroughly discussed.

"Brad," she said, cloaking her objections in a delicately phrased question, "why did you decide on Hawaii? Was there any specific reason for that particular choice?"

Brad couldn't tell from her voice whether Jennifer was for or against his idea, but he needed her as an ally. He swallowed his belligerent feelings toward Gwen and answered Jennifer.

"For months, I've listened to our resident fashion authorities predict that the tropics will be a major design influence. Hawaii is America's tropical paradise. Why not be the first to play it up? California has been done to death, and Florida doesn't have the mystique to launch a fashion trend."

Jennifer still wasn't convinced, but she shared Brad's urgent need to do something to prevent *Jolie* from changing hands.

"I'll need total editorial coverage," Brad was saying. "Every department will be involved. College and Careers should evaluate jobs on the island, as well as the universities. I want articles on food, drinks, diets, furniture, and, of course, fashions."

"Brad, *darling*." Gwen's hostility was always easily measured by the affectation in her speech. The more contrary she felt, the more British she became—no easy feat for a girl from Brooklyn.

"You have a problem, Madame Editor?" Brad asked, a sour grimace washing across his face.

"No, Monsieur Publisher, you do. I've just returned from Paris, and I don't recall hearing even the slightest mention of muumuus for summer."

Her sarcasm angered Brad.

"Somehow, I don't think you've fully grasped the situation, Gwendolyn. Your finely clothed bottom is as much on the line as anybody else's. If this magazine bellies up, your Charles Jourdan shoes are going to pound plenty of pavement, so I'd suggest you give this project your all."

Gwen harnessed her fury. She detested being told what to do with her magazine, particularly by Brad Helms. When pushed, Gwen might acknowledge that she fell short of being the best in the business, but over the years she had been successful more often than not, and she steadfastly believed she knew more about what sold at the newsstand than Bradford Helms. Indignation was etched on her face, but Brad had turned his attention to Jennifer.

"I want to support this issue with more in-store promotions than we've ever done," he said, making notes as he spoke. "I know that's Brooke Wheeler's province, but you, Jennifer, will have to team up with her for some imaginative ideas—hula dancers, flame throwers, something really exotic. I also want mailing pieces and ads to hit the trade. Plus, I think a big bash in the showroom would help pry some advertising out of those short-pockets in the rag business. Don't even think about budget."

Brad's enthusiasm was building. It was obvious that he had every intention of steamrolling his idea through. Jennifer felt compelled to brake the momentum with a dose of reality.

"I'm sorry, Brad," she said, "but we have to think about budget. This party has stretched us to the breaking point. We don't have a penny to spare."

Terk Conlon had been sitting in bemused silence. Something in Jennifer's posture and her voice caused him to turn and look at her. He noticed how her lithe body changed from sensuous to purposeful with a gentle shrug of her shoulders. He had seen that pose before, and he knew she had something to say that would be worth listening to.

Brad had noticed also. He hoped for unquestioning support. He anticipated honest opinion.

"I've been concerned for a long time about the reversal in leadership which now places *Allure* firmly ahead of *Jolie*, and I agree that drastic measures are called for." Jennifer's voice was soft, but firm. "I'd like to offer a suggestion. I think we should charge a fee for the April promotion."

Gwendolyn Stuart began to sputter. "Brooke Wheeler would faint if she heard you say that. We've never charged a fee for promotions. Our live events are always free, compliments of the magazine. I couldn't go along with that, and I'm sure Brooke won't either. It's unheard of. It's never been done before!" Her face was flushed, pinking her normally pale complexion.

"I understand your concern, Gwen," Jennifer said. "But we've never been in this position before. The fact is, we can no longer afford to pick up the tab."

"It's positively demeaning." Gwen turned to Terk for approval. His eyes were still focused on Jennifer. "It's so déclassé. Don't you think we're above that sort of thing?"

Jennifer pivoted toward Gwen. "When one is down, one is not above anything," she said. "Besides, it's all a matter of interpretation. You see this as a last-ditch effort. I view it as a sign of absolute confidence."

"It's begging," Gwen insisted.

Jennifer was enjoying the interchange.

"To help put this into perspective," she said, "let's examine the Gucci school of salesmanship. They close their doors during lunch hours, the peak selling time of the day, forcing customers to wait until they're once again permitted to spend outrageous sums of money on Gucci products. Do they lose customers? Not a one. They've created an aura of exclusivity, and it sells like crazy. If we bill this April issue and the tie-in promotion as the most exciting thing ever to hit a selling floor, we'll have more stores than we'll know what to do with."

Jennifer started to outline a two-pronged plan in support of Brad's newly conceived April issue. Though she still harbored doubts about the idea, she was willing to defend it, at least until someone offered a better solution. She had made some tentative notes during the meeting, and as she continued, she embellished them, thinking as she spoke. Part one of her plan involved the in-store events which would translate the issue into retail sales. She proposed following their tried-and-true format of a fashion show with hair and beauty professionals doing makeovers on audience volunteers, but she urged plumping up the entire event, enlarging its scope. She suggested a more elaborate stage, offering the services of her art department for set designs and backdrops. She promised that the fashion coordinators and merchandising people in each store would still receive a *Jolie* store kit with press releases, newspaper ads, resource lists and tie-in suggestions, but, she announced, she wanted a super kit, hyping the promotion to Hollywood proportions—more posters, customer giveaways, buttons, radio spots, and whatever other gimmicks her creative staff could devise.

The second part of Jennifer's master plan required stores to buy four full-page national ads in *Jolie* along with the promotion. One ad would run concurrent with their event, the other three spaced out over several months. *Jolie* would help them arrange cooperative money from fiber or clothing companies if they wished. The fee to each store, probably in excess of ten thousand dollars, would cover all staff traveling expenses, production costs, and advertising space charges. She estimated that they would break even on the promotion, but would come out way ahead on their advertising quotas for the year.

"Brilliant! The woman is brilliant!" Terk Conlon was on his feet, applauding. Jennifer blushed, startled by his reaction.

Brad placed his hands on his desk, considering Jennifer's suggestion. He was grateful to her for offering support and only slightly annoyed that he hadn't thought of charging a fee himself.

"Your idea blends well with mine," he said, eager to link himself to her proposal. "They're both firsts, and that's how *Jolie* became famous. For daring to be first." Brad was warming to his subject, his broad shoulders pulled back, his voice brimming with confidence. "Terk," he said, "work out the figures for the advertising package. Ten thousand sounds too low. Gwen, meet with the editorial staff and tell them about the change in the concept for the April issue. Jennifer, get your creative staff thinking native."

They had been dismissed. As the three of them filed out of his office, none of them could have imagined the waves of relief washing over the person of Bradford Adamson Helms. He knew he had marched into this meeting costumed in bravura, hiding behind the mask of a hastily conceived idea. As he had so often in the past, he had banked on the cleverness of others to bring his idea to life. More to the point, he had hoped that no one would blame him for *Jolie*'s crisis. Most of the staff had little to fear from a sale. They were a talented assembly capable of impressing any new owners. It was his neck that was on the line, his job that was in jeopardy. And at that moment, he felt eternally grateful to Jennifer Cranshaw for granting him a stay of execution.

Jennifer lowered herself into her chair, adjusting the small cushion she used to support her back, and massaged her temples. Terk plunked his burly body into the chair facing her and roared with laughter. Jennifer looked at him through half-opened eyes.

"Terk, your sense of humor is truly demented," she said. "A magazine may be on the block, this magazine in particular, and Brad's tossed us a Big Pineapple. I feel a moment of silence for his dear, departed sanity is in order, and you respond with ghoulish guffaws."

"Moment of silence, my ass!" Terk slid down in his seat and rested his feet on her desk. "If Bradford Adamson Helms would study his elegant family tree carefully, he'd discover that he's a descendant of the fuck-up branch. I'd suggest that he give in to his heritage and stop thinking he's a genius. He should just sit back and let it all happen."

"You know he can't do that," Jennifer said.

"You're right," Terk said, leaning forward. "Instead, we're going to witness history in the making! I can see it now." He splayed his hands in a grand pantomime of a bogus Hollywood director. "First, there was Napoleon's Waterloo. Then, Custer's Last Stand. And now, ladies and gentlemen, Helms's Hula Hoop."

"Professor Conlon," Jennifer interrupted Terk's hilarity. "I think you've overlooked one major fact in your brilliant, but limited study of abortive military maneuvers. In each case, there were battalions of innocents who died fighting those losing battles. That's why I offered my support. I don't want to depart prematurely in red, white, and blue."

"Nobody's going to be draped except Generalissimo Helms, and Lord knows, he deserves it." The hard edge in Terk's voice was unmistakable. "And why you waste your brain power on saving that moron is beyond me."

"Because it's *Jolie* we're saving, not just Brad. What's more," she said, "you're going to help me."

"No way, pretty lady. I'd love to see someone buy this rag and toss Helms out on his custom-made derriere."

"And what if the new owner cleans house?"

"He won't," Terk said.

"What makes you so sure?"

"Trust me, he won't."

"Terk, do you know something I don't?"

"Plenty, but I've never been a kiss-and-tell kind of guy," he said, telegraphing messages with his eyebrows.

"Cute. A bit coarse, but cute."

"Listen, Cassandra, I'm feeling so good I'm going to buy you lunch. You name the place."

"I realize I'm probably passing up the chance of a lifetime, but I already have a lunch date."

Terk lifted his large frame with mock effort, one hand clutching at his heart.

"Now I know how Arthur felt when he found out about Lancelot." He gripped his heart one last time as he closed the door.

Jennifer felt her own heart flutter. She loved flirting with Terk. It was all very innocent, but deep down she had to admit that he affected her and had ever since he'd first arrived at *Jolie* over two years before. Jennifer had been instantly charmed by his sharp wit and easy manner; fascinated by his street sense and pugnacious personality. Also, if asked, she could never deny that she found him disturbingly attractive. Just under six feet tall, Terk was a strapping figure of a man, his body broad and muscular, his face ruggedly square and determined. He was fair with thick sandy hair and a ruddy complexion that reddened with anger or excitement. His jaw was firm, his mouth full and generous, but it was his eyes that dominated his face. They were dark, a blue so intense they were sometimes hypnotic. Terk was a primitive, a bright man with an earthy quality that seemed to fill a room with an animal scent. Jennifer and Terk had spent many a lunch hour parrying with each other, but he was married and she was married and office affairs were traditionally messy.

As she walked around her office, working out the stiffness in her back, she wondered if Terk ever really entertained thoughts of a relationship with her. She left the question unanswered, concentrating instead on the few pieces of litter Mimi had missed. Her office was a large square room with one window wall and ordinary gray carpeting. The rest of the decor was a testimonial to Jennifer's independence. Fellows Publications imposed rules for everything ranging from salary structures to the number of pictures that could be hung on a wall. Jennifer had adhered to the one-couch-plus-one-chair, or three-chairs-no-couch proscription, but she had deliberately neglected to request a copy of the list of acceptable color schemes. Aside from the chair that sat behind her huge black Parsons table desk, she had three other bergères, all upholstered in a tiny French provincial print of black with specks of red and yellow. For additional seating, she had a stack of massive floor pillows in the same print. A wrought-iron baker's rack stood in a corner, housing her collection of good luck owls and ceramic cachepots filled with greenery. The wall opposite the window was all bulletin board, holding examples of her department's work displayed with schoolteacher precision. As she returned to her desk, she rearranged the fresh irises resting in a stoneware vase. Every three days she bought fresh flowers from the corner florist.

Jennifer picked up *Fashion Report*, folded open to the article Brad had read during the meeting, searching for hidden clues or between-the-lines meaning. Unfortunately, she knew that if any Fellows magazine were for sale, *Jolie* was the likely candidate. *Jolie* was a fashion book edited for young, career-oriented women, well-educated, single, and upwardly mobile. *Allure* was *Jolie*'s major competition, but Jennifer had always felt that the two magazines ran on separate tracks. The women who read *Allure* fell into the same age bracket as those who subscribed to *Jolie*, but their demographics were as different as polyester from silk. *Allure* was edited for Middle America. *Jolie* was a "city book." *Allure*'s readership worked. *Jolie* devotees pursued careers. *Jolie*'s fashion pages were chic and slick, heavy on designer clothes, while *Allure*'s editorials featured middle-of-the-road clothes at more popular prices. Jennifer felt confused. For years, *Jolie* had been the top-selling magazine for women eighteen to thirty-four, bursting with advertising. Two years ago, the trend had reversed itself, putting *Allure* in first place.

Fellows also published *Elegante*, the doyenne of fashion magazines, *Mariee*, a bridal magazine, and *Gracious Living*, a decorating book with the same elevated audience as *Elegante*. Every magazine, except *Jolie*, was currently making money. Jennifer wished she could adjust the figures and redraw the bottom line. The more she thought about it, the more sense the article in *Fashion Report* seemed to make.

She was not especially concerned for herself. She felt secure in her position, confident in her talent and ability. Even if there were a mindless purge, she believed she could have her choice of jobs. Over the years, she had been offered many other positions. That wasn't the problem. The problem was that Jennifer adored *Jolie*. Would a new owner love *Jolie* as she did? What if they didn't understand that this was more than a magazine, that it was a living entity with a personality uniquely its own? *Jolie* was a woman, an intensely female being with a love of beautiful clothes, well-cared-for bodies and artfully made-up faces. Sometimes it was petulant, forcing its opinions on a hesitant public. Other times it was inspirational, setting trends and generating excitement. *Jolie* had a sense of humor, an inquisitive mind, a zest for life, a feeling of sisterhood with other women, and the courage to take a stand—and Jennifer couldn't imagine working anywhere else. No! She wasn't going to let *Jolie* wither. It had been the best for too long, and Jennifer was determined it would be again. She wasn't sure how she was going to accomplish this as yet, but she was certain that she could help.

The phone startled her, displacing her vision. She picked up the receiver, allowing Charles Cranshaw's voice to intrude on her thoughts.

"I thought I'd check in on my other half and see how you were faring," he said. "You were up and out so early this morning, I didn't get a chance to speak to you."

"I know. I'm sorry." She tried to remember how many times she had apologized to her husband lately. "The model selection went well, but then Brad called an unscheduled meeting and dropped a bomb. An article in *Fashion Report* claims a magazine might be for sale, and the consensus of opinion is that it's *Jolie*."

"I'm surprised I haven't heard anything about it," Charles said. He could hear the concern in her voice, and he wished he could share it with her, but his world was one of writs and torts. The inner workings of a magazine remained a mystery to him even after eight years of marriage to Jennifer. "An acquisition like that would normally produce rumblings down here on the Street."

"I thought about that. In fact, I wondered if you would poke around for me and try to wheedle some information out of your contacts."

"I could try," he said. "Are you upset?"

"A little, but I want to think it through before I panic. Speaking of panic," she said, lightening the mood, "are you coming home tonight, or would you prefer taking a frazzled woman out to dinner?"

"I'd love to, but I have a five o'clock meeting, and I'm not sure how long it will last. Shall I call you?"

Jennifer sensed he was battling with himself, debating

priorities and feeling guilty about refusing her. His hours had lengthened a great deal recently, and it was rare that they spent more than two nights in a row together during the week.

"You know what they say about all work and no play?" she warned.

"If you're telling me I'm becoming a dull boy, you're right, but I can't help it, Jen. Things are piling up to where I can't see over the file folders stacked on my desk. I promise, I'll get caught up soon, and then we'll play. How's that?"

"Better," she said, disappointed. "You do realize that the wheels of commerce would not grind to a screeching halt if you took a night off?"

"Jennifer, I already said I was sorry. I'll try to make it. I can't do more than that."

The sharpness in his voice felt like a slap. She apologized again, assuring him that she understood, and hung up feeling somewhat guilty herself. Charles had always been supportive of her career—"Climb whatever ladders you want, hon, I'm right behind you"—but she had her moments of wishing they had more time together, more conversations that didn't hinge on their business lives. When they were first married, their outside interests had balanced their office hours, going to concerts and the theater, attending and giving parties; but in the last few years their social life had dwindled, and she was as much to blame as he. She had been feeding her ambition, concentrating her energies on the magazine when she might have been concentrating on Charles. She wondered if perhaps she had forced him to become compulsive about his own work, encouraged him to view her as something secondary. The thought disturbed her. She didn't like to fail at anything, and the fact that her marriage seemed to be faltering depressed her.

She pushed her chair away from the desk, turning toward the window to survey her appearance. She grabbed bunches of hair, pulling them up and letting them fall in huge fluffs, as if that action alone would make everything better. She smoothed out the creases in her skirt and headed for the door. Why was she so convinced that she could save *Jolie* and so unsure about how to salvage her marriage? The question nagged at her all the way down in the elevator. She only hoped Josh's mood was brighter than her own.

Three

The rolling table from room service sat unobtrusively in the corner. Half-eaten croissants languished on gilt-edged china while curls of butter floated in a bowl of melting ice. Once-crisp damask napkins lay across the corners of the table, used and forgotten, draped atop marmalade-coated spoons and greasy knives. In the midst of the elegant debris, a candle flickered softly in the darkened room.

The heavy gold brocade curtains were drawn, blocking the midday light, leaving a twilight haze to veil the richly furnished suite. Strains of Glenn Gould playing Bach drifted over the room. A man's suit hung limply over the back of a desk chair, the shirt and tie slung carelessly over an arm, reaching down to touch the pastel-patterned rug. A tufted bench held a woman's maribou-trimmed dressing gown and a lacy silk teddy.

Brooke Wheeler lay naked on the pink satin sheets, her painted toes snuggling the plump comforter that was crushed against the end of the bed. Her head was propped by several pillows, and she was watching the look of ecstasy grow on Clint Rogers's face as she slowly, deliberately poured Dom Perignon over her body. The champagne splattered over her full, round breasts, causing her to shiver from the impact of the chilled wine. It foamed slightly and then dissipated into a dozen rivulets winding their way over her flesh. She arched her back and invited Clint to indulge himself, lifting her breasts to his hungry mouth. He licked at her, lapping at the champagne and growing strong and hard with each delectable taste. His lips closed over one of her rising nipples, his teeth biting, sucking, greedily possessing her.

Brooke pulled back, urging him to go slowly, all the while pouring the champagne until it covered her with a thin coat of ecru bubbles. As Clint's tongue explored her, she marveled at how easy it was to control men. Clint Rogers was a wealthy, successful businessman, owner of a large chain of specialty shops in the southwest, yet here he was, panting and pleading like a leashed puppy. *And that*, Brooke thought, *was as it should be.*

Brooke's hand gripped Clint, stroking him and sliding her wet fingers over him again and again. Her hips started to undulate, twisting and turning with snakelike rhythm, pushing against him, rubbing and stimulating until his insides quivered. Before he was aware of what she was doing, Brooke slithered under his erect body and placed him between her dampened breasts. Her hands sandwiched him as she squeezed and kneaded, pressed and then released. Her breasts were firm and hard, and he felt himself grow hot and feverish. He buried his face in the pillow and groaned.

Brooke listened with pleasure. As she watched Clint writhe in anticipation, she wished she could manipulate women as easily as she did men. Women required careful plotting and clever connivance, especially strong women like Jennifer Cranshaw. But Brooke was not one to admit defeat easily. She wanted Jennifer's job, and somehow, she was going to get it.

She turned her attention to Clint, jockeying them into a position that freed her to mount him. She placed herself on top of him, sitting upright and emptying the last of the Dom Perignon on his body. She rubbed it into him, causing his chest hair to mat and glisten with a mixture of sweat and champagne. Her hands moved in slow, steady circles, covering his broad shoulders, then moving down along his sides and beneath his waist. She lowered herself to within a millimeter of him, tantalizing, teasing, tempting. She inched down, touching and retreating until Clint was reduced to begging.

"I'm so glad you're staying for the *Jolie* party Thursday night," she said incongruously, holding him against her.

Clint moaned, his eyes closed, his breath catching.

"I don't have anything to wear," she whispered, leaning

over and licking his chest. "And it's a very important occasion."

"Anything you want!" Clint practically screamed as she
lowered herself onto him.

She felt triumphant, and she rode him with the fury of
a cowboy breaking a wild stallion until she felt his body
jolt, shudder, and then go limp.

Brooke detached herself and lay alongside him on the
bed. He was still breathing heavily, his eyes shut, his face
covered with cooling beads of sweat. He was spent.
Brooke eyed him carefully. Quietly, furtively, she leaned
down and kissed him. She caressed and kissed, waiting for
a reaction she knew was impossible.

"Brooke, haven't you had enough?"

"I didn't come."

"You have to be kidding." Clint's eyes were wide with
astonishment.

"You were selfish again. I took care of you, and you left
me hanging. It's my turn now."

"Brooke, I would if I could, but I haven't got an ounce
of strength left."

She didn't answer him, but continued to fondle his flaccid body. Clint raised his shoulders off the bed so he
could look at her.

"Okay," he said, resigned to the inevitable. "Let's go
shopping, and I'll buy you that Saint Laurent you saw the
other day. Then we'll come back here, and I promise to
fuck your little brains out."

"What a marvelous idea!" Brooke bounced out of bed
and headed for the shower.

Clint threw his head back on the pillow.

You get what you pay for, he thought as his eyes
closed.

Four

As Jennifer closed the door of the taxi, her face was brushed by the brisk crosswinds whipping across Second Avenue. It was late October, and this snap of early winter whistled about her. Cars and buses weaved their way through a maze of double-parked delivery trucks while lunch-hour crowds rushed from one place to another.

Jennifer's hands went up to protect her hair as she stepped under the billowing brown canopy of L'Olivier. She pushed open the heavy wooden door and stood in the tiny foyer until her eyes adjusted to the darkness. She waited, allowing shadows to define themselves into recognizable shapes and faces. Slowly, the restaurant's rustic interior came into focus. The walls of the long, narrow room were splashed with swirling stucco, interrupted every few feet by mahogany-stained hand-hewn beams. On the ceiling, thicker beams crossed the width of the room, dotted here and there with a hanging basket or bunch of dried country wildflowers. Small pastoral paintings framed in distressed oak tattooed the walls, their bucolic scenery reflected in the mirror behind the bar.

He was already there, his strong body straddling a leather bar stool, and Jennifer immediately felt the jumble of emotions that enveloped her whenever she saw Joshua Mandell. She smiled at the sight of him, this man who had been such an important part of her life. He looked very different now, and she thought he was more handsome than ever. High, sculpted cheekbones lofted above a dimpled chin, and an olive complexion gave him an almost Mediterranean look. His nose was broad and slightly bent, his mouth wide with full lips that moved easily into an engaging smile. Large, hazel eyes suggested sincerity and honesty, the chameleon blend of green and brown constantly alert and assured. His black hair, sprinkled with gray, was razor-cut to tame a persistent curl, and his navy pinstripe suit bore the elegant fit of a European tailor.

She walked up behind him, slid her hands over his eyes, and whispered, "Boo!" in his ear. She startled him, and he swiveled around in his seat.

"Jennie Sheldon and only half an hour late. Will wonders never cease?" He gave her a soft kiss on the cheek and wrapped his arms around her in an embrace.

Jennifer hugged him eagerly, drinking in the sandalwood scent that had become his signature. She loved the fact that he still called her "Jennie." He was the only one who did.

"Every time I see you, I find it hard to equate this glamorous woman standing before me with the little, white-aproned baker's daughter from Bayonne." He looked her up and down with obvious admiration.

"We are one and the same, and I'm ravenous! You promised me a super lunch, and if you don't deliver, I'll tell your mother."

"Once a snitch, always a snitch," he teased as he steered her toward the end of the bar.

Claude, the maitre d', led them into the garden room. Sunlight streamed down from a greenhouse ceiling, washing the dining area with a diffused, veiled luminescence. Bentwood chairs and fresh bouquets of flowers balanced the lush greenery that hung suspended from the ceiling in moss-covered baskets. In one corner, a massive tree trunk rose, pushing its way through the roof and spreading its foliage over the skylight. L'Olivier was the kind of restaurant Josh always chose for their noontime meetings: small, atmospheric, and intimate.

When they were both comfortably seated, Jennifer looked up. Her eyes met Josh's and lingered. Thirteen years ago, just days after Jennifer had turned twenty-one, she had channeled their lives onto separate paths, forging a distance between them that narrowed only when mutual friends or circumstance brought them together. Last April, they had found themselves guests at the same dinner party. It was the first time she had seen him in several years. Josh's wife had died two years before. As Jennifer spoke to him that night, she detected a loneliness in the otherwise confident tycoon that even his facile humor couldn't conceal. It was Jennifer who suggested that they meet occasionally for lunch. She and Josh had shared too much together for her to deny him her friendship. Their past encouraged involvement. He would have done the same for her.

"Joshua Mandell, you are just what the doctor ordered," she said. "It has been an absolutely beastly morning!"

"Beastly mornings happen to be my specialty. How about something to drink?"

"White Lillet on the rocks with a slice of orange, and when it comes, just pour it directly down my throat."

Josh gave the waiter their order and turned back to Jennifer, who sat spotlighted by a beam reflected through the skylight. Her hair was still a bit tousled from the wind, and a few undisciplined ringlets caressed her cheeks. Her skin looked flawless, even under the harsh gaze of the sun, but Josh noticed a weariness cloaking her eyes. He leaned forward to light her cigarette and picked up the delicate floral of her perfume.

"I'd invite you to exorcise your demons, but the food is too good here to spoil with gothic tales of blood and gore."

Jennifer caught the concern in his voice. She puffed on her cigarette and then proceeded to relate the morning's events, confiding her anxiety about a potential sale and Brad's proposal.

"The Fellows family might be selling Jolie for reasons totally unrelated to the magazine," Josh suggested. "They own a newspaper chain and several radio and television stations, and it's conceivable that they're looking for money to finance a new venture. Besides, it might be the best thing to happen to Jolie."

"You're the second person today to express that opinion," she said, wondering why she didn't see any advantages to a sale. "How about explaining it to me?"

She listened attentively as Josh explained that new ownership usually felt bound to inject substantial sums of money into a purchase. Certainly, Jolie could benefit from an infusion of funds; Jennifer's own department might well enjoy a budget boost, he said.

"Or a bloodbath."

"Not likely. At least not immediately. When I go into a company, I spend months studying the staff," he said. "It's the only way to know who's really responsible for the red ink on the bottom line."

Jennifer twisted her cigarette around in the ashtray, watching the smoke rise in small, puffy circles as she tried to digest everything he said. Josh was probably right, but his logic hadn't lightened her mood a bit.

"You're probably right." She admitted the thought aloud. "You usually are, you know. That's one of the things I find most infuriating about you."

"What else do you find infuriating about me?" he asked, moving closer to her.

"That 'gotcha' smile you now have spreading across your face."

He responded with a hearty laugh, his eyes crinkling at the corners and causing Jennifer's thoughts to shift once again from the self-assured millionaire back to the little boy whose parents had owned the children's store next to her family's bakery. She still had a hard time grasping the fact that Josh had created an empire, especially when she recalled the hundreds of childhood discussions that had passed between him and her brother David. She used to hide on the stairs and eavesdrop, fascinated by how fervently the two boys planned their futures. David wanted to be a doctor, healing bodies and saving lives. Josh's bent was business. Not just the debit and credit aspect of commerce, but the construction of a conglomerate, the formation of a group of companies that interacted with each other. David and Josh had fueled their youthful dreams with adult determination. David was now a surgeon at Hadassah Hospital in Israel, and Josh was head of JM Industries, a *Fortune* 500 company that had started out as a scrappy little factory producing hydraulic machinery. Both men were considered leaders in their fields. Both had had an enormous influence on Jennifer's life.

"When is the eminent Dr. Sheldon returning to his native land?" Josh asked as if reading her thoughts.

"I don't know." She was embarrassed to tell him she hadn't heard from David in months. "You correspond with him. How come you don't know?"

Josh heard the defensive tone in her voice. He knew

that brother and sister had drifted apart. David hadn't told him the details, but Josh had guessed that it had something to do with Charles Cranshaw. Jennie and David weren't doing battle anymore, but Josh surmised that their peace was tentative.

Josh signaled the waiter for menus. As he studied the French, Jennifer studied him, zeroing in on his hands. They were broad and strong, and Jennifer couldn't help remembering how good those hands had once felt on her body, how firm and loving they had been. Those hands had been the first to explore her, and they had done it gently and tenderly, introducing her to the singular experience of sharing her body with another. The reminiscence prompted her own hand to stretch across the table and come to rest just near enough to his to achieve a moment of contact. Her face flushed, and she sipped her Lillet as if that might erase the memories flooding her consciousness, but she didn't remove her hand.

"Are you having trouble translating the French?"

"Order for me," she said, putting her menu down. "I'm sorry if I seem distracted."

Josh eyed her carefully. There was a tightness about her lips and something about the way she held her head that disturbed him. She had finished her drink in what he considered record time.

"Would you care for another pacifier?" he asked.

"I'll take two and call you in the morning."

"You'll have one and tell me what's bothering you."

He flagged the waiter and ordered Jennifer another drink, white wine for himself and sole Veronique for both of them. Jennifer lit another cigarette, fumbling with the match and busying herself with her napkin. He waited for her to finish smoothing the square white cloth over her skirt.

"Anyone watching you fidget like that would think I had asked you to rush off to a room at the Hotel Dixie. I do have my reputation to consider, so would you mind telling me what is behind those snaky lines in your forehead?"

"I'm planning a crusade," she said, finally. "I have decided to turn *Jolie*'s birthday party into a kickoff for Brad's invasion of Hawaii. If we're going to stage an extravaganza, we may as well make it work for us."

"I thought you didn't like the idea of dedicating an issue to Hawaii."

"I didn't, at first, but it may be offbeat enough to attract attention. The problem is finding a way to do it by Thursday night, when I have a captive audience of industry movers and shakers. But I'll pull it off," she said, more to herself than to him. "I have to. This is very important to me."

"Another step on the stairway to heaven?" Josh said quietly, anticipating her knee-jerk reaction.

"Let us not debate the plusses and minuses of ambition," she said, feeling the old anger creep into her body. "It's a subject that has not served us well in the past."

He leaned across the table, taking her hand in his without taking his eyes off her face. He could see the anger and, more than anyone else, he believed he understood it. His gaze was steady and unwavering, his voice subdued, but stern.

"You're wrong, you know. You think I find fault with the concept of ambition. In fact, I thrive on it. I applaud it. But," he said, stressing the word, "there's a difference between ambition that motivates and ambition that consumes."

"You didn't get where you are by being a Goody-Two-Shoes, you know. Why is it right for you and not for me?" Jennifer's eyes were blazing, and she pulled her hand away from his.

"Don't try and twist my words into some sexist debate. I've always been drawn to talented, aggressive, independent women. That's probably what I find so devastatingly attractive about you." He could tell that she was as sorry as he that the discussion had ever begun, but it had, and it deserved to be finished. "The point, my darling Jennie," he went on, "is that you're so blinded by fairy tales that I think you underestimate your present success when compared to your fantasies. You're a star, but you won't admit it. You're still groping for more. I think you're fascinated with ambition for ambition's sake, just as some people fall in love with the idea of love. It's not real, and it's certainly not fulfilling!"

His words stunned her, forcing an involuntary shudder

to surge through her body. He was right. Each accomplishment seemed to require another. Somehow total satisfaction eluded her. She'd reach for it, stretch for it, yet she never truly captured the sweet sensation of fulfillment.

This was not the first time they'd had this discussion. She wondered now if perhaps he was correct to view her desire to save *Jolie* as another quest for success that would leave her still wanting . . . what? She shook her head, sloughing off the frightening thought, reaffirming that she would—could—have what she wanted.

Josh remained silent, allowing Jennifer time to wrestle with herself. He watched as she regained her composure. She sighed, and her silk blouse caught against the swell of her breasts, making him think back to the nights they had spent wrapped in each other's arms, making love over and over again. Afterward, they would lie beside each other, naked and open, talking. He told her of his dreams in a voice that was bold and determined. Jennie's voice would strain and falter as she revealed her needs, her desire to leave her parents' bakery and all it stood for. She had wanted better. He had promised to give it to her. He loved her then, just as he knew he loved her now.

"How's Charles?" he asked.

The question caught Jennifer off guard.

"He's very busy," she said. "You know how it is when you're a big time corporate lawyer."

"No, I don't. How is it?"

"Difficult. How's that for Girl Scout honesty?"

"I'll mail you the badge. Is there something going on that you might like to talk about?"

Plenty, she thought to herself, but it was too abstract, too undefined to put into words. Something had driven a wedge between her and Charles, that much she knew, but what it was remained a mystery to her. Where they had once been loving, they were now considerate. Where they had been attentive, they were now polite. They still supported each other emotionally, but they no longer excited each other physically. They had, in effect, become companions. Maybe because it was comfortable, or maybe because she had had so little time lately to give to her marriage, Jennifer had armored herself against feeling what she knew, deep down, she was missing. How much easier it was to wonder vaguely what was happening than to acknowledge the loss and try to do something about it.

"Let's just say that our late nights at the office and our business trips aren't coinciding. We keep missing each other."

Josh detected trouble, and a part of him was strangely elated. He would never wish Jennifer any unhappiness, but the idea that all was not blissful with Mr. and Mrs. Charles Tyler Cranshaw produced thoughts that he had to struggle against. A door that he had considered securely locked had just opened a crack.

"If you ever feel the need to confide," he said gently, "I'm always available."

"I know," she said, looking at her watch, avoiding his eyes. "But right now I have to meet with a caterer."

Josh paid the check, and they both rose, each reluctant to leave the other. It occurred to Jennifer that there had been a time when she couldn't wait to get away from Josh. But that was long ago, and she didn't have the energy to dwell on history. There were too many things in the present that needed her attention. Besides, it made no sense to look back. *What's done, Lady Macbeth,* she thought, *is done.* One had to live with one's decisions, even if they turned out to be wrong.

Josh hailed a cab and helped Jennifer in. When he kissed her good-bye, he held himself back, reminding himself that she still belonged to someone else. But her kiss clung to him as he watched the taxi turn the corner. There was more on her mind than Hawaiian luaus and disco parties. He knew he shouldn't get involved, but he had been involved with Jennie Sheldon for a very long time. He wasn't about to uninvolve himself now.

Five

Jennie Sheldon spent her early childhood surrounded by babkas and streusel cakes. Every shopper on Broadway knew Jennie. Each day, they expected to find her sitting in the window of her parents' bakery, waving to them from behind the glass, her reddish-brown curls bobbing and bouncing about her head. She was a cheerful figure, an icon drawing them into the store.

Everyone found something special about Jennie. Some were charmed by the big, dark eyes glinting with mischief, the wide mouth spread in an impish grin. Others responded to the innocent candor and the contagious laugh. Sometimes, they'd find her out of the window, perched on a wooden stool with a large white apron covering her overalls and dropping way below her shoes. Then, her face was as serious as it was possible for a child's face to be, and she used her most grown-up voice to ask if they really preferred onion rolls to honey buns. As much as these neighbors loved seeing Jennie in the bakery, Jennie loved being there. Her mother and father were there; her brother was in and out; there were goodies to munch, and she was adored by everyone. Jennie had no complaints. She was still too naive to have anything to complain about.

The bakery was small and in need of a paint job, its pale green color graying wherever time had touched it. On the wall behind the long glass cases hung colorful pictures of tempting cakes and pies. Behind the cash register, there were family snapshots and scraps of paper taped to the mirrored alcove in a haphazard collage. Across from the cake counters stood a refrigerator case, its frosty glass door obscuring ice cream containers, frozen cakes, and milk cartons. Nearby was a candy case displaying wrapped packages of gum balls, jawbreakers, chocolate bars and mints. The Sheldon's Bake Shop of Jennifer's earliest memories was a lively place where warm, inviting smells wafted in from the back, encouraging indulgence and promising satisfaction.

The short, plump woman who lived behind the bakery counter was a veritable dynamo, darting back and forth from bin to bin, window to register. Rose Sheldon had a round, open face with cheeks flushed a light pink, just a shade softer than her crisp uniform. Her hair was a mass of dark auburn curls, pulled back from her face by two five-and-dime barrettes. A few stray ringlets refused to oblige, and she was constantly pushing them off her face with whichever hand was not tying packages or making change. Her smile was warm and genuine, but underneath the bouncy, genial exterior was a tough, determined businesswoman.

There was no madness to Rose's methods. If someone asked for a hunk of cheesecake, her hand conveniently slipped, to the tune of an extra quarter pound. Even though she apologized profusely, no one ever asked her to trim off the excess. If a customer ordered a half-pound of assorted cookies, Rose deliberately put them in a pound box, making them look skimpy and spare. Predictably, the customer asked her to fill the box. If she was pressured into giving a local charity group a break on price, she made certain that their discount purchased day-old goods.

The front of the store was her domain, and she ran it like a field commander, scrutinizing each salesgirl, stepping in swiftly whenever one of them failed to complete a sale. No one walked out of Sheldon's Bake Shop empty-handed. She worked her girls hard. Rose never understood that to them, the bakery was just a job. To Rose, it was her life.

Marty Sheldon kept to himself in the back of the store. His was a world of flour and fillings, icings and recipes. He baked in large quantities, turning out pie after pie, cake after cake. Whenever Jennifer thought about her father, she pictured his hands: huge and gnarled, discolored from years of constant abuse.

His joys were few: his wife, when she wasn't in the bakery; his children, all the time; any hours spent inside a synagogue; and birthday cakes. He loved making them, fashioning roses on his little stand, spinning the small metal circle around and around in his fingers, gently squeezing pink, blue, or yellow buttercream out of a cloth tube and deftly forming sweet-tasting flowers in various stages of bloom, or shaping slender branches and graceful leaves that looked as fresh as those born in April. Whatever message was requested, Marty wrote it in a flourishing script.

He was a good man, Marty Sheldon, and an honest man, but a silent one. He had made his choices a long time ago, and, right or wrong, he was locked in. His children would have alternatives.

Jennie felt no need for alternatives for a long time. As a seven-year-old, her world was small, its perimeters determined by which streets she was allowed to cross and which playgrounds were out of bounds. The circumference of Jennie's world measured fifteen blocks, that area from the house on Twelfth Street and the Boulevard, to the bakery on Twenty-fourth and Broadway. In between those two points were the Temple, the elementary school, two playgrounds with giant swing sets, and everyone she cared about.

She was a shy child who hadn't uttered her first word until she was almost three. She'd point and grunt and cry and gurgle until the family did exactly what she wanted. When, after much coaxing and numerous visits to the pediatrician, she did speak, she astounded everyone by using complete sentences and pronouncing her words without a trace of baby talk. And once she started to talk, as her mother was fond of saying, she spoke endlessly. Before long, Jennie had developed the disarming, effervescent exterior that drew people to her and cloaked her timidity in second-grade banter. She had, unconsciously, armed herself against patronizing customers who pinched her cheek and indulged in that infuriating adult habit of discussing children as if they were not present.

In school, she was at the top of her class. Her report cards glowed, and her teachers' evaluations were filled with praise. They predicted, and correctly so, that she would excel in English and struggle with math, adore languages and abhor science.

Jennie was too young to know the difference between "rich" and "poor." Even though she knew "more" and "less," it was a day-to-day distinction that defined itself only when a school friend acquired an extra pair of Mary Janes or two new dresses instead of one. She also understood, on the periphery of her young consciousness, what "in" and "out" meant. As the baker's daughter, she was "in." Any friend of Jennie's could dip her hands into the cookie bins or stuff her pockets with candy. Jennie loved the fact that her friends envied her Rose. Whereas other mothers frowned on sweets, Rose endorsed them. Other mothers limited snacks: Rose distributed them freely. And in return for Rose's largesse, Jennie was invited to every birthday party and picnic in town.

Another benefit to being Jennie Sheldon was being allowed free rein in the land of enchantment that was the back of the bakery. She never tired of watching her father spin the magic metal circle that made roses. She never ceased to be amazed at how a lump of rubbery dough grew into a glorious mound of rich-tasting bread. She loved opening the large freezer door and scooping out handfuls of whipped cream. And she never turned down the opportunity to help frost petit fours, dipping a big ladle into steaming copper vats and slowly pouring thick syrup over tiny sponge cakes. The frosting hardened the moment it touched the cake, forming a crunchy covering and bringing Jennie instant delight.

She had just turned thirteen when her sugar-dipped existence began to sour. Her parents' business was growing, but available help was dwindling. Out of necessity, David was recruited to man the deliveries, and Jennie was expected to help out behind the counter.

One afternoon she lingered too long after school. Everyone was teasing and laughing, and she just couldn't tear herself away from the warm friendly circle. Suddenly, she looked at the clock. She was late. Her mother would be waiting, worried, perhaps even angry. She ran from the school yard, racing down the street, sprinting across the playground and cutting corners. She never saw the light change. She was only a block away from the store when a green station wagon made a quick left turn and hit her, flinging her onto the sidewalk.

When she regained consciousness, she was in the recovery room of Bayonne Hospital, strapped to a bed with metal sides, wired with tubes connected to glass jars and

plastic bags that hung from high poles. Her ears rang with
the constant beeping of the machine that monitored her
heart, counting beats like a metronome, droning,
thumping. Round shapes loomed over her, hovering,
speaking in echoes. They had foggy faces with distorted
features, white-capped angels telling her how lucky she
was to be alive. She didn't feel lucky. She wasn't even
sure she felt alive. She was groggy, her body was numb,
and her toes refused to wiggle. From time to time, she felt
a cool hand touch her wrist, hold it, and then place it
gently at her side.

Everything was so vague, so clouded. Her head was
swimming. Slowly, her vision cleared, and a man's face
crystallized. The doctor leaned over her, his voice sooth-
ing, and told her that she had just come to after a four-
hour operation. He patted her hand and told her she was
a very brave girl. She tried to smile, but the muscles were
too weak to do anything more than twitch. He explained
that her vertebrae had been fractured, narrowing the
space between the bones of her spinal column, pressing on
the arteries, veins and nerves that radiated from the central structure and into the trunk. He had inserted a plate
between the two injured vertebrae, screwing the metal to
the bone itself to separate them so they couldn't pinch
and force the bones apart.

She understood little of what he told her. Her aware-
ness had been interrupted by pain, throbbing, bewilder-
ing pain shooting up her legs and pressing against her
shoulders. Her face twisted, and her head jerked from side
to side until one of the nurses stuck a needle into her arm
and returned her to mercifully anesthetized sleep. For
three days, she drifted in and out of consciousness, oblivious to the bedside vigil of her family. When she opened
her eyes on the fourth day, Rose's face broke into a smile,
releasing Jennie's tears. Rose held her as she cried, stroked
her head and kissed her cheeks, reassuring Jennie that
there was no permanent damage and no hideous scars.
The operation had been successful and in three weeks,
Jennie would come home. Jennie turned her head, relieved that she felt no pain, and smiled at her father, who
stood silently at her side weeping.

Jennie wanted them to stay with her, to sit by her bed

every single minute until she was released, feeding her, bathing her, caring for her, but the bakery made that impossible.

David came that night and every night, holding her hand, reading to her, listening, speaking, calming. He understood that the unknown terrified her more than the thick wad of bandages on her back. Jennie was certain that they were hiding things from her. David began chasing the doctors, hounding them for information, badgering them and burrowing through medical books. He read everything he could, studying charts and diagrams he barely understood, forcing himself to learn. Jennie's case was typical, no complications, no cause for worry.

As David presented his diagnosis to Jennie, she noticed the triumph in his sixteen-year-old face. He had discovered his calling.

As Jennifer began to have longer periods of pain-free wakefulness, she became more alert to her surroundings, more attuned to the cacophony of sounds in the ward she shared with seven other patients. Time passed slowly, and she watched the clock constantly, waiting for David to come, needing his calm and desperate for his comfort. Her parents' visits were always rushed. Rose brought boxes of cookies for the ward and looked bright and cheery in her pink uniform and crisp white apron. She was everyone's darling, but Jennie felt something chafe inside of her, a niggling resentment.

When she left the hospital it was the end of May, and the world seemed especially beautiful to Jennie. Everything became precious. Her bed, her pillow, the familiar stuffed animals, even an old doll she had discarded years ago. The wound had not totally healed, and so, on her doctor's advice, she remained at home for the rest of the school year, ferrying her assignments back and forth with David and trying to maintain her average. Her friends came to visit, often at first, and then sporadically. They were wrapped up in being teenagers. Jennie's accident was unfortunate, but inconvenient.

The only constants in her life were David and his best friend, Joshua Mandell. Whenever David had to work, Josh substituted, tutoring Jennie and keeping her company. Josh had been around for years, but before her illness, she had barely noticed him. Now, Jennie was fourteen, he was seventeen, and that summer she fell in love. She didn't recognize the feelings. They were new, but wonderful. She was convinced that Josh was just doing David a favor, but it didn't seem to matter. She was experiencing sensations she had never felt before, and he was responsible for them.

Josh and David had been at college for a month when Jennie returned to the hospital for a second operation. Her wound hadn't healed properly, and pus was draining into her body, causing high fevers. Her body had rejected the metal plate. Her confinement was shorter this time, but the pain was greater. Without the plate, the vertebrae fused, clamped together, and squeezed the nerves and veins that ran between them. Jennie suffered terribly, but she willed herself to mend. Six weeks later, she returned to school. Each day was a battle against the agonizing thorns that pinched her back. Her friends were uncomfortable around such pain and soon stopped searching for excuses to avoid her. Jennie was more alone than she had ever been. Josh wrote to her often, and his letters provided the one bright spot in an otherwise bleak existence. David called and wrote. He kept track of her progress, offered encouragement, but the pain was cruel. For lack of any other distraction, she began to fill her empty hours with writing, penning frequent letters to Josh and keeping a diary. What had started as therapy soon became a joy. She was intrigued with the pleasure of words, writing secret poems filled with innocent lust and uneducated sensuality.

For nine months she was alone with her wretchedness, and bitterness festered. Try as she would, she couldn't fight the resentment she felt for her parents' catch-as-catch-can company. They were putting in very long days in an effort to pay her medical bills. That Jennie understood, and she suffered from guilt. But she was angry as well. She spent her time spinning fantasies of a life as rich and frothy as the whipped cream she had loved as a child. She fancied herself a grand lady who wore expensive clothes instead of uniforms and who strolled up and down Fifth Avenue instead of hopping a bus on the Boulevard. Her present life was only a starting point. She would have more, she told herself. She had earned it.

By June, the pain had become unbearable, and Jennie was steps away from being crippled. Yes, there was something the doctors could do. They could remove part of the femur from her thigh and insert the bone in between the grinding vertebrae. Rose and Marty were skeptical. It was a long and tedious operation with few guarantees. Jennie had grown sullen. She had endured so much already that they questioned the validity of subjecting her to further agony. But Jennie spoke for herself and demanded the operation. Once again, she submitted to the scalpel. She spent another six weeks in the dreaded ward, yet this time she didn't mind. Josh was there. Occasionally, she presented him with her poetry, watched his face as he read it, and felt his lips on her cheek mark his approval. By the time Jennie left the hospital for the last time, vowing never to return, she was hopelessly in love with Joshua Mandell.

Six

Jennifer unlocked the door to her apartment and groped for the light switch. Juggling her key, her purse, and the mail, she flicked on the lights and then gratefully dropped her paraphernalia on a snakeskin Parsons table. She shuffled through the mail, hoping for a letter from David, separating the day's installment of bills from the letters that began "Dear Occupant." Two neat piles were left for Charles.

She was in a marvelous mood, buoyed by her successful meeting with the caterer and the surprise she had arranged for Thursday night: champagne, caviar (at a reasonable price!), and something more.

Humming a made-up tune, she stripped down to her underwear and laid out her exercise mat. She felt elated, but the stinging in her back attested to the pressure she had been under the past few weeks. Head and shoulders

up off the floor. Twinge. Arms extended. Reach. Try to
touch the toes. Don't strain. Reach. Her spine cringed, but
she continued. Down. Breathe. Up again. Stretch. Reach.
Pain.

Forty sit-ups and fifty bends later she was finished. Her
back throbbed. She showered quickly so her muscles
didn't tighten up again and slipped into a white terrycloth robe. In the living room, she switched on the stereo
and let Neil Diamond fill the air with his haunting baritone. She reached for the telephone, then remembered:
Charles had said he had a late meeting.

Jennifer put the receiver down. She was disappointed.
Disgruntled. Somewhere, deep inside, she had hoped that
Charles would cut his meeting short and come home. On
impulse, she walked over to the bar and selected a
Mouton-Cadet from the small refrigerator hidden within
the lacquered unit. She popped the cork and poured herself some of the dry, white wine, raising her glass to the
disembodied voice coming from the stereo.

"Here's to a lovely dinner, Madame Cranshaw. Oh? Are
you dining alone?" she said, her voice deliberately mock-
ing. "Why yes, Mr. Diamond. I'm a party of one."

Drink in hand, she paced the large room, drifting
toward the sweep of windows overlooking the East River.
Floor-to-ceiling vertical blinds tilted at a forty-five-degree
angle, obscuring the twinkling lights of the city below.
She pulled them to the side, hypnotizing herself with the
blur of commuters' headlights streaming up the FDR
Drive. How many of them were husbands rushing home
to aproned wives and freshly bathed children? How many
had left meetings early to please their families? That's not
fair, she thought. After all, she wasn't in the kitchen
preparing a well-balanced meal or perfuming the air with
a special dessert. She was a career woman, and if she had
had a late appointment, Charles wouldn't have acted like
this. He wouldn't stand here blinking back at the commercial laundry sign on the other side of the river, counting
seconds between each flash of red. He would understand.
He would accept the fact that sometimes her job required
her to be late. He would fix himself something to eat and
spend the evening reading the latest political memoir. He

wouldn't question her motives as she was questioning his. And he certainly wouldn't take it personally.

Jennifer turned back to the interior and leaned on the window sill, looking at her apartment as if for the first time. Charles had selected the furniture, an expensive collection of ultramodern pieces. Everything was white. Stark, blinding, antiseptic white. An L-shaped sofa dominated the room, daring her to be comfortable on it. The low-backed couch was covered in cotton that had been stretched and pulled into wide, stiff cushions that never had to be fluffed. It squatted on short, gleaming chrome legs, its lines too hard to ever look inviting to Jennifer.

Facing the sofa were two white leather chairs with wide bottoms and gently swayed backs tufted into ridges that reminded her of a corrugated box. A lucite and glass coffee table held center stage, with an assortment of precisely stacked art books providing the room's only touch of color. In the corner, by the windows, four white suede chairs circled a round stainless steel game table. There were track lights, and one lone painting, awash with light from an overhead spot.

Jennifer kicked off her slippers and tried to curl up in a corner of the couch, adjusting the cushions to support her back. She closed her eyes, letting the music take hold of her. She longed for softness, for big oversized chairs that embraced you as you sat in them; for knickknacks that collected dust, but contained memories; for a fireplace with fat logs spitting sparks and exuding a rosy glow. Suddenly, she had a disquieting thought. She realized that her office suited her more than her home. There, she had surrounded herself with warmth, and within its walls she felt strong and sure of herself. Here, a chilly elegance enveloped her, and for the moment, it felt unsettling.

As she sipped her wine and debated with her environment, a picture of her parents' home flashed through her mind. She closed her eyes again, drawing the image closer to her consciousness. In her mind's eye, it appeared cozy. It made you feel welcome. There were no pretensions about Rose and Marty Sheldon's house. It was honest and real. Maybe that's what was wrong, Jennifer thought. Maybe this apartment fit her more than she cared to admit. Hadn't she acquiesced to an image? She had vowed to live in an Upper East Side flat one day, an apartment decorated to the nines. She had achieved that goal, but just as Josh had reminded her at lunch, it hadn't given her fulfillment.

She retreated further into the couch and deeper into the past. The more she reflected, the more she knew that the cozy image she had conjured of her parents' loving home was false—or so it had seemed when she was nineteen.

In the Sheldon house, the bakery had always come first. The hours were long, and the main concern was the end-of-the-day take, but until she went to college, Jennifer had never realized the effects of such single-minded preoccupation. Then, home from Vassar for Christmas, she felt dulled and resentful at the drabness of life in Bayonne.

She sat in the dining room with her parents, her brother David, and his girlfriend, Sarah, a lovely brunette who was trying hard not to let Rose intimidate her. It was late, and everyone was lingering over coffee and the inevitable selections from the bakery. All during dinner, Rose had badgered and probed to try to understand what was suddenly so different about her daughter. Instinctively, she knew she was being rejected. She also knew that this time the tension between them went deeper than the usual mother-daughter bickering.

"So, Jennie. What are your fancy friends doing over the holidays?" she asked, cutting Sarah off in midsentence. "You really should have asked a few of them over for dinner."

Jennifer scraped the frosting off a piece of seven-layer cake, hoping her mother would drop the subject, but Rose never gave up. She asked again, and this time, Jennifer answered.

"Because I would die if you were as discourteous to them as you're being to Sarah. That's why!"

Jennifer scowled at her mother, transmitting waves of disapproval from wide, angry eyes. Rose ignored both Jennifer's look and her outburst. She spooned the last of the cherry vanilla ice cream onto her crumb cake. David motioned to Jennifer to restrain herself.

"And what is it that you find in your *shiksa* friends that

you think is so terribly lacking in me?" Rose demanded, deliberately oblivious to Jennifer's antagonistic silence.

Jennifer leaned toward her mother, looked her straight in the eye, and forbade any love to soften her intention to hurt.

"Class, Mother. Class. They have it. We don't. Classy people do not come to dinner dressed in a uniform, for one thing. Classy people do not insult their guests or keep pushing food onto them or monopolize every conversation. Classy people care, really care, about others."

Years of resentment poured out as she sought the reasons and words to blame her mother for all the things their lifestyle had deprived her of.

"You see, Marty," Rose said to her husband, as if she had just been proven right on a testy issue. "I knew we shouldn't have let her go to Vassar. I told you she wouldn't meet the right kind of people."

Jennifer knew what was coming next: Rose's standard lecture on the benefits of attending a local college and living at home. Whenever this argument arose, Jennifer reminded her parents that David had gone to the University of Virginia with their blessings, but their response was always the same. It was different for a boy. Boys should go away to school. It wasn't as important for a girl.

Jennifer pushed her chair away from the table, as if that single action could remove her from everything she found distasteful. Then, she got up and lowered the lights, knowing it would annoy her mother and using it to gain further distance from the family. David remained quiet. Duels between his mother and his sister were not uncommon, but he had little sympathy for them. He believed that each generation had its own peculiarities and that the younger should avoid antagonizing the older on issues that could never be resolved. He understood what Jennifer was trying to say, but he disagreed with the way she was going about it. Independence was fine. Impudence was not. He didn't realize how deep her hurt was.

"For years, all I ever heard was how important a good education was and how lucky I was to be so bright and so clever. Over and over again, you told me to make the most of what God had given me. Well, that's what I intend to do. You're hypocrites. Both of you!"

Marty put his cigar down and glared at his daughter.

"Jennie, your mother and I work too hard to take abuse from you. We don't deserve it!"

"And I suppose I deserved the humiliation of having my tuition checks bounce two years in a row? Did you ever think about how that made me feel? I was mortified. Positively mortified. If you couldn't afford to send me to school, then you shouldn't have. Don't you blame your failures on me!"

Marty stood up and gripped the table. He didn't bother to wipe the tears running down his cheeks.

"It was unavoidable." His voice was pained and soft. "We had two bad summers, and I hoped that by the time the school cashed the checks, I would have enough in the bank to cover it. Eventually, I did. I'm sorry you consider me a failure, Jennie, but I won't be made to feel guilty by an ungrateful child."

He left the room, his body heavy with disappointment. Sarah, feeling that she had intruded where she didn't yet belong, started clearing the table, eager to escape to the safety of the kitchen.

Jennifer could feel the criticism in the air, but she refused to back down.

"Are you happy now?" Rose asked with a ring of triumph in her voice.

"How could I possibly be happy living in this house?"

"What's wrong with this house?" David asked.

"Everything!" Jennifer marched into the living room. "Just look at it. It's disgusting! Those friends of mine that Mother is so quick to put down live in magnificent homes with expensive furniture and baby grand pianos. They don't have bargain dining room sets with everything dyed-to-match or fake French chairs made in Japan. Their homes reek of money. This house reeks of day-old pot roast and cheap carpeting!"

David was staring at her. His face had hardened, and his dark eyes had become cold with rage.

"And that makes them better people? Just who the hell do you think you are? Mom and Dad have worked their asses off to provide for you. What more do you expect?"

Jennifer stood at the entrance of the dining room,

feeling the alienation she had created. Somehow, she didn't care.

"How about coming home from school and finding my mother there? That would have been nice. Other children remember coming home to mommies who shared milk and cookies with them and helped them with their homework and read them bedtime stories. Not me. *My* mother was never home. *My* mother never took her daughter on shopping sprees in the city or out to lunch. My big treat was sharing a sandwich in the back of the bakery and tracking down half-price sales at factory outlets."

Jennifer could feel the tears welling up in her throat, but she swallowed them, determined not to cry. She felt denied, and she wanted them to know it.

"And what about this close family you're all so busy telling me about? Did we ever go to the theater or to the opera or even to a movie together, or to anything more enlightening than a cousins' club meeting? No! We never went anywhere. We never did anything!"

"Jennie, I think you're getting carried away."

"Am I?" David's warning had no effect. She was shouting, her voice reverberating with all the unsaid accusations of a dozen years. "I've watched my friends go out on dates. They borrow their mothers' jewelry and sometimes even their furs or a designer dress. And what did my mother share with me? Her apron!"

Rose was just as angry as Jennifer, and fighting back the tears just as valiantly.

"Is that why you enjoy spending your vacations with those people?" she said. "So you can play dress-up?"

"Why not? I love it. They belong to country clubs and dine at fine restaurants and serve beautiful, elegant dinners. Not frozen vegetables and overdone turkey. They eat things like milk-fed veal and artichokes vinaigrette. They drink fine wines and speak in cultured tones. Everything they do is refined, and that's the way I intend to live. You may consider this a good life, but to me, it's hardly living."

"Your bullshit is making me sick!" David was pacing. He always paced when he was angry. He hated losing control, and physical motion was the only way he knew to harness his temper.

"Say what you will, my do-good brother. You have no right to get so pompous. Why are you breaking your back to get through medical school? And Harvard, no less? So you can donate your services to some free clinic? Who's bullshitting whom? Deep down, what you really want is money and success. Maybe I'm just verbalizing what you don't have the nerve to."

"You're the one with the nerve. I'm in med school because I want to be a doctor, not because I'm looking to impress people with a collection of meaningless possessions. You're becoming a climber, Jennie, and it's ugly!"

Jennifer struggled with herself. She did want the life of which she spoke, and it angered her that no one understood. It wasn't a crime to be ambitious and to dream and to want to better herself. Their vision was narrow and hers was grand.

"You're entitled to your opinion and to your life," she said. "But I'm going to have a drop dead home with beautiful clothes and lots of jewelry. What's more, I'm going to be a smashing success, and people are going to respect me. I want luxury and stardom, and I'm going to have it."

"Well, Jennie. Oh, excuse me," David said sarcastically. "I forgot that even your given name isn't lofty enough for you. It's Jennifer these days, isn't it? Well, *Jennifer*, let me give you a little piece of brotherly advice. Until you make peace with who you are, you'll never be content with what you have."

Even now, so many years later, Jennifer could feel the contempt that had raged through her as she stormed out of the house. The memory of the disapproval in her brother's voice and the hurt in her mother's eyes jolted her back to the present. She was shaking, just as she had then. She refilled her wine glass and took it to the bedroom, trying to escape the guilt that hung like a pall over the living room. As she lay down on the bed, she wondered if, in fact, she had ever made peace with herself and if perhaps that was why she wasn't content with all she had. Here she was, handsome husband, elegant home, and still, she felt obsessed with the idea of rescuing *Jolie*. She thought, too, about the party and her overzealous dedication to its success. Was that just more of the same? To most, the evening was nothing more than a convenient excuse for a good time. She feared that, to her, it had become yet another starting point in her search for superficial celebrity.

Her back was beginning to ache, and she rose from the bed, walking inch by inch to the bathroom in search of something to relieve the pain. Through bleary eyes, she noticed it was after one. Charles still wasn't home.

Seven

T erk Conlon wandered into the library as the last of the limousines drove away. Across the hall, servants began to clean up after a lavish dinner party. China and glassware were loaded onto rolling carts. Rented tables and chairs were stacked and piled into a corner. Ashtrays were emptied, linens inspected, centerpieces disassembled, and rugs lightly vacuumed for stray crumbs.

A welcome silence greeted Terk as he closed the library doors behind him. Deirdre never used this room for entertaining. According to her, it wasn't properly set up for company. There wasn't adequate seating for large groups. It wasn't convenient to the powder room. The color wasn't always flattering to older women with less than flawless skin. Although Terk disagreed with each reason proffered, this was one issue he refused to debate with his wife. This was his sanctuary, and he didn't want it violated by unwanted visitors.

Here, the walls were lined with books, the floor covered in plush, plaid carpeting. Plump couches strewn with needlepoint pillows flanked a huge fireplace boasting a fieldstone hearth and carved oak mantel. Towering wing chairs upholstered in red and black checks posed majestically before lushly draped windows, and family photographs in antique frames sat neatly arranged on skirted

tables. The only artwork in the room was a primitive landscape painted by Deirdre's mother.

In contrast, the living room, dining room, salon, solar-
ium, even the entrance hall, had a look-but-don't-touch
perfection. Valuable antiques and priceless works of art
accessorized vast spaces filled with elegant furnishings.
Each item had been carefully authenticated, each piece
precisely placed. This was Deirdre's showcase. The house
was impressive; Terk didn't deny that, but on the rare occasion when he was asked for an opinion, his response
was an irreverent, "It's a nice place to visit."

He removed his dinner jacket and untied his bow tie,
tossed them onto the nearest available chair, and poured
himself a brandy. His eyes stung from fatigue and cigar
smoke, and his jaw ached from forcing himself to smile at
people who held little interest for him. It had been a long
day and an even longer evening. As he eased himself onto
one of the sofas, he closed his eyes, resting, feeling the
warmth of the fire, allowing the brandy to anesthetize his
body.

"What an incredible party!"

Deirdre Conlon entered the room with a triumphant
flourish, her jade green gown swirling around her legs, her
face pink with excitement. Her tall, slender form stood
framed in the doorway, the wide portal accentuating the
nobility of her pose. Her neck glistened with a collar of
diamonds, but the glitter paled in comparison to the
sparkle in her eyes as she waved a parcel of checks in the
air and read off the numbers, one by one. "Half a million
bucks for one night's work! What a haul!"

Terk whistled with admiration as he saluted his wife
with his brandy.

Deirdre accepted the compliment with an imperious
smile. Then, with a flippant wag of the checks, she said,
"Don't be so boorish, darling. You make this sound like a
heist."

Terk laughed. "Exactly what would you call it when
you invite forty people to your home with the express purpose of fleecing them?"

Deirdre sat on the sofa opposite him, took off her shoes
and rubbed her feet, wriggling her toes to encourage circulation.

"I call it charity," she said. Her tone was flat, her manner preoccupied, as if his question, perhaps even his presence was an intrusion.

Terk should have been used to her penchant for patronization, but he was not a man who accepted rebuffs easily. Each time it happened, no matter how slight the snub, his automatic response was retaliation.

"Retarded children. The underprivileged. The handicapped. *Those* are charities!" His voice demanded her attention.

"How about the tired and the poor? The huddled masses yearning to be free?" Still, she refused to look at him.

"How about them?" he insisted.

"My dear Terk." Deirdre finally condescended to shift her gaze from her feet to her husband. "Tonight we raised a sizeable amount of money for the Westchester Museum of Modern Art. According to the United States government, it is a legitimate, tax-exempt, charity."

"According to me, it's an exercise in aristocratic indulgence!"

Deirdre's shoulders stiffened, her original buoyancy replaced by annoyance. "You're either being deliberately narrow-minded and argumentative, or you are displaying an embarrassing lack of class."

"I am being none of the above," Terk said with affected defensiveness. "My only point is that if we're going to put forth this sort of effort, it ought to be for a really worthwhile cause."

Deirdre removed her diamond choker, dropped it on the table behind her, and turned to Terk with an exasperated sigh. "Museums are worthwhile. They are houses of beauty and culture, which, my precious barbarian, feed the soul and enrich the spirit."

"The only thing these donations feed are the bloated egos of the rich."

"Don't be such a snob," Deirdre snapped.

"Then don't be naive. Terminal cancer patients and orphans don't spend their Saturdays hanging around museums discussing the genius of Picasso!"

"It wouldn't hurt you to spend a Saturday in a museum," she sniffed. "It might improve your mind."

Terk chuckled and moved forward on the couch, leaning on his hands and smiling at her. "You didn't marry me for my mind, so why the sudden concern with its wellbeing?"

Deirdre's face assumed a pose of extreme patience, but Terk caught the flicker of amusement in her eyes.

"I don't understand why you're making such an unnecessary fuss about this evening," she said. "You had nothing better to do anyway."

Terk's eyes widened in disbelief. "You're unbelievable! Don't you remember the rather heated discussion we had before *your* guests arrived? I told you there was a serious crisis at the magazine and that I was under a lot of pressure. I told you I needed to work tonight!"

"I needed you with me."

"And your needs always come first, don't they?"

Deirdre turned away, but before she did, Terk thought he saw a hurt look wash over her face. He was about to say something, but she spoke first.

"I shall ignore your sarcasm and allow you to fix me a brandy." The momentary softness was gone.

Terk rose and walked over to the small bar in the corner. As he did, Deirdre's gaze followed him, studying, observing, mentally comparing him to the other men they had entertained that night. Her friends' husbands were all lean and lanky, with smiles as neatly pressed as their pants. Next to them, Terk appeared uninhibited and aggressive, his conversation sometimes brash. Even his wavy, butterscotch hair appeared untamed. The other men were pleasant, but predictable, and ultimately, that made them boring. Terk had his faults, and Deirdre could recite each and every one of them with the precision of a catechism, but Terk was never predictable. And never boring.

He handed Deirdre her brandy and sat on the edge of the coffee table near her. It was late, and though he felt rumpled and weary, she was as splendid and sleek as she had been at the outset of the evening. Her long, straight blonde hair still retained a freshly brushed sheen; her creamy complexion still carried a powder-puff paleness. A bewitching scent surrounded her like a perfumed aura, and just then, Terk thought she looked uncommonly delicate and vulnerable. Her relaxed posture encouraged the fabric of her gown to drape and fold over her body, accentuating the fullness of her breasts, the narrowness of her waist. Their relationship was a complicated one, often antagonistic, but no matter what else existed between them, Terk had always found Deirdre an extremely sensuous woman. Tonight was no exception.

"I know you loathe this sort of function," she said, keenly aware of his closeness, "but you are a formidable fundraiser. I had given Ellis Anderson up for lost, and you talked him into a fifty-thousand-dollar contribution. How on earth did you manage it?"

Terk's hand began to slide along her leg, pushing her gown up on her calves. "I simply gave him the full thrust of my Irish charm. Most people find me irresistible. Present company excluded, of course."

Deirdre couldn't decide whether the glint in his eye was laughter or longing. Truthfully, she didn't care, as long as his hand continued to stroke her. As he did, she permitted herself a moment of reflection. He was right. He had been charming. He had flattered the women and impressed the men, cajoling them all with his quick wit. He would never say so, but he had made a special effort tonight, on her behalf. She would never say so, but she was grateful.

"Obviously, the people who find you irresistible don't know you as well as I do," she said instead.

"And what is it you know that the populace at large doesn't?" Terk's nose burrowed around in the bodice of her gown as his lips sought the warmth of her flesh.

Deirdre felt a contented purr rise in her throat, but she stifled it immediately. "I know that you're a phony." She shifted slightly, moving his mouth nearer her breasts.

"In what way?"

She heard the huskiness in his voice and felt his tongue on her skin. For an instant, she toyed with the idea of saying nothing more, of just giving herself to him, but as quickly as the thought came to her, she dismissed it. That was not the way it was between them. Kissing. Touching. Fondling. That was too gentle, too mild for the Conlons. For them, abrasion was the essence of passion, and debate was the most stimulating method of foreplay.

"For one thing, you love mingling with the wealthy,

talking stocks and bonds and supply side economics. It's such a change from your usual pedestrian conversation."

Terk didn't respond, except to reach behind her in search of the zipper to her gown. Slowly, he undid her dress.

"For another," she continued, "if *Jolie* is as all-fired fascinating as you constantly insist it is, why don't you ever discuss it with my friends? They might find it amusing."

Terk had started to unbutton his shirt, but he stopped, a rising anger curbing his desire.

"I think you don't discuss the trials and tribulations of *Jolie*," Deirdre continued, "because even you know that in the real world, the fate of one dinky fashion magazine is totally unimportant."

Terk leaned forward, his eyes boring through her. "It's important to me."

"Why?"

"Because it's mine! Because your money didn't get me the job and because no one there gives a shit that I'm Parker Walling's son-in-law or Deirdre Walling's consort. I'm Terk Conlon, and that's good enough for them!"

Deirdre sat up slowly, clasping her dress against her, moving her face close to his. "In my world, darling, good enough is merely an excuse for not being the best."

"In my world, I am the best!" he shouted. His face was flushed, and his mouth was rigid. "But you wouldn't know that because you've never taken the time to find out what I do or what I want. You're too wrapped up in what you want."

Deirdre's blue eyes glared at him, but her mouth curved upward. "You're wrong. From the minute we met, Terk Conlon, it was quite obvious that we both wanted the same thing."

She leaned forward and put her arms around his neck, letting her gown slip to her waist. As she drew him to her and he felt her bare chest on his, Terk experienced the familiar sensation of surrender. He tried to resist her, but only briefly. Though he denied it fiercely, both to himself and to Deirdre, she was right. He had wanted her from the day he met her. And he wanted her now.

Deirdre Ainsley Walling was the premiere leaf on an illustrious family tree. Her father was Parker Walling, an ardent capitalist who had parlayed family holdings into a startling real estate empire. Even his detractors admitted that he possessed an innate divining rod, an ability to sniff out valuable parcels of land with the accuracy of a hunt dog, and then lunge after deals with a passion most men reserved for women or sports. He was an imperialist, a man comfortable with risk, accustomed to triumph and contemptuous of failure.

Deirdre's mother, Winifred, was Philadelphia Main Line, a frail and mystical woman whose mild, modest demeanor made her the perfect foil for her aggressive husband. Although her family was well-to-do, Parker Walling was a definite step up, and for most of her married life, everything she did was in an effort to please her husband. She was an outstanding hostess, an accomplished equestrienne, and an active member of every socially important organization from the Greenwich, Connecticut, Garden Society to the D.A.R. She voted a straight Republican ticket, drank only sherry, and never questioned her husband, even when she heard him stumbling around his bedroom at three in the morning, having just returned from an evening with one of his women. Winnie Walling was a religious woman and, therefore, at peace with herself. She reasoned that God in all His infinite wisdom would watch over her. If this life did not fill her with happiness, the next life would.

Deirdre had inherited both her mother's delicate features and her father's overbearing personality. As a child, she had tried to emulate her mother's breathy speech and elegant carriage. She took piano and dance lessons. She even dabbled in art and flower arranging, but the role of retiring female never quite suited her. Her father was far more exciting.

By the time she was a teenager, Deirdre had become Parker Walling's protégée. She became a leader without ever having been a follower. She was spoiled, self-centered, and firmly convinced that there was nothing in life she couldn't own. She manipulated people with the same skill that her father manipulated money. And if Deirdre became a bane to her mother, she was a source of unending pride to her father. The only time his strong face

ever soured with disapproval was the day she announced
she was marrying Terk Conlon. A nobody.

Terk was the eldest of four children. There were two
younger brothers, Ian and Sean, and a baby sister, named
Megan. Their parents were Irish immigrants who had
struggled for years to scrape together enough money to
open the Shamrock Bar & Grill in Woodside, Queens. To
them, sacrifice was habit and success meant meeting the
monthly mortgage payment and having enough to put in
the collection plate on Sunday. Terk's father tended bar;
Terk's mother ran the kitchen, and Terk and his brothers
worked every day after school.

Terk never knew when the Shamrock began to turn a
profit, because Thomas Conlon believed that denial built
character. While Terk might have forgiven his father his
penury, he could never forgive what his obsessive frugal-
ity did to his mother. Years of unrewarded drudgery had
weakened her, draining the life from her eyes and rounding her shoulders. Years of exclusion from Thomas's world
had created a growing loneliness. She filled her evenings
with whiskey and died when Terk was fourteen.

Terk blamed his father, and vowed he would have
more out of life.

A friend introduced Terk to Deirdre. He had insisted
that Terk accompany him to a dance at his parents' club
in Greenwich, promising him an introduction to the
heiress of his choice. Terk found it was not difficult to
court Deirdre. She was beautiful, tall, and willowy, with a
cool, blonde aristocratic face. Her paleness struck Terk as
ethereal, and in the beginning, he treated her like a china
doll. Then he got to know the real Deirdre Walling.
Beneath her socialite's demeanor was an insatiable passion, a lust that put him off balance. He had met her at a
time when "nice girls" only dreamed about sex. He was
totally amazed when, on the third date, she invited him
back to her apartment for a drink.

It was late when they arrived. She fixed him a cognac
and disappeared, reentering the room naked and eager.
From that night on, their relationship was intensely, insa-
tiably sexual.

And so, despite her mother's tears and her father's vehement objections, Deirdre Ainsley Walling became the wife of Terkel Michael Conlon.

Terk waited until he was sure Deirdre was safely asleep before he removed the tin box from a locked drawer. His broad chest was heaving, and his breathing was labored. For a minute, he thought he heard Deirdre out in the hall. He gripped the edge of the desk, closing his eyes, listening. When he had assured himself that she was in bed, he opened the box and flipped through a batch of file cards. Then he wrote some names and numbers on a sheet of paper, returned the box to its hiding place, and relocked the drawer. Small tricklets of sweat dripped down his face.

As he attempted to steady his nerves, Terk wondered how much longer he could withstand this pressure. It would have been nice, he thought, if he could have confided in Deirdre and shared his fears with her, but he didn't have that kind of marriage. Deirdre wasn't that kind of wife, and, in a way, he knew he couldn't fault her for that. She was who she was, and he was who he was. His greed had courted and wooed her. His avarice had accepted her gifts, knowing they were tied with emotional strings. He had charmed his way into this marriage. If he was coming close to destroying himself trying to get out, there was no one to blame but himself.

Eight

"Good morning, ladies and gentlemen, and welcome to *Jolie*'s Fashion Forecast of Spring and Summer Trends. Everything that's going to be a fashion statement tomorrow is in our showroom today. Fashion is getting bolder, echoing the demands of liberated women who reject the notion of one look or one hem length. Individualism is what they want, and, according to our editors, it's an idea whose time has come. Watch for a season of alternatives. Choices. Personal interpretations. Evening runs from shy to sexy with clingy crepes sharing the same rack as delicate lace. Daytime shifts easily from business to pleasure with executive suits and jogging suits, preppie classics and sporty moderns. As for colors, the passion for warm-weather neutrals continues with shadings of beige and white popping up in linen, silk, one hundred percent cotton and lightweight suedes. Another grouping we call 'Refreshments,' the pales that seem so right for soft, flirty fabrications. And 'Firecracker Brights' are daring, gutsy colors that mix like never before. You'll see makeup tune into the brights. Intensifying. Exploding. Jewelry is either ultra rich or plastic punk. Shoes go strappy at night, sensible by day. And hair is the accessory of the season. So, sit back and enjoy the show. It's the shapes of things to come!"

A large screen dominated the far wall of the showroom, transforming it into a small theater in which more than a hundred people sat shoulder to shoulder, pencils poised over *Jolie* notepads, eyes facing front. Jennifer sat in the back next to Brooke Wheeler, whose merchandising department had coordinated the show, while one of Brooke's four assistants stood off to one side, behind a podium equipped with an intricate control panel. She switched the house lights off, the platform lights on, and activated the tape recorder that pumped low rock music out of four ceiling-height speakers.

Click. Title slide. "Sultry Nights." Fuchsia background with white type.

Click. Strapless black, ankle-skimming dress with three-quarter-length kimono.

Jennifer had approved all the sketches months ago, but she loved seeing them blown up on the big screen. The illustrations were inspired. Sweeping lines and elongated bodies jumped out like three-dimensional figures. Faces were half drawn, and torso proportions were deliberately distorted. The clothes were vague, stylistic impressions rather than tight drawings—they were intended to indicate and suggest, not to dictate and define.

Preceding both the fall/winter and spring/summer selling seasons, *Jolie* invited the trade to partake of the magazine's expertise. Two shows were produced for each season, each running two weeks, with two performances a day. Today's presentation was Fashion Forecast I for spring and summer with the emphasis on trends. Designers, manufacturers, and fabric people made appointments weeks in advance so as not to miss *Jolie's* predictions. Fashion Forecast II, three months later, in January, would zero in on actual merchandise, giving buyers an opportunity to stock their inventories with predestined sellers. The same procedure was followed in May and August for fall/winter fashion.

Jolie's fashion forecasts were regarded as the best of all the magazine presentations. Most of the credit for this reputation belonged to Marnie Dobbs's uncanny success in picking winning looks. *Jolie's* senior fashion editor possessed a sixth sense about what appealed to young women. If she gave the nod to a particular look, that look sold. The applause that greeted many of the slides told Jennifer that the audience thought Marnie had been right again.

Click. Red suede walking shorts, oversized purple suede T-shirt.

Click. One-shoulder black taffeta dance dress ruffled at the knee.

"You don't actually believe that stores will buy that Hawaiian promotion, do you?" Brooke Wheeler whispered.

"I hope so," Jennifer said. "I'm having a meeting later this morning to go over some of the plans. I'd love for you to be there."

"Let me warn you, Jennifer. This promotion had better be incredibly special if you intend to charge a fee. My stores don't like paying for something they've always gotten for free." An unmistakable, but not unexpected, challenge underlined Brooke's words.

"I think retailers are more flexible than that," Jennifer said. "We'll charge them, and what's more, they'll pay."

Brooke sank back against the cushioned banquettes and chided herself for having missed Brad's meeting. True, she had gotten a stunning Saint Laurent gown and a commitment from Clint Rogers for several full-page ads, but if she had been there, she could have mounted an immediate campaign to discredit Jennifer's idea. Not that she disagreed with the principle of charging a fee for promotions. But Jennifer had suggested it. Brad had accepted it. And no one had bothered to consult with her.

Click. Turn-of-the-Century white cotton blouse with crisp white linen pants.

Click. Calf-length striped cotton skirt, fanny-hugging string knit sweater.

The commentary for the show was pure *Jolie* "telegraphese"—fashion magazine shorthand. Quick. Punchy. No sentences. Just words. Phrases. Exclamations! It transmitted excitement via verbal dots and dashes, and it was as effective in editorial and promotion copy as it was here in the showroom.

"Normally, I give a rundown of the promotion schedule at the end of each show," Brooke said, as if talking to herself, "but I think this time I'll skip it."

"Why?"

Brooke tossed her mane of honey-blonde hair and stared at Jennifer in amazement. "Because I have nothing to report. As far as I'm concerned, we don't have anything at all."

Click. Petticoat cotton skirt, lacy camisole top.

Click. Passementerie. Four examples of fancy trims: Ornamental braiding. Bugle beading. Metallic threads. Delicate cording.

"Tell you what," Brooke said, her tone more cordial than before. "I'll ask some of my friends what they think of the idea at the party Thursday night. Most of the top executives from the major stores will be there. I invited them personally, you know."

"Yes, and I appreciate it," Jennifer said.

As merchandising director, Brooke's sphere of influence was the retail community. Her function was to act as liaison between stores and those manufacturers who advertised in *Jolie.* She fed the retailers constant updates on trends and merchandise currently in production, keeping them abreast of whatever was new and exciting. In addition, she advised them on the most effective ways to reach the elusive, but affluent contemporary woman. She surveyed *Jolie*'s readers on their buying habits—Where did they shop? How much did they spend? What did they think of store displays? Mail order shopping? From these interviews, Brooke had discovered that young women give shoes a higher priority than lingerie, that window displays did in fact pull people into the stores, and that interesting boutiques prompted a great many impulse purchases. Brooke's biggest claim to fame was that her in-store events brought thousands of potential customers onto the selling floor and thereby produced tremendous sales. These events, mostly fashion shows and makeover sessions, were conceived by Jennifer's department and carried out by merchandising's personnel.

Brooke knew her business and her people. One could name a city anywhere in the United States and within seconds, Brooke could tell you every store in that city, its branches, and the fashion coordinator in charge. It wasn't lack of knowledge that caused criticism of Brooke Wheeler. It was her blatant quest for power. Although she headed a vast and important department, it was considered a service arm of the magazine rather than a money maker and placed her lower on the masthead than she felt she deserved.

Click. "Sport Cuts." Red type on chrome yellow.

Click. Pleated white pants with cotton knit polo shirt.

Click. Wide-leg khaki walking shorts, man-tailored leather vest.

"Now how does Brad expect us to make styles like that come off Hawaiian? The concept is doomed," Brooke grumbled. "These looks just don't make it. I haven't seen a grass skirt yet."

"But there have been bold prints and island colors. I've noticed lots of magenta and purple," Jennifer announced, wondering why she was being so defensive.

"That's not enough to build a magazine around."

Jennifer hated to admit it, but Brooke was right. So far, there had been nothing on that screen that said "Hawaii." If Brad's idea was going to work at all, the fashions had to verify the magazine's point of view. No matter how effective sales pieces were, the fashions had to support the notion of dedicating an entire issue to Hawaii. It had to appear as if Hawaii was inspiring a major fashion trend. Otherwise, the whole thing would come off as a phony advertising ploy.

Click. Vivid green maillot and wrap skirt.

Jennifer thought, *what if that were a sarong?*

Click. *Spaghetti strap sundress in lemon-slice print.*

How about parrots or other tropical birds? She almost said it aloud.

Click. *Big flower earrings.*

Click. *Shell necklaces.*

There it was! Small touches, perhaps, but there, nonetheless. It just had to be enlarged upon. Jennifer scribbled some notes to herself, her mind working faster than her hand. She watched the rest of the show impatiently. When the lights finally went on, Jennifer hastily excused herself. She closed the door to the showroom just as Brooke took her place behind the podium and welcomed her guests. Jennifer practically ran to the elevator. If her research panned out, she just might have come upon an idea to make April the most successful issue ever!

Jennifer spent the next hour making phone calls, checking both the legality and the feasibility of her idea. Once she had some answers, she began to think about how her plan would be received. Terk and Brooke might raise some objections, but fortunately, Jennifer didn't need their approval. She needed Brad's, but she wasn't worried about him. Thanks to Ivy Helms, Brad would do anything to save *Jolie* and his credibility. Gwen Stuart would have to be counted. She was normally resistant to change. A conservative by nature, Gwen was content to repeat past successes. She was still grousing about dedicating the April issue to Hawaii, but she would come around. When push came to shove, Gwen was devoted to *Jolie*.

Just then, Charles called. "Hi, sweetheart," she said. "You were sleeping so soundly this morning, I didn't have the heart to wake you. I hope you got to work on time."

"I did. Thanks for letting me sleep." His voice was tinged with apology. "I'm sorry about last night. I couldn't help it."

"If you don't slow down, we're going to have to print 'I couldn't help it' on your tombstone. In order to prevent that, doctor Jennifer is prescribing rest and relaxation for two. I have even decided to reacquaint myself with the kitchen and whip up a fabulous gourmet meal. How does that strike you?"

"I'd love it," he said in a voice that warned Jennifer something else was coming, "but Mother's invited us to dine with her and father. I tried to refuse, but we haven't seen them in so long, I just couldn't get out of it gracefully. Do you mind?"

"Yes, but I'll go." A familiar disappointment welled up inside her. "What's the mode of dress?"

Charles laughed. His parents adored giving formal dinner parties in the middle of the week, and both he and Jennifer found the practice pretentious. They took turns inventing elaborate excuses.

"Your beige silk will be fine. It's just the four of us. I think they've caught onto our little game."

"Well, thank goodness for that. My next excuse was going to have to be that I was taking the night shift at the bakery, and I don't think I could have gotten that one out of my mouth!"

They continued to chat for a few more minutes, and by the time Jennifer hung up the phone, she felt better. Charles seemed more at ease than he had recently. She knew he hated visiting his parents, but so did she, and their mutual discomfort had always brought them together. Maybe tonight would be just what they needed. She hoped so.

Before she'd had too much time to dwell on the matter, Terk Conlon marched into her office.

"I have a proposition," he said.

"And I have a meeting."

"My passions have been stilled by the harsh voice of a business woman." He began to rearrange the flowers on her desk. "But you have jumped to the wrong conclusion. I have to go to Boston to pitch a big shoe company for some advertising, and I need you to come along. Brad wants us to visit Jordan Marsh while we're there. How's your schedule?"

"Tight, but I'm sure I can work it out." She flipped the pages of her desk calendar, starring appointments that would have to be changed.

"Good. This shoe company doesn't part with a bloody dollar unless they think they're getting something in return. I'd like you to give them a spiel on how we would merchandise their advertising and all that. Then, I guess we'll have to charm Jordan Marsh."

"We've done it before," Jennifer said.

Many times, she and Terk had worked in tandem to sell an account or entice a store into taking one of *Jolie's* promotion packages. Jennifer looked forward to the trips, both for the selling and the celebrating afterwards. After a successful venture, she and Terk usually treated themselves to a night on the town.

As Terk left, Jennifer's office began to fill up with members of her creative staff. Some grabbed the floor cushions in front of the bulletin board, others perched on the radiator ledge. Patrick Graham took one of the French chairs near Jennifer's desk and pulled a large glass ashtray in front of him. Brooke Wheeler swept toward another one of the bergères and proclaimed it hers.

Jennifer opened the meeting by complimenting all those who had contributed to the Fashion Forecast. Yesterday, she had briefed them on the new theme for the April issue and now asked if anyone had any thoughts on how to best promote The Big Pineapple.

"I've worked up a poster," Patrick said, holding up a huge piece of stiff posterboard. "As we discussed," he said, looking at Jennifer, "the best approach is a memorable graphic that could translate down into every phase of this April push. I can't claim any genius, because the use of a pineapple is so obvious it hurts."

He had painted an oversize pineapple with broad strokes. The shadings were masterful, and Jennifer could tell he had spent hours on it. Running across the bottom, Patrick had printed the words, "APRIL JOLIE" in the same vibrant green as the leafy crown. It was typical of his work, she thought—well-designed and on-target.

"It may be obvious, but it works!" Her voice was a mixture of appreciation and relief. "I was having nightmares about what you would have to do in order to satisfy Brad, but this is truly sensational."

"I'm glad you like it," he said. She knew he meant it.

Jennifer took the board and walked around the room with it, holding it at arm's length and examining it with the same delight as a toddler with a brand new toy. She showed it to the others, encouraging their enthusiasm. She sat down on the front of her desk and propped the poster up alongside of her as it faced her audience. Then she opened the floor to suggestions.

Everyone agreed that The Big Pineapple needed a fashion show commentated by one of *Jolie*'s own people, including makeovers by professional hairdressers and makeup artists. They also decided that Jennifer's idea to beef up the stage area was a good one.

"How about hiring some Hawaiian dancers to travel with the team?" one young woman from the art department asked. "They could teach the hula as a form of exercise. It might be fun."

"I know where we can get some cheap pineapple pins we could use as giveaways."

"As long as we're adding to the team, how about a career woman to talk about jobs unique to the islands?"

Jennifer was excited. Her staff's enthusiasm was building. Ideas popped out of every corner, for everything from customer giveaways to window displays.

"Let's teach the audience how to tie a sarong."

"How about posters?"

"Maybe a raffle for a free trip to Hawaii?"

"Could we get Don Ho?"

One of the copywriters suddenly interrupted, an inspired grin on her face.

"Let's get the stores to declare the week of the event, 'Big Pineapple Week!, Get their restaurants to feature Polynesian dishes. Do table settings in the china department that feel tropical. Get local cooks to give demonstrations in housewares. If they have a furniture department, get them to do Hawaiian patios. Spread the theme throughout the store! It could be incredible!"

Patrick Graham put his hand on the young woman's forehead and clucked his tongue. "Poor dear. She's coming down with pineapple fever. It's dangerous, but rarely fatal."

"Not to do it would be fatal!" Brooke Wheeler's voice silenced the laughter. "You could never sell a major store an ordinary promotion, but something as all-encompassing as this might justify a fee." Jennifer breathed a sigh of relief. She had hoped that Brooke would respond to the excitement and she had. Though there was a negative ring in her voice, she had begun to offer a few suggestions of her own. "There are so many resorts in Hawaii that sporting goods equipment is a natural tie-in. So is luggage. And don't forget that most of the big stores have book departments. Get them to feature travel books. Total saturation is the key."

Everyone spoke at once, agreeing, throwing out new ideas, embellishing those already given. Slowly, Jennifer was becoming convinced that Brad's concept was workable. If they paid attention to every detail, it could be fantastic.

"I have another thought I'd like to share with you," she said. "How about a secondary promotion? This event is going to cost the stores a bundle of money, and for that fee, they have the right to an exclusive in their area, but if we're really going to sell this issue, we need more than one store in each city. Don't you agree, Brooke?"

Brooke sensed that, once again, Jennifer was going to trespass on her territory. She nodded in agreement, knowing there was little else that she could do.

Jennifer saw the hesitation, but she continued anyway. "What I'm proposing is a paper promotion for the smaller 'momma-poppa' stores. No giveaways, no team, no show. Just a kit with ad suggestions, display ideas, and a few sketches for them to use in and around their stores. This way, they get to tie-in with a big issue, they get all the benefits of the *Jolie* name, and we get lots of exposure."

She was greeted by a unanimous moan. It meant a lot of extra work, but by the time the meeting broke up everyone had consented to give it a try. Everyone but Brooke Wheeler.

The halls were quiet. Salespeople and executives were enjoying expense account luncheons, and most of the secretaries were catching buses to Bloomingdale's or hunting bargains on sale at Saks. The clicking of an occasional typewriter broke the hospital stillness, belying the corporate complaint that for two hours each day Fellows Publications paid for services not rendered. Outside each group of offices, a secretary took her turn monitoring the phones while dribbling bits of tuna salad or cottage cheese on pages of the latest paperback romance.

Terk Conlon's office was adjacent to Brad's. Though he knew there was no one to overhear his conversation, he had closed his door, just in case. He wedged the phone between his chin and his shoulder, curling and uncurling the cord with one hand, doodling on a yellow pad with the other.

"I can't make it today, Eben. I know I'm late, but things have been tight."

The voice on the other end was cold. "You have until Friday."

"I'm not sure I can raise it by then. How about Monday?"

"If you're truly strapped, ask your wife for a loan," the steely voice said. "I don't care how you get it. Just be here Friday at twelve-thirty!"

The phone went dead. Terk stared at the receiver, holding it out in front of him and glowering at the instrument that had connected him to Eben Towers's hatefulness. He slammed it down, feeling the vibrations from the crash mingle with his anger.

The yellow pad rested on his knees, and he continued to scribble, drawing thick lines and sharp designs, creating an intricate maze that twisted and turned into impenetrable dead ends. Black angles jerked into fierce lightning bolts, reminding Terk that the storm his own swollen arrogance had caused was about to break over him. For almost seven years, he had been chained to Eben Towers, starting from the day he had been appointed national sales manager of Morceaux, Towers's Industries' largest sportswear division. Terk wasn't the first man to take kickbacks, and he knew he wouldn't be the last, but for him it had proved to be calamitous.

It had all seemed so simple, he thought, again seeing the faces of the buyers who had clamored to participate in the bogus close-out operation. And why not? It was a natural. Slick and fast. After each selling season, fashion manufacturers found themselves burdened with surplus goods. The only way to turn a profit was to peddle them to retailers as sale items, ridding the factories of costly inventory and providing stores with customer come-ons. Morceaux was no different; no matter how careful the planning, racks of slacks and jackets lingered in the warehouse. Terk's scheme was elementary. A pair of wool gabardine slacks that retailed for sixty-two dollars bore a wholesale ticket of thirty dollars. At season's end, Towers's policy was to offer stores a twenty-dollar-an-item, closeout price with the understanding among the sales staff that if the customer was willing to purchase in large quantities, the inside price dropped to eighteen. Terk convinced his contacts to commit their stores for twenty. He, in turn, went back to Towers claiming that he had been bartered down to eighteen. Terk and the buyer split the difference. In five years, Terk had amassed a quarter of a million dollars.

No matter how profitable the scheme was, he should have known better. His various partners in fraud were too scattered, subject to pressures Terk couldn't control. Family obligations. Mistresses. Medical bills. And greed.

When one of his conspirators in Detroit got hungry and tried to squeeze Terk for another fifty cents per item, Terk balked. He threatened and bullied the man until he felt sure of his silence. But Terk had seen only one side of the Janus from Michigan. Within three days of their blistering conversation, Eben Towers had stormed into Terk's office, brandishing ledger sheets and intoning the penalties for embezzlement. If convicted—and Towers had more than enough evidence to extract a guilty verdict—Terk faced a possible five years in prison as well as stiff fines. And if, by some miracle, he was acquitted, he still wouldn't be free. In the garment business, occasions of petty thievery might be overlooked as well as certain instances of manipulation, but taking kickbacks wasn't so praised, but double-dealing your employer was shocking.

Terk had pleaded with Towers. At the time, Towers's decision had seemed benevolent. He would not prosecute. Double-dealing the competition was easily forgiven. He would keep the matter private, but Terk was to repay every cent, with interest.

It was the interest that made him a slave. In exchange for waiving a time limit on the repayment of the $250,000 debt, Terk was obliged to perform certain services for Towers.

Eben Towers adhered to a strict philosophy of human utility. To him, each person possessed certain talents that, if properly directed, were worth more than money. He spotted in Terk a street sense that could serve him well. He never asked Terk how he fulfilled his assignments, because method was unimportant.

Now, Terk wanted out. He wanted to finish paying his pound of flesh and be done with Eben Towers once and for all.

His eyes fell on the antique filigree frame that held a formal picture of his wife. Her piercing blue eyes mocked him. He stared at her image, recalled Eben's gibe, and sensed frustration take hold of him. It was a recurrent emotion that flared up without warning like malaria, seizing control of his body and leaving it weak. He knew others believed what Towers had implied: that he had married Deirdre solely for her money. Certainly, her wealth had been a plus. It was also true that he had gladly accepted large cash gifts for birthdays and anniversaries, but, difficult as it was to fathom now, he had loved Deirdre when he married her. It was later that her money became more desirable than Deirdre herself.

Terk left his desk, unable to look at the still likeness of his wife. He paced back and forth, trying to quell the anxiety that nagged at him. How much longer could he stand the pressure of finding the funds to repay Towers? The years of pressure had taken their toll. Outwardly, he remained the same: full of bravado. But stress had tempered his bulldog personality and reduced his braggadocio. Caution had moved in. And self-pity.

In a few months, his debt to Eben would be paid, and he would be released from the bondage that had clouded his life. *Jolie*'s impending sale had complicated matters, but that too would be resolved. And then, he would be free. The thought made him grimace. Free to do what? Divorce Deirdre? That had been his motivation for getting involved with Towers in the first place, but then there had been someone waiting for him. There was no one now.

He sat in his chair and surveyed his office, a boxlike room carpeted in navy blue, with a beige leather Chesterfield sofa resting against a grasscloth-covered wall. Above the couch, an array of photographs framed in half-inch strips of beveled chrome contained memories that went far beyond the eight- by-twelve-inch borders. The Daibutsu held center court. The massive Buddha sat in repose with teal blue shadows resting on his lap, shading the folds of his stone toga. His face was green, tinged with the moss of age, and Terk unconsciously narrowed his eyes so he could see the three tiny specks on the Daibutsu's crown. They were sparrows caught in flight, the only touch of reality in an otherwise majestic still life. Beneath it was a grand vista that captured the awesome beauty of Mt. Fuji, its soaring, snow-bonneted peak reflecting itself in the choppy, midnight waters of Lake Hakone. Terk stared at the picture, feeling self-pity well up inside him once again. Lake Hakone was where he had first met Zena Welles, ten years ago.

The trip to Japan had been a vacation planned and paid for by Deirdre. But Terk had little interest in her endless shopping excursions, so they decided to go their separate ways. The arrangement was amicable, with Deirdre content to spend her days browsing around Tokyo antique shops and visiting the thousands of art galleries that dotted the ancient city.

Terk went alone to Mount Fuji, taking the Bullet, Japan's sleek, super-fast train, to Hakone, one of the five lakes surrounding the mystical mountain. At the train station in Hakone, he hired a car to drive him the five miles to Kowakien, a hotel tucked beneath the far-reaching gaze of *Fuji-san*. It was autumn, and as the black Toyota climbed the winding mountain roads, hoards of lush green pines intermingled with autumn trees already fully coated with the colors of nature's palette. The air was clear, contrasting sharply with the stagnant skies of Tokyo, and it felt crisp, inviting Terk to drink it in.

Before he knew it, he had arrived at Kowakien, a sprawling one-story structure of stone and blond wood, landscaped with sculptural hedges and bushes sprouting up from multitoned pebbles. The entrance doors had large uncovered panes of glass and were adorned with huge brass doorknobs; all the other windows in the hotel were covered with shoji screens.

He wandered around the garden for a long time, amazed at the precise mathematical shaping of the bushes and trees, the exactness of each stone-filled oasis. He was working his way toward the outer perimeter of the hotel's property when he spotted a young American woman standing in the middle of a jumble of camera equipment. She was short, with waist-length, raisin-colored hair falling freely down her back. She was dressed in jeans and a plaid flannel shirt; her feet were strapped into worn leather sandals. Her face was obscured by a telephoto lens, which she was aiming in the direction of Fuji, snapping the shutter furiously and moving her position inches to the right after each take. He stood watching her for some time, observing the way the muscles in her curvaceous behind tightened each time she shifted position. Even from a distance, he could see that her hands were extremely delicate, with long, tapering fingers. He approached her cautiously, not wanting to upset her concentration. He introduced himself and began asking her about her equipment, declaring himself a stranger in the world of shutter speeds and lens openings. He saw that she wore no makeup. The wind had pinked her cheeks, and her bow-lips appeared slightly chapped. Her eyes were green, emerald circles sparked with orange flecks, and an unconscious self-assurance shone out of them, captivating him.

Her name was Zena Welles and she was a free-lance photographer on assignment for Cook's Tours. She was doing all the work for their new travel catalogues, and Japan was the midpoint of her swing through the Far East. After several minutes of conversation, she agreed to accompany Terk back into town to help him purchase a camera.

It was late afternoon by the time they returned to the hotel, and Terk invited Zena to join him for a drink. They arranged to meet again in an hour. Terk went to his room with an odd feeling stirring inside of him. He had had a wonderful afternoon in which he had met an enchanting, beautiful young woman with whom he felt completely relaxed.

He was already seated at a window table when she entered the bar. Her hair was pulled back into a long braid, and her face had hints of makeup on it. Her lips were moist, but still uncolored, and he assumed the glisten came from Vaseline. Her eyes were outlined in mint green, intensifying the verdancy of their natural color, and her cheeks were faintly blushed, the rosy powder heightening the impact of her strong bones and small, rounded chin. While she was still yards away, the clean, fresh scent of her cologne drifted around him. Somehow he had known that if she wore perfume at all, it never would have been something cloyingly sweet.

Their conversation was easy. Drinks led to dinner, and over tea, Terk invited Zena to spend the next day with him. When he dropped her off at her room, it was all he could do to leave.

The next morning, Zena insisted on spending an hour teaching Terk camera fundamentals, reminding him that her pictures were business, his for pleasure. After Terk had mastered those lessons, they rode down to the lake where they were greeted by a group of black-capped men eager to rent them shiny motorboats. Zena selected a red one, and off they went, bounding along the perimeter of the pine-sheltered lake. The wind was blowing, and the water kept invading their craft, sloshing up over the sides and splashing their clothes. Zena teased Terk about his natty tweed trousers, making him laugh at his own pretentiousness. He tried to explain what life was like as an ambitious young man masquerading as an up-and-coming tycoon; his tales of tedious sales trips and uptight buyers sent her into fits of laughter. The sound of her spontaneous delight struck him as something he had not heard for eons. They were so engrossed in themselves that they might have ignored Mount Fuji altogether if not for their boat captain yelling at them in Japanese and pointing behind them. He had jockeyed the boat into the middle of the lake to provide an unobstructed view of the majestic peak. They both grabbed their cameras—Zena expertly manipulating hers, Terk fumbling with his. His eagerness to get the perfect shot almost capsized them, and they collapsed into spasms of giggles. For Terk, it was the most exhilarating day of his life.

That night he didn't leave her at the door, but instead made love to Zena Welles with a tenderness he never knew he possessed. Her pale, ethereal coloring was bathed by the moonlight pouring in through the open screens, making her look like a fragile doll whose body had been carved out of ivory. Her hair cascaded over her shoulders, draping her breasts. She was thin, but her body was sturdy. Her breasts were small, but firm with dark aureoles circling pink, responsive nipples. As he lay alongside her, wanting to feel and see her at the same time, he kissed her lips, her eyes, her ears, her neck, all with a hesitant gentleness.

Her skin was cool and smooth, and he felt as if he could stay there forever, just feeling its alabaster luxury. Her long fingers stroked him, making him shiver with sensual delight. They ran the length of his body, titillating him and exciting him beyond anything he had ever experienced. Her rounded fingernails lightly grazed his inner thighs while her lips caressed his stomach, her hair brushing against him and feeling like silk.

She seemed so tiny that he was afraid his weight might hurt her, so he lifted her on top of him, letting her hair form a shawl over his shoulders. Her eyes were closed, and he watched her as he moved his body back and forth. Her legs straddled his, her wetness teasing him, sweeping over him until he thought he would lose control. They explored each other for a long time, prolonging their anticipation and heightening their desire, until her body shuddered. But she was not complete, and she remained with him, coming again and again. He strained against the onslaught of his own orgasm until he was certain she was satisfied. Finally he gave in to the rapture of their togetherness.

As he lay with her in his arms, her head nestled against him, he felt his eyes mist. He had experienced unselfish giving for the first time. Throughout the night, he tried to focus on what it was that he found so entrancing about Zena. Sometime toward morning, he knew he was falling in love with the woman beside him, and he was helpless to stop it.

From that night on, he managed as much time with Zena as he could, considering his circumstances. He had confessed his marital status to her, and to his amazement, it didn't seem to matter. Zena loved him and wanted to be with him. Whatever time they could share was all that was important to her. She waited for him in Thailand and Hong Kong, Greece and Rome. In each place, Terk managed to escape to the pleasure of Zena. He saw the world through her eyes and found it beautiful.

Zena kept a tiny studio in an old brownstone in Greenwich Village, and for two years, they carried on the perfect affair. Terk feigned late meetings and an occasional business weekend, but during those times that Zena had to travel, Terk was desolate, counting the minutes until she returned. After one extended trip to India, he confessed his utter loneliness without her.

They were in her apartment, relaxing on her overstuffed couch and watching the candles from their dinner flicker softly.

"Zena, this is difficult for me to admit, but I'm unable to function without you. I wander about aimlessly, missing you too much to do anything constructive."

"Traveling is part of my job," she said quietly.

"I know that. Really, I do, but it's hard enough trying to see you when you're in town, let alone dealing with your absences."

"Terk," she said, sitting up and facing him. "I've never asked you this, but the subject is simply screaming to be discussed. I know you're unhappy with Deirdre, and I know you're happy with me. Why don't you leave her? Live with me. Love me. Be a part of me."

Her voice wrenched his insides. He had known this moment had to come, and yet he was unprepared.

"I don't know how to explain it to you. Deirdre is a very powerful woman. In her own way, she's paving the way for my success. I'm afraid to leave her. I'm scared to death that if I do, I'll find myself back in some Queens gutter."

"Why?" Zena asked, her green eyes filled with confusion. "We're young, and you don't have any children. I do pretty well, and you have a good job. Maybe we wouldn't live as high off the hog as you do now, but we wouldn't starve."

Terk got up off the couch and walked to the window. His hands were in his pockets, and his head was lowered.

"Zena, I never thought I could love anyone the way I love you, but something inside of me is terrified. You were brought up in a nice, comfortable, middle-class home, and to you, moderate success is acceptable. I suppose it should be for me too, but it isn't. I was a poor kid, always scraping and snatching dimes. My childhood fed my ambition. I want to be wealthy. I need it! And I don't know if I could give it up."

Zena walked over to him and rested her head on his back.

"We won't discuss it anymore. Just come and love me."

That was the last night he ever experienced the joy of being part of Zena Welles. Two days later she was supposed to meet him for lunch in Central Park. He waited there for her for four hours. She never came. A wonderful chapter in his life had ended.

Terk stared at the pictures; his stomach knotted. He shook his head, dismantling feelings of regret and wasted opportunity. Then, he picked up the phone and dialed a number, hating what he was about to do. With *Jolie* in the midst of a crisis, he should have been calling prospective advertisers, but the sale of *Jolie* was not his greatest fear. Not meeting Eben Towers's payment schedule was. As he waited for someone to answer, his thoughts returned to Zena, and for the first time in years, he was grateful for their parting. Knowing who she was and what he had become, he didn't think he could face her now.

Nine

J ennifer felt as if she were being swallowed up by the steam from the shower. The thick vapor streaked the mirrored walls of the bathroom until the glass looked as if it had been frosted with liquid sugar. She took a towel and mopped a circle on the mirror above her dressing table. Then she reached for her hair blower, turning it on high, and letting a rush of heat attack the soppy ringlets. She shook her head and fingered her way through the wet mass until it felt completely dry. The results delighted her. Her coppery-red highlights sparkled in the bright light bouncing off the mirrors, and as she brushed, her hair grew into a wild titian fluff.

She adjusted the towel knotted over her breasts and took her seat at the marble dressing table. Bottles and jars of every description stood at attention, a cosmetic army awaiting orders. She primed her face with a spray of mineral water and a light moisturizer and then set to work on her makeup. As she did, she thought about Josh, the memory of him still vivid in her mind. He still cared for her and in a way, she felt guilty. She didn't deserve his affections, and she shouldn't court them, not even subtly. Then again, she argued, Josh was a grown man with a mind of his own. He wasn't a schoolboy. More than anyone else, he knew her faults. Yet he accepted them. Jennifer stared in the mirror, checking her eyeshadow. Maybe that was what she found so comforting and so disconcerting at the same time. The loyalty. The acceptance. The caring. All without a price and without demands. For a moment, she wished Charles were more like Josh. As she mascaraed her lashes, she chided herself for even having such a thought. Hadn't she married Charles because he was the antithesis of Josh? Josh was open and gregarious. Charles was polished and sedate. Josh wrestled with life. Charles adjusted to it. And at the time when Jennifer had been ready to marry, Charles had been there. Josh had not.

She was applying the last touch of lip gloss when she heard the door open.

"Charles? I'm in here."

Charles Cranshaw gave his wife a casual greeting. The days of kissing hello and good-bye had long since passed. She went to fix him a brandy and soda and rattled off the day's events while he prepared to shower. His silence bothered her.

"Hello. Are you in there? The voice you are listening to is that of your wife. Blink if you hear me."

Charles looked at her, sensitive to the effort she was making.

"I'm sorry, darling. It's been a tough day, and I can't say I'm looking forward to this evening. I'll feel better after I change."

He stroked her cheek and disappeared into the shower.

Jennifer adjourned to the bedroom, turning her attention to the beige silk dress hanging from her closet door. As she slipped it over her head, she considered Charles's mood. She had to accept his explanation. She too, dreaded any time spent in the company of Charles's parents. She fixed the fabric-covered buttons and smoothed down the shawl collar, adjusting the waist so the slit in the skirt wasn't overly revealing.

"We wouldn't want to expose too much leg," she said to her reflection. "The Cranshaws would never approve."

She located her double strand of pearls and fastened them around her neck so the diamond clasp rested at the back. Pearl earrings, a gold bracelet, and beige shoes completed her outfit. As she spun around, she flirted with herself in the mirror.

"Jennifer Sheldon Cranshaw, you're one hell of a good-looking woman," she said, winking at the lady in beige.

She went into the living room to wait for Charles and positioned herself on the couch so she could observe him as he dressed. Charles was a splendid-looking man, elegant, with a bearing that spoke of private schools and privileged upbringing. He was six feet tall with flaxen hair clipped Wall Street short and blue-gray eyes set close to a slim, patrician nose. His frame was lean and firm, strengthened by regular workouts at a gym and occasional exercise sessions on Jennifer's mat. His taste in clothing was as conservative as his investments, and as she watched him don a white shirt and a three-piece navy suit, she knew his tie would be a solid burgundy silk. Charles's wardrobe was understated and predictable, much like Charles himself. He looked exactly like a partner in a prestigious law firm: tasteful, well-groomed, terribly respectable.

Charles slipped his wallet and keys into his pocket and joined Jennifer in the living room.

"Tell me I look fabulous," she said. Jennifer stood and pirouetted.

"As a matter of fact, you do." He took her face in his hands and placed a soft kiss on her cheek.

In the cab, between spurts of small talk, Jennifer observed her husband. She studied his face in hopes of reading his mind. *He looks troubled,* she thought, and she reached for his hand, trying to bridge the distance she felt separated them. She needed to make contact with the man she had married. That man had been controlled, but not cold. He had been prone to introspection and solitude, but never selfish. And even during those times when he had been preoccupied, he had continued to be loving. *I hardly know this man sitting beside me,* she thought sadly. He had changed in the last year or so, and she felt somehow responsible. His reticence reminded her of her father, and the comparison hurt. She had always accused her mother of being more married to the bakery than to her father, and now she wondered if perhaps she was more married to *Jolie* than to Charles. She worried that her own ambition had precipitated the erosion of her marriage, but then she noticed he was still holding her hand, and she felt encouraged.

Wyatt and Celeste Cranshaw lived in a spacious apartment on Upper Park Avenue, boasting ten rooms decorated by Elie Winters, one of the city's more distinguished designers. Huge double oak doors opened into the foyer. An antique brass chandelier cast its light on a floor of brass inlaid marble. Tones of parchment beige had been ombréed on the walls, and an elegant console table flanked by twin Louis XVI fauteuils sat across from the doors. A Grecian urn filled with a breathtaking display of silk flowers sat atop the table, and a mirror framed in distressed wood was guarded by two brass sconces with tiny white pleated shades.

Jennifer handed her wrap to the Cranshaws' butler, a kindly old gentleman who took the lynx boa in practiced silence. He led them into the living room and disappeared as if by magic.

Celeste Cranshaw was seated in front of the fireplace. She rose regally to greet them, a stately woman, slim to the point of being bony, with pale gray-blonde hair pulled back into a tight chignon. Her carnelian silk dress rippled against her long legs as she came toward them, and a delicate smile parted her lips as she took her son's face in her hands and kissed him on both cheeks. She held him for a moment more, admiring him, and then she offered her hand to Jennifer.

They exchanged pleasantries and seated themselves

around the fire, waiting for Wyatt Cranshaw to make his entrance. The butler served them a chilled Chardonnay and a few minutes later returned with a silver tray of canapés. Jennifer sat stiff-backed on a French brocade armchair, keeping her feet tucked close so as not to mar the lacquered Chinese table positioned between her and the couch where Celeste sat holding her son's hand. As she sipped her wine and nibbled on a cracker spread with curried shrimp, she tried to lose herself in the splendor of the room, leaving Charles and Celeste to their own conversation.

An enormous red and white French rug covered most of the parquet floor, establishing the borders for the two separate seating areas. Opposite the fireplace was a magnificent Coromandel screen, its Oriental imagery and shiny black background bathed by ceiling spotlights. In front of the antique screen was a long white sofa with red and white throw pillows tossed into either corner. A low mahogany table showcasing a collection of dinner bells sat before the couch, with two more French chairs like the one Jennifer occupied, on each end. All about the room were Louis XV footstools with petit point cushions and gilt legs, on which Jennifer's imagination placed ladies-in-waiting and royal visitors with diamond tiaras and ermine wraps. Two crystal chandeliers glittered from above, and several large areca palms added softness to the formal setting. The artwork was traditional, but original, part of a collection Celeste had acquired from years of traveling in Europe and cultivating an eye for promising young artists.

Jennifer's stomach was beginning to nag when Wyatt Cranshaw finally made his entrance. He bounded into the room. As Jennifer looked at him, she saw a handsome face streaked with lines attesting to his sixty-nine years, a full shock of carefully groomed gray hair, and an aura of complete success.

"Sorry I'm late," he said, his voice booming. "I was compelled to soothe the rather nervous condition of one of my clients. He still believes another crash is in the offing."

He marched over to Charles, who had risen the instant his father entered the room, and grabbed Charles's hand, pumping it heartily.

"You're looking well, son, though still a bit on the

scrawny side. Jennifer, you should try harder to fatten
the boy up," he said, turning to where Jennifer was standing. Jennifer could see Charles's face tighten, and she felt
for him, knowing how much he hated it when his father
treated him like a little boy. Wyatt wrapped Jennifer in a
strangling bear hug, his large hand hurting her side.

"Fine-looking woman you've got here, Charles." He
winked at his son and placed himself in the chair that
matched Jennifer's. "Well, how are things going, boy?"

"Fine, Father. The firm is doing well." Charles's words
were clipped, yet respectful. "You're looking fit, as always."

"Well, I keep myself active. You know, you really
should come out to the club and golf with me sometime.
It's very invigorating now that there's a bit of a nip in the
air."

"I don't play golf, Father, but thank you for asking."

"Right. Right," Wyatt muttered absently. "How's old
Claiborne? He hasn't been at the club lately."

"He's been quite busy. The office is handling some very
important matters, and Claiborne is involved with most of
them."

"Jennifer, are you still working, dear?" Celeste said,
directing her soprano voice toward her daughter-in-law.

"Yes, I am."

"Why don't you resign from that job and get down to
the business of making babies?" Wyatt said, slapping his
knee for emphasis. "You certainly don't need the money,
what with the income from Charles's trusts and your own
sizable inheritance."

Jennifer saw Charles's face go white, his eyes becoming
almost slits.

"I work because I enjoy it," she answered pointedly.

Charles nodded his approval.

"Jennifer has a key position at *Jolie*, and she's an ex-
traordinarily capable woman. Besides, Father, you have
enough grandchildren to keep you busy."

"That I do," Wyatt chuckled. Charles's elder brothers,
Wyatt Jr. and Willie, each had three little ones, all boys.
"Rough and tumble boys at that."

Celeste glanced sideways at her son, sensing his hostility and hoping they would be summoned to dinner

shortly. Her heart filled with sympathy toward her youngest, and she watched his face carefully while the others chatted about the political situation in Europe. She knew Charles was too old for her to protect him, but her instincts kept his hand in hers, trying to shield him from his father's barbs. Charles had always been her child, the one on whom she had lavished the most attention. Wyatt Jr. and William, so much older than Charles, were the sole property of her husband. They looked like him; they had followed in his athletic footsteps and on to Wall Street as partners in the family brokerage firm, but Charles had been the one Celeste had taken to concerts and galleries, swelling with pride at his keen intellect. She had spoiled him, she knew that, but she couldn't help herself. After William had been born, she had given birth to a beautiful little girl. The child had been born with only one kidney and had died at eighteen months. Celeste had been devastated. It took her eight years to conceive again, and instead of a daughter, she bore Charles. By then, Wyatt had become totally involved with the older boys, and Charles had been neglected. Celeste picked up the slack, doting on him. Looking at him now, so handsome and successful, she felt assured that she had done well.

They sat in the starched formal dining room listening to Wyatt recount his adventures as a pilot during World War II and his outstanding career as a fullback for Princeton. Jennifer spied Charles stifling a yawn, and she prayed the evening would come to an end. But Wyatt had not yet completed his litany. Jennifer knew his speech by heart. Wyatt Jr. and Willie were low-handicap golfers, and they were the newest wizards on Wall Street. Their children were brilliant and beautiful. Jennifer felt her husband's pain and wanted to hold him and console him, but his father kept talking.

She begged herself to concentrate, but her eyes kept drifting to the portrait on the wall behind Celeste's chair. It was an enormous oil of Celeste's father, Tyler Stanfield. Tyler had been captured in profile, and Jennifer thought how inaccurate that was. Tyler Stanfield never turned away from anything. He had been a swashbuckler, an intrepid pioneer who had accumulated his riches by steamrolling his competition. He had built an empire on plastics, having seen the miracle even before the Du Ponts, and had never abdicated his throne until the day he'd died, three years before, at the age of ninety-two.

Jennifer and Charles had spent many pleasant hours with Tyler at his Westchester estate. Jennifer and Stanfield had taken to each other immediately. She, because Charles's maternal grandfather had been the only one to accept her without reservation. He, because of her dogged determination to succeed. Once, he had insisted she take him to the bakery. What a day that was! There they were, standing in the back of the store next to her father, Tyler Stanfield leaning on his gold-handled cane and allowing Jennifer to tie a crusty white apron over his custom-made suit. Marty taught the old man how to make dinner rolls, showing him how to knead the dough with the heel of his hand, rolling it so it was thin and tight enough to braid. Tyler had waited by the oven for his batch of rolls to bake and proudly wrapped them himself in a waxed paper bag.

Tyler Stanfield was no stranger to manual labor. In his youth, he had stacked crates and swept factories to help support his family. He knew what it was to earn a living with one's own sweat. He spent hours telling Jennifer of his early days peddling plastics from door to door, pleading with disinterested customers. He used to say that he and Jennifer were the only ones who knew how many doughnuts one had to make to earn a dollar, the only ones who grasped the correlation between sweat and salary.

Of his three grandsons, Charles was clearly his favorite. The other two impressed Tyler as money-grubbers who expected everything on a satin cushion, not unlike the boisterous man who had married Celeste, his only child. In his grandfather's estimation, Charles had shown tremendous spunk by refusing to join Wyatt in the market. He had insisted on fulfilling his own dreams and his own ambitions, and Tyler had supported him. His only complaint was Charles's Republican attitude toward money. Charles refused to gamble or take risks, something in which Tyler wholeheartedly believed.

Jennifer turned away from the portrait to study Wyatt Cranshaw, remembering the hostility that had raged in his eyes at the reading of Tyler's will. A sizeable portion of the estate was bequeathed to Celeste, with trust funds established for each of her three children; Charles's legacy was greater than the others', bolstered by prime parcels of real estate. Wyatt certainly did not go unremembered, but it was a crushing blow when the attorney read a codicil written several years before Tyler's death. Jennifer Sheldon Cranshaw was to receive Tyler's entire collection of Ezra Gallway paintings, valued at several million dollars. Tyler had found Gallway in the mountains of West Virginia and had been immediately impressed with his powerful portraits of the American working man—coal miners, factory workers, farmers, fishermen. Only Charles and Celeste had been pleased by the gift, understanding the affection behind it. The rest of the family was outraged. Wyatt Jr. even tried to contest the will, but to no avail. Jennifer owned the collection, whether Wyatt Cranshaw liked it or not. And she refused to sell even one of the paintings, whether Cranshaw liked it or not. She did what Tyler had done, allowing the collection to tour museums across the country. Gallway's paintings had been bestowed upon her by a man who had long possessed a corner of her heart. Tyler had earned that place with his humanity, even though others thought he had bought it with his generosity. Charles knew, and she knew, and that was all that mattered.

"You were marvelous tonight, Jennifer," Charles said as they entered their apartment. "I hate to subject you to my father, but I can't bring myself to refuse my mother."

"I understand sweetheart, really I do. It's just that your father is so sanctimonious and frankly, so boring. Sometimes I wonder how your mother tolerates him."

Charles was unknotting his tie. His face was pensive.

"I've never understood it either. The woman is a saint. If not for her, I don't think I would have survived."

Jennifer walked over to him, put her arms around his neck and kissed him.

"I'm glad you did," she whispered, taking his shirt off and rubbing his back. "Come to bed." She removed her clothes and slithered under the covers.

"In a minute," Charles replied, hanging up his suit and placing his shoes in their proper place on the bottom of the closet. He turned off the lights and moved close to her, allowing her to kiss him deeply.

Jennifer ran her hand down his back, tracing the line of his spine and stroking his buttocks, just the way he liked her to. She licked his ear and pressed her body against him, feeling her own body moisten with excitement. She raised her chest, waiting for him to touch her, to rub her with his sensuous fingers. His arms went around her back instead, and he turned so that she could continue stroking his bottom. She ran her hands along his sides, pressing her pelvis against his, waiting to feel his hardness, but nothing was happening. He was soft and flaccid, and she opened her eyes. He was straining, concentrating on pleasing her, but his own body would not respond.

"I'm sorry, Jennifer. I guess I'm just tired."

She heard the pain in his voice, but it didn't salve her longing. He took his arms away from her, kissed her gently and turned over. For a long time she just stared at his back, small tears trickling down her face. He had been tired so many other nights. She wondered if it was a physical fatigue or an emotional vacuum that had caused his impotence; if, in fact, he was merely tired of her. The thought depressed her and she felt a chill. She got out of bed, slipped into her nightgown, and walked quietly into the den so as not to disturb him.

As she stood in the darkened room smoking a cigarette, she felt afraid. There was a chasm between them. She sensed it growing wider and wider, and she felt helpless to close the gap. At that moment, all she knew was that she felt an incredible loneliness sweeping over her. Her carefully constructed existence was crumbling. This marriage, once so supportive and secure, was coming apart, bit by bit. And *Jolie*, once a bastion of stability, was threatened with destruction. She looked out at the stars blinking in the blackness and wondered where they were leading her. More than that, she wondered if she would be happy when she got there.

Ten

It was a little after seven when Jennifer pushed open the doors to Cloud 9. The lobby was dim, lit by two small lamps that cast strange shadows on the ceiling. It was quiet, almost eerie, and Jennifer walked the length of the long entryway hugging the wall. Large buffet tables were already set with enormous glass beakers rising high above empty platters bedecked with silver doilies. The bright colors of the lilies were subdued by the darkness, but every so often a twinkle of light caught on a bead of water still clinging to the freshly picked flowers. Jennifer groped her way to the entrance of the main room where she heard people chattering and glassware clinking.

She hung back, drinking in the moment. Soon this massive area would be alive with pulsating music and excited voices. Laughter would fill the corners, and beautiful people would animate the stillness. Now, it was hushed, gray and lifeless, like a Broadway stage with its props in place, waiting for the actors to bring the scenery to life and give it meaning. The difference was that tonight she was the director.

For a moment, she felt afraid. So much of herself had gone into this that she dreaded even the most minute failure. She stilled her anxieties by wondering how many business deals would be made tonight and how many affairs would begin or end on this dance floor.

For the next hour, Jennifer commandeered her army. She rehearsed the models and checked costumes, oversaw the placement of food, banished the "talent" to the balcony, and tested the special effects she and the disc jockey she had hired had arranged.

Just minutes before the first guests arrived, Jennifer positioned herself at one side of the entrance and Brad at the other. As she glanced over at him, she marveled at how splendid he looked. The worry that creased his features so often these days seemed to have disappeared. He was in his glory, shaking hands and making light conversation, welcoming everyone with a personal comment.

As she greeted her share of guests, her eyes searched the crowd for Charles. So far, he hadn't arrived. Brooke Wheeler glided by, stunning in a Saint Laurent gown of sapphire blue taffeta. Gwen and Frank Stuart were stationed inside, mingling with several Fellows executives and playing host and hostess with practiced ease. Gwen was dazzling in an André Lang suit of black velvet trousers, a plain satin shirt, and short satin quilted jacket to match. She looked radiant standing next to her husband and exchanging quips with Selwyn Fellows, the son of *Jolie*'s owner.

Jennifer was admiring Bettina Kharkovsky, *Jolie*'s beauty editor, when Terk Conlon arrived. He was approaching on Brad's side of the lobby, so Jennifer had to strain to see his wife. Her pictures did not do her justice. She was ravishing in a black velvet jumpsuit jacketed in gold-and-black striped lamé, opulently ruffled at the neck. Her gleaming blonde hair fell freely, one side pulled back, the other swooped over one eye, à la Veronica Lake. She looked, Jennifer thought, like a goddess sculpted in ice.

She turned her attention back to the receiving line in time to catch Diana Ross's entrance. The photographers were all over her, flashbulbs popping. Then the arrival of the mayor stole the attention of every media person in the room. He moved through the lobby with a politician's ease, dodging some questions and answering others. One reporter kept asking why His Honor hadn't brought a date. The mayor, a confirmed bachelor, looked around at the crowd, then back at the reporter.

"Why bring a sandwich to a banquet?" he said.

Truman Capote followed, a huge black cape swirling behind him. He made a point of telling reporters that *Jolie* had been one of the first magazines to publish his work, a comment that greatly pleased Jennifer. She checked off Ali McGraw, a former *Jolie* covergirl, Bobby Short, Marvin Hamlisch, Norma Kamali, George Plimpton and his wife Freddy, and the irrepressible Norman Mailer.

Slightly after ten, Jennifer moved inside, concerned that she had missed Charles in all the confusion. She pushed her way through the crush of people hovering near the bar, stopping to talk to Patrick Graham and several other members of her staff. Suddenly her eye caught Brooke Wheeler, who was talking with a tall man in a beige tweed jacket. Something about the man was strangely familiar, and she walked toward them. She was only a few steps away when the man laughed. Even above the music, Jennifer knew instantly who Brooke's companion was.

"Charles! I was afraid I missed you. What time did you get here?"

Charles brushed her cheek lightly, his mouth still caught in a smile.

"About an hour ago. I tried to get to you, but you were surrounded by hordes of people. I didn't want to interrupt the meeting and greeting process." He took her hand and twirled her around. "You look exquisite, darling, and from what I've seen so far, you throw one hell of a party. I don't think there's room to breathe on that dance floor."

Jennifer accepted his compliments, but she couldn't take her eyes off his outfit. It was definitely a departure from the Charles she knew. The tweed jacket covered a café au lait silk shirt open at the neck, and he wore camel gabardine slacks. Charles watched her appraise him.

"I didn't think you'd want the hostess' husband to look out of place in this high-chic crowd."

Jennifer struggled with her reaction. His outfit and his enthusiasm surprised and pleased her. He was obviously into the spirit of the party, but something just didn't sit right with her.

"You do look marvelous," she said sincerely. "It's just very *Gentlemen's Quarterly*, and you are usually *Wall Street Journal*. I guess it took me back a bit."

"A little element of surprise is good for a marriage, don't you think?" Brooke said, smiling at Charles.

Jennifer wasn't sure what she thought, but before she could respond, Charles had drawn her aside to explain that he had left a business meeting to attend, and soon he would have to return to the office. His tone was sympathetic and regretful, but once again, she became aware of that wedge, that indefinable force that seemed determined to come between them. Call it selfish, spoiled, demanding, whatever. This was her night, and so far, it was fabulous.

She wanted him to stay, to share the excitement with her. He insisted he had to leave. When he put his arm around her in a gesture of comfort, she still felt dissatisfied. She wanted more than a gesture. She wanted a kiss, a hug, some physical reassurance that he wanted to be with her as much as she wanted to be with him.

"And don't feel as if you have to entertain me," Charles was saying. "You're the hostess, and I know you have obligations. Just enjoy yourself." He gave her a playful push toward the dance floor. "I'll be fine."

Jennifer headed for the bar, still feeling uneasy. As she turned toward the crowd, her eye caught the figure of one of the most incredible females she had ever seen. The object of Jennifer's attention was truly exquisite, with Nefertiti eyes and silky black hair that hung halfway down her back. She was wearing an exotic burgundy dress striped in shimmering gold threads. It had no sleeves and practically no sides. Jennifer didn't know whether it was even correct to call it a dress. It was more like a sarong that exposed long, lithesome legs to their fullest, the center draping provocatively. The effect was dazzling. The specific effect on Jennifer was unsettling. Standing next to this vision was Josh Mandell. She had started toward them when Terk Conlon and his wife stopped her.

"Terk tells me you're the mastermind behind this extravaganza."

"That I am," Jennifer said, sensing that Deirdre was not a woman impressed with false modesty.

"I think it's fantastic. What a night!" Terk boomed.

Just then, a model sauntered by in a scanty mini dress covered in shiny paillettes. Deirdre looked shocked.

"Please tell me that was a costume. Otherwise, I shall be compelled to assume that that poor, misguided young woman has been locked away in someone's basement for the last fifteen years."

"That," Jennifer said, stifling a laugh, "was one of our models, costumed to represent the forty years Jolie has been in business. The clothes are all authentic."

Deirdre's eyes were still glued to the model, who was pirouetting for a nearby sixsome.

"Personally, Deirdre," Terk said cheerfully, "I think the

look is super. I'm all for those skimpy numbers coming
back. You know I've always been a leg man."

"I also know you have no taste, precious. Now if you'll
both excuse me, I see an uncostumed banker friend of
mine." Deirdre walked off in the direction of a perfectly
correct gray flannel suit, complete with vest and club tie.

Terk and Jennifer looked at each other, neither knowing what to say. Terk stopped a waiter and lifted two
glasses of champagne from the tray.

"And to the gladiator, a libation for bravery under fire,
valor in the line of duty, and courage in the face of a cyn-
ical woman." He handed her the glass with great ceremony. She smiled in response.

"May I tell you how outstanding you look this evening,
Madame Cranshaw. In fact, I almost didn't recognize you
without your clothes on. What lovely clavicles you have,
my dear."

Instinctively, Jennifer's hand went to her bare throat,
and she laughed, both at Terk's comment and her response.

"You always know just how to make me laugh," she
said.

She held her glass up to his, and they smiled at each
other.

"I hope I'm interrupting something."

Charles's voice startled her, causing her to spill some of
her drink.

"I don't believe you've ever met Terk Conlon, *Jolie*'s super sales manager," she said, drying her hand with her
cocktail napkin. "Terk, my husband, Charles."

As Charles grasped Terk's hand, Jennifer thought he
appeared a bit stiff. She wanted to believe that he was
ever so slightly jealous.

"You have a delightful wife, Mr. Cranshaw. Talented as
well as beautiful." Terk was doing fine. Maybe Charles
would be jealous after all. Conlon was a handsome man.

"Did you say your name was Conlon?"

"That's correct."

"Are you by any chance Deirdre Walling's husband?"

"It is true that in certain circles, Deirdre Walling is
known as Mrs. Terkel Conlon. Why do you ask?"

"I'm a partner with Stark, Brooks and Trumble. Your

wife's family has been associated with our firm for years. I believe her father and Claiborne Stark are old Harvard classmates."

"Also true."

"I've had the pleasure of working with your wife on several matters. She's exceptionally bright."

The situation amused Jennifer. Where Charles had been ever so formal at the outset of the conversation, she knew him well enough to recognize the subtle change in his voice as he shifted into his be-nice-to-the-client's-husband manner.

"Deirdre's intelligence is what drew me to her when we first met," Terk said with a sly smile.

While Charles and Terk engaged in small talk, Jennifer surveyed the room. Everywhere she looked, there were gorgeous women luxuriously gowned and expensively jeweled. It was as if the pages of *Jolie* and *Elegante* had magically sprung to life. The music was blaring, and on the dance floor, hundreds of people moved in time to the beat. Luscious fabrics swirled in a kaleidoscope of color and texture.

When Jennifer turned back, she saw that Charles had left and another man had taken his place. She would have excused herself, eager as she was to mingle with the crowd, but something about this new man intrigued her.

"Eben, how nice to see you." Terk was smiling a little too broadly, Jennifer thought.

"Good evening, Terk."

Terk seemed nervous. Jennifer coughed softly so that someone would remember her.

"I don't think you've met our hostess, Eben. Jennifer Cranshaw, this is Eben Towers."

Jennifer recognized the name instantly. She shook his hand.

Eben smiled at her, a patronizing, pat-on-the-head smile.

Terk moved away from Jennifer and threw his arm around Towers. He was fawning, something Terk rarely did, and Jennifer was dying to know why.

"Eben is head of a very large conglomerate of better sportswear houses," Terk pointed out unnecessarily, raising his voice so Jennifer could hear him over the music.

"Savvy, Helen Dean, Gold Rush. You know him, Jennifer. They advertise in *Jolie*."

"*Used* to advertise in *Jolie*," Towers said emphatically.

It was a party, and Jennifer really didn't want to engage in business discussions, but Towers had created the opening, and she felt compelled to follow it up. Maybe she could unearth some clue as to *Jolie*'s sudden lack of advertiser appeal.

"And why don't you advertise with us any longer?"

"Because *Jolie* is having a passionate love affair with name designers. They've forgotten their position in the market and forsaken the very people who kept them in business all these years."

Jennifer was puzzled. Towers seemed angry, and she didn't understand why.

"I don't think that's necessarily true. Yes, we show designer fare, but our magazine's foundation is the young career woman, and she can't afford closets filled with fancy, expensive labels."

Eben Towers drew in his nostrils, as if he found her attempt to pacify him distasteful. "I'm gratified to hear that you recognize that, but your editorial staff is of another opinion altogether."

"Perhaps they're feeling consumer pressure." Jennifer was glad that the D.J. had switched to softer music.

"Perhaps they just want to wangle a discount for themselves. Frankly, I find it criminal that today's consumer has been brainwashed by the likes of *Jolie* into believing that one pair of designer slacks is a better investment than two or three items from one of my companies. These poor dears are settling for fewer clothes while spending more money for them."

His voice had risen, and several people nearby turned to look at him. He was oblivious to their stares.

"*Jolie* used to be a wonderful magazine," he continued. "Classier than *Allure* and less pretentious than *Elegante*. Somewhere, somehow, someone has run amok!"

Terk shifted his weight from one leg to the other. He sought to change the subject.

The men began to chat about the prime rate, and Jennifer took the opportunity to study Eben Towers. He was an imposing figure, although he was not tall. His custom-made suit was elegantly accessorized with a Turnball & Asser shirt, ribbed silk tie, and Cartier watch. Eben Towers was an important man and clearly, he knew it. Terk knew it too. At that moment, Jennifer didn't realize how important Eben Towers really was.

Brooke Wheeler had hustled Brad Helms onto the dance floor the minute the D.J. changed the mood from mellow back to rock. As they danced, Brad found himself staring at Brooke's chest, watching her breasts jiggle against the low-cut neckline of her gown. Her mouth was set in a seductive smile, and her eyes refused to wander away from his. Every once in a while, he caught snatches of shouted conversation. Something about how attractive he was and what a shame it was about his divorce. She swooped down, bending at the waist and swaying from side to side, alternately singing along with the record and saying something about great ideas for the promotion department. As he watched her, he, too, had a great idea, but it had nothing to do with the office.

Suddenly, Brooke moved up against him, her arms flying over her head, her hips pushing into him. Driven by a mix of champagne and party spirit, and her tantalizing nearness, he put his arms around her. For Brooke, the signal needed no decoding.

Gwendolyn Stuart had spent the evening attending to every celebrity and executive in the house. Now, she plunked herself down on one of the banquettes and loosened her shoes, perfectly content to be a spectator for a few minutes. Just as a pony-tailed blonde in a 50's felt poodle skirt and angora sweater be-bopped past her, someone joined her on the couch. It was Serge Beidermeyer, artistic consultant to all the Fellows magazines. Serge was a painter who had impressed Joseph Fellows years ago and had wheedled himself into a very cushy position. He was responsible for the look of each magazine—layout and typeface, column setups and photographic techniques. Many considered him a genius. Gwen thought he was trapped in a time warp, his taste level having stalled somewhere around 1955. She argued with him constantly that the pages of *Jolie* were too busy, but he held firm. Deep down, Gwen felt Serge's meddling was partly responsible for the drop in *Jolie*'s newsstand sales, but she knew better than to say so. One didn't mess with Joseph Fellows's in-house genius.

"*Jolie* should get some great publicity out of this," she said, pointing to a Jean Harlow look-alike in a sultry white satin gown and ostrich feather boa. "The reporters and photographers haven't stopped for a minute, and the TV crews are setting up for a spot on the eleven o'clock news."

"Clair would never allow *Elegante* to be exploited like this," Serge said, his bulbous nose pointed skyward, referring to Clair Corelli, *Elegante*'s imperious editor-in-chief. "She has such high standards."

"And I suppose I don't," Gwen hissed to herself.

"Don't you think Clair looks splendid this evening?"

"*I don't look like a Barbie doll myself*," Gwen thought as her eyes followed his to the lady in question. Clair did look superb in Calvin Klein's dramatic crepe-de-chine dinner suit with black bugle beads gleaming from the collar and cuffs. She was holding court by the bar, surrounded by a large Seventh Avenue contingent, her industrialist husband standing devotedly by her side. One *FR* photographer after another approached the group, asking Clair to pose for another picture.

"If I open tomorrow's *Fashion Report* and see her face plastered all over that paper instead of mine," Gwen vowed to herself, "I'll cancel my subscription!"

"How much longer is this organized debaucherie going to last? I'd like to know when it would be polite to leave." Serge billowed his nostrils like a Victorian gentleman suffering from an overdose of snuff.

"It might last all night, so leave any time." Gwen rose from the couch. "At your age, you need your rest."

She turned away from the surprised man and headed toward the bar.

Terk was all charged up. He loved parties, and despite his run-in with Towers, this one was exceptional. The music never stopped; the people were super-stylish; the food was excellent, and every one of Jennifer's ingenious devices was coming off without a snag. Just then, he was

watching a huge man dressed in a gorilla suit stalk one of
the models. The apeman stomped his feet and pounded
his chest, playing King Kong. On the other side of the
dance floor, a muscular young man in a leopard print bi-
kini and chains juggled bowling pins. There were magi-
cians, a couple dancing on roller skates, a flame eater,
several clowns, and a snake charmer. This was the new
rage, Jennifer had told him, discos with bizarre live entertainment meant to blend in with the scenery, creating
diversion and filling the air with a sense of circus. The gorilla had just swept the girl up into his arms and was giving out a wild Tarzan yell. The crowd loved it.

He was still laughing when he caught sight of her. He
looked twice, just in case his eyes had deceived him, but
they had not. Standing a little more than fifty feet away
from him was Zena Welles. There was no mistaking her,
but it had been so many years that he hesitated, unsure of
how she would react to seeing him.

"Zena! What a pleasant surprise. I can't believe it." He
embraced her self-consciously, testing to see if she'd pull
away. She didn't.

"Hello, Terk." Her voice was soft.

He felt awkward, as if he were suddenly unable to find
a suitable place for his hands or the appropriate words to
speak.

"You look wonderful, Terk. How've you been?"

"Fine. Just fine. How about yourself?"

The conversation was inane, but he couldn't help himself. He wished he could think of something pithy, something to which she would have to respond in a way that
would allow him to read her thoughts.

Instead, he mumbled, "Why are you here? I mean, who
are you with?"

Zena laughed, her green eyes twinkling and hypnotizing
him.

"I was a *Jolie* award winner a few years back."

"Right. I remember now. You had done a terrific book
on African wildlife." He wondered how she could appear
so relaxed when he felt so tense. "I felt proud, Zena. I almost dropped you a note, but, well, I didn't."

"I understand."

Terk was sweating. He felt like a college freshman at his first mixer. The fact that every few seconds someone bumped into them or stopped to say hello didn't help.

"Zena, I have to speak to you. Come have a drink with me somewhere else."

"I'm here with someone," she said. "And so are you. By the way, she's very beautiful."

It took Terk a minute to realize she was referring to Deirdre. Before he could respond, someone slapped him on the back. He turned around to face Randy Webster, an old acquaintance who chattered away about his marriages, his divorces, and his business, completely unaware of the scenario being played out around him. It was Randy who had introduced him to Deirdre, a hundred years ago it seemed. But Terk barely heard a word. The nearness of Zena was stifling, like an overpowering perfume. He tried to speak to her, albeit silently, attempting to send messages with his eyes. He was certain that she had answered him, making him wish for a magic wand that could accelerate time, end this evening, and spirit them into tomorrow when he could call her. There was so much he wanted to say. So much he needed to know. Odd as it seemed, the moment he saw her, he had felt old emotions rise up within him like a riptide. Just as he had so many years ago, he felt bewitched by Zena Welles.

Terk wasn't the only one surprised to see Zena Welles at Cloud 9. Deirdre had spotted her an hour before and, since then, had stalked the young photographer. She watched Terk embrace Zena, and a cold anger prickled at Deirdre's skin, as if an Arctic wind had rushed through the crowded room. She slid into a corner where she could maintain distance from them and still keep them clearly in view.

Terk thought she never knew about him and Zena, but she had been aware of their affair almost from the start. It wasn't the late meetings or frequent business trips that had tipped her off. Rather, it had been Terk's lack of sexual enthusiasm. No matter how often they had fought or how bitter the arguments had been, their bed had always been a passionate meeting ground. Terk had continued to perform his husbandly duties, but their lovemaking had become quiet, almost perfunctory, minus the animal lust that Deirdre had been used to from Terk.

At first, Deirdre had concluded that Terk's distraction was the result of stress. He had always been obsessed with the idea of making a name for himself, of proving himself worthy of marrying a Walling, so she had held her tongue. Then, when he had begun to forget social engagements and neglected to show up at certain functions, she had become even more concerned.

Her mother had noticed Terk's absences as well as the tension between her daughter and her husband. When she had mentioned it to Deirdre one day over lunch, she had hinted at the possibility of another woman. Deirdre had scoffed at the idea. Yet she knew that Winnie was qualified to read those kinds of signals. The word "fidelity" had never been a part of Parker Walling's vocabulary.

"What if he is having an affair?" she had asked. "What do I do?"

"Nothing," Winnie had said with the authority that comes from experience. "Wait it out. You don't break up a marriage over a fling."

The next day, Deirdre had hired a detective. When she had a name and an address, she had conceived a plan. One night, after Terk had taken a taxi, supposedly to go to the airport for a flight to Atlanta, Deirdre had followed him. Terk had entered an old building, suitcase in hand, and Deirdre had waited. Hours passed and still she waited. It had been almost noon the next day when Terk and Zena had emerged, arm in arm.

Even now, so many years later, Deirdre remembered the rage she had felt then, the hurt and the fury of betrayal. She remembered wanting to jump from the car and confront him right there on the street. But she had done nothing. For two years, she had continued to get reports from the detective. For two years, she had choked on her pride. Then, one day the detective came to her and said that Zena Welles had closed up her apartment and left town. Winnie had been right. You didn't break up a marriage over a fling.

But Terk's fling had changed their marriage. They fought more and loved less. She carped at him. He ignored her. Now Zena Welles was back and so was the smitten look on Terk's face. Deirdre had stood by once before. She had no intention of standing idly by again.

At five minutes before twelve, Brad Helms climbed up into the D.J.'s booth where Jennifer was waiting for him. It was time for his speech, and the special effects. While they waited for the stroke of midnight, Jennifer searched the crowd. Charles, to her surprise, was still in attendance, laughing and joking with a small group stationed behind the dance floor. On the other side of the dance floor, she spotted Josh and his companion, the black-haired woman in the fabulous dress, who was holding her hands up to her face, fending off a horde of persistent photographers. Who was she that the boys from *FR* were plaguing her so? And why was it bothering her to realize that Josh had not come to the party alone? She watched them dance. Josh was marvelous. He looked wonderful, and she decided that even if she didn't know him, she would have stared at him. For a moment, she wished she were the woman in the sarong.

Finally, the D.J. gave the signal for the music to stop. The lights dimmed. All motion ceased, and soon, the room was quiet. Brad moved to the microphone, adjusting it to accommodate his height. He looked over at Jennifer, who smiled and urged him to begin.

"Ladies and gentlemen. We interrupt the festivities for a brief commercial message."

The audience laughed and Brad relaxed.

"Tonight, we are celebrating the fortieth birthday of *Jolie*. For those of us who work on the magazine, it's a very special occasion, for it means we have come of age. On behalf of the entire staff, I'd like to thank our friends for accepting our invitation and sharing this night with us."

He paused, waiting for the applause to stop.

"For forty years, *Jolie* has honored America's young women, feasting them with the best of fashion and the latest in beauty. Our goal has always been to keep abreast of current trends, and, I'm proud to say, over the years *Jolie* has been responsible for starting many trends of its own. Our editors are blessed with the knack of catching the pulse of a nation and presenting the most exciting fashions Seventh Avenue has to offer.

"Recently, we've increased our health and fitness pages, because we firmly believe that inner health has everything to do with outer beauty. Our fiction pages have provided a forum for some of the finest authors and poets in the country, and many of those whose first works appeared on our pages are here tonight. We congratulate them on their success and ourselves on our foresight."

Another round of applause. Brad was beaming. His hands were shaking, but his voice remained strong.

"Our nonfiction has always been timely, aimed at helping our readers deal effectively with their lives. We've discussed everything from good sex to bad dates. We've shown them how to organize their closets and urged them to come out of their closets. We've taught them to decorate their homes as well as themselves. And we've given them invaluable tips on how to climb corporate ladders and what to do with their power once they've reached the top. *Jolie* is the magazine of the young career woman. We own her. And we're not going to let her go."

His voice was firm, and he underlined his last statement, making it sound almost like a dare.

"We feel we owe it to these women to remain in the forefront, and so, in keeping with the spirit of the occasion, *Jolie* is about to launch another trend. Once again, we're going to forge ahead and dare to be different. It's our birthday present to you."

He took a deep breath and then continued.

"The April issue of *Jolie* marks a first, not only in fashion, but in magazine publishing as well. The entire issue is dedicated to Hawaii. Everything from fashions to food will have a tropical flavor. We sense a mood, a feeling, that young people today yearn for a touch of paradise, and *Jolie* is prepared to give it to them. Our Big Pineapple is destined to be the most exciting single issue ever to hit a newsstand!"

His stomach fluttered as he watched hundreds of people exchange comments with their neighbors. He noticed Jennifer watching also.

"And now, before you change channels on me, I'd like to thank my entire staff for making this night possible, especially *Jolie*'s Promotion Director, Jennifer Cranshaw, who put this incredible evening together."

He held out his hand and brought her forward. Jennifer's ears filled with the thunderous applause from the appreciative crowd.

"If," Brad continued, keeping Jennifer by his side, "it's true that life begins at forty, let me assure you that everyone at *Jolie* is ready for it. I wish us all a happy birthday and aloha."

The instant Brad's speech ended, hundreds of balloons imprinted with *Jolie*'s logo dropped from the ceiling onto the dance floor. Behind them, an enormous neon sign was being lowered, its bright lights illuminating the room. It was a giant outline of a green and orange pineapple which surrounded the phrase, "JOLIE GOES NATIVE" crafted in white neon script. Then, all thirty models paraded onto the dance floor, preening in their costumes and tossing trinkets into the crowd. They were plastic pineapple pins, and people scooped them up as quickly as they fell. The screams and wild applause that greeted the finale thrilled Jennifer, and she shivered when all twelve hundred guests sang "Happy Birthday" along with the record the D.J. had turned on. A bubble machine dropped glistening circles on everyone's heads and a smoke machine spewed fog along the floor. It was the most spectacular sight she had ever seen.

Josh had avoided her all evening, but the minute the hoopla died down, and his date went to the powder room, Coral Trent headed straight for him. He toyed with the idea of walking the other way, but he knew she would track him down wherever he went.

"Joshua Mandell, shame on you. I think you've been hiding from me." She tickled the underside of his chin with long, red-painted nails.

"I've been mingling." He moved back a step, but she moved too.

"It's been years since I've heard from you."

Her face was heavily made up, and her lips were thick with hot pink. Her hennaed hair had been combed into a huge bowl cut and long bangs covered her eyebrows.

"Coral, I was never the only man in your life, and you

know perfectly well why I stopped calling you, so cut the bullshit!"

His voice was harsh. Hers was cloying.

"I felt terrible about your wife, really I did, but I assumed your mourning was over long ago. You certainly don't look like a grieving widower tonight, sugar."

Her mouth was pulled into a tight sneer, and Josh had to control an urge to smear her lipstick all over her face.

"Did anyone ever tell you you're a very trashy lady?"

"You did, many times, but you seemed to love rolling around in the trash."

"Drop it, Coral." His words squeezed through clenched teeth, and he tried to maneuver his way around her, but she blocked him, throwing her arms around his shoulders.

"Don't tell me you've become a monk. Not the Josh I knew."

"That man doesn't exist anymore!" Josh pulled her arms off him and flung them down at her sides.

"I don't believe that for a minute. Especially since I checked out the piece of ass you've been cuddling with all night."

"It was over a long time ago, Coral. It never should have been."

"Maybe not, but it was. And it was something else!"

"I'm sure you've found plenty of other beds."

She looked at him and laughed, a low, sinister chuckle.

"Some were too big, and some were too small. Yours was always just right."

"Do us both a favor and make a hasty exit before this turns ugly."

"Whatever you say. But if you ever feel the need, give a call."

She sauntered off, her laughter burning his ears. He swallowed his drink quickly, his eyes aflame with anger. He felt dirty and longed to run to the men's room to wash his hands. Coral Trent was filth, but she was right. He had been all too willing to wallow in it.

Jennifer's curiosity was aroused. She had witnessed the entire scene between Josh and the model, and she couldn't imagine what Coral could have said to upset him so. His face was a study in anguish, and it took a lot to unsettle

Josh. That girl had done it, and Jennifer wanted to know why.

She elbowed her way through the jumble of bodies, excusing herself as she went. Several times, people stopped her, offering congratulations and begging to know more about The Big Pineapple. She could feel enthusiasm for the project sweeping through the room—more than one plastic pineapple had been pinned to a lapel. Jennifer steered each person who asked about the promotion toward a *Jolie* salesman, leaving the potential customer seconds after the sales pitch began. By the time she reached Josh, his mood seemed somewhat restored. Jennifer wondered if it was due to the saronged woman, who had reappeared at his side.

"Is this the most fabulous party you've ever been to in your whole entire life?" Jennifer flashed her most captivating smile at Josh. "Do not be shy. Feel free to rave about the neon pineapple and the balloons and the bubbles and the glitz and the whole thing!"

Josh took Jennifer into his arms and hugged her. "I must admit," he said, still holding her near, "I haven't been to anything so outrageous since Sidney Sulcov's bar mitzvah!" He backed away, retreating until only their fingers remained entwined. "There is only one problem."

Jennifer's face immediately responded to the seriousness in his voice.

"I think I'm falling in love with the guy in the King Kong suit."

Jennifer's smile returned, broader than before.

"We're being rude," she said. "I don't know your date, and I'd like to."

"Forgive me," Josh said. "Jennifer Cranshaw. Elyse de Marco."

The name registered.

"Elyse de Marco. Of course. No wonder *FR*'s shutterbugs have been hounding you all night."

"They do make me extremely nervous," Elyse said. "I hate publicity, and usually, I avoid places where I think the press will be out in full force. It's a tribute to you and your party that I haven't locked myself in the ladies room."

Elyse de Marco was not only breathtaking, she was exceptionally talented as well. The de Marco name signified the most imaginative design in New York. No wonder Josh seemed so enchanted with her.

"I've been trying to convince Elyse to go into her own business," Josh said. "I've offered to take her away from her tony little boutique and make her a millionaire, but she keeps turning me down. I must be losing my touch."

Jennifer looked from one to the other. From what she could see, Josh hadn't lost his touch at all.

"I've gone over this with you a dozen times," Elyse said, seeming embarrassed at having to discuss this in front of Jennifer. "I like my boutique. If I had to mass produce, I'd never be able to indulge my fantasies the way I do now. My designs are not typical mass market merchandise. Do you really think the great American public is ready for this?" She pulled at her dress, emphasizing the sarong design.

"Josh may be right." Jennifer sensed that Elyse wanted to end the discussion, but an idea prickled at her, prompting her to continue. "The de Marco name already means super-chic. Who's to say what the American public is or is not ready to accept? Now might be the perfect time to go nationwide. Besides, you could always keep the boutique for one-of-a-kind items."

Elyse tensed. In an instant, the easy friendliness she had displayed faded behind a tight mask.

"I couldn't do that."

Jennifer couldn't imagine what she had said to trigger such an abrupt response. She stole a sideways glance at Josh, but he appeared as confused as she. "I almost forgot," she said, turning to Josh and hastily changing the subject. "My mother called tonight before I left. David and Sarah are coming home next week."

"No kidding!" Josh was still eyeing Elyse. "That's great. Make sure Davey Doctor calls me."

"It's entirely possible he'll call you before he calls me," Jennifer replied, half to herself.

"Don't be silly. Whatever went on between you two doesn't matter anymore. I've never known David to hold a grudge for more than a millennium, so forget it. Besides, this is your night. Your Big Pineapple is off to a flying start, and I, for one, am excessively proud of you."

He leaned forward and kissed her, partly because of the party, partly because of the distress that had washed across her face when they spoke of her brother. As his arms went around her, Jennifer felt blanketed by warmth and support. She also felt a strong impulse to return his embrace, to give in to those flutters of emotion that danced inside her whenever they were together. Even with the music blaring and people swirling around them, snatches of memories fringed her consciousness, flashing bits of moments shared and years lost before her eyes. She pulled away.

"Is this a high school reunion?"

For the second time that night, Charles's voice had startled her. This time, she turned to find him smiling at Elyse de Marco. Jennifer made the introductions, and for a few minutes they chatted amiably. Then for some reason, Jennifer stole a look at Charles's watch.

"I thought you had to be back at your office," she said.

"Actually, that's what I came to tell you. I called in, and the negotiating is still going on. Much as I hate to leave, I must."

Three photographers suddenly invaded their group, snapping at Elyse, asking Josh's name, clicking and demanding until Elyse covered her face and turned her back to them. When they left, Elyse was visibly shaken.

"Josh, would you mind if I left? I really can't take it anymore."

"I'm leaving anyway, Miss de Marco. May I drop you off?"

Jennifer looked at Charles, her face expressionless. His gesture was gentlemanly and just what she would have expected of him, but somehow she felt less than gracious.

"I don't want to take you out of your way, Mr. Cranshaw," Elyse said.

"On the contrary. It would be my pleasure. I'm dropping Brooke Wheeler off. Another passenger would be no bother at all."

"That's very nice of you, Charles," Josh said. "I must admit, I'd like to stay. If Elyse wants to leave, I'd feel better about it knowing you were seeing her home."

Charles turned to Jennifer and kissed her lightly on the cheek. Then he held her face near his and spoke to her softly.

"I can't tell you how proud I am. All evening, I've listened to people sing the praises of my wife. You deserve every word of it. The party was smashing, my darling, and so are you. I only wish I could stay until it's over."

"I understand," she said, wishing that she did.

"You and Josh enjoy the rest of the party. If the meeting drags on too long, I'll stay over at the office."

Jennifer and Josh watched them leave.

"Charles is right. Let's enjoy your success. You haven't danced once tonight, and I happen to be a summa cum laude graduate of the Fred Astaire Dance Studio."

Josh took Jennifer's hand and led her onto the dance floor, maneuvering her in such a way as to keep her eyes off the door.

A little after two, Josh found Jennifer in the Cloud 9 office. Most of the guests had left, and the winding down of the party had affected Jennifer. She felt sad, deflated. Her night was over, and though it had been everything she had wanted it to be and more, endings had always depressed her. She recalled her mood when Charles had left and chided herself for being petty. She decided to call him, to tell him how glad she was that he had come at all, that she understood how difficult it must have been for him to get away, and to say good night.

"Going over the final figures?" Josh asked, noticing a grimace on her face and massaging her back.

"I'm going to call Charles to see if his meeting has ended," she said, grateful that Josh was helping ease the pain in her back. "I just want to find out if he's going to make it home tonight."

"It's not necessary," Josh said.

"It'll only take a second."

Jennifer dialed Charles's office and sat, listening to the phone ring. It rang and rang and rang. After several minutes, Josh reached over her shoulder, took the phone out of her hand and replaced it in its cradle.

"They must have disconnected the switchboard," Jennifer said without conviction. "They're probably so wrapped up in their meeting, they never heard the phone." Her tone was disheartened and even a bit embarrassed.

"Probably. Now let me take you home."

Jennifer just sat there, staring at the silent phone. She dialed the number one more time and let it ring until the sound of it buzzed inside her head. She put down the phone and looked at Josh.

"Take me to your place," she said.

Eleven

Jennifer felt awkward. She had never been in Josh's apartment before. She wasn't sure what she expected, but what she found was quiet luxury, and it startled her. Large rooms sprawled over half a floor in one of upper Fifth Avenue's most stately buildings. He led her through a darkened formal living room and into the kitchen. There, Jennifer felt the warmth of family life surrounding her, like the pungent smell of pot roast simmering on the stove or brownies baking. Elementary school art patchworked one entire wall with rudimentary sketches and fingerpainted abstracts. Math papers and spelling tests boasting happy-face stickers and colored stars clung to the refrigerator door, under plastic fruit-shaped magnets, vying for space with bus schedules and shopping lists. A child's step stool rested beneath a counter populated by a Big Bird cookie jar Jennifer guessed was always filled, a Cuisinart with all its attachments, a mayonnaise jar overflowing with broken crayons, and a big bottle of Flintstone vitamins.

Jennifer fingered the straps of a Snoopy knapsack, silently congratulating Josh. Although she knew it was a housekeeper who battled the crowds at the A&P and folded underwear, it appeared as if life in the Mandell household simply hummed along. Still, as she watched

Josh rummage through the refrigerator, she wondered who checked the children's homework and who took them for checkups at the dentist. She wondered if they were allowed to play at friends' homes after school and if they were ever punished. Without realizing it, she voiced her thoughts.

"Does your housekeeper tell them stories and buy them sneakers?"

Josh stopped his scavenging and looked at her.

"Jennie, what is this? Are you a social worker in disguise?"

Jennifer laughed self-consciously.

"No. I'm sorry. I'm very fond of your children."

"They're fine, honest. If you'd like, you can see for yourself."

Jennifer watched as Josh visited his children. She smiled at the way he crept first into Rachel's room and then into Scotty's, tucking blankets under chins and leaving soft kisses on puffy, sleepy-pink cheeks. She stood in the doorway while Josh retrieved a fallen teddy bear and gently placed it in the crook of Scotty's arm. A sense of envy gripped her throat until she coughed, swallowing as if a too-big piece of apple were crowding her esophagus.

Josh motioned for her to join him, and she took a tentative step forward. She wanted to kiss the sleeping child, to feel his warm breath against her face, but she didn't. She couldn't. She wasn't the boy's mother. No matter how warm and loving Josh's children were when they saw her, she was only an occasional accessory to their lives. Deep inside of her, Jennifer began to hurt.

Jennifer snuggled into one of the loveseats in Josh's studio, tossed her shoes off, and cuddled one of the pillows. Josh had removed his jacket and tie and sat next to her, his feet propped up on an ottoman, his expression relaxed. Jennifer felt strange. Here she was sitting with a man she'd known almost all her life, and she was struggling to make simple conversation.

"I hope you don't mind. I mean, I did invite myself."

"Not at all," he said, smiling at her. "As long as you don't ask to see my etchings."

"Is that what the women you bring here usually do? Ask to see your etchings?"

"I don't bring women here," he said.

Jennifer lowered her eyes. She was angry with herself for sounding so coy. It was ridiculous to pose in front of a man who knew her so thoroughly. For several minutes, she took an inordinate interest in the patterns of light dancing in her wine, reflected from the fire Josh had built.

Josh rose and went to the fireplace, poking at the smoldering logs and causing them to sputter and spark. He stood silently, his face clouded with memories, scanning a mantelpiece crowded with family pictures. He studied each one carefully, as if to assure himself that those times had really existed. Jennifer followed his gaze, staring at shots of Laura and the children frolicking in the ocean; Josh and Laura beaming down at a newborn Scott; Laura and Rachel feeding each other sandwiches; Scotty tossing a football to his mother's outstretched arms. It was a poignant gallery.

"Laura was a beautiful woman, Josh. Inside and out. I wish we could have gotten to know each other."

Josh turned to her and swirled his wine around in his glass, a sadness invading his face.

"She was special. Very special. The two of you would have liked each other."

He returned to the sofa, and Jennifer felt a presence between them.

"Jennie, do you love him?"

"What?"

"Do you love Charles?"

Jennifer didn't answer.

"Do you love Charles?" he repeated.

"I'm not sure."

"Did you ever love him?"

She hesitated, but his eyes bored right through her, insisting.

"Not the way I loved you," she whispered.

Josh nodded, almost matter-of-factly, as if he had anticipated her response. He took a long sip of his wine. When he looked at her again, his face was tight.

"Why did you reject me?"

There it was. It had been stalking the atmosphere,

hovering over them, skulking in corners, waiting for just the right moment. Jennifer knew the cage had sprung open. Their past had just burst into the room.

"Jennie, I asked you a question." His voice was harsh.

Jennifer shivered. She had avoided that question for years, fearing the effect of her answer. She shifted in her seat. Finally, she looked at him.

"I did love you. Believe me, I did. But . . . I had known you for years, and we just weren't exciting anymore. You were too available. Too stable. Too acceptable. My parents loved you. My brother worshipped you. And my friends adored you. I felt trapped. Almost manipulated, as if my parents and yours had signed a contract when we were toddlers. I wanted to escape. To rush out and experience life."

Josh laughed, a forced chuckle that gave Jennifer chills.

"That's odd," he said. "I had the mistaken idea that we would experience life together."

"Please. Let's not dwell on this. It happened so many years ago." She reached out for his hand, and when he pulled away, she felt confused. "You didn't exactly pine away for me, you know."

He leaned back, pursed his lips, and considered her last remark.

"I suppose that depends on how you look at it. I was hurt for a very long time. Angry too. You had made it abundantly clear that I was not part of your master plan. Several years went by, and then I met Laura. I fell in love with her, deeply in love, and I pursued her doggedly. She made me a happy man, even though I wasn't worthy of her. She gave me purpose and fulfillment, not to mention two marvelous children. I can't possibly regret the eight years I spent with her."

"I know. I'm sorry. That was unfair of me."

"Yes, it was. Did you think I was going to remain celibate because you had given me the heave-ho?"

An embarrassed smile crossed Jennifer's lips.

"Yes, I did. How immature that was! I had rejected you, but somewhere in the back of my mind, I expected you to wait for me. When I heard you had married, I felt you had deserted me. That's insane, don't you think?"

Josh laughed and refilled both their glasses.

"Not really. But I didn't desert you. I replaced you. I can even say that I still loved you, but I had to put you into another place. A place where I could love you and Laura at the same time."

Jennifer became pensive, spinning her wedding ring around her finger in slow, hypnotic circles.

"Josh, when Laura died, did you ever think about us?"

"You were married by then. You were Mrs. Charles Tyler Cranshaw, and what God hath joined together, let no old boyfriend put asunder," he said. Then, suddenly serious: "Jennifer, what's going on between you and Charles?"

She sighed deeply. When she spoke, her voice sounded remote, almost detached.

"Not much. We're like polite strangers, begging one another's pardon and things like that. It wasn't always this way, but now we're drifting, and I don't know what to do about it."

"Leave him."

"What?"

"Leave him. Why is that idea so shocking to you? You seem very unhappy, and I would venture a guess that so is he."

Jennifer stared at him. There was something in his tone that unnerved her.

"I can't."

"Why the hell not?"

"Because I made a commitment and because I don't like to fail."

Josh looked at her carefully.

"You're afraid of what people might say, aren't you?"

Jennifer lowered her eyes.

"You'd rather live a life that's making you unhappy than admit you made a mistake!" Josh's mouth tightened into a straight line. "Are you afraid divorce would hurt your chances of getting a bigger and better job?" His voice rose. "It's your fucking ambition that's keeping you chained to this farce you call a marriage, isn't it?"

"Leave my ambition out of this! That's your answer to everything. Ambition. You make it sound like it's something filthy. Well, you have no right to do that. You think you got all this without ambition? Bullshit."

They both shrank back into their respective corners and glared at each other. Josh softened first.

"Okay, do you want me to tell you how I see it?"

"Is this going to be another one of your lectures?"

"No. This is going to be a discussion. A conversation between two consenting adults. All right?"

"Fine."

"I see ambition as a straight line. It extends up and up. It's a thin line, like a tightrope, which makes it hard to keep one's balance. What's more, this line is a continuous one. It has no conclusion."

"Wrong, Herr Professor. Success is its conclusion," Jennifer said.

"Aha! But what is success?"

"I feel as if I'm taking a quiz."

"You are, and there are no marks. Just pass and fail. At some point, Jennie, you have to start shaping that straight line into a circle. If you don't, you'll never be happy."

"And you don't think I have any circles in my life?"

"No, I don't. You and Charles certainly haven't created a circle."

She made no comment.

"And you've spent most of your life standing outside your family circle."

"That's not true!"

"Yes, it is. For as long as I've known you, you have fought your background. You've done everything you could to deny the fact that you're a nice Jewish girl from Bayonne with two hardworking people for parents."

"I don't deny that!"

"You certainly do. Wasn't that part of the reason you rejected me? Didn't I represent the life you wanted to escape?"

Jennifer remained silent.

"Jennie, you're a beautiful, talented woman, but you've made hasty decisions based only on how far up the straight line they would take you. You've never looked to the right or left of you."

"You're angry, aren't you?"

"You bet! You loved me, but you left me and married a man you now say you weren't sure you loved. You claim you couldn't accept me. Well, I'll tell you why. You couldn't accept yourself!"

Jennifer just sat there, trying to absorb what he was saying, feeling his words sting and stab at her.

"You've told me many times how much you love my children. Why don't you have any of your own?"

"Charles doesn't want children," she answered in a small voice.

"Don't pull that victim routine on me, because I don't buy it. The Jennie Sheldon I knew would have made a wonderful, caring mother. Jennifer Cranshaw doesn't care enough."

Josh was pacing, consumed with rage. Jennifer stayed put, watching him cross the room, his face grim, his body taut. He looked like a panther stalking his kill, his muscles tightening with each step, and pushing against his slacks. Jennifer found herself getting excited. He was so strong and so vital. Suddenly she wanted him more than she had ever wanted anyone or anything in her whole life. Her stomach fluttered and her heart pounded, filling her head with demands. She rose from the couch and approached him, hesitantly. He stopped and looked down at her.

"Hold me," she said. Her voice was low and pleading.

Without a word, Josh took her in his arms, held her roughly at first, and then gently kissed her hair and stroked her neck. He held her face in his hands and searched her dark brown eyes. Delicately, he removed the hairpins and released the topknot, letting her hair cascade about her shoulders. Her eyes didn't leave his as he slipped her dress off and tossed it on the couch. She felt the heat of the nearby fire against her back, but it didn't compare to the scorching sensation she experienced when he touched her breasts. His strong fingers cupped her, and he bent down, kissing each breast softly, nuzzling them until they stood erect. His hands slid down to her hips, pushed her hose off, and left her naked before the fire.

He undressed quickly and came to her, stroking her back and kissing her deeply. For a while, they just stood there, holding each other, feeling each other's presence. Jennifer's knees trembled as she followed Josh to his bed. His face loomed above her. His hands felt warm against her flesh, and she wrapped her arms around him, drawing him to her. She clung to him, shivering each time he caressed her, feeling herself grow moist. His fingers were narcotic, drugging her, exciting her to the point of giddiness, until she thought she would cry with pleasure.

His mouth explored her and left a trace of heat wherever his lips touched, branding her and binding her to him. Soon, her body began to throb, pulsating until all thought was eliminated. She lifted her hips to his and pressed against him. His hand went under her, his arms around her, and then, he lowered himself onto her, thrusting and driving, filling her with himself until she felt delirious. Their bodies were damp, and she felt as if they were glued to each other, moving in passionate unison, rising and falling, rising again to the ultimate crescendo. Her nails gripped his back as they loved each other, thoroughly and completely. Jennifer wished the night would never end.

Twelve

Elyse de Marco stood barefoot on her workroom floor, draping a bolt of soft peach jersey on a figure dummy. Her teeth clamped on a cluster of straight pins, and scissors dangled on a long slice of ribbon around her neck as she wrapped and tied the supple fabric. She was working more from habit than inspiration, because today, Elyse's mind was focused on Jennifer Cranshaw. She had called Jennifer's office earlier, but Jennifer wasn't in. A polite young woman had asked if Elyse wished to leave a message, but Elyse had declined. She had promised she would call back, but now she wondered if she would. Ostensibly, she had called to congratulate Jennifer on a wonderful party and to thank her for allowing Charles to play White Knight to her Lady in Distress. As Elyse stretched the jersey around the dummy's back, she admitted that the call was probably otherwise motivated, but the truth was still murky, and she needed time for it to define itself.

She dismissed the notion that her interest in Jennifer was related to Josh. Jennifer couldn't be considered a rival, because there was no need for competition. Josh was a companion for Elyse. He was a dancing partner, a dinner partner, and a very satisfying bed partner. But they were both free agents. Love was out of the question.

Elyse looked at the dummy in disgust. She took a deep breath to cleanse her head of extraneous thought and refocused her attention on the fabric and the form. She took the jersey in her hands and allowed the buttery cloth to glide through her fingers. Elyse only worked with fabrics that possessed an innate sensuality. To her, clothes were an erogenous zone. They touched the body and held the body and embraced the body and therefore, the act of dressing and undressing became a sensual experience.

Elyse's designs were never unbuttoned or unzipped. There was nothing but fabric, yards of luscious cloth that had to be gradually and leisurely undone. Women who rejoiced in their womanliness bought de Marco. Women who demanded attention. Violets never wore Elyse's clothes. Orchids did.

She stood back and admired her latest creation. It was a striking dress with a neckline plunged to the waist and delicately pleated over the breasts. It flowed softly down between the legs, pulled close and secure around the waist, and reappeared as a loose shawl over one shoulder. It was a toga worthy of Aphrodite, and Elyse loved it. She spit a bunch of pins into her hand and began to secure all the pleats and folds. As her fingers moved deftly over the dress, her thoughts returned to Josh and his entreaties to allow him to set her up in business. The offer was more tempting than Josh could ever know, but it was impossible. Josh didn't understand, and she didn't expect him to. She couldn't tell him the whys. She had inferred and implied, but she never had been totally honest with him. She couldn't afford to be. There was too much at stake.

Charles was worried. It was almost noon, and Jennifer still hadn't arrived at her office. What's more, she hadn't even called in. It wasn't like Jennifer to be negligent. He had called the apartment earlier, and Hattie, the house-keeper, had told him Mrs. Cranshaw had left a little after nine. Where the hell was she?

It was guilt that stabbed him, and he knew it, but he couldn't control himself. What if she'd called the office last night? What if someone had answered and told her there was no meeting? What if someone had seen him?

Charles rubbed his hands together, squeezing them un-til they were bone white. He had never meant for it to come to this. Duplicity was destroying them. Still, he wasn't sure how to write the ending or even if it was time for a denouement.

His intercom buzzed. Before he had a chance to pick up the phone, Deirdre Walling Conlon swept into his of-fice.

"Mrs. Conlon. What a lovely surprise. What brings you here?" He walked out from behind his desk to greet her.

"A whim," she said, removing a glove to shake his hand.

Charles closed the door and offered her a seat. Deirdre put her gloves and handbag on a table, tossed her mink coat on one chair, and slouched into another, crossing her legs so that her skirt separated, revealing shapely thighs.

Charles positioned himself in a chair opposite her, curi-ous. He had met Deirdre Conlon many times, and al-though she had always been charming, her presence unnerved him. For one thing, she was incredibly self-possessed, one of those women who wore her assurance like $100-an-ounce perfume. Charles had known many women like her. Rich. Willful. Self-centered. And deadly.

"Do you happen to have a bar hidden somewhere in this stodgy office? I've been with Claiborne Stark for sim-ply hours, and I'm parched."

"What's your pleasure?" Charles slid a panel aside and uncovered a small, but well-stocked bar.

"Something stiff."

Charles's sensors picked up a warning, but he ignored it. He filled the two glasses with ice and Stolichnaya, handed her the drink, and sat down, waiting.

"Claiborne and I have been going over my investments

until I'm positively drained." She laughed, a cultured chuckle with a throaty, hollow sound.

"How did you enjoy the *Jolie* party?" he asked.

"Personally, I prefer smaller gatherings, but each to her own," she said, raising her glass in a toast. "It was a shame you had to leave so early," she continued. "The party really blossomed after one."

"I had to return to an all-night business meeting."

"Return? That explains why you didn't escort your charming wife to her soiree."

Charles wasn't certain where this conversation was headed, but the direction was ominous.

"Yes," he said guardedly. "I had someone cover for me while I made my appearance at Jennifer's gala. It was a difficult evening. Conflict of interest, you might say."

"Your wife must be a very understanding woman."

"She is."

"Terk thinks a lot of your wife. He was so concerned about that party that you'd think they were more to each other than just coworkers."

Charles refused to be baited.

"I wouldn't think that at all," he said. "I would merely assume that your husband's concern was for the magazine. They all had a stake in that party."

Deirdre studied Charles over her glass.

"I think we have some mutual friends."

"Do we?"

"Wilson Gifford? Spencer Dearborn?"

"College friends. How do you know them?"

"We travel in the same circles, darling. After all, you and I were both to the manor born."

"I'm not sure I know what you're driving at, Mrs. Conlon."

"Deirdre. We have so much in common that it's silly to be so formal."

"What is it that we have in common, Deirdre?"

"For one thing, we both married beneath us, didn't we?"

"I never ran a Dun & Bradstreet on my wife, if that's what you mean."

"Obviously. Be a dear and get me another?"

Deirdre held out her glass, using her free hand to run

long, tapered fingers through her blonde hair. As Charles refilled her glass, he looked at her reflection in the mirror behind the bar.

She was staring at his back, her blue eyes lit with pleasure. Her mouth was moist, merely tinged with color, and she had a habit of running her tongue along her upper lip. Charles bent to refill her glass. He didn't see her rise from the chair and walk over to him. He became aware of her presence when he felt her body press against him.

"You're a very attractive man, Charles Cranshaw," she said, her warm breath caressing his neck. "I like attractive men."

She refused to move, forcing Charles to turn around, their bodies still touching. She took her drink from him, sipped it slowly, and looked directly into her eyes. Then, she stroked his cheek with the back of her hand.

"Deirdre, please." Charles tried to move out of her way. She responded by putting her drink down on the bar and rubbing her hands on his arms.

"Don't you like me, Charles? Wilson and Spencer adore me."

"You're a lovely woman, Deirdre, but this is an office and you are a client."

"Then service me," she said, moving her hands lower. He attempted to move away, but she held onto him, issuing low, throaty sounds.

Charles took refuge in the chair behind his desk.

"I would never have imagined you a tease, Charles."

"I am not teasing."

"Neither am I." She leered at him from across the desk. "I am a very important client, Charles, and I am not accustomed to being denied. Claiborne will be distressed to hear that I asked you for a small favor and you refused."

Charles summoned his most businesslike tone.

"I'm afraid it would be impossible for me to accommodate you at this time, Mrs. Conlon."

She chuckled.

"You think you could accommodate me at any other time? I doubt it!"

She retrieved her gloves and her bag, draped her mink coat over her shoulders, and stalked out of the office, leaving Charles bewildered and upset. He didn't doubt for an instant that she was on her way to Stark's office with some woeful tale of rejection tucked under her arm. He knew that she was banking on the fact that he could never tell his senior partner the truth. Deirdre had been after something more than his body, of that he was certain, but what? And what purpose would it ultimately serve?

He had been surprised to hear that she knew his Yale comrades, but not shocked. She had been correct. They did travel in the same circles, and it was not unlikely that she knew most of his acquaintances. After all, money provided the best introductions. But what was her relationship with these men? How often did they talk and how much?

Wilson Gifford was a highly successful commodities broker with a major firm. Married. Three children. On the Board of Governors of Winged Foot Country Club. Member of the Rye City Council. And still partying, if Deirdre's insinuations were fact. He saw Wilson for lunch occasionally or to discuss periodic investment possibilities, but they had had no social involvement for years. Jennifer felt uncomfortable around Wilson and Sybil Gifford, and frankly, so did Charles. What could Wilson have said? Nothing particularly damaging. No, Charles wasn't concerned about Wilson Gifford. Spencer Dearborn was another story.

Terk Conlon entered Eben Towers's private dining room at precisely twelve-thirty. A square glass table was set for lunch in front of the windows. Gold-rimmed bone china emblazoned with Eben's corporate initials sat on suede place mats, accompanied by Waterford goblets, antique sterling, and Irish linen napkins. Fresh mums filled a silver basket, and a bottle of dry white wine rested in a Lucite ice bucket. To an outsider, the scene might have appeared elegant and inviting, but Terk was not an outsider. He viewed the room as an affectation—an expensive, unnecessary assertion of wealth. Most Seventh Avenue moguls, even those who frequented Côte Basque or Le Cirque, didn't indulge themselves with private dining rooms.

He moved to the window and was watching the lunch

hour pandemonium on Broadway below when Eben entered the room.

"If you're planning to jump, wait until after lunch. I've ordered poached salmon, and I'd hate to see it go to waste."

Terk stifled an urge to lunge for Towers. "You're a regular Milton Berle, Eben. A laugh a minute. Now how about giving me a drink and getting down to business?"

"Eager little beaver today, eh, Terk?"

"I've got a lot to do."

"Anything other than what you have to do for me is unimportant. I thought you knew that."

Terk bristled.

"Right, mein commandant. And what Herculean task do you have on tap for today? I cleaned out the stables yesterday."

Eben laughed as he fixed their drinks. His laugh was guttural, more like a cough. He motioned for Terk to take a seat on one of the leather couches and pressed a button to alert the kitchen staff.

"What's happening at *Jolie* these days?" Towers asked, draping his arm on the thick brown leather.

"The Big Pineapple."

"Excuse me, please?"

"It's Brad Helms's latest brainstorm. He plans on dedicating the entire April issue to Hawaii. He figures this brilliant maneuver will bring thousands of advertisers crawling to his door."

"He's a fool. An utter fool."

"No debate there. I think the bit in *Fashion Report* shook him up."

"Yes, I'm sure it did. Any other reactions?"

"Panic," Terk said, pausing to take another sip of his drink. "Everyone's afraid of losing his job."

Towers jiggled his glass, thinking. "How well do you know Jennifer Cranshaw?" he asked.

"Fairly well. Why?"

"Just curious. Before last night's soiree, I had never had the pleasure of meeting her. Tell me about her."

There was something strange about this conversation. Eben never asked idle questions, and he detested small talk.

"Jennifer is your basic fabulous lady. She's talented. Beautiful. Ambitious. Head of the Promotion Department. Terribly inventive."

"Interesting." Eben was more impressed with the admiration in Terk's tone than he was with the complimentary nature of his words. "Go on."

"The day *Fashion Report*'s article appeared, Helms came up with this Pineapple number, and the natives were ready to boil him in oil until Jennifer created an advertising/promotion package that I wish I had thought of. Why are you so interested?"

"I told you. I'm curious." Eben downed his drink in small, jerky sips.

"You're never just curious. What's the fascination? Does the lady turn you on?"

"Excuse me, please?"

Terk didn't bother to repeat himself. Eben had a habit of whispering, "Excuse me, please" whenever a bit of conversation surprised or displeased him, a mannerism that annoyed the hell out of Terk. Maybe it was the *sotto voce* way in which it was said. Or perhaps it was the timing, the way he truncated discussions with the use of that phrase. Or maybe it was Towers himself.

Towers had pressed another button, and several white-coated waiters stood quietly as the two men moved to the table. Without a word, the waiters filled the plates, poured the wine, and then retreated. Terk and Towers ate in silence, both deep in thought, neither one appreciating the salmon.

"Do you have the money?"

"Right here. In unmarked bills." Terk reached into his breast pocket, pulled out a thick envelope, and handed it to Towers, who put it on the table alongside his plate.

Terk ripped open a packet of Sweet 'n Low, poured it into his coffee, and stirred slowly. "I'm almost all paid up," he said.

"I'm aware of that." Towers's lips twisted into an uneven crescent. "You make me sound so cruel," he said. "Our little arrangement was agreed upon by both of us, Terk, or doesn't my memory serve me correctly?"

"Don't bullshit me, Towers. You know I had to go

along with whatever you said, and I did. But let's not make a charade out of this."

"Fine. It doesn't really matter anyway. It's almost over. Soon, you'll be a free man, Terk. I wonder if you'll know how to handle it."

"Your concern is touching. Just don't forget your part of the bargain."

"Would I be so dishonorable?"

Terk's stomach turned. Would Towers be dishonorable? There wasn't a doubt in Terk's mind. But he was prepared. He had planned on being betrayed and had insured against it. He knew that Towers thought he held all the cards. Maybe once he had, but Terk had wangled one ace out of the pack, and when the time came, he would use it. With pleasure.

Friday mornings were usually hectic in the bakery, and this Friday was no exception. The place was jammed with women clutching shopping lists with one hand and fidgety preschoolers with the other. Voices exchanged gossip and called out orders, their high-pitched tones mingling with the ring of the cash register and the persistent whirr of the bread slicer. Rose Sheldon stood center stage, orchestrating the mayhem, overseeing two other saleswomen while waiting on three customers herself. Jennifer had been in the store fifteen minutes before Rose even spotted her.

"Oh, my goodness! What a surprise," she squealed above the din. "How long have you been here?"

"I came in three days ago for a seedless rye, but I forgot to take a number." Jennifer leaned over the counter and kissed her mother hello.

"Such a tease. Let me see how you look." She waved Jennifer back and gave her daughter an approving once-over. "Mrs. Feinstein, you remember my Jennifer, don't you? Isn't she stunning? She's a big shot now, too. Practically runs *Jolie* magazine."

Mrs. Feinstein nodded, mumbled something about Jennifer having been a pretty child, and asked for half a dozen Danish.

"So? The party was a success?" In between speaking to Jennifer and boxing the Danish, Rose managed to answer a question from the younger sales clerk as well as cajoling a stout Polish woman into buying more rolls than she wanted.

"It was incredible! I can't wait to tell you all about it!"

"How about some cheesecake?" Rose said to Mrs. Feinstein. "What did you wear?"

Jennifer didn't even bother to answer. Trying to conduct a conversation with Rose in the store was like showing a new dress to a man in the middle of a football game. Instead, Jennifer stepped away and watched in bemused silence. Though it had been a long time since she had been in the bakery, the scene was immediately familiar. Nothing had changed and in a strange way, Jennifer found that comforting. Other segments of her life seemed to have entered a stage of flux, but this place and the woman behind that counter remained a constant.

Jennifer had forgotten how hard Rose worked and how skilled she was at her job. One by one, bags and boxes were filled, money was put into the cash register drawer, and another eager customer begged to be served. A smile of admiration crossed Jennifer's lips. She realized that this was probably the first time in her life she hadn't been openly hostile at being pushed aside in favor of a three-dollar sale.

Ordinarily, she walked into the store with the fantasy that Rose would drop everything in order to cater to Jennifer's needs. She supposed she had felt that way today as well, but oddly enough, she didn't feel hurt or compelled to compete with strangers for her mother's attention. Maybe this change in attitude signaled a new maturity? Or maybe it had to do with Josh. There was no question that, thanks to him, her mood this morning was deliciously mellow.

"I'm waiting to hear what happened last night."

Rose's voice startled Jennifer. A blush rouged her cheeks. For the moment, she had forgotten that Rose was referring to the party.

"You and I are going out for breakfast," she said firmly. "We'll talk then."

"But it's Friday."

"That depends on how you look at it." Jennifer grabbed

her mother's coat from a hook near the refrigerator. "To me, this is just the day after Thursday."

Several people had stopped to listen. Even Natalie, Rose's assistant for more than fifteen years, risked her employer's wrath by turning away from a customer and nodding encouragement to Jennifer.

"I'd love to darling," Rose said with a saccharine sweetness, "but I can't. Mrs. Kronski is having a brunch, and we're trying to decide between an almond horn and an apricot tart."

Rose telegraphed Jennifer a look that said she had every intention of selling the woman both and not to interfere. Jennifer ignored her mother's admonition, walked behind the counter, and draped Rose's coat over her shoulders. Then she turned to Mrs. Kronski.

"Personally, I believe in giving my guests a choice. I also believe that occasionally, mothers and daughters should spend some time together." She began to nudge Rose away. "So, if you'll let Natalie complete your order, we shall bid you a good day." Taking Rose by the hand, she piloted them to the door. "And don't forget cookies for the kids!"

With that, Jennifer steered a resistant Rose out of the store and down the block to the nearest luncheonette. By the time they had settled into a booth and ordered, Rose's protests had slowed to a sputter.

"Now, isn't this pleasant?" Jennifer asked.

"It's very nice. But I haven't even checked on whether or not Daddy filled all the special orders."

"Stop grousing! I'm sure he did, and what difference does it make what day this is. We haven't had breakfast together in ages and, in spite of you, I'm enjoying it." Rose smiled, and Jennifer felt rewarded. "In fact, I've decided we're going to do this more often."

"Fine. Make it on Tuesdays when the store is closed."

Jennifer moaned and threw up her hands in mock exasperation.

"Mother," she said patiently. "In case you haven't noticed, I'm not at work either. I have a ton of obligations at the office, especially the day after such an important party, but I took the morning off. If I can do it, certainly you can."

Rose's forehead crinkled as she debated the issue.

"You're right," she said, smacking the table for emphasis and shaking her head as if ridding herself of other considerations. "This is a treat, and I'm giving you a hard time. I'm sorry, sweetheart. I won't mention the store again."

She would. Lifelong habits couldn't be broken that easily, but Jennifer recognized the effort and appreciated it.

"There isn't anything wrong, is there?" Rose asked. "I mean, you're not here to tell me something horrible, are you?"

"I just wanted to spend some time with you. It's as simple as that!"

Rose looked relieved. The waitress brought their food, and Rose turned her attention to organizing the table. She asked for extra packets of jelly, rifled through the sugar bowl for artificial sweeteners, sniffed the cream, and examined the toast.

"It was thoughtful of you to call last night to wish me good luck," Jennifer said between bites of an English muffin. "I know how busy Thursday nights can be."

"I always have a few minutes to wish my daughter well."

"You should have come to the party, Mom. You would have loved it. I don't know why you and Daddy refused."

Rose buttered her toast carefully. "We wouldn't have fit in."

"What would make you say a thing like that?"

"You."

"Me? I invited you."

"True, but you've always made such a big thing about how different your father and I are from your friends. We didn't want to embarrass you."

"You're embarrassing me now." Jennifer took her mother's hand and forced Rose to look at her. "Next time I invite you to something, you'd better come!"

Rose put down her fork and patted her daughter's hand.

"I'll tell you what. Next time, I'll even let you go shopping for me."

"How about if we go shopping together? On a Tuesday."

"Terrific! It sounds like fun."

Jennifer was beaming. It did sound like fun. Immediately, she began to think about which stores she would take her mother to, which restaurant she might like for lunch. They had never spent a day like that, and Jennifer wanted it to be perfect.

"What's with Charles? Did he have a good time last night?"

The change of subject was so abrupt and so pointed that Jennifer's breath caught in her throat. She reached for her cigarettes and fussed with her lighter, avoiding her mother's eyes, regrouping her own thoughts. Last night, while she had been with Josh, she had allowed her mind to go blank. She had experienced no doubts, suffered no pangs of recrimination, yet suddenly, sitting across from Rose, she felt guilty. She saw it as Rose would. She was a married woman, and she had made love with another man.

Hastily, she constructed a defense for her dalliance. She cited a diminished sex life and the probability that Charles had spent the night with Brooke Wheeler as just cause for her actions. But as quickly as she made her case, she ruled against it. None of that mattered. It didn't exonerate her, especially since she knew that sleeping with Josh had nothing to do with justice. It didn't even have anything to do with Charles. It had to do with closeness and caring, need and fulfillment.

"He must have been very proud of you," Rose said, studying her daughter. Jennifer had flinched when she had mentioned Charles's name, and Rose wanted to know why.

"He was proud. He thought everything was wonderful."

Jennifer's response was too swift, her answer too pat.

"How are things between the two of you?"

"Good. We're fine."

Rose nodded and finished the last of her breakfast. Jennifer sipped her coffee. She was tempted to confide in Rose; to talk to her about her marriage, her feelings for Josh. For a minute, she was even willing to risk the expected I-told-you-sos. She started to speak and then stopped.

"Your brother should be home any day now."

Jennifer couldn't believe that her nervousness had gone unnoticed by Rose. Why hadn't she pursued the subject? What would Jennifer have said if she did?

"I know. You told me last night." She had to force herself to sound excited.

Rose began to prattle on about David and Sarah; how they had looked when Rose and Marty last saw them in Israel; how she planned to welcome them home with a big party; and how much it meant to her to have her family together again.

Jennifer wished she could lose herself in her mother's enthusiasm, but the thought of a face-to-face reunion with David unsettled her.

"The children must be so big by now," Rose said. "I can't wait to get my hands on them!"

Jennifer had seen her niece and nephew only twice.

"I wonder if they'll know who I am," she said.

"Don't be ridiculous! They know all about their Aunt Jennie. I send them pictures of you all the time. Whenever you're in the paper."

Jennifer was truly touched. She had heard her mother brag about her in the store, but she thought that was for effect. She would never have imagined that Rose would have taken the time to leaf through newspapers and cut out clippings.

"In fact," Rose continued, "save everything about the party. The kids will love it."

"As long as we're finally on the subject, can I tell you about my gala?"

"I know all about it. With the neon pineapple and the balloons and everyone dressed up in old-time clothes."

Jennifer was shocked. "Who told you? Was there something in the local paper?"

"Josh called me first thing this morning."

"Josh?" Jennifer had to struggle to maintain her composure. "Why would he call you?"

"He calls me all the time."

Jennifer was positive that she had detected a note of triumph in Rose's voice.

"Why?"

"Why not? He's called me twice a week for years." Rose was delighted with Jennifer's response. "He comes out to visit occasionally too. Daddy and I haven't seen his apartment because we don't go into the city too often, but we used to go to the house in Alpine when he and Laura and the children lived there. What a house that was!"

"You went to his house?" Jennifer had been there once, to pay her respects after Laura died.

"Why are you so surprised? Josh has always been like a third child to me."

Jennifer was more than surprised. She was confused. And she was angry. She was hurt. It was as if her mother had established an intimacy with Josh as a way of punishing her for rejecting his proposal. No matter how she felt about him now, she resented her mother's self-righteous tone. It was all too familiar: Rose insisting on having her way; insisting that she knew what was best for Jennifer; withholding her approval whenever Jennifer argued or disagreed.

"I can't believe you did that!"

"What's not to believe? Laura was a wonderful girl. When she invited us, we went, and we always had a lovely time. What a hostess she was! What a cook! It's still hard for me to accept the fact that she's gone."

Once again, Jennifer was tempted to tell Rose that she had spent the night with Josh, but not because she wanted advice.

"I don't think it was right. Josh and I were practically engaged. Going to visit him and another woman was disloyal." Jennifer was visibly upset.

"You weren't engaged, and you weren't married." Rose was paying close attention to Jennifer's reactions. A part of Rose was thrilled. After all, she reasoned, if their romance was ancient history, none of this should bother Jennifer. "If you were foolish enough to toss him out of your life, that's your mistake. It doesn't mean I have to be foolish and toss him out of mine!"

"I didn't toss him out of my life. I wasn't ready to get married then. I had other things I wanted to do."

"Fine. And you did them. Meantime, Josh settled down with a lovely wife and had two lovely children."

Again, Jennifer heard echoes from the past. "You always make it sound as if what I wanted to do with my life was equivalent to chasing butterflies! I got married. And I pursued a career. What's so wrong with that?"

"I never said there was anything wrong."

"But you hint at it a lot!"

Rose leaned forward and rested her arms on the table so her face was nearer to Jennifer.

"Okay. You want me to be honest? I'll be honest. I think a baby might be nice. Before you get too old."

Jennifer's eyes widened, and she had to stop herself from screaming.

"I am not too old. Charles and I are waiting."

"For what? The stork?"

"Let's change the subject."

Rose inched her way to the end of the bench.

"To what? You don't want to discuss your brother. You won't let me talk about Josh. You're obviously touchy about your marriage. And overly sensitive about your career. What's left to discuss? The weather? It's late, and I've got a store to run."

She stood up and went for the check. Jennifer snatched it from her hand.

"Fine. I have a job also!"

She spun on her heel and marched to the front where the cashier sat. She never heard her mother's comment.

"I just wish you had more."

Thirteen

J osh was a Gemini, and even though he paid little attention to astrology, he was a true child of Mercury: witty, enterprising, perceptive, forceful and chameleonlike. As with most people born under the sign of the twins, Josh was cursed with duality. Mood shifts were not unusual for him. Often, intellect tugged at emotion and conviction strained against impulse.

There was no question about the joy he felt being with Jennifer. He loved her, and he had felt her love him in return, reviving a sense of fulfillment that had been absent from his life for a long time. Now, alone at his desk, he felt her presence and experienced a rush of desire. He fought it, dismissing it like a rude interruption. He had come to his office to escape distraction; to surround himself with the trappings of his success; to fuel himself with reminders of his strength. It was all there, the massive desk, the luxurious appointments, yet still, he struggled with insecurity and weakness. He was tired, he knew that, but it was not fatigue that was dragging him down.

Other forces nagged at him: Jennifer's reluctance to commit herself; her vacillation about Charles; her single-minded obsession with success. Josh had spent every minute since she had left sorting out his emotions. He relived the past. Rethought the future. Reviewed his options. But no matter what approach he took, one fact kept surfacing, over and over again. If memories had brought them together, memories were destined to push them apart.

Josh wanted Jennifer, but he would deny himself, and her, a relationship until she had freed herself from her marriage to Charles. The decision was painful, but Josh knew he would stick to it. He had to. He owed it to Jennifer, to himself, and most of all, to Laura.

Laura. First, she had decorated his office. Then, she had furnished his life.

He had been in business for himself for two years when his company finally began turning a profit, and he had decided to reward himself with some new furniture. His small apartment didn't permit grand purchases, but he had squirreled away enough for a new couch and a coffee table, prices permitting. For two days, he explored the D&D building, wandering in and out of every showroom. He had begun to feel like Goldilocks in the three bears' cottage. Everything was either too big, too small, too hard, too soft, or simply too expensive. He was tiring of the whole adventure when he noticed her near the back of a small showroom on the tenth floor.

She was tall, with turquoise eyes and glistening sable hair cut in a feathery cap. An older woman stood next to her, shaking her head from side to side. Laura kept pointing to a particular couch, her attitude patient, but insistent. The other woman continued to shake her head and point to another couch, equally insistent. Laura reached into a huge canvas bag and laid out fabric samples and paint chips on the couch. For a minute, the older woman hesitated, but then she shook her head again, threw up her arms in disgust and walked out of the store.

Josh didn't know whether it was because he admired her beauty or felt compassion for her defeat, but he went over to her and touched her arm.

"Listen," he said. "I'm a desperate man, and you've got to help me."

He had startled her. She spun around, her wide-set eyes narrowed with caution.

"I think I've found the couch of my dreams."

"I hope you'll be very happy together." She picked up her swatches and put them back in her bag.

"Please?" he implored.

She remained skeptical, but she let him lead her toward an overstuffed, skirted loveseat covered in a bold pink and green floral chintz. He positioned her in front of the couch and sat down, his posture rigid, his hands clasped before him, prep-school style.

"Well, what do you think?"

She just stared at him.

Then, he stretched out, his long legs hanging over one of the arms.

"It's me, wouldn't you say?"

She didn't smile. She didn't say a word. She stood there like a theater critic, letting him play out his act. Undaunted, he changed positions again. Still, she didn't respond.

"Maybe it's the colors you don't like. How about green flowers and pink leaves?"

At that, she turned and started for the door.

"How about if we forget flowers altogether and go for birds?" His voice was playful, his green eyes soft.

For a minute, she didn't speak. When she did, her mouth spread in an easy smile. "Better yet, how about we go for lunch?"

Their marriage was a good one. Laura was a Sagittarius, as frank and outspoken as her Gemini husband and equally determined to maintain personal freedom. Her mind was keen, her sense of humor droll, and her attitude open and honest. She was also the first woman since Jennifer who had stirred Josh's emotions.

In addition to being lovers, Josh and Laura became helpmates and friends. They often disagreed, but rarely fought. She understood his driving need to succeed and never intruded on his work. Her time was spent building the decorating business she owned with her two sisters. It was not unusual for Josh to find an extra lamp in his study or a chair missing from the living room. It was also not unusual for Laura to cram her schedule with extra clients in the early years so that Josh could continue putting money back into his business.

By the time Rachel and Scotty were born, Josh had sold his business and begun to think about relocating the family. Since Laura couldn't bear the thought of being confined in an apartment, no matter how many rooms it had, they built a magnificent retreat in the New Jersey Palisades, close enough to the city for Josh to commute, far enough away for them to have a sense of country. They joined a country club, played golf and duplicate bridge.

But then, Josh lost track of himself. In New York, power was the prized commodity, and Josh was one of the power brokers. He was a captain of industry, a deal maker, a man who bought and sold large companies. In the inner circle of New York's financial elite, he was touted as a giant, and for a while, he got caught up in the glittery allure of his own importance.

He had purchased a failing women's sportswear concern because he had been convinced that, with good management, he could turn it around. He personally supervised the project and, little by little, became intoxicated by the world of fashion. His showroom became his downfall. Nubile models roamed in and out, dressing and undressing without modesty, making it clear that they would do anything to please their boss. For months, Josh toyed with temptation, and then, as if it were the most natural thing in the world, he allowed himself to get caught up in the sport of cheating on his wife.

At first, it was a model here and a model there, but soon he drifted into a six-month affair. Gradually, his conscience returned. He went to Coral Trent's apartment one Thursday night in December and told her it was over between them. She was difficult. She screamed, cried, threatened, and begged, but he remained firm. It was over. It never should have happened.

That same night, Laura had had her steady bridge game at the club. About eleven, she started home. It was snowing, and the roads were slick. She drove carefully, but it was difficult guiding her sports car around the treacherous, unlit curves. Suddenly, a bright light blinded her. She jerked the steering wheel. The car skidded. She hit her brakes. A truck swerved, and Laura's car spun on the ice. The other driver tried to steer his truck away from her car, but he lost control. Laura died instantly.

By the time Josh reached the hospital, Laura's body was draped in a sheet. He touched her. She was so stiff, so cold. This wasn't his Laura. His Laura ran through piles of leaves and built sand castles on the beach. His Laura illuminated rooms with her laughter and brightened his life with her love. Now, his children had no mother. He had no wife.

He stood over her, paralyzed by grief and guilt. He had betrayed her. He had been unfaithful, and for no good reason. He couldn't say his wife didn't understand him, because she did. He couldn't say his wife had been unresponsive, because she never was. He had sought the pleasures of another woman because of ego. Nothing more. Nothing less.

The day of the funeral, he asked for a few minutes alone with Laura. When all the family had been ushered into the chapel, he opened the coffin, expecting to be comforted by her peacefulness. Everyone had said that she would look as if she were sleeping, but in life, even when Laura slept, she had appeared vibrant. She was dead, and his heart ached. Slowly, he removed his wedding band and wrapped it in the lace handkerchief Laura had carried on their wedding day. Along with the ring, he placed two beaded baby bracelets beside her. Tears blinded him. When he touched her hair, his hand shook. Silently, he closed the coffin.

At that moment, and many times after that, he wondered if Laura had known about his affair. His question could never be answered, but in a way, it didn't matter. He knew. He knew that he had cheated. He knew that his wife had died without anyone to hold her hand. And he knew that he would never disregard anyone's marriage vows again.

It was almost four in the afternoon by the time Jennifer had a chance to call Josh. She should have been exhausted from the strain of too little sleep and so many congratulations, but she was exhilarated. As she listened to Josh's private phone ring, she examined the state of her desk. Dozens of newspapers were stacked up, each one folded open to a show-and-tell report on the party. Phone messages were clipped together in a thick pack, and every other inch of available space was taken up with flowers.

Brad Helms had sent a bouquet of spring blossoms accompanied by a charming note of thanks. When she had stopped by his office, he told her that several accounts had called first thing this morning to find out more about The Big Pineapple. Gwendolyn Stuart's offering, a fat-bottomed crystal bud vase with oddly mated flowers and twigs, bore Vincent Matteo's ikebanalike stamp, and her note also mentioned post party approval of *Jolie*'s upcoming April issue. Jennifer's own promotion department had expressed their appreciation with a double-stemmed gloxinia, fluffy and plush with magenta petals and wide, jungle green leaves. They were all lovely, but it was the simple, squat terracotta pot of parrot tulips that affected her most. Tulips were her favorite flowers, and these were from Charles.

"Could it be that the missing heiress has returned?"

Jennifer smiled the moment she heard Josh's voice. She swiveled her chair toward the wall, away from Charles's flowers, and greeted Josh.

"Frankly, I had been expecting some gravel-voiced thug demanding a fortune in ransom money," he said. "Where the hell have you been all day? And what possessed you to disappear like that?"

Jennifer was silent for a moment. "I didn't disappear. I

knew where I was all the time. I went to Bayonne to visit my mother," she said quietly.

"I'm glad," Josh said, and she could hear the sincerity in his voice.

"I thought you would be. Mom and I had breakfast together, catching up on lots of gossip about old friends and things. And speaking of old friends, in between bites of her whole wheat toast, she happened to mention that you and she are regular phone pals."

"Guilty."

"I had no idea that I'd have to fight my own mother for the heart of Joshua Mandell." At that moment, she would have fought anyone for him. "Exactly how long has this torrid romance been going on?"

"Since I was eleven," Josh said, straining to keep his tone casual. "I've always had a thing for short redheads."

"I can assure you the feeling is mutual. She adores you, although for the life of me, I can't understand what the fatal attraction is."

Josh gave no response. His silence surprised Jennifer, but she stumbled on, filling the void.

"And what is this about you having some long distance chat with my brother this morning?"

"I just called to see if I could do anything to help out with his return to the motherland."

"Always the Good Samaritan, aren't you?"

"No. Not always." Josh wished she would get to the point. All he wanted to know was whether or not she had considered his suggestion that she leave Charles. For an instant, he was tempted to ask, but he decided to let her do this her own way.

"Am I to assume from this bouncy repartee that the entire staff of *Jolie* gave you a standing ovation?"

"You may," she said, her voice ringing with self-satisfaction. "I can't tell you how marvelous this day has been. There are flowers all over the place and phone messages and telegrams, the works! I even got my picture in the New York *Times*!"

"That's wonderful. I'm proud of you, Jen."

"Good! Then you'll be more than willing to celebrate my triumph over dinner tonight, won't you?"

His answer was three beats too slow.

"I'm not sure."

"What do you mean, you're not sure? You have no choice. I have this craving, you see, and you're the only one who can satisfy it."

Again, the long, unexpected silence.

"What about Charles?" he said flatly.

"I've thought it all out. Don't worry, it'll be fine."

"I'll meet you at seven," he said. "Is that convenient?"

His choice of words jarred her.

"You sound odd. Am I embarrassing you?"

"No."

Still odd. Stilted.

"Should I meet you at your apartment?"

"I'd prefer meeting you at a place on Hudson Street. The Village Green. Can you get there by yourself?"

There's nothing wrong, she told herself. *There's someone in his office, and he can't speak freely.*

"I think I can manage it," she said aloud. "I can manage anything today. Want to know why?"

No response.

"Because I'm going to be with you tonight."

"I'll see you at seven," he said.

"Sure. Seven. See you then."

Jennifer hung up the phone slowly. Something wasn't right, but she didn't know what it was. How could there be any problems now? They had found each other again after too many years apart. Wasn't the joy of that enough? Couldn't they just love each other and let everything work itself out? She felt happy for the first time in months, and nothing was going to spoil what had already been a perfect day. She had one more call to make, and then she would go home to pack. She had every intention, she suddenly realized, of spending the weekend with Joshua Mandell.

She dialed Charles's number and waited for him to come on the phone. His secretary said he was on another line and would be with her in a minute. While she waited, her mind raced, searching for a way to buy time with Josh.

"Jennifer! I've been trying to reach you all day."

"I know, darling. I'm sorry, but before I explain, let me thank you for the tulips. They're gorgeous! I'll take them home so we can both enjoy them."

"That will be nice. Now, would you mind telling me where you were?"

"I went to Bayonne," she said. Then it came to her in a rush: "I got a phone call from my mother this morning. My father's had an accident. He fell and dislocated his shoulder rather badly. Mom was stuck in the store, and I had to run to take Daddy to the doctor."

"How serious is it?"

"He doesn't have to stay in the hospital or anything like that, but I'm going to have to spend the weekend taking care of him. Mom would never trust Natalie to run the store, and Daddy certainly can't fend for himself."

"No. Of course not." Charles felt impatient. "Couldn't you hire someone? I had thought we would spend a quiet weekend together. Just the two of us."

Jennifer had finished with most of the papers. She was saving *Fashion Report* for last.

"We haven't had much private time lately."

There was something in Charles's voice that made her pay closer attention. He sounded jumpy, almost pleading. Jennifer considered cancelling her evening with Josh, but she couldn't do that. She had to be with him.

"I know, sweetheart," she said, covering her own case of nerves. "I feel terrible about all this, but you know my parents. They'd never spend the money for a private nurse, and they won't let me pay for one. We'll spend next weekend together. Maybe we'll even go away."

"When are you leaving?"

"I thought I'd go back to the apartment in about an hour, shower and change, and leave about six-thirty or so. I have to take the car. Do you mind?"

"No."

"What will you do?" She was fighting her guilt.

"Catch up on some work, I suppose."

Forgive me, she thought. She said, "Better yet, why not catch up on some sleep? I'll see you Sunday night."

Her hand shook as she replaced the phone. She couldn't believe how easily she had lied to him, how facile her betrayal had been. Last night she had been unfaithful, and today she had lied. She felt guilty, but oddly enough, she didn't feel shame. She had never been unfaithful to Charles before; even during those long months of rationed

sex, she had remained loyal. She had convinced herself
that her husband's unresponsiveness was temporary and
would one day disappear, but she couldn't deny the rap-
turous afterglow of making love to Josh. The naked truth
was that no man had ever made her feel the way Josh
did. She hadn't realized it before, but she knew it now.

Charles stared at the silent phone, conflicting emotions
battling each other. Unwittingly, Jennifer had just pro-
longed their marriage. It was all so ironic. Throughout the
day, Charles had agonized over their situation, fighting
the guilt that had invaded his soul. For hours, he had
been trying his own case, prosecuting himself on charges
of deceit, defending himself on the grounds of survival.
Only minutes before Jennifer had called, he had sen-
tenced himself to a total confession of his sins. Now, it
had to wait, and he was petrified. Delay increased the
chance that he would lose his nerve.

He pushed himself away from his desk and, turning
toward the window, swept aside the heavy tie-back drapes
and peered at the stone landscape that was Wall Street.
Outside, evening cast antagonistic shadows over his office.
In neighboring buildings, windows blinked from bright to
black as people left their offices to join the traffic that
snaked its way through the narrow streets of New York's
financial center.

To Charles, there was something very pure about Wall
Street and its single-minded devotion to business. There
were no residential buildings here; no parks with mothers
wheeling prams and strollers; no delivery boys juggling
bags of groceries in bicycle baskets; no school bells ringing predictably at eight and three o'clock. The only bells
of significance were those that signaled the opening and
closing of the Stock Exchange, and even if they weren't
actually heard by everyone on the Street, they were felt.
This was a world of three-piece suits and grim expressions, bulging briefcases and closely cropped hair. It
was a world where colossal success roomed with abysmal
failure. A world where power was key and money was
power.

Charles turned away from the window, his lean, angu-
lar face expressionless. Restless, he began to pace. He put

some pencils back in their holder, adjusted a lampshade that had dared to tilt, evened out some books, and restacked a few undisciplined file folders. Eventually, he dropped into a leather wing chair and glanced at the small drop-leaf table next to him. On it was a picture of Jennifer, a Bachrach portrait encased in a silver Tiffany frame. She was sitting totally erect, her posture more perfect than it ever really was, her eyes gazing off to one side, and her lips parted in a faint smile. It had been difficult to convince her to sit for the picture, and as he looked at it, he was certain he read resignation on her face. Funny, he had thought his request for a portrait would have pleased her. He had just been made a partner in the firm and noted that all the other senior attorneys had similar portraits of their wives. He had explained to Jennifer that it was expected, part of the trappings, like the traditional furnishings and the hidden bar. She had responded by saying she felt silly, that only the newly engaged posed gleefully for white-blouse-stiff-smile likenesses. Ultimately, she had relented, as he had known she would.

He looked at her now with a mixture of tenderness and remorse, remembering how they had been, regretting what they had become.

He picked up the picture, seeing moments from their past swirl around Jennifer's still image. Out of the jumble of memories, it was their first meeting that stood out most of all.

By the time Charles had arrived, Wilson Gifford's Sutton Place duplex was overflowing with exaggerated pre-Christmas cheer. Most of the guests looked to Charles as if they had been hired through Central Casting. And most of those assembled were either rich or socially prominent or both. Charles was both. Jennifer was neither.

He first spotted her standing slightly apart from a trio clustered in the far corner of the living room. While the others talked, he saw her quickly empty her drink into the base of a ceiling-high ficus tree. Despite the tangled mass of people between them, he thought he saw amusement in her eyes.

He watched her take a sip from her empty glass, as the threesome dispersed, leaving her standing by herself. Slowly, he elbowed his way across the room.

"I don't care for eggnog either."

Her head turned sharply, a pinkish glow spreading across her cheeks.

"I won't tell if you don't," he said, as he poured his drink into the already intoxicated plant.

Her laugh was spontaneous and sincere, her teeth white and even.

"I'm Charles Cranshaw, sometime friend of our host and a reluctant guest."

"I'm Jennifer Sheldon, sometime friend of a friend of our host and here under threat of bodily harm."

"May I ask if the friend is male or female?"

"Female."

"And would she object if I spirited you away for a quiet drink at an underpopulated bar?"

"No, she wouldn't, and yes, I'd love to!"

Charles stared at Jennifer's picture, recalling how they had sat in that small, dimly lit place on First Avenue drinking white wine and talking until closing time. When they left the bar they elected to walk to her apartment on Seventieth and Third, a decision that astounded the few cabbies who offered their services. She linked her arm through his and occasionally burrowed her face into his coat to avoid the brutal winds whipping about them. When they reached her door, they kissed—naturally and easily, as if a relationship had already been established. Her lips were soft, hesitant. He held her gently, and her body felt shy against his. As he opened the door for her, he promised to call—and he did, the very next day. That call had changed the course of his life.

The memory faded. Suddenly, Charles felt frantic, as if something terrible would happen if he didn't see her, if he didn't say what he had to say. He needed her presence, her reassurance that they were indeed going to be all right and that they could resolve their problems. He reached for the phone, but there was no answer. She had gone.

Charles let the phone continue to ring until he felt hypnotized by its precisely timed buzz. He pressed the button, and the dial tone hit his ear like a command. He listened to it. He debated with it. And then he made another call, one that would change his life again.

Jennifer arrived at the Village Green fifteen minutes early, and she considered her timeliness a triumph. It hadn't been easy locating the restaurant amid the winding pathways of Greenwich Village. Each street she had turned down ended in a one way going the wrong way, forcing her to make endless circles until finally, she found Hudson Street. She deposited the car in the nearest parking lot and walked the rest of the way. Under ordinary circumstances, she would have opted for a taxi, but to strengthen her alibi and store her suitcase, she had needed the car. Right now, she needed a drink.

The bartender placed her drink on a small paper napkin in front of her. The wine and cassis had been mixed in a tall, tulip glass, a coincidence she found amusing. She wondered if Charles had believed her story. He must have, she thought. He had no reason not to; she had never lied to him before.

The small lounge was filled. Every bar stool was occupied, and each of the tables that buttressed the wall was surrounded by customers engrossed in conversation. Where was Josh?

She finished her drink and ordered another one. She glanced at the door and then checked her watch. It was only a few minutes after seven. She cautioned herself against impatience. But all she wanted was to be with Josh, to love him and have him love her, to lose herself in the exquisite pleasure of his touch and the luxurious sensuality of his being. Where was he?

"I'm sorry I'm late." He startled her and caused her to topple her glass. He caught it just in time and stood it safely upright, smiling at her. "It's raining out, and I had a tough time getting a cab, but it was worth it. You look gorgeous!"

"You look pretty stunning yourself," she said.

He had just ordered a drink when the captain offered to show them to their table. Jennifer followed him down the steps past a roaring fireplace and into the small, cozy dining room that nestled beneath the lounge. A waiter placed their drinks in front of them and rattled off the various specialties of the evening. Jennifer barely heard him; her total concentration was focused on the handsome man across from her. She took his hand.

Josh's smile faded. He could tell from the poetic gleam in her eyes that her perspective on their relationship bordered on fairy tale. Inside, a premonition swelled. She looked lovely bathed in idealism and scented with the perfume of expected romance.

"I checked the *Times*," he said, steering the conversation. "Your picture and the write-up on the party were impressive. You should feel very proud of yourself. In fact, I would paste the entire page in your scrapbook."

"Maybe I should put it alongside the latest stomach rumbler in *Fashion Report* about that magazine for sale." Her hands went up and she shook her head. "Nope. I refuse to think about that tonight. Forget I said it." She smiled broadly. "I'm not going to let business interfere with what is definitely pleasure." She paused.

"You'll never guess what I found," she said, after a moment. "I had to search the entire top shelf of my closet for this, and believe me, that's no easy task, but it was worth it. I wanted to surprise you."

She held up her hand and shook her wrist, drawing his attention to a gold link bracelet with a circular disc dangling from the center. It was the bracelet he had given her when she graduated from college. He touched it, rubbing the two raised initials on the front, tracing the overlapping "J's" with his fingertips. He turned it over, knowing that the inscription on the back read, "two for one." He smiled at his youthful attempt at poetry and poked at the shiny sphere, his face softened by the ever-present past.

"I never dispose of anything," Jennifer said in a hushed voice.

His eyes grew intent, belying the smile on his lips.

"I'm glad. I'd hate to think that my tips from an entire summer bussing at Grossinger's had been tossed into some unfeeling trash basket."

"Never! I saved lots of mementos from that time in my life when Joshua Mandell dominated my every thought."

"Was there ever such a time?"

"Almost my whole life," she said seriously. Then her face brightened and her tone became girlish. "In that old cigar box, I have the big gold letter from your high school sweater, your fraternity pin, the hood ornament from your old Chevy, several not-so-passionate love letters, a dried wristlet from my senior prom, and the key to our room at the Paul Revere Inn in Bethlehem."

She looked at him and then looked down at the bracelet.

"I spent an hour going through that box tonight," she said half to herself, "reliving our past. It was a lovely past, wasn't it?"

"Yes, it was."

"You won't believe this, but as I sat on the floor and touched my memories, I cried. More for me, I think, than anyone else. I've made plenty of mistakes in my life, especially when it comes to judging people, but nothing even comes close to letting you get away from me."

"Jennie, don't."

"I can't help it," she said, her eyes misting. "I kept thinking about those things you said to me last night about making circles. It made a lot of sense. I was a fool to reject you."

"Jennie, it's past."

"Maybe, but don't you find it strange that I kept pieces of the past? I threw you away, but I held onto our memories."

"They were worth saving," he said, kissing her hand.

The waiter interrupted, served their dinner, poured the wine and left. Neither one of them ate very much. They picked at the food, nibbling and pushing things around on their plates.

"What did you tell Charles?" he asked.

"I told him I was spending the weekend in Bayonne."

Josh ordered coffee for both of them, his face minus expression.

"That's not what I meant. When are you telling him you're leaving?"

Jennifer looked shocked, almost insulted.

"I don't know. I hadn't thought about it."

Josh took a long, thin cigar from his breast pocket, unwrapped it, clipped the end, and lit it with deliberate ceremony. He puffed on it until its pungent aroma surrounded their table.

"I thought we discussed this last night. I thought we had an understanding."

"You *discussed* it," she said. "And I don't want to discuss it now."

"We have to."

"Why?"

"Because we spent a glorious night together making love, and unless you're honest with Charles, it can't happen again."

He can't mean that, she thought. *He can't mean what he's saying.*

Jennifer pulled her hands away from him. Tiny beads of sweat had gathered at the nape of her neck.

"Jennie," he continued. "I'm not trying to be noble, believe me. I just don't think it's wise for us to plunge into an affair, though God knows, I'm more than ready to plunge. You're married and it's wrong. Don't you see that?"

Her head reeled. *I lied to my husband. I packed my clothes and morality in a suitcase for you. Don't you see that?*

"I only see that we're right together," she said aloud. "All I can think about is how much I need to be with you. The way we were last night. Is that so terrible?"

He pulled his chair closer to the table, leaned toward her and spoke in a voice just above a whisper. His face was taut.

"To some people, maybe not. But for reasons I'd rather not explain, I can't get involved with a married woman. Not even you."

All my plans. All my lies. You can't say no. You just can't.

Jennifer moved back against the banquette and glared at him. Her back throbbed, and a thin blue vein near her temple was pulsing.

"I was a married woman last night or have you forgotten that? We made love, and if my memory serves me correctly, we were both more than consenting. Why are you acting so moral all of a sudden?"

He moved even closer, took her hands and held them firmly, forbidding her to pull away.

"Because I've loved you for too long to let us drift into a temporary arrangement. Last night meant the world to me, holding you in my arms and loving you that way. But it stirred up too many memories of too many unfulfilled promises. I can't go through it again. I can't sneak behind closed doors to love someone I want to love openly."

Jennifer couldn't look at him. She felt dizzy and faint, as if the air around her had stopped moving.

"I need time," she said. "I just need a little time. Why can't we be with each other now? I'll work this out."

Josh saw the pain in her eyes, and for a moment he felt his resolve ebb, but recollections of another pain filled his head, a pain he thought he had calmed.

"I can't," he said quietly. "I can't do it. And neither can you. Besides, you're not the type for clandestine meetings."

She snatched her hands away from him, her eyes flashing.

"How chivalrous of you! How nice of you to protect me from being branded a modern-day Hester Prynne!"

Josh didn't respond. They both sat there, not daring to look at each other.

"Jennie, if you were happy with Charles, you wouldn't have spent the night with me. You wouldn't have slept with me unless you were playing some very cruel joke, and I don't think you were."

You're pushing me into a corner, and I can't breathe. I can't deal with all this. I'm not strong enough.

"Charles and I do have problems," she said. "I've admitted that. But I just can't jump into a divorce. It frightens me. I have to live with the idea, get used to it, understand its consequences."

"And what am I supposed to do in the meantime? Go back on the shelf?" Josh's face wrinkled with anger.

"Love me. Be with me." She was pleading, but she didn't care.

"No. You're turning this into some perverse, egotistical contest. You want to stay married to Charles and have an affair with me. You can't have it both ways. Charles and I are not in competition for the hand of fair Jennifer. Charles is the husband of record, and therefore, he wins. Until, that is, you decide otherwise."

Jennifer's heart pounded. She had expected comfort and support. She couldn't deal with accusations. She had been certain that Josh would see it her way and give it time. She looked at her watch and twisted the dial until it wouldn't turn anymore. Why wasn't he more sympathetic? What were those reasons he mentioned? And why wouldn't he explain?

"You know, Mr. Mandell," she said, holding onto the banquette but trying to sound contained. "You sound like a patronizing parent. The next thing I know, you'll tell me that this hurts you more than it hurts me. Well, you can spare your advice to the lovelorn. My mistake was believing we were special."

"Jennie, you're taking this all wrong. I'm not deserting you."

"Aren't you?"

"No. If you're going to try and work out your problems with Charles, I'd only be in the way. I owe it to you to give you the chance to salvage your marriage, if that's what you want to do. But, I also owe it to myself to guard against being hurt."

"You want a decision?" She stood up and leaned against the table on wobbly arms. "I'll tell you what I've decided. I was right to leave you before, and I'm leaving you now."

She grabbed her purse and stormed up the stairs, hoping he couldn't see the tears welling up in her eyes. Josh ran after her. He reached her just as she was about to open the door. He grabbed her arm, but she pulled away.

"Don't touch me. I wouldn't want you to dirty your hands, Mr. Boy Scout!"

She spun on her heel and ran out of the restaurant without looking back. Josh watched her go. He could have caught her, but he knew he wasn't even going to try. He had done the right thing for both of them.

But if I'm so right, he thought, *why do I feel as if part of me just died?*

Fourteen

N ew York City abounds with homeless people, part of an enormous subculture of vagabonds who claim no permanent address other than the piece of sidewalk on which they stand. Most of them are vagrants whose days start and end with a swig from a bottle in a brown paper bag. Some are elderly, penniless and sick, forgotten by their families and rejected by a society that venerates everything old except its people. Some are weak and beggarly. Others are crafty Artful Dodgers who prey upon the pockets and purses of passersby and then disappear into the crowds. Finally, there are the disenchanted, the disenfranchised youth enslaved by their craving for exquisite escape and mindless oblivion.

They're everywhere and yet they're nowhere. New Yorkers ignore them and hurry on past. It's the ones who have homes, yet still rove the empty streets who invite curiosity. The well-dressed man or woman who lingers in a bar too late or window-shops past midnight or watches the movement of the river at three in the morning.

That night, Jennifer Cranshaw was one of those people. It was raining, a cold, raw steady rain that seeped through to the skin and chilled the bones. Despite the elements, she sat on a bench in Washington Square. Her hair was sopping wet, and mascara had made squiggly lines down her cheeks.

She had left the restaurant propelled by outrage, wandering through the zigzag streets until a grinding pain had invaded her spine, forcing her to find a place to rest. She had been there for hours, unable to move, unwilling to cry. Aside from the burning soreness, she was experiencing the entire range of her emotions. Love. Hate. Fear. Guilt. Pity. And others which jumbled together in such an intricate web that she couldn't sort them out. Over and over again, she repeated Josh's words, feeling the impact of his rejection. He had accused her of playing a cruel joke. She tried to force herself to believe that he had been the one playing the joke, that he had taken advantage of her, paying her back for her rejection of him so many years before.

Thirteen years ago. August. The heat was oppressive. Not even a small breeze poked through the thick curtain of humidity that hung over Bayonne. Jennifer and Josh were on the patio of the Skyline Beach Club, listening to the band inside play its last set. Josh had removed his jacket and tie, unbuttoned the top of his shirt, and was fanning himself with his hand. Jennifer was stretched out on a lounge chair, shoes off, dress hiked up over her knees. She sipped the last of her iced tea, held the cold glass to her cheeks, and then lay back, eyes closed.

Josh moved over to Jennifer's chair. "I hope the heat didn't ruin the evening," he said softly, running his finger down Jennifer's bare arm.

"I'm a little wrung out, but I had a great time." She felt him kiss her neck. She didn't respond.

"Good. I wanted tonight to be perfect." Josh nuzzled under her ear, kissed her gently on the mouth, and sat up.

Jennifer sat up also. Her dark, almond-shaped eyes studied his face. All night he had been acting strangely—smiling when nothing amusing had been said, kissing her affectionately in front of strangers, asking her constantly if she were enjoying herself. She had guessed the reason behind his behavior. Although her answer had been prepared weeks ago, now that the moment was upon her, she felt a spurt of nervousness.

"Jennie." Josh took her hand and held it tentatively, shyly. "We've been together for a long time, and it's no secret that I'm wildly in love with you." He smiled. Jennifer pulled her hand away, wiping her sweaty palm on her skirt. Josh reached into his pocket and pulled out a small box. With great ceremony, he got down on bended knee, opened the box so she could see the diamond ring inside, and took her hand again. "Jennie Sheldon. Will you marry me?"

He expected her to throw her arms around him, to grab

the ring, maybe even to giggle a little. She didn't move. She didn't even smile. She just shook her head.

"I can't."

It took a second for Josh to comprehend what she had said. Then, shock registered on his face. Disbelief resounded in his voice. "You're out of school. I've got a good job. There's nothing standing in our way. What do you mean you can't?"

She had rehearsed this scene at least a dozen times, but knowing her lines did not dispel her horrible stage fright. She had anticipated his anger as well as his confusion. She had planned on him questioning her, demanding answers. But she hadn't expected to feel this awful.

"I don't love you," she said, forcing herself to look at him.

Josh stood up, turned away from her and then back. "I don't believe you!"

"Believe what you like. It's true."

He stared down at her, his green eyes wide with incredulity. "I've been on the road a lot this summer. Did you find someone else while I was gone?"

She slid off the lounge chair and stood on the far side of it, away from Josh. "Yes, I did," she said. "Me! Next week I start with Young & Rubicam Advertising as a copy cub."

"You got a job? Mazeltov! What does that have to do with marrying me?" He was shouting, his voice filled with an intensity born of frustration.

"I'm starting more than a new job. I'm starting a new life."

"And being Mrs. Joshua Mandell is not what you had in mind. Is that correct?"

The band had stopped, and his voice echoed against the sudden silence. Jennifer saw the strain in his jaw, the rigid set of his shoulders. If only she could do this some other way.

"Right now, I don't want to be Mrs. Anybody. I want to find my future. And it's not here in Bayonne!"

He looked as if she had slapped him. Hurt spread across his face, flushing it like a sudden fever. "For years, you said you loved me. When exactly did you stop?"

"I was young, and I felt grateful to you. You were always there, and that's the problem. I think we just became a habit."

Josh wanted to close his ears to her words and the cold, detached way in which she said them, but there was a finality in her voice he couldn't ignore.

"I'm glad I could be of service," he said bitterly. "Lucky for you some habits are so easily broken."

The drive home was short and excruciatingly quiet. Josh never got out of the car. He never even looked at her. He simply dropped her off in front of her parents' house and drove away. She hadn't seen him again until two years ago.

"Are you all right, Miss?" A policeman tapped her shoulder.

She looked up at him, her eyes bleary and bloodshot. She was surprised to see him and suddenly, she looked embarrassed.

"I asked if you're all right," he said again.

"Yes. I'm fine. Fine. Yes."

Her teeth were chattering, and her speech was uneven, but he could tell she wasn't drunk, nor was she on drugs.

"What are you doing here so late?"

"I . . . my car. The garage closed. I can't get my car. I have the ticket, but I can't get my car." She reached into her purse, searching for the stub that would verify her story.

"Don't bother, Miss," he said, closing her purse and rubbing her frozen hands between his. "Would you like me to get you a cab?"

She looked at him again, like a runaway child, reluctant to go home for fear of being punished.

"Do you have someplace to go?"

"Go? Yes. Yes. I do. And a cab would be nice. I'm very cold. Could you help me up? My back is a little stiff."

As he lifted her to her feet, she cried out in pain. Slowly, he walked her to the corner near Waverly Place. He motioned to an oncoming taxi and gently helped her in.

"Do you have any money?" he asked.

She nodded, starting to open her purse again.

"What's your address? Tell the driver."

She told him, then looked at her watch. "Officer, what time is it? My watch has stopped."

There was something so sad about the way she shook her watch next to her ear and polished the face on her coat.

"I'm sure it can be fixed, Miss. It's twelve-thirty. How long have you been walking around?"

"Three, four hours. Something like that. I'm all right, though. Really. You've been very kind. Thank you." She smiled weakly, blowing into her hands and letting her warm breath thaw her frozen fingers.

"You'll be all right now?"

"I'll be fine. Thanks."

He closed the door, said a few words to the driver and tapped the side of the door, as the cab pulled away. As Jennifer's shivering subsided, her mind began to function. She fumbled in her handbag, pulling out a mirror and assessing the damage. A tissue removed the blotched makeup, but she didn't have the strength or the desire to repair it. It was irrelevant. Once again she tried to convince herself that tonight was Josh's revenge, but she couldn't make it stick. She knew better. She even understood what he had been trying to do and why he hadn't followed her. He wanted her to take charge. He wanted her to be as forceful and uncompromising in her personal life as she was in business. She understood, but that didn't salve her feelings of loneliness and isolation.

The taxi was speeding north on the FDR Drive. Soon, she would be home. As she watched the city fly by her window, she wondered what she would tell Charles. How could she explain her appearance? The missing car? Her father's sudden recovery? It was just the kind of situation her father used to warn her about. If you told one lie, you'd have to tell another to cover it and then another and another until, eventually, you forgot the first lie and caught yourself in your own trap.

She paid the driver, and rushed into the building, avoiding the doorman. As she pushed the button for her floor, she hoped that Charles was asleep. She was too exhausted and worn to make excuses. When the doors opened, she limped down the hall. Her right foot was swollen, and her shoe was pinching her toes. Outside her apartment, she put her ear to the door and listened for sounds. There were none. Inside, it was dark. She eased into the foyer and took off her shoes, kicking them into the closet. From memory she found a thick wooden hanger and put her dripping coat on it, hanging it on the closet door to dry. Hugging the wall, she groped her way to the bedroom. The door was closed, but she could see that that room too was dark. Slowly, she slid the door open, just enough for her to creep quietly to the bathroom.

She closed the door behind her, flicked on the lights, stripped down, and wrapped herself in a terrycloth robe. She washed, towel-dried her hair, and splashed on a little cologne. She had opened the door and was about to turn out the light when something moved. Her eyes went to the bed. Charles was there. She could see his blond hair caught in the one slash of light that had pushed through the half-opened door. He was sleeping, curled up on his side. But he was not alone. There was another body lying there. In her bed. Next to her husband. She felt numb. As if in a trance, she stood watching. Waiting. Charles wriggled next to the other body and draped his arm around the adjoining lump. Jennifer felt sick, weak and sick, and she hung onto the wall for support.

The instant the lights went on, she wished she hadn't turned the switch. The two bodies jumped up, rubbing their eyes and turning in the direction of the door. For the moment, she was dumbstruck, her tongue thick and speechless. But then, she was angry. Wildly angry, like an animal clamped in the teeth of a steel trap. In her bed, naked, lying next to her husband, was a man.

"Get out! Get out of my bed! Get out of my house! Get your filthy, disgusting body out of my bed!"

Weeks of office pressure and personal doubt released themselves in an explosion that started deep within and raged toward the surface with volcanic force. She was screeching. Her body was quaking, and her voice quivered with fury. Charles stared at her, the color drained from his face. The other man hurriedly wrapped himself in a sheet and ran past her into the living room where he must have dressed. Jennifer never took her eyes off Charles. They both heard the front door slam, and it was as if a grenade went off inside her head, driving her to that brink of insanity where logic disappears and raw emotion rules. She ran to the bed with her fists clenched and pounded at Charles, beating his head and his back. She was screaming and crying, shouting senseless, hateful words. She thrashed at him, pummeling him, missing occasionally and slamming her fists into the headboard. At last, she fell into the chair near the bed and sobbed. Charles put on his robe and waited for the convulsive spasms to subside. She felt his hand touch her knee, and she recoiled, pulling both legs under her, protecting herself from him. The crying stopped, but in its place was seething unabiding venom.

"Don't touch me, you goddamned faggot! How could you? How dare you flaunt your perversity in my face like that, bringing that thing in here, into my bed?"

"Jennifer, please. Let me explain." His voice was strangled and pathetic, but Jennifer felt no compassion. She felt nothing but hate.

"What's there to explain? Those late nights? Your business trips? I thought you were working. Hah! You must have loved it. What a fool I was." She rose from the chair, pacing back and forth. "How many men have you brought to my bed? Ten? Twenty? Did you do it when I traveled or when I worked late?"

"No. Never before. Never here," he said, his eyes pleading.

She continued her frenzied pacing, spitting words at him.

"Once in a while I wondered if there was someone else. I just couldn't understand why you were always so tired. I told myself you were overworked and sick. It turns out I was right."

She turned to him, her teeth bared, eyes wild.

"You are sick! You're demented."

Suddenly she laughed, an hysterical, creaturelike howl that frightened Charles. She sounded as if she had lost her mind, and he rose from the bed, starting for her.

"Don't come near me," she said, backing away. "Don't ever come near me." She laughed again, and it was a hollow, bitter laugh resounding with hostility and disgust. "I

thought you might have had another woman. I thought
you slept with Brooke Wheeler. No. Not you. That would
be normal. But you're not normal! And I hate you! Do
you hear me? I hate you! I want you out of my house and
out of my life!"

Thoughts and emotions were crashing around inside her
head. Why was this happening? What had caused the
foundation of her life to crack and heave? Everything she
had considered solid and secure was crumbling. She was
overtired and overwrought, still reeling from Josh's unexpected rejection. She felt herself sinking. She tried to hang
on, to grab reality and push it back to where it once was.
At that moment, she wasn't even sure whether it was
Charles's homosexuality or his infidelity that appalled her
more. It was finding him, here, with someone else that
stung her. Seeing him sleeping so peacefully when she felt
so miserable and alone. Later, she would determine to survive and search her soul for new and stronger resources.
Later, she would reevaluate her goals and redefine happiness. But now, she was shaken and trembling with rage.

She reached behind her and grabbed anything her
hands touched, flinging objects across the room. Perfume
bottles, picture frames, books, anything that found its way
into her hands slammed against the opposite wall. Charles
held his hands up to protect himself, crouching on the
floor beside the bed. When he looked up, she was
clutching herself, her body wrenching from the trauma.
Her color looked strange, and then her legs began to
wobble. He caught her as she fell. Gently, he picked her
up, at first turning toward the bed, but then heading for
another room. He lay her down on the couch in the den,
rushing to cover her with a blanket. He ran to the kitchen
in search of something, anything to revive her and returned with a bottle of ammonia. He opened it and passed
it under her nose, watching her snap her head from side to
side to avoid the stinging odor. Her eyes opened. She
stared at him. His hands gripped her shoulders and held
her down.

"You fainted," he said quietly. "You have to rest. And I
have to talk."

"I don't want to hear it."

"But I have to say it."

She turned her head away, covering her ears with her hands. Charles sat back on his knees, his eyes filled with tears.

"I never meant for this to happen, Jennifer. You must believe that. I've fought it. God knows, I've fought it. But I'm gay. I am what you say I am. I'm a faggot, and there's nothing I can do about it."

His voice was low and choking. Jennifer turned toward him cautiously, the anger still present.

"How long?" she said. "How long have you been cheating on me this way? How many times have you come to me after being with a man?"

"Jennifer, try and understand. It's only been the past year or so when it overwhelmed me. Before that, I had it under control."

"Did you?" she said, sitting up and glowering at him. "And when you married me, was it under control then? Did you know then as you promised to love and honor me? Did you?"

He sat silently, staring at the floor. He breathed deeply, shoring up his strength. Then, he faced her, and he was calm.

"I wasn't sure then. I don't know, maybe I was repressing, but I did love you. I wanted to make you happy, and I prayed that you could do the same for me. You almost succeeded."

"Spare me the soap opera. I don't want to hear it. I just want you to get out!"

He retreated to the bedroom where he dressed and packed. When he was ready to leave, he stopped in the doorway of the den. She was still sitting there, blank and sober.

"We have to talk, Jennifer. I'll call you."

She jerked her head away and fixed on a spot on the wall. She didn't even dare to blink until she heard the door close and knew that he was gone. Her back was throbbing, and her eyes ached, as if they had suddenly grown too large for their sockets. Yet she remained mute, not moving, not thinking. Her head began to feel sweaty and feverish, but her body was shuddering uncontrollably.

Her first instinct was to call someone. Josh. She needed him. She needed to talk to him, to have him hold her and

tell her it would all go away. She reached for the phone
and listened to the dial tone. Slowly, she put the phone
down. What would she say? How could she tell anyone,
especially Josh, the truth? It was too awful. Too disgusting. She felt more alone than ever with no place to turn
for help. The tears came again, large puffy tears that
rushed unchecked down her face. She leaned back and let
them come. They continued almost all night, even when
at last, she slept.

Fifteen

Nature has a way of demanding order. For each
loss, there has to be a gain. For each death, a
birth. For each separation, a coming together.
Some call it fate. Others say it is coincidence. And still
others view it as the working of an omnipotent force.

Terk Conlon wasn't the type to consider cause, only effect. To whatever or whomever was responsible for bringing Zena Welles back into his life, he was grateful, but he
felt no need for cosmic explanations. She was there,
willing to see him and nothing else mattered. Not his
work, not his wife, nor the clawing reality of Eben Towers. He felt like a schoolboy as he stood nervously on the
steps of Zena's Chelsea brownstone, clutching a handful of
roses in one hand and a bottle of Mouton-Cadet in the
other. When she opened the door, his breath caught in his
throat. Her face was backlit by the hall chandelier, and he
thought he had never seen anyone as lovely in his life.
Her skin was a creamy white, the color of cultured pearls,
and her celadon eyes were bright and clear. Her long,
raisin-brown hair was richer and fuller than he had
remembered it, and it hung luxuriously down her back.
Her scent was the same fresh-spirited fragrance she had
worn when they first met.

She invited him in and relieved him of his packages. As
if to put him at his ease, she took him on a tour of her

house. It was a small, but comfortable, two-story building with boxy rooms decorated in International Eclectic, a blend of antiques and souvenirs from her travels. He followed her into the living room where she had a fire blazing in a fieldstone hearth. A bottle of wine had already been chilled and opened.

Zena offered Terk a seat on one of the couches. She joined him, but remained two cushions apart. He poured wine for them both and held his glass up to her, toasting without words. His eyes enveloped her, and she let him stare, never looking away or past him.

"You're still the most exquisite woman I've ever known."

Zena started to say something, to warn him not to take too much for granted, but instead, she merely smiled.

Terk longed to hold her, but he suppressed his urge and stuck to amenities. He felt awkward, and his conversation was stilted. The room was filled with her photographs, so he asked her about each one, pretending to listen to stories about safaris in Africa and digs in Egypt. They had just about finished the wine when he screwed up the courage to ask her about Randy Webster.

"Are you living with him?" he said, searching the room for telltale signs like pipe tobacco.

"He's a friend." She watched Terk carefully. She knew he was uncomfortable, and she felt for him. She too wanted to hold him, but too many years had passed. They had to contact each other psychically before they could touch each other physically.

"I, uh, got the impression the other night that he considered you much more than a friend."

"We have been lovers, if that's what you mean, but I have no room in my life for commitments. Randy understands that. He's divorced, and right now, he's a freewheeling bachelor. I suppose I'm number one, but there are many others on his list."

Terk nodded, trying to appear casual and finishing his wine in beer-stein swallows. Zena was staring at him, and a calm smile carved half-circles into her cheeks. Her eyes were soft, but they bore through him and searched his soul.

"And what about you?" she said. "What's happened in your life?"

"A lot and yet nothing. So much has happened, and so little has changed." He sounded uneasy, almost pained. "I'm still married to Deirdre, but it's a flimsy structure."

"I'm sorry." She moved toward him and took his hand. Her touch burned his skin, and he felt desperate. He covered her hand with his own.

"Why didn't I grab you when I had the chance? You're the only good thing that's ever come into my life, and I didn't have the sense to hold onto you."

He lifted her hand to his mouth, kissing it and pressing it against his cheek. He closed his eyes, relishing the feel of her skin. Gently, she pulled away.

"Let's have dinner."

Throughout the meal, Terk restrained his impulses to tell her everything. He discussed business and politics and the sagging economy as best he could. They had finished a second bottle of wine when Zena suggested they have their coffee in the living room. The fire had dwindled, and Terk added more logs, stoking them until they were fully flamed. He waited for her to sit, placing himself immediately beside her and losing himself in the smell of her. He felt his hands move, as if something outside of himself had taken control. He cradled her face and brought it toward him. His lips brushed hers.

"I need you," he said, afraid to tell her how much.

Zena held him in her arms, rocking him and feeling his back tremble. She hadn't planned on this, but she knew she couldn't deny him. Even after all these years, something about Terk affected her deeply. She knew that inside this bulky bear of a man was a floundering child, a little boy who still suffered pain and loneliness, carrying it with him like an eternal torch. It had been that tiny spot of vulnerability that had made Zena fall in love with him in the first place. As long as it still existed, so did her feelings for him.

She glided off the couch, taking his hand in hers and leading him up the stairs to her bedroom. He started to speak, but she placed a finger on his lips, silencing him. He watched as Zena went to the dresser and lit several fat candles, placing them on either side of the bed. The room became a dream, a dusky Elysium with light beaming and fading like a nova in a winter sky. She removed her clothes slowly, keeping her eyes locked on his and casting a spell over him. When she was naked, she came to him, sliding into his arms. He stood statue still while she undressed him with bewitching deliberateness, elevating the act of disrobing to an almost mystical art form. Her hands moved slowly, dawdling over a button and idling over a sleeve as if it were all part of an ancient tribal ritual. Finally, he stood before her, embarrassed by his readiness. She said nothing, but used silent gestures to summon him to her bed.

The candles cast long shadows over her body, fingering her skin and caressing her limbs. She rose above him, her face tranquil and serene. As she did, she leaned forward, granting him the pleasure of her cascade of hair washing over his chest. Her lips explored him, pressing against his neck and his chest. His hands gripped the sheets in an effort to retain control, but it was a battle. Her tongue had discovered hollows in his body he never knew existed, and she caressed him, licking him, sucking on his skin. His arms went around her, attacking her, pressing her to him until he thought their bodies had become fused. His mouth found hers. He was starved for a taste of her, and he satisfied his hunger. He felt her body tremble, and he was ecstatic. She wanted him as much as he wanted her. He could feel it in her legs as they stretched out beneath him, digging into the bed and becoming rigid and stiff. Her hips had begun to move, undulating, swinging and shifting, enticing him to follow. He joined her, thrusting himself inside her, losing himself in the warmth of her, the wet of her, the beauty of her. He buried himself in her body, grasping at her flesh with the fury of one who fears loss, holding her to him even when their bodies had nothing more to give. He remained on her, in her, holding her face and watching the dim light play with her features. She smiled up at him, and he kissed her lips, softly and sweetly. He felt her fingertips outline his face. They traced his eyes, his nose, and then his lips. His mouth closed around her finger and sucked on it like a nursing infant. Finally, she eased him off her, onto his side. His eyes remained fixed on her face. For a long time, neither of them spoke.

"I won't let you go this time, Zena." His voice was husky and low.

"You won't have to. I won't ask you to choose the way I did years ago. Your situation may be the same, but I'm not."

She explained to Terk that she had come to realize that her work was the *primum mobile* of her existence, the altar on which she was willing to sacrifice anything, including the security of a permanent relationship. She spoke softly, but her words rang with conviction. Terk listened, feeling old and provincial in the face of such dedicated independence. She still loved him, she said, and she wanted to be with him, but there was no need for ties, and there would be no demand for promises. Terk let her speak, unable to comment, but inside he was struggling. He wanted ties. He wanted marriage. He wanted to possess her, totally and completely. He had dreamed of nothing else, and here she was telling him that an affair was all she asked. She was establishing the rules, and he knew that he would abide by them.

The candles had exhausted themselves. Zena left the bed and padded about the room in search of replacements, the slim lines of her body forming a blue-gray silhouette against the dark walls. She was unaware of her effect on him, oblivious to the stirring he felt inside each time her body passed in front of him. It was as if she were a magic amulet, swinging back and forth before his eyes, and lulling him into a hypnotic trance.

She lit the candles and kissed him on the forehead, leaving the room and returning a few minutes later with a bottle of brandy and two snifters. She poured some of the amber liquid in each glass, and held the fat-bellied goblets over the candles' flame for a few seconds. She handed him the glasses and slithered back into bed. The window was open, and the room was chilly. Her nipples were tight and erect from the cold, and his first impulse was to warm her with his hands, to pull her down beneath him and love her all over again. But Zena had pulled the sheets up under her arms and was sipping her brandy. As if sensing his mood, she announced that she wanted to talk.

"At the risk of embarrassing you," she said, "why did Deirdre marry you in the first place?"

The question had caught him off guard and at first, he couldn't answer.

"You're from two completely different worlds. I would've thought her family would have forbidden such a match."

He laughed, a deep, bearish growl that came from somewhere behind his throat.

"They tried, but Deirdre is a very determined woman."

"I assumed as much," she said, her green eyes reflecting the orange glow of the candles. "But why you? Why not some Lochinvar from Sutton Place?"

Unfortunately, the answer was far more complicated than the question. How could Terk tell her that, according to Deirdre, his main qualification for husbandhood was his lower class sexuality? *Sex is the tie that binds*, she had told him. *And when that goes, so do you.*

"I guess I was the prize in a Cracker Jack box," he said.

"I beg your pardon?"

"Deirdre is a rebel dressed in diamonds and furs. She loves nothing more than laughing in the face of tradition. She takes great delight in shocking people, especially her parents and others who travel in elevated circles. I was a nobody. What could be more outrageous than an heiress marrying a bartender's son?"

Zena looked into her brandy glass and then lifted her eyes to meet his. Her hand stroked his cheek.

"But you've been married a long time. Isn't the game over?"

"Sweet Zena. You don't play nasty games so you couldn't possibly understand. Deirdre is a master. She's involved in a constant battle of wits with her father, and I am the pawn. Parker Walling hates my guts. He has ever since the day we met."

"I would think that that would be reason enough for Deirdre to let you go." Zena looked confused.

"Normally, you would be right, but the Wallings are not your average folk. Deirdre and her father love and respect each other, but both of them are highly competitive animals. If Deirdre left me, for whatever reason, her father would win. She'll never allow that to happen."

"Then why don't you leave her?"

"Because then I lose. Family is family and Parker Walling would not take kindly to a bartender's son walking out on his precious daughter. He's a powerful man with his hand in hundreds of pies. I'd never know when that hand was going to grab hold of my neck."

"It's sort of a Mexican stand-off, isn't it?"

"I guess so. Every time I think I've found a way out, I run smack into another roadblock."

Zena sat very still. She knew it wasn't easy for Terk to bare himself like this. Zena was not as innocent as he believed, but neither was she sophisticated enough to understand the machinations of a creature like Deirdre. Zena was forthright. She shied away from puzzles. This was one, and the pieces didn't fit.

"Terk, you can't go on like this." Her face was serious. She put down her brandy glass and folded her hands on her lap. "You're a condemned man, and it doesn't seem as if you've committed any crime other than having been born to the wrong parents."

Terk cringed. Everything he had told Zena was the truth, but only part of the truth. And he couldn't tell her the rest. Finally, he said, "I have a plan, Zena. Soon I'll be free of Deirdre and her father and anyone else who thinks he has a hold on me. I just need to know that you'll be there."

The tremor in Terk's voice set off an alarm in Zena's brain. She knew Terk better than he thought she did. He was motivated by desperation, and she had seen too much not to know that desperation made people careless. The thought caused small bumps to pop out on her skin. Terk took her in his arms.

"You're cold. Let me warm you." He put his glass down on the table beside the bed and held her.

"I love you, Zena Welles, and nothing is going to prevent me from being part of your life. Nothing!" he said.

Sixteen

Beneath the glossy cover of every magazine, a complex machine grinds its gears like a giant, self-winding watch, ticking, ticking, ticking toward the monthly deadline. At *Jolie,* the April issue dominated all conversation and activity. Each department was immersed in the tedious process of culling information, planning pages, assigning articles and selling space. Whereas one floor agonized about filling the front of the book with advertising, the other floor fretted about the editorial content in the back of the book. The goal of each group, however, was the same—to outdo the competition and lure both advertisers and consumers into spending their dollars on *Jolie.*

Marnie Dobbs waited impatiently in the Fashion Closet, the hub of her chiefdom, and the focal point of the magazine. She had called a nine-thirty meeting, but it was nearing ten and the members of her department were still dribbling in. As she watched the clock, she wondered why Jennifer Cranshaw had asked to attend the Fashion Department's regular Monday morning work session. She knew that Jennifer was concerned about the April issue, but so were they all. Marnie's curiosity mingled with a vague sense of annoyance. Promotion had nothing to do with fashion selections. Jennifer had never intruded before. Why would she start now? When she called, Jennifer had said something about them all pulling together and turning The Big Pineapple into something special. Marnie had assured her that she had shelved her own personal reservations about the concept and would do her best to support it. What more could Jennifer want? And what could she possibly contribute? Marnie conceded that Jennifer was a smashing-looking woman with a definite sense of style, but she likened Jennifer to someone who learns to play the piano by ear without ever learning to read a note of music; she respected the talent, but was suspicious of the actual working knowledge.

Marnie sipped her coffee and watched the seats around the conference table fill up. As she did, she surveyed the large square room. Every inch of wall space was taken up with "cubbies," each box stuffed to overflowing with shoes, handbags, hats, scarves and other accessories pertinent to the present fashion season. She let her eyes blur, enjoying the interplay of color and texture. It was in this room that clothes for the editorial pages were selected and accessorized before every photographic shoot. Huge, double metal racks stood on one side, jammed with garments supplied by manufacturers eager to have their labels touted in *Jolie*. It was the job of Marnie's staff to scout the market, view the lines, solicit samples, and, on occasion, provide styling advice to smaller companies who wanted their products to have the *Jolie* look.

Once the racks were filled, Marnie and the fifteen women who comprised her department judged each piece, critically assessing them for style, excitement, chic, and potential salability. Marnie was a very organized woman, and she insisted that the clothes be categorized immediately according to use (evening, business or sport) and then further sorted to fit the theme of each issue. She was one of the few industry higher-ups who defended the system of standardized issue themes. Most of the senior fashion editors at the other Fellows books, as well as those at Fellows' major competitors, Hearst and Condé Nast, claimed the practice stifled creativity. Marnie laughed that off as hogwash. It gave order to what might easily have been chaos. There was more than enough room for creativity within each issue of the magazine to suit her. She recited the list over and over to herself like a mantra, finding comfort in its repetitiveness: January was resort, February and October spotlighted beauty, March and September dealt with career, May and June zeroed in on warm-weather garb, April was active sportswear, August, back-to-college, and November and December meant holiday. It was simple, direct.

The large table was already strewn with early morning litter—plastic lids dripping coffee, waxed wrappers from buttered rolls. Marnie glanced at the clock. Jennifer would be there any minute. Marnie turned to the women at the table. She had watched the faces change many times over the years, but the basic personality somehow remained constant. The girls in the fashion department were devoted to their jobs, completely enthralled to be part of *Jolie*'s elite. They flocked to the magazine from all parts of the country, willing to start out doing secretarial chores or working reception desks on the faint chance that one day they might take a seat around Marnie Dobbs's famed Closet table. Marnie didn't award seats to very many, but each one she assigned held someone gifted with that inexplicable, innate faculty known as "style." Dash and flair attracted Marnie's attention. Poise and the ability to think on one's feet were other criteria, but the most important quality an aspiring fashion editor could possess was a genuine love of the business. Marnie didn't tolerate dilettantes.

As she watched her troops assemble, she saw that they were dressed in what Marnie tongue-in-cheek often called "outré chic," the staffers' penchant for taking *the* style of the day and treating it with supposed indifference. If big blouses were in, fashion editors wore big blouses, but with an attitude that said it didn't matter, that the wearing of that blouse had been nothing more than a spur of the moment decision. This was what differentiated them from the general public, who treated trends as edicts. Magazine people didn't have to carbon copy. They had the knack. Marnie refrained from telling them that while they might have removed themselves from the herd, they had fallen into the conformism of the fashion editor, which was just as imitative.

Marnie loved this business, even with its reverse snobbism and its overexaggerated sense of importance. It was more than a business to her. Marnie believed that pretty clothes and makeup artfully applied did more for a woman's psyche than years of analysis. If she didn't believe it, she would never have been able to do her job as well as she did.

The last girl had just taken her seat when Jennifer entered the Fashion Closet. Marnie's keen eye tagged the crunchy tweed jacket as Ralph Lauren and the expression on Jennifer's face as haggard. Her eyes were watery, without their usual fire, and she looked as if she had a cold.

"I'm sorry I'm late," Jennifer said, her froggy voice

confirming Marnie's armchair diagnosis. "I had a number of calls to make."

"My girls are never on the button anyway," Marnie said with criticism in her voice. She led Jennifer to a seat next to her own. "You sound as if you have a brute of a cold."

Jennifer nodded.

"I got caught in the rain over the weekend," she said, feeling compelled to explain and then wondering why she had bothered.

As she took her seat, Jennifer could feel the younger women staring at her and whispering among themselves, wondering why she had been permitted to attend this sacred gathering. Sensing an explanation was in order, she told Marnie she needed some input to help her flesh out her promotion proposals, and added that they should proceed as if she weren't there. Marnie remained curious. Why was Jennifer willing to take so much time out of her own schedule if it were just to observe?

Marnie called the meeting to order and went straight to the point. Her staff's job this month was to comb Seventh Avenue for fashion with a Hawaiian flavor. She briefed them on Brad's brainstorm, gingerly, sensitive to the grimacing faces she saw before her. She tried to infuse the task with a sense of challenge, ever conscious of Jennifer's presence.

Each time Marnie stressed the importance of supporting The Big Pineapple, she was greeted by a unanimous groan, prompting Jennifer to smile in sympathy. Jennifer listened carefully as a few suggestions rose out of the grumbling. One painfully thin woman, with her hair rolled in the style of the 40's, knew where to find island-print shirts and natural fabric skirts and pants. Another suggested they theme the portfolio around color, using the flowers of Hawaii as their guide. One of the older women in the department proposed contacting a source on the islands about unique accessories unavailable on the mainland as well as the least overdone locations. Jennifer wrote everything down in a spiral pad, keeping her face clean of expression. The sportswear editor still clung to the belief that the active sportswear traditionally featured in April could be transported to a Hawaiian setting, using the various resorts on Maui and the Big Island as background.

Marnie agreed, turning to Jennifer and throwing out the idea of asking Terk Conlon to coordinate hotel editorial credit in return for free accommodations. Jennifer nodded, adding that perhaps they could tie in with a resort and an airline to create a four-page advertising section.

Finally, Marnie turned to Jennifer and invited her to comment.

Jennifer looked at their faces and knew they were going to be difficult to win over.

"I know it's not easy for any of you to swallow this Big Pineapple idea," she said. "I'll be honest and tell you that my initial reaction was out and out horror, but facts are facts. *Jolie* is in trouble, and Brad is the publisher."

"And if this is his idea of a cure, it's no wonder we're dying!" The sardonic voice came from a pinched-nose curly-headed woman at the other end of the table.

Jennifer saw many of the young woman's cohorts shaking their heads in agreement, and she decided the time had come to stand. She rose quietly, keeping her hands on the table and leaning toward them. Her chin was set, but her eyes remained gentle.

"I'm not here to defend Mr. Helms," Jennifer said, "but I think that perhaps we're all conditioned to complain without giving his ideas our full attention. I've done a lot of thinking about this, and I've come to a startling conclusion." She paused, allowing everyone an anticipatory moment. "I think it can work!"

At least ten staffers had slouched down in their chairs, signaling to Jennifer that she would have to present a very solid case to win their support. She noticed that a few of them were attentive, and she directed her next comments to them, deliberately excluding the others.

"Consider this from the point of view of a first. That's how Brad sees it, and in a way, he's right. Not that I'll ever admit it that easily."

Smiles came to many of the faces, and a few more sat up, warming to the woman at the head of the table. Jennifer had enticed them into her corner.

"Why not continue with the concept of creating a first? Why not do something *Jolie* has never done before? Something no other magazine has ever dared to do?"

The atmosphere changed dramatically. Jennifer had dared them to be great, and suddenly, it was as if she had turned a switch, forcing electricity to flow throughout the room, sparking everyone present. Marnie was staring at Jennifer, uncertain as to where she was headed, but instinct told her the direction was on target.

"Let's commission a famous designer to create a native *Jolie* line."

It was the first time she had aired the idea that had formed during the Fashion Forecast. She held her breath, waiting for reactions.

Several of the women hooted openly. Others shook their heads as if in the presence of a madwoman. Only Marnie was bobbing her head contemplatively. The idea was outrageous; there was no question about that. It was unheard of, and Marnie wasn't even sure if it was ethical, but the magazine was in danger of being sold, and she would do anything to help save it.

"Are you suggesting a couture-priced line?" she asked, her strong voice silencing the tabletop debates.

Jennifer was grateful Marnie was being cooperative.

"No. I think the appeal comes with a high-priced name designing a popularly-priced line. We'd feature it in the April issue, launching it at the perfect time for April/May selling in the stores. I'd also recommend using it as the basis for our live fashion shows in The Big Pineapple promotions. The publicity value alone would be worth its weight in gold."

Marnie felt a flutter of excitement. Jennifer had come up with an idea that could push *Jolie* to the forefront of the fashion industry, and she loved it, but she had to know more before she gave her support.

"Do you have anyone in mind?"

"Yes, but I haven't approached them, and I don't think it's fair to mention names at this point."

"When will you tell us?" asked a quiet blonde two seats away from Jennifer.

"I don't mean to be secretive, but we can't afford to have this leaked to the press ahead of time. My plan is to have this designer meet privately with Marnie. They'll put the line together themselves."

"We'd need models, and they'd know. So would the photographer. Why do we have to be the only ones in the dark?"

Jennifer turned to a short redhead in an army jacket and fatigue pants.

"I have a model, and the photographer would know that he was to keep his mouth shut or risk losing his place in *Jolie's* roster book."

The force of Jennifer's statement put an end to the questions and an end to the meeting. She turned to Marnie and started to discuss the details with her as the room emptied.

"I know all this sounds wild, Marnie, but I think we have to dive in head first, or we're all going to pay the penalty."

Marnie was filled with conflicting thoughts. The first was jealousy. Why hadn't she thought of this? Why hadn't she seen the possibility of uniting her talents with those of a designer to create something spectacular? Because she was too busy doing her job, she told herself defensively. The second emotion was joy. It bubbled inside her like carbonation, rising to the surface in a rush. For years, she had promoted fashion; this was her chance to graduate, to become an architect of fashion.

"How much input would I have?" she asked Jennifer.

"Style direction, fabric selection, colors. I need you to share your knowledge of what sells. Will you do it?"

"I'll do whatever I can," Marnie said, finding it an effort to sound calm. "This could be the coup of the century, Jennifer. I hope you can pull it off."

"We're going to pull it off. You'll see."

Jennifer checked her watch. She had forgotten that it had stopped. Suddenly, the events of the past weekend covered her like a leaden shroud. She hadn't slept very much, and for the moment, she felt woozy. As she stood up, she staggered and felt Marnie's hand grip her arms.

"Are you all right?"

Jennifer looked at her, lost in her nightmare. She forced herself back into the present.

"It's this cold," she said. "I'll be fine, really I will. Thanks for everything. I'll be in touch."

"Thank *you*," Marnie said as Jennifer rushed off. Marnie stood in the empty room. She could still feel the electric current Jennifer had generated.

I'm not sure she realizes it, she thought to herself, *but that lady with the tissue box in one hand is holding the future of this magazine in the other.*

Gwendolyn Stuart had a headache. She had had an early morning visit from Jennifer Cranshaw, who had convinced her to push for a Hawaiian model on the cover of April *Jolie*. Gwen had flatly refused to even consider such heresy, but Jennifer held firm, wearing her down with argument after argument. Gwen eventually relented. Any woman who could put together a party of the magnitude of *Jolie*'s birthday bash and have it go off without a single hitch had to know what she was doing. For more than an hour now, Gwen had been pleading with the head of the Circulation Department to agree to the idea.

She paced the perimeter of her all-beige office, half-listening to his endless recitation of cover facts. He didn't have to tell her that certain models sold more than others. She knew that. She knew that each month it was the job of the Circulation Department to tally the number of newsstand copies sold nationwide for each magazine, carefully noting the cover model, the color of the magazine logo, and the colors of the lead lines. Then, they documented their findings and fed them to Gwen and the other editors-in-chief, encouraging them to select only those faces and colors which paid off in substantial sales. Within any twelve-month period, *Jolie* used, at most, five models to grace its covers. The logic was that certain faces possessed a *je ne sais quoi*—an appeal to the harried consumer who grabs a magazine off a rack. Why take a chance when one could bet on a sure thing? Gwen listened patiently as Jack Kingsley explained that a native girl with a flower in her hair was an untried commodity. Gwen shook her head in hesitant agreement, but she knew she had to fight Jack, or she'd be fighting both Brad and Jennifer. Jack was the lesser of the evils.

"I understand what you're saying Jack, but you felt the same way when we started using black models on the cover."

Kingsley nodded.

"True. Very true." He stroked his chin and drew his hands forward until they puckered his fleshy lips. "But Gwen, that was different. We have a large black readership."

Gwen stopped short in front of her built-in bookcase, giving the starched man with the crew cut her most dazzling smile.

"Jack, *darling*. I don't think you totally understand the situation. I'm not suggesting that we start a trend. I'm not advocating an ethnic group of the month for the cover of *Jolie*. But this is a special issue, dedicated body and soul to the Aloha state. It would be ludicrous to boast about Hawaii with a pale blonde grinning at you, now wouldn't it?"

"But statistics show that blonde-haired, blue-eyed models bring the best results." He crossed his legs so that she was forced to notice his spit-shined, black wing-tips. "We even resist models with brown eyes because they don't pull as well at point-of-sale."

Gwen had returned to her desk. She hated arguing a point in which she didn't wholeheartedly believe. Half of her wanted to sabotage Brad and insure the issue's failure, but the other half kept reminding her that her name headed the masthead; if she screwed Brad, she screwed herself.

She turned to Jack Kingsley once again and summoned her most patient voice.

"Jack, dear, I can't be concerned about statistics on this issue. Brad has demanded a native girl on the cover, and our head of promotion is in total agreement. If you have any reservations about it, I wish you would discuss it with them."

Jack glared at her, springing up from his seat and practically clicking his heels as he headed for the door. He opened his mouth to say something more, and then left, mumbling to himself. Gwen watched him leave, pleased with her performance. She knew that no matter how distasteful Kingsley found the idea, he would do exactly as she requested. She was a powerful woman, and he was a cog in a vast machine. Cogs didn't question queens, according to Gwen; they merely did as they were told. It just didn't seem fair that Gwendolyn Stuart was only a queen when *Elegante*'s Clair Corelli was obviously an empress.

Jennifer inched her way down the hall in the direction of the Beauty Department, hoping her legs didn't buckle before she got there. She smiled at anyone who passed her en route, but she had to hug the walls for support. Her spine was throbbing, and her head was reeling. She knew she should have stayed home, at least until her fever subsided, but she couldn't stand the sight of that apartment. It had become a vile sore, a gaping wound oozing humiliation and despair. She had spent the entire weekend holed up in her den, nursing her cold and trying to dress her emotional wounds, but none of her ministrations had effected a cure.

Charles had called a dozen times, and she had slammed the phone down the minute she heard his voice, eventually disconnecting the phone altogether. He must have contacted their housekeeper, because late Saturday morning Hattie appeared, letting herself in with her own key and insisting on lending a hand. Jennifer could still see the questions in Hattie's eyes as the woman returned from the bedroom holding pieces of broken picture frames and shattered vases in her hands. Without saying a word, she stripped the room, throwing out all the bed linens as Jennifer had instructed her to do. Intuitively, she shut the door when she was finished, locking in whatever had caused such destruction. Hattie made up the sofa bed and retreated to the kitchen, cooking soup and bringing Jennifer tea and toast, hovering over her until she finished. While Jennifer slept, Hattie sat beside her, waking her occasionally for aspirin and more tea. By ten o'clock, Jennifer couldn't take it anymore. She begged Hattie to leave, promising to take care of herself. She was unable to bear being in anyone's company. More than once, Jennifer entertained the thought of running away and hiding out until the grinding pain abated, but she knew there was no escape from her reality.

Sometimes hours slid by and she felt calm, almost suspended, her mind empty, swept clean of all thought. And then, without warning, the hurt would return, battering her until she felt sore and ravaged. The wretchedness refused to go away, no matter how often she cried or how loudly she screamed. At one point, she left the den, drawn to the bedroom as if some giant magnet were pulling her there. Her hand shook as she opened the door, confronting the room and the ugliness within. She didn't know how long she stood there, or even what went through her mind as she relived her horror, but suddenly she was on the floor, crouched in a corner by the door, sobbing and pounding her fists against the wall. When she had exhausted herself, she fell into a merciful sleep, huddled in the shadows, shivering with fever and fear.

When she finally awakened from her hideous nightmare, a plan to do battle with the goblins infesting her brain had taken shape. As she had done so many times before, she would turn to her work. She had convinced herself that she and the magazine were intertwined, connected to each other by some spiritual link. Her union with Charles was over, but her marriage to *Jolie* continued. *Jolie* would fill the emptiness. *Jolie* would give her comfort.

Bettina Kharkovsky and her two assistants were waiting for Jennifer, clustered around Bettina's desk at the far end of the long, narrow office. The room was painted standard, flat, office-white. Bettina's desk backed up to a large window, the only one in the room, and she had created a hanging jungle in front of it, massing together asparagus fern, Swedish ivy, purple hearts, and two small baskets of donkey's tail. One entire wall was taken up with metal filing cabinets, topped by a counter with three light boxes and stacks of slide trays. The other side of the room housed Bettina's assistants, Esmé Phillips and Natalie Lewis, who had used their ceiling-to-desk bulletin boards to declare themselves, push-pinning tear sheets, personal photographs, ticket stubs, and other memorabilia.

Jennifer took a seat alongside these three young women who controlled the magazine's second most important editorial department. Beauty accounted for a great deal of the advertising in the front of the book and for good reason. The eighteen-to-thirty-four-year-old market spent two billion dollars a year in beauty and health products, and it was this department's job to see that the large outlay of money continued.

"I want you to check with Lauder, Arden, Revlon, and the others," Bettina said to Esmé, her Slavic accent changing w's to v's and vice-versa. "See if we can get our hands on their new color lines immediately. Find out if they have any new product launches scheduled and if, by any chance, they could be tied in with Hawaii."

Esmé, thoughtful, twirled her raven hair around her index finger, but Natalie jumped right in.

"I think we should explore the fragrance market," she said. "After all, one of Hawaii's claims to fame is their flora, and there have to be at least fifty floral scents already on the market. We could theme our entire beauty section around flowers. The colors for the makeup and the scents for fragrance."

"It sounds good to me." Bettina turned to Jennifer and wondered why her face seemed so tight. "What do you think?"

"It's exactly what I had in mind," Jennifer said, her voice scratchy and hoarse. "It also gives me an idea, if you don't mind me making a few suggestions."

"Not at all."

"It might be very effective to incorporate flowers with your hair pages. Vincent Matteo—he did the flowers for the party—could work with your hairdressers to create some special *Jolie* looks using fresh flowers. Sort of a 'Native New Yorker' feature."

Esmé's eyes brightened instantly.

"I love it! I can picture all kinds of sophisticated twists and rolls with big fat flowers tucked in, and long, flowing hair braided with tiny, white florets. Jennifer, that's great!"

"Thank you," Jennifer said to the willowy brunette with the large sapphire eyes. "I don't know if my other idea is feasible, but I'd like to give it a shot. I'd love to have a fragrance geared especially for this issue."

"Fragrance is my thing," Natalie said, "but I'm not sure I know what you mean."

Jennifer turned to face the slim ash-blonde with the serious expression.

"What if we spoke to a major house and asked them if they were planning to launch a new fragrance? If it's an exotic scent and they agree, we would push the hell out of it in the April issue. We would herald it as the *Jolie* scent for summer. Let them name it for a volcano or a lagoon or even a city. All Hawaiian words sound romantic. The bottle has to be drop dead elegant and the scent a smoldering, yet delicate floral blend."

Natalie listened intently, pursing her thin, highly arched lips.

"It's possible," she said. "But it's going to take some doing. I might need a dummy campaign and some spec promotion material to sell it. Can I count on your department?"

"Absolutely! And if you need me to go along with you, that's fine too."

Natalie grabbed a pencil from Bettina's desk and started scribbling notes to herself. Jennifer saw Esmé's face darken and began to feel a current of competition electrify the room.

"I'm sure Brad wanted makeovers." Esmé cut short the discussion of the perfume. "I'll take care of the hairdresser and the makeup artist."

"Wonderful," Bettina said, obviously tuned in to the rivalry between her assistants. "But no prima donnas this time. Bargain for price. They're getting a free trip to Hawaii, and that's worth plenty!"

Jennifer signaled her approval of Bettina's concern for cost.

"Who's traveling on the shoot?" Natalie asked.

Bettina considered the question. She knew both girls were dying to do the job, but only one of them could accompany her.

"Nat, you went on the last assignment. I think Esmé is up."

Jennifer was fascinated by the silent exchange of looks. Envy on one, triumph on the other.

"Terrific," Natalie said, a definite bite to her words. "I get to go to Motor City and makeover assembly line workers, and you guys get to go to Hawaii."

"I'd love it if we could all go, but budgets are tighter than eighteen-hour girdles," Bettina said absently. She was still thinking about the makeover story. Those were her favorites. She found it miraculous to watch a pair of skilled scissors and a conglomeration of grease pots transform someone from blah to beautiful. Naturally, the subject had to have solid bone structure, good, but not perfect, facial features, and unblemished skin. Usually, she looked for someone who struck her as plain. Ugly was hard to help. Plain was nothing more than an unused canvas.

Bettina was evangelical about makeovers. It aggravated her to see women suppressing their natural beauty just because they were lazy or frightened of change.

By the time Bettina rejoined the conversation, Jennifer Cranshaw was moving toward the door. Something about the stoop of her shoulders made Bettina worry. Something was wrong with Jennifer. Bettina wished she knew her well enough to ask, but her European-bred respect for a person's privacy held her back. Later, she would regret not exercising her American-learned aggressiveness.

Brad Helms had sequestered himself in his office. In front of him were Jennifer's proposals for The Big Pineapple. He supposed he should have been encouraged. On paper, it looked extremely promising. But was it promising enough? Dread swept over him. What if someone did buy the magazine? The figures were terrible, and he was the most obvious target for blame. Total support from his coworkers or absolute proof that the backslide had been caused by circumstances beyond anyone's control might exonerate him, but he possessed neither of these things. His only hope rested on the bottom line. The figures had to be reversed.

He took several long, deep breaths and concentrated on relaxing the muscles in his body, freeing himself to think clearly. As he meditated, he felt a strange suspicion. Figures. They kept appearing before his eyes. He had to check the figures. When did the sales begin to drop? Where did they fall off from? Was there a pattern?

He forced himself to review his tenure at *Jolie*. The first three years he was publisher, everything was fine. Then, two years ago, sales had begun to drop, only slightly, not enough to worry about. Magazine sales reflected the economy, and during times of inflation and recession, sales dropped off. Advertisers slashed budgets and waited it out. When the economy became healthy again, magazines reaped the benefits. For a while, he had tried to comfort himself with that thought, but the truth nagged at him. He had not kept a firm hand on the balance sheets. And both Jennifer and Gwen had urged him to take drastic steps, advice he had chosen to ignore.

But somewhere in the back of his mind, he believed that he alone was not responsible for the severe downward curve. Deals he had considered wrapped up had suddenly, mysteriously fallen through. It was almost as if something or someone was working against him. Brad came to attention and began scribbling unconnected phrases on a piece of paper, writing down anything that came to him, creating his own free-association test. It was there someplace, he was sure of it. He was the victim of a weird conspiracy. He knew it, but he also knew he had to prove it. He only hoped it wasn't too late.

Seventeen

B y Wednesday, Jennifer felt slightly better. Her fever was gone, and her body was stronger, even if her spirits were still weak. She had met with every department at the magazine, made suggestions, taken notes, encouraged support, and succeeded in rallying the entire staff around Brad Helms's Big Pineapple campaign. She and Terk had confronted the sales people, pushing them, feeding them speeches, offering to help in any way they could.

Though Terk had been cooperative, he seemed to be mouthing his words, saying the right things, but without conviction. It was strange, unlike him, and it confused her. From the very beginning, Jennifer had known that she couldn't possibly do this by herself. She needed Terk's uncanny sales sense, his bold, aggressive style, and his head for figures. But each time they met, he appeared reluctant, hesitant, almost defiant. Once, she even accused him of wanting *Jolie* to fail, of wishing it sold. His "no comment" had frightened her. She needed Terk, and she had told him so.

Since she knew that there was no one who loved a fight more than Terk, and since she had never known him to back away from anything, his hedging set off an alarm in her brain. Whenever people changed course, Jennifer became suspicious. On every occasion but one.

For the past few days, Jennifer had been reprimanding herself for not reading any of the signals that might have told her the truth about Charles. She had searched her memory for clues, hints that she had neglected to pick up. Should she have questioned his late nights at the office or his trips out of town? Were those "clients" who called after ten really businessmen or were they lovers? It had been there all along, and somehow she should have known. She felt like a fool, and she hated Charles for making her feel that way. She despised him for what he had done to her. He had betrayed her, lied to her, and what was worse, she felt that he had disgraced her.

Sometimes she had the urge to go running through the streets, screaming, announcing Charles's perfidy to the world. She imagined a frothing, Puritanical mob stoning him. But for now, she couldn't tell anyone. She kept it bottled up inside of her, afraid as much of what it said about her as what it implied about the marriage.

So many times in the past few days she wondered what, if anything, she had done to encourage his homosexuality. She found herself avoiding mirrors, fearful that if she looked, she would see a woman not responsive or sensual enough, a woman so preoccupied with her career that she might have pushed her husband into the arms of other men. She gripped the edge of her desk and tried to control herself, but hot tears forced their way to the surface.

She heard the knocking, but it seemed distant. When the sound persisted, she wiped her eyes, pulled her hands through her hair, and fluffed it as best she could. The door opened, and Mimi came in carrying several large posterboards.

"Mr. Helms and Miss Wheeler are on their way," she said, placing the boards on Jennifer's desk. Jennifer's eyes were red and bloodshot. "Would you like another cup of tea?"

"No! What I want to know is what these are and what meeting you're talking about." Her voice was gruff, agitated.

"These are the roughs on The Big Pineapple sales piece. Mr. Helms and Miss Wheeler have an appointment to go over them with you."

"But I haven't had a chance to look at them!" She sounded frantic, so unlike the Jennifer Cranshaw that Mimi had come to know.

"Would you like me to cancel the meeting?" Mimi asked quietly.

It was too late. Brooke and Brad were already there, taking their seats. Jennifer stared at them. Brad was finishing up a story, and Brooke was listening to him intently, her tall, well-shaped form perched decorously in one of Jennifer's bergères. Suddenly, Brooke's presence, her assurance, her haughty sense of her own sexuality angered Jennifer beyond reason. Brooke, with the long, honey-blonde hair and gray cat eyes. Brooke, who always had some man lapping at her heels. She wouldn't have been fooled by Charles. She would have known right away he wasn't a real man.

At first, no one noticed how distracted Jennifer was. Brad took the boards, looked at them carefully, handed them to Brooke who also studied them and then gave them back to Jennifer. In a fog, she tried to concentrate.

The layouts indicated a four-color sales piece with two side flaps closing over a large centerfold. On each of the sides was a ticket slanted like a tree trunk, spouting luxurious palm fronds. The headline, split between the two flaps, read "TWO ON THE ISLE." She went to the next board which represented the inside of the piece. Above Patrick's free-form pineapple were the words: "WELCOME TO THE BEST-SELLING SHOW THIS SIDE OF PARADISE—THE BIG PINEAPPLE!" The third board showed the back side of the front folds, repeating the ticket motif and encasing the copy. Jennifer never read it. If she had, she would have noticed that her advertising program was detailed on one ticket, the in-store promotion plans on the other.

"I think it's wonderful," Brooke cooed, looking at Brad.

"I think it's awful!" Jennifer's voice snapped with disgust.

"How can you say that?" Brad asked, confused by her rage. "It's clean and crisp. The copy is exciting. Your staff has done an admirable job."

"It's slip-shod," Jennifer insisted.

Brooke watched Jennifer's mouth tighten and her skin fade to a shocking chalk white. She had also seen Jennifer's lips quiver and her hands turn into fists. For some reason, Jennifer Cranshaw was out of control.

"I don't know about either of you," Jennifer continued, "but I won't accept work like this. When I get something *I* approve of, I'll let you know. Now, if you don't mind, I have other things to attend to."

Jennifer's body began to shiver. What possessed her to behave like that? Her performance was ugly, and she knew it. Somewhere in the periphery of her fury, she knew that Brooke was not to blame for her torment, that she was not responsible for the agonizing twist in her back. But she couldn't help herself. She felt small and inadequate next to Brooke.

Brad rose from his chair. "I know you haven't been feeling well. Let's talk about this later." His voice was gentle, filled with concern.

Brooke Wheeler followed Brad out of Jennifer's office. She couldn't believe her good fortune. She couldn't imagine what had prompted the unusual display of temper, but it didn't matter. Ever since Brooke had heard that *Jolie* was in trouble, she had accelerated her plan to take over Jennifer's job. Up to that time, she had gone along at a slower, more subtle pace, intimating that she, not Jennifer, had the talent and aggressiveness to make *Jolie* a force in the industry. Brooke had never fashioned herself an underling. The fact that Jennifer held the position of power meant nothing except that Jennifer was her target.

First, she would endear herself to Gwendolyn Stuart and Brad. Then, she would nudge Jennifer into a corner where she might make that one mistake that would put her job in jeopardy. Jennifer's record of achievement and her personal popularity were formidable stumbling blocks, but Brooke believed that even the strongest towers could be toppled if the right brick were pulled. Now, Jennifer's attitude told Brooke the time was right to pull the brick.

The buzz of Jennifer's intercom upset her. Why hadn't she told Mimi to hold all calls? What if it were Charles? She picked up the phone gingerly.

"Hi, squirt!"

For a moment, the voice didn't register. When it did, she felt her spirits lift for the first time in days.

"Who is this?" she teased.

"This, my misinformed wench, is David Sheldon, doctor of orthopedic surgery, formerly of Hadassah Hospital in Israel, newly appointed chief of orthopedic services at Bellrose Hospital, Big Apple, U.S.A."

"I can't believe how good it is to hear your voice!" she said, letting the deep baritone that had calmed her so many times before soothe her now.

"I'll bet you say that to all your doctors."

"Only those related by blood." She wiped a tear from her eye. "How are you? *Where* are you? If you didn't just step off the plane, I want you to know what a shit I think you are for not calling me sooner!"

"Hostility registered and accepted. Excuse following. I tried to call you all day Sunday, but you must have been out. Then Sarah took the kids to see her parents in Great Neck, and I flew to Boston to give a seminar at Mass General."

"Charles and I were out on Sunday," she lied. "I feel terrible that we missed your call. We would have come to see you immediately. How are Sarah and the kids?"

"You can see for yourself. Mom would like you both to dine at the family manse tomorrow night. Can you make it?"

Jennifer began to sweat. She hated lying to her brother. Not only did he deplore dishonesty, but he always seemed to ferret out the truth. Still, she had to chance it.

"Charles has the flu," she said calmly. "He got caught in the rain Friday night, and he's in terrible shape. I, however, am fine and shall be there. With bells on, I assure you."

"Tell Charlie I hope he's feeling better. It's a shame he can't join us, but I guess we'll just have to make do."

Jennifer winced. Even after all these years, David's hostility toward Charles hadn't abated. David had never accepted Charles as a substitute for Josh. Calling him "Charlie" was his way of voicing his disapproval. Jennifer could almost see Charles cringing at the nickname.

"Listen," David was saying, "I have to be in New York tomorrow to settle on office space, so why don't I drive you out? I'm feeling exceptionally charitable."

"In that case, I'd best take advantage of the mood while I can. I'll meet you downstairs at five."

"Super. I'll wear a carnation so you recognize me."

Jennifer was elated. David was home, and she felt like hugging herself from the joy of it. She felt as if she had just found a childhood security blanket that had been stored in the attic. It seemed like kismet that David and his family had chosen this moment to return. She couldn't remember a crisis when her brother had not stood by her side. This time, she might not be able to confide in him, but she could absorb his strength, and use it to refuel her energies. She grabbed for her purse and headed for the elevator, feeling suddenly giddy with relief. David would fix things up, make everything better. Hadn't he always?

The de Marco boutique occupied the second floor of a white stone building. The façade bore the scars of multiple renovations though the building had managed to hold its ground despite the soaring co-ops which surrounded it on all sides. The lower level housed a beauty salon distinguished by a bold yellow and white striped awning and its name splashed across the front window in a flourish of script. In contrast, the window above was clear except for the de Marco name printed in white lower-case letters in the right-hand corner.

Jennifer climbed the dark stairway and pushed the heavy glass door that led into the shop. A young salesgirl appeared from behind one of the many metal racks suspended from the ceiling by large link chains. She was California blonde and very skinny. Her slight form was poured into a cerise bodysuit, belted and topped with a starched, man-tailored shirt, cuffs rolled, collar up. She asked if she could interest Jennifer in something, but Jennifer's "just looking" banished her to a plump leather ottoman in the back and the latest edition of *People* magazine. Jennifer approached one of the hanging display units and reconnoitered the clothes until a gentle hand touched her shoulder.

"Jennifer Cranshaw. What a pleasant surprise!"

Jennifer swiveled toward the alto voice and matched Elyse's smile with one of her own.

"I called you last week to compliment you on your fabulous party," Elyse said, "but you were out. I'm sorry I never got back to you."

"It's all right. It was sweet of you to think of it."

"Can I help you with something?"

"Actually, I came here to present you with a business proposition, but I got waylaid by the clothes. If you have time, we could talk now, and I'll shop later."

"Why not shop first?" Elyse said with enthusiasm. "Are you looking for anything special? Daytime? Dressy?"

"How about anything and everything?"

Rack by rack, Jennifer toured the shop, absorbed in the clothes and trying to erase the sight of herself ripping into her closets and throwing out everything Charles had helped her select. It had been Monday night, and her fury had set her off. She had gone on a rampage, tearing into every neatly arranged group of garments, emptying whole closets of skirts and suits. She rejected anything with Charles's handprint on it, every item he had ever approved. Even the next morning when she was calm and rational, she stood over the heap of expensive clothing eager to rid herself of Charles's lingering presence. She folded everything carefully, solemnly packing four large cartons to be given to charity, as if she were clearing out the belongings of someone who had died.

Elyse ushered Jennifer into one of the dressing rooms and for an hour, Jennifer went about the task of creating a new persona. Without realizing why, she chose the most sensual of Elyse's creations—soft pants that hugged her hips and narrowed at the ankles, luxurious silk blouses that plunged to the waist and billowed at the sleeves. She even bought several jumpsuits in slinky fabrics that left little to the imagination.

Elyse stood to the side and watched respectfully, noting that Jennifer's fashion instincts were keen. She never took anything that overwhelmed her, nor did she hide behind anything "safe." Elyse also marveled at Jennifer's sense of color. She united reds and purples; masterfully blended three different shades of green into a verdant ombrée; mixed roses and pinks until they were exciting and new. The only color that seemed to displease Jennifer was blue, and after much debate, she finally consented to one royal blue sweater and only because she felt it added a surprise to a creamy white suit.

After they had dropped everything at the register, Elyse led Jennifer into the back room where she offered her guest coffee.

"You amaze me," Elyse said when they were both comfortably settled. "I had you pegged as elegantly classic."

Jennifer still felt exhilarated by her adventure, and her voice was buoyant. "It was time for a change!"

"Well, I'm glad you chose de Marco for your metamorphosis."

Jennifer smiled a "you're welcome" and studied Elyse as she went to a stereo cabinet and adjusted the volume. Even in baggy tweed pants and a suede sweatshirt with her hair pulled back in a ponytail, Elyse was splendid. She was a sultry woman, exotic in face and animal in body. Jennifer felt Elyse's sexuality across the room, and a sudden damper fell over her. It was impossible to look at Elyse and not think about Josh. For almost a week, Jennifer had managed to repress all thoughts of him, but seeing this stunning creature brought memories rushing back, stinging and hurting all over again.

"Now." Elyse returned to the art deco sofa facing Jennifer and tucked her legs beneath her like a cat. "What is this business proposition you spoke of earlier?"

Jennifer gulped her coffee, swallowing hard. She wanted to remove Josh from her consciousness, and she did, replacing him with business.

"*Jolie* is producing a special April issue this year, dedicated to Hawaii." She had decided that for the moment, there was no need to mention that this issue was born of desperation. "I've come up with an idea that might benefit both you and the magazine."

"Sounds interesting," Elyse said, her eyebrows arched.

"I'd like you to design an exclusive collection for *Jolie*. Something young and exuberant and tropical."

Elyse's voice dropped. "Under the de Marco label?"

"No. An entirely new label." Jennifer wondered why Elyse suddenly appeared stiff and ill-at-ease. "I'm looking to launch a concept and a collection at the same time. The issue would promote the line, and the line would promote the issue."

"Did Josh put you up to this?" Elyse left the couch and walked toward the stereo again.

"We may have to use Josh's money as backing, but it was my idea. I haven't even spoken to him about it yet."

Elyse's eyes filled with questions, only some of which Jennifer understood.

"I'm convinced that this is a unique idea, something worth doing."

Elyse clicked off the music.

"I can't," she said.

"Why not?"

"I just can't, Jennifer. But thanks for the offer."

Elyse walked over to a window and leaned against the sill. Even though Jennifer could see only her back, she knew Elyse was agonizing about something.

"Is it because Josh would be fronting the money?"

"It has nothing to do with you or Josh. Could we please drop the subject?" Elyse kept her back to the room.

"I can't drop it, Elyse. It's too important to me, and I had thought it could be important to you. Frankly, I concocted this whole idea with you in mind. I had even planned on asking you to model for the editorial portfolio. You're fabulous looking, and our readers would love to see a designer in her own clothes."

Jennifer couldn't tell if she was getting through. "You can't turn me down."

"I have to." Elyse's voice was barely more than a whisper.

Jennifer recognized the sound of a troubled soul, and she felt a wave of sympathy wash over her. She put her coffee down and went to Elyse, wrapping an arm around her.

"Why?" Jennifer said softly. "Why have you turned

Josh down each time he's asked and now me?" She kept
her voice low, hoping to draw Elyse out. "It doesn't track.
You're a brilliant designer, and I think you know that.
Why deny yourself the opportunity to be staggeringly
wealthy?"

Elyse struggled with herself, feeling her secret rise up
in her throat. She had repressed it for such a long time,
but the need for release was becoming more urgent every
day. She lifted her face to look at Jennifer, examining her
eyes, searching for trust.

"My husband controls this business," she said, speaking
so quietly that Jennifer had to lean forward to hear her.
"He's a difficult man, and he keeps a tight rein on me. I
couldn't possibly go out on my own, which is what you
and Josh are asking me to do."

Jennifer's head reeled. She hardly heard anything after
"my husband." Josh didn't date married women, he said.
He couldn't. Wasn't that why he had rejected her? Wasn't
that his reason? That she was married? He had lied! He
had told her he loved her and lied in the same breath!
She tried to leash her anger, but the word "husband"
reverberated in her ear, as if she were standing inside an
enormous clanging bell. She looked at Elyse carefully.

"I didn't know you were married," she said, alert for
the most minute reaction. "Josh never mentioned it."

"I don't live with my husband," Elyse said.

Jennifer folded her arms across her chest and began to
pace. "How long have you been separated?"

"Years, actually." Elyse didn't understand. She sensed
an accusation underlining Jennifer's questions, but she
didn't know what, or why. She didn't feel any personal
animosity coming from Jennifer, so she continued. "I think
we've been apart more years than we were together. I
work for him, and we speak often about the business, but
we each maintain our own apartments."

"Then why can't you just quit?" she said. "I'm offering
you another job. Why not think of it that way?"

"It's very complicated, Jennifer, believe me. I'm tied to
Mario in more ways than just marriage and a boutique. I
can't leave him."

Elyse's eyes were shadowed. There was another chapter

to this story, but Elyse chose not to tell it. Jennifer continued to walk back and forth across the small room, her mind racing.

"Elyse, I need you to do this for me. I don't know what you're hiding, and it's none of my business, but I'm looking to save my magazine, and I think you're the one who can help me." She took Elyse's hands into her own and held them tightly, speaking as convincingly as she could. "It'll be strictly confidential, I give you my word. I don't want any publicity on this until late March anyway. That gives you almost four months to find a way out of whatever hole you're in."

"It's not that easy."

"It's never easy," Jennifer said. "But if you're drowning, you have to be willing to fight for your life. Believe me, I know."

Elyse felt a surge of energy suffuse her, as if Jennifer were a force drawing her into a magnetic field. She felt strong for the first time in years, and the feeling was so overwhelming that she began to cry. She stood facing Jennifer, a wobbly smile on her lips and big, pear-shaped tears gliding down her cheeks.

"I'm scared to death," she said. "But if you'll help me, I'll do whatever you want."

Jennifer led Elyse to a seat, keeping a grip on her hands. She sensed a current running between them, welding a bond of friendship. For a long while they sat without speaking, each imprisoned by secrets, dark, painful bonds that held them back and restrained them like silent handcuffs.

"We'll help each other," Jennifer said half to herself. "We'll help each other."

Eighteen

"**Y**ou look incredible!"
Terk stood in the doorway to Jennifer's office and bellowed his approval of one of her new ensembles. Jennifer acknowledged the compliment with a delicate bow of her head and invited Terk to join her at her desk.

"I'm glad you like it," she said, genuinely pleased at his reaction.

"It's impossible for you ever to look bad, but this is outstanding!" He took a seat and motioned for her to spin around and give him a one-woman fashion show.

Jennifer was wearing the creamy white pantsuit and royal blue sweater she had bought at de Marco, and she felt wonderful in it. She sauntered to the center of the room, pirouetted and exaggerated her movements. The pants were gently pleated in the front with tapered legs, the trim line ending in medium-height pumps in the same color as the sweater. She closed the jacket for him with the single white button and shrugged her shoulders so he noticed the padding. She then removed the jacket with a burlesque toss, revealing the vivid blue cashmere sweater. It was pinch-pleated at the shoulders as if it were the most supple silk, and the neckline swooped down just low enough for Terk to see the rounding of Jennifer's breasts. As he watched her turn, he drank in the fullness of her, her lush vitality. The vibrant blue heightened the red glints in her hair, and her dark eyes flickered with light. She appeared incandescent, transmitting warmth like an August breeze that waved over him and aroused his senses.

"Wait until they see you in L.A.," he said, ogling her as she took her seat behind the desk.

"Los Angeles? Who's going to Los Angeles?"

"You and I, my pretty, are jetting off to la-la land next week."

"What happened to Boston?"

"I sold it to the highest bidder."

"Terk, sweetheart. You're not making any sense. Would you care to translate all of that into English?"

"Certainly," he said with the gleam of someone springing a surprise. "In line with your all-out effort to make this Pineapple thing the success of the century, I've lined up the big guns at Neiman-Marcus. We are going to meet them in L.A. as well as the people from all The May Company stores. I'm sending another team to Boston to deal with Jordan Marsh. Now! Feel free to tell me how much you love me."

"A lot!" Her eyes sparkled with excitement. "When do we leave, and how long are we staying, and oh, my God, that's fabulous!"

"We're leaving Monday. We're staying four, five days, and I've booked us into the Beverly Wilshire."

"Do you realize what a bonanza it would be to get Neiman-Marcus?"

"It did cross my mind," he said smugly.

"I've got to get all the sales pieces and promotional material into the works immediately. I'm going to need samples to take with us and copies of the business proposals and budgets and how the hell am I ever going to be ready?"

Terk started to laugh, a hearty burst of sound that made Jennifer smile at her own hysteria.

"I know you thought I wasn't giving my all to your fruit campaign," he said. "Now do you believe I'm behind you?"

"I'm glad you've finally admitted that you've been a pain in the ass. What made you change your mind?"

"The Big Man told me to support Jennifer Cranshaw and to help her catapult *Jolie* into the major leagues," Terk said. "I always do what the Big Man tells me."

"Well, I'm glad. In the meantime, this little woman is about to chase you out of here so I can get some work done. And on your way out would you ask Mimi to come in?"

"Your every wish is my command," he said, bending low at the waist.

She watched him strut over to Mimi's desk, and lean over to whisper in her secretary's ear. She was surprised to see Mimi's face tighten. Jennifer assumed he was making a suggestive remark, but Mimi should have been used to that. They exchanged a few more words, and Mimi's face was stiff and pale when she entered Jennifer's office.

"Mimi, I need ten copies of all the Pineapple proposals," Jennifer said, scrutinizing the young woman as she spoke. "That's the good news. The bad news is that I need them tomorrow afternoon."

Mimi nodded, keeping her eyes on her steno pad, her hand jerking across the page.

"And could you get hold of the roughs for the sales piece?"

The blonde head bobbed up and down in response, but the eyes remained fixed on the pad. Jennifer studied her secretary. On her upper arm, Jennifer spotted a deep purple blotch that looked like the result of an awful bruise.

"Mimi, if Terk said something to upset you, just tell me, and I'll ask him to leave you alone."

Jennifer waited for an answer, but none was forthcoming.

"Did he upset you?" she asked gently.

"It was nothing. I haven't been feeling too well lately, and well, I guess my sense of humor isn't what it should be."

"Take care of yourself," Jennifer said, watching Mimi walk out the door.

Instinct told her Mimi was lying. For weeks she had been listless and short-tempered. Jennifer knew from her own recent eccentricities that uneven behavior could be a symptom of emotional upheaval as well as viral infection. But she couldn't remember the last time she had seen Mimi smile, and it bothered her. Perhaps it was more trouble at home. Mimi Holden was the eldest of four daughters in a wealthy Houston family. Her parents were pillars of Texas society. From what Mimi had told Jennifer, Mimi was her powerful father's favorite, his "sunshine child," and he had plotted her life with the intensity of a general charting a war. He had selected her schools, her clothes, her friends and eventually her fiancé. Mimi had allowed herself to become engaged, but two days before the wedding, she fled to New York. Her father followed her, tracked her down like a hunt dog, and after much discussion, they effected a tentative truce. Holden gave Mimi two years to make it in New York, but he cut off her allowance as incentive.

Jennifer craned her neck to see Mimi's desk. Mimi was sifting through a stack of papers, her face still tight. She had lost weight. Jennifer was convinced that something was eating at Mimi. It couldn't be easy living on a secretary's salary when one had been used to an abundance of money, but Jennifer had thought Mimi had adjusted. Maybe the pressure was getting to her.

Jennifer made a notation on her calendar to take Mimi out to lunch when she returned from California, underlining it three times after Mimi dropped the posterboards on her desk without saying a word. Jennifer watched her retreat to her desk. There was another purple welt on the back of her leg.

Along with the original boards were three thumbnail sketches, hastily drawn on white tracing paper and clipped together with a note from Patrick Graham. Patrick had redone the mailer, under orders from Brooke Wheeler. Jennifer's embarrassment surfaced as she studied the two pieces.

The original had been perfect, targeted to the point and shot with the sort of play on words Jennifer had always encouraged. As she read the copy and reviewed the layout, she realized that she hadn't even looked at them when they were first shown to her.

The second version was effective, but plodding, minus the clever snap of the first. It was factually correct, but definitely less creative. Jennifer had no doubt as to which proposal she would take with her. The question was why had Brooke taken it upon herself to request a revision? And why had Brooke's request been granted without anyone checking with Jennifer?

Terk had a surprise waiting for him when he returned from lunch. There on the sofa in his office sat the cool, confident person of his wife. Seeing her, perched so comfortably on the couch with one arm casually thrown over the back, the other fingering her blonde hair, made him immediately defensive. Deirdre could do that to him too easily, he thought. Trying to regain his momentary loss of composure, he entered the room.

"Well, this must be my lucky day," he said, moving toward his desk. "What brought you into the city? Did Bergdorf's send a car? Are they falling behind in their profits?"

Deirdre smiled. "I was having a love attack, my precious. I thought I'd just pop in, and my devoted husband would take me out for an intimate lunch. But lo and behold, my devoted husband was already gone. Were you dining with someone exotic?"

"I was grabbing a sandwich with one of my salesmen," Terk said, his voice snapping. "Is that exotic enough for you?"

"Each to his own," she said.

"Deirdre, I'm busy. I have to get ready for a trip to California. Now, what do you want?" Terk leaned forward, his hands clenched.

Deirdre moved to the edge of the couch, rested her chin in her hands, and let her long hair fall forward, framing her face. Her wide-set eyes stared at him. Her lips were pursed, the edges turned up in what was the beginning of a smile. When she spoke, her voice was husky.

"What I want is you and the games we play. Those wonderful, exciting games we play with each other. You remember them, don't you, darling?"

He could feel himself getting excited, and he hated himself for it. Deirdre sensed her effect and rose from the couch in one long sensuous stretch. She walked over to the door and closed it, locking it. Then she moved toward him, slowly, never removing her eyes from his. She was taunting him, and she knew it. He knew it, and still he couldn't help himself. The warmth spread, and he began to throb from the nearness of her.

"It's been a long time, my love." Her voice was low and throaty.

As she glided to the front of his desk, one side of her pale silk blouse dropped down and revealed the upper part of her breast. His eyes left hers and traveled to the swelling peeking through the open shirt and stayed there, watching her nipples harden. She stood in front of him and leisurely, languidly, opened her blouse. Each deliberate movement of her fingers acted as a tease. She was smiling, staring at him, and letting the tension build. When her shirt was completely opened, she lowered herself onto his lap and in a single motion put her full breast near his mouth, rubbing him, massaging him, making him hurt with the pleasure of it all.

Terk could no longer control himself. Whatever else Deirdre was, she was the most sensuous woman he'd ever known, and for the moment, his hatred dissolved into passion. He lost himself in her, mouthing her exposed body, following her hands as they slipped her skirt off as well. He fumbled with his zipper like an inexperienced schoolboy. He felt awkward and clumsy, but he brought her to the floor and stretched her out on the carpet, his body hot and tense. His hands moved over her long, taut body, each touch heightening his desire.

Her body was perfect for lovemaking, full breasts that responded to his eager tongue, small hips that moved in such tantalizing ways that he barely had to move his own. Her legs, long and sleek, wrapped around him, pulling him into her. Her mouth was all over his neck and chest, breathing on him, biting him, seducing him with swift, snakelike swipes of her tongue. Every part of him was pulsating. He moved on instinct, trying to cover all of her, trying to capture and control her.

They performed like finely tuned instruments; they rose and fell in concert, and created a harmony they never achieved outside of sex. This was what they did best, this was the only time they really understood each other.

Deirdre felt him tense, and she pulled him closer, raising her hips and drawing him even further into her. He felt flushed. Tight. Drunk with pleasure. As he felt Deirdre's body quake in climax, he too erupted, releasing the molten liquid of passion.

And then he was limp, and his breathing was labored. Deirdre was quiet. Terk lifted himself up on his elbow and looked at her. For an instant there was something approaching love in his eyes. In the next instant it was gone.

"I told you I wanted an intimate lunch," she said, "and I always get what I want."

She rose in triumph and dressed herself with the same detachment one might have in front of the family doctor. She ran her fingers through her hair, refreshed her lipstick, and went to the door.

As her manicured hand touched the doorknob, Terk realized he was still on the floor, half-naked. He scrambled to his feet, embarrassed and angry.

"Where are you going?"

He juggled with his zipper, trying to tuck in his shirt at the same time. He was fumbling, and he knew he looked absurd.

"I'm going shopping. Don't be late for dinner."

She turned and left, leaving him there still tucking in his shirt. She had won again. She always won. He felt as if he'd been raped, but he knew he had been all too willing. If only he could detach himself from her sexually, he'd be free. But that was the hardest part. Personally, they had never been together. They had never shared emotions, only sex. Only flesh. Never any happy moments, never even any sad ones.

Terk felt suddenly depressed. He thought about all the years he had spent with Deirdre, years he could have been with Zena. He thought about his own lack of strength, his terrible lack of conviction. Deirdre was right, after all. He wasn't a man. When Deirdre wanted him, he complied. When she didn't want him, he suffered without comment. The house was hers. The money was hers. The cars were hers. And he was hers. He collapsed on the couch, desolate. He wanted to be his own man, and he wanted to make a life with Zena Welles. He had promised Zena they would. Twice. He knew he wouldn't get a third chance.

Brad Helms was daydreaming at his window when he spotted Jennifer leave the building and run into the arms of a sturdy sun-bronzed man. The stranger held her tightly, kissing her face and spiriting her into a car. Brad had met Jennifer's husband many times at industry functions, and that handsome, dark-haired man was definitely not Charles Cranshaw. He wondered if the man was Jennifer's lover, and the thought intrigued him. He knew

Charles's reputation for legal brilliance, but Brad had always thought that Charles didn't appear lusty enough for Jennifer. He remembered thinking several times that he, Brad, was, but it was a fantasy he had never pursued.

As he watched the car pull away from the curb, he realized that Jennifer had been on his mind a great deal lately. Via the office grapevine, that intricate system of whispered communication, Brad had learned of Jennifer's attempt to spearhead a campaign that would insure the success of his Big Pineapple. For that, he was grateful. She certainly had the talent, the energy, and the enthusiasm to pull it off. He thanked her also for possessing the grace to link his name to hers when offering suggestions, helping to create the illusion that he was intimately involved in every phase of this project.

Yet Brad suspected that some of the staff knew his contributions had started and stopped with the original idea. Without Jennifer's razzmatazz, most of the senior editors would have dismissed it entirely. Jennifer had salvaged his concept and therefore his integrity. The problem, as she saw it, was that if the concept salvaged the magazine, where did that leave Bradford Helms? Jennifer was the one coaching and guiding the plays. He was on the bench, and his pride was beginning to itch.

It was imperative that he solve the mystery of *Jolie's* dizzying downward spiral. He had to be the one to fit the pieces together. If he could prove that there had been a conspiracy, a concerted, premeditated effort to sabotage the magazine, he could maintain his grip on the publisher's chair, whether *Jolie* was sold or not. He couldn't even count the number of hours he had already spent going over figures and accounts, trying to find a trend, hoping to unearth a connection. So far, there were just traces, nothing concrete.

Tonight would probably be more of the same, digging for clues, searching for answers, but it did help fill empty hours between the end of one work day and the start of the next. Brad detested solitude, rebelled against silent rooms and empty beds. He had had more than enough of that during his marriage. He and Ivy had shared a palatial home, a country club membership, a joint checking account, and the care of their children, but they had slept in separate beds and led separate lives. Even now, his monastic existence was Ivy's doing.

Brad picked up a ceramic ashtray molded from a child's handprint. His son had made it for him last summer in camp. As he looked at it, matching his fingers to the clay impression, animosity for Ivy churned inside him. He would wait out this purgatory. He would go to court and sue for custody of his children. And he would win.

"Do all publishers sit in their offices until everyone else goes home?" Brooke Wheeler walked into the room and took a seat across from him.

"I've got pineapples on the brain," he said, grateful for the interruption.

"Me too," she said, hiking her skirt to uncover a dimpled knee. "That's one of the reasons I stopped by. I'm concerned about the way the project is going."

"Aren't we all?" His nose tickled from the overpowering rush of her perfume. "What specifically is bothering you?"

Brooke sighed, and as she did, her breasts pushed against her sweater.

"I don't know how to say this without sounding bitchy, but Jennifer seems intent on doing this whole thing single-handedly."

Brad had to force his eyes off her chest and onto her mouth which glistened with claret-red lipstick.

"From what I heard," Brooke continued, fully aware of the effect she was having, "she's taken over fashion meetings, beauty meetings, sent lists to every editor on what she wanted from their departments. I may be wrong, but isn't that overstepping her bounds?"

"Yes and no," Brad said. "This April issue is unique. It's heavily tied into promotion and advertising. I suppose she's just trying to pull the whole thing together."

Brooke flicked her long caramel hair onto her back. Her gray eyes studied Brad.

"I'm afraid Jennifer's on a glory trip. Didn't you notice the way she dismissed the two of us the other day? I can't help but think that the only reason she rejected that sales piece was because I said I liked it. She's a bit power-hungry. I know how much *Jolie* means to you and how badly you want this issue to succeed. I'd like to help, but Jennifer seems to be piloting a one-woman ship."

Brooke's comments revived Brad's earlier questions about Jennifer's role. Maybe her motivations weren't as altruistic as they seemed. Maybe her bravura performance was nothing more than an elaborate charade to put him off his guard. Maybe her ultimate goal was, as Brooke implied, simply to feather her own nest. If he stood by and let her, it was possible that he could be thrown out of the tree entirely. He had never viewed Jennifer as a credit-grabber before, but they had never been faced with disaster before. Crisis did strange things to people.

Brooke watched as Brad considered what she had said. She could see that she had planted a seed of doubt. It had been easy, even easier than she had thought it would be. Now all she had to do was convince him that she was the perfect helpmate—solicitous, talented, capable, but respectful of his position. That, too, should be easy. Everyone knew about Brad's divorce and the precarious position he was in. Brad was vulnerable and Brooke was available.

She stood and walked toward the door. "I guess I'll be on my way," she said. "I hope I didn't keep you from anything."

Brad rose from the couch and came toward her.

"Listen. It's five-thirty, and according to my inner watch, a drink is in order. Do you have some time?"

Brooke smiled. She had all the time in the world.

Nineteen

It was only the beginning of November, but like so many other streets in Bayonne, Avenue E was already aglitter with twinkling Christmas lights. Houses bedecked in party-colored bulbs illuminated the evening sky with jewellike outlines. Santa waved holiday greetings to passersby from nearly every rooftop. Front lawns were festooned with elaborate creches. And outside each house, city-sparse evergreens burst into electric display.

Bayonne was a working-class town. Its per capita income was modest, except for those who occupied the big Victorian homes bordering the park, and its leadership took the form of a patriarchy shared by the Democratic party and local Church Fathers. This was a city of immigrants—Polish, Czech, Lithuanian, and Ukrainian, with substantial numbers of Jews, Irish, and Italians sharing the busy streets and overcrowded schools. Strict parish boundaries segregated one neighborhood from the other. Only on the main shopping thoroughfares did the various groups bump shoulders. There, butcher shops declared their predilections by featuring sausage, kielbasa, or kosher calves' liver. And everything from shoe stores to furniture emporiums revealed their customers' heritage with marquees blazoning a jumble of colorful names.

As David steered his car through the familiar streets, Jennifer balanced a past eagerness to escape these surroundings with her present anticipation at returning to her childhood home. Throughout the ride, at Jennifer's insistence, David had monopolized the conversation, providing her with a vivid synopsis of the five years he and Sarah had spent in Israel. Jennifer prodded him for details, especially about the children and about his work, and David complied with stories. Jennifer knew he was editing, relating those incidents he thought would amuse or enlighten, deleting those that might have given her cause for concern.

When David asked about her, Jennifer found she had surprisingly little to say. Having made the decision to sidestep anything related to the current state of her marriage, she concentrated instead on the mystery surrounding *Jolie*. As she talked about sliding sales figures and possible conspiracies, she was struck by the hollow timbre in her voice and the shallowness of her conversation. Five years of her life had been reduced to the fate of a magazine, and even to her ear, it sounded like a feeble commentary.

Here they were, she thought, sister and brother, born of the same parents, subjected to the same deprivation and inattention, yet somehow, David had managed to translate the negative effects of his childhood into positive adult commitment. He approached life as if it were a glass half full, confident that life would reward him with a goblet brimming with success.

In contrast, Jennifer's glass was half empty. She still winced from the early sting of denial and isolation, still felt punished by circumstances beyond anyone's control. She had entered into battle with herself long ago, seeking victory in the form of success. As they drove past the houses of her high school friends, she realized that while they now station-wagoned to supermarkets and den-mothered cub scout troops, she hobnobbed with celebrities and rode to elegant parties in chauffeured limousines. She knew that she had triumphed. She had fame and money and position, but it was only expensive wrapping on an empty package.

Jennifer stared at her brother. He had shared the same background, minus the accident, but it did not appear to haunt him the way it did her. She suddenly felt like a child again, looking to David for example and guidance, perhaps even solace. He had always been there for her, and he was here again—and so too was the urge to have him tell her a bedtime story with a happy ending and to put a Band-Aid on her hurts. This time, however, she feared her story was too complicated for happily-ever-after, her hurts too deep for a mere strip of adhesive.

"Jen. I think we ought to clear the air between us." David kept his eyes on the road, but his hand reached across the seat for Jennifer's. "I know we made peace via the mails, but I'd like to seal the pact with a face-to-face apology."

When Jennifer had announced that she was not going to marry Josh, the family had become one voice to object. Especially David. He accused her of flightiness, of rejecting his friend on the basis of distorted dreams and misplaced values. After her wedding to Charles, he had refused to welcome his brother-in-law into the family. Jennifer had demanded that David reverse his attitude, warning that if he continued to criticize her life, he didn't have to be part of it. They did not speak for three years.

Jennifer, too, had thought that an apology was in order, but she lacked the courage to bring it up. Lately, she lacked the courage to do a lot of things.

"I was out of line challenging your relationship with Charles." David's use of Charles's real name did not go unnoticed by Jennifer. "You had every right to decide with whom you wanted to spend the rest of your life."

How ironic, Jennifer thought, David giving his blessing to a marriage that no longer existed.

"I guess I took it personally," David said, unaware of Jennifer's uneasiness. "I took your rejection of Josh as a rejection of me."

"It had nothing to do with you," she said, noting that, in a way, it had had nothing to do with Josh either.

"I know that now." A sheepish grin took hold of David's mouth. "I had always thought of Josh and me as a team, just as I always thought of Josh and you as a couple. I expected you to see it the same way. You didn't, and I'm sorry. I only wanted whatever was going to make you happy."

Jennifer couldn't bear to look at him. She feared that if she did, he would be able to read the truth in her eyes. Charles had not made her happy. And Josh was no longer willing to try.

Before she could give in to the impulse to tell David what had happened, his car stopped at the small gray house. The moment had passed and, in a strange way, Jennifer felt relieved. There would have been questions, and she still had no answers. David took her arm and led her up the front steps. As he did, the pungent aroma of Rose's brisket wafted into the street. Both of them smiled. Without saying a word, they knew that the door would be opened before they pressed the doorbell.

The instant she stepped inside, Jennifer found herself caught up in tearful embraces and heartfelt greetings. Rose bounced from one to the other while Marty wrapped his arm around his son. Jennifer went straight to Sarah, hugging her sister-in-law, then holding her at arm's length, and then hugging her again. Standing there, feeling Sarah's warmth envelop her, Jennifer realized how much she had missed her. The other women in Jennifer's life were business associates, people to whom Jennifer revealed only a part of herself. Sarah knew the total Jennifer, her history, her dreams, her frustrations, and her flaws. She was a bright, caring woman, and Jennifer welcomed her home with almost selfish enthusiasm.

Somewhere between "you'll never believe . . ." and "wait till you hear about. . . ," Asa and Lia pushed their mother aside and demanded affection from their aunt. Lia was ten now, Asa, seven. Lia had long, dark hair and big brown eyes like her father's. Her body was lean and long-legged, and it was easy to see that she was going to be a beautiful young woman. Asa was blonder, impish, and still bronze from the sun. Jennifer welcomed them into her arms and allowed them to tug at her until she fell back on the couch, laughing. They each competed for her attention, reciting poems in Hebrew, counting to one hundred in Arabic, telling tales of heroic adventures, and drawing her into intricate folk dances that had Jennifer tripping over her own feet. At the end of their impromptu recital, Jennifer rewarded each of them with a shopping bag filled with gifts from F.A.O. Schwarz. Finally, the two children settled down amid piles of crinkled paper and discarded ribbons, one nestled under each of Jennifer's arms.

The rest of the adults had settled also, Sarah in one of Rose's faux-French chairs, David on the couch with Jennifer and the children, and Marty in an overstuffed gold brocade club chair. Only Rose refused to light. She bustled around the room, going from one to the other with a tray of chopped liver and Saltines, ordering Marty to get up and fix drinks and smiling nonstop. Having one's family together after such a protracted separation was cause for jubilation, and in honor of the occasion, Rose had taken the entire day off, something she had done only three times before: for President Kennedy's funeral and her two children's weddings. She had fluffed pillows, filled candy dishes, polished silver and cooked as many courses as she had pots and pans. The table was set with the good china, the sterling and the cut-crystal wine glasses David and Sarah had sent for their parents' anniversary two years before. Even the plastic flower arrangement that usually sat in the center of the dining room table had given way to a bowl of fresh pink carnations. It had been a long time since her house was full. Tonight it was, and so was her heart.

A profound closeness filled the house on Twelfth Street, and the person who felt it most keenly was Jennifer. Inside these cluttered rooms was warmth and security. There was also honesty and feeling, laughter and affection, tenderness and support. It was all part of blood reestablishing its connection, and Jennifer yearned to lose herself in it, to grab it and press it to her until it seeped inside her body and healed the terrible loneliness in her soul. But she had come to this gathering accompanied by a lie and burdened with guilt. Although she was tempted to confess that she and Charles were separated and to accept their comfort and advice, the familiar pull of inhibition kept her a prisoner of her own pride.

Because it was a Sheldon custom for everyone to speak at once, the decibel level was loud enough to obscure the sound of the doorbell. When Josh and his children strode into the room, their presence came as a complete surprise to everyone, except Rose. David bolted from his seat and ran to embrace his friend. Rachel and Scotty accepted quick hugs and kisses from the adults and then lavished their full attention on Asa and Lia. Only Jennifer hung back.

She watched as Josh and Sarah and David clutched at each other and wiped tears from each other's eyes. Rose and Marty descended on Josh also, and still, Jennifer waited. She needed time to sort out her feelings. This was the first time she had seen him since that horrible night almost a week ago. Every nerve ending jangled as anger mingled with anticipation and longing touched hands with restraint. One minute she worried that he might ignore her, and then the next worried that he wouldn't.

Suddenly, she was grateful for all the people surrounding them, preventing them from touching or talking. There would be no private moments to rehash their argument. It was David and Sarah's night, and Josh would costume whatever he was feeling in good manners and party chatter. Jennifer only hoped she could do the same.

As he came toward her, she prayed that a blush would not betray her.

"Old sawbones looks pretty good, don't you think?" Josh looked away before she could answer, before she could read his eyes. "He doesn't look bad for a guy who's been piloting four cylinder camels."

"Five cylinder," David replied with an air of mild offense. "With adjustable humps."

Jennifer's fingertips touched the edge of Josh's tweed jacket as he inched back toward David and Sarah. She thought he stopped for a second, but now he and David were taunting each other with the tender gruffness of two lifelong friends. They seemed oblivious to her presence, and once again, she felt left out. She retreated to the kitchen.

"You didn't tell me you invited Josh," she said to her mother.

"You didn't ask." Rose continued to baste the turkey, patting the golden bird with her wooden spoon.

"I thought this was going to be a family night."

"It is and he is." Rose opened the oven and peeked inside to check the progress of her noodle pudding. "Besides, what difference does it make?"

"No difference. I was just surprised, that's all."

Rose eyed her daughter carefully. She was fussing with the fruit salad as if it were an intelligence test, spooning the same number of pieces into each of the small glass bowls. Her jaw was set, and her eyes were glassy. Rose had learned a long time ago not to muscle in on Jennifer's private life, but she was a mother, and concern was part of the job.

"I called Josh when you said Charles was too sick to come," Rose said. "You know how I hate to have a half-filled table. How is Charles feeling?"

"It's just a simple cold, Mother. Don't make a big deal out of it. He'll be fine."

"I'll send some soup home with you. A little Jewish penicillin will fix him up as good as new."

"I am not schlepping chicken soup home in a leaky plastic bowl!"

"Just offering. No need to bite my head off." Rose lifted the turkey out of the oven and placed it on the table.

Jennifer regretted her outburst. She kissed her mother on the cheek.

"I'm sorry, Mom. I don't mean to snap, but I've been

under a lot of pressure lately, what with the magazine and the party and all."

Rose patted her arm, and Jennifer went back to ladling fruit salad. Not for one moment did Rose believe that Jennifer's testiness had anything to do with the office. Jennifer thrived on pressure. She always had. No, this was something else, something deeper. Rose had never infringed on Jennifer's privacy. She wondered now if it was not the time to break that unwritten pact.

For some time Rose had suspected that her daughter's marriage was in trouble, but she had said nothing. Part of her was anguished at the thought of a possible divorce, yet another side of Rose was delighted. If asked, she would own up to the fact that she had never really approved of Charles as a suitable husband for Jennifer. First of all, Charles was not Jewish. Rose was too traditional for a difference in religion not to bother her. Second, his aristocratic bearing clashed with her proletarian openness. And third, Rose had never believed that Jennifer truly loved Charles. In Rose's mind, Jennifer belonged to Josh, and if, through a tragic chain of events, they had the chance to reedit their lives, so be it. It all made sense to Rose. Josh needed a wife and mother for his children. Jennifer needed a family. She needed to feel the circle of a family unit nourishing and protecting her. She had none. That was not what Rose wanted for her only daughter.

"Are we eating anytime within the next century?" David poked his head into the kitchen, holding his stomach as if death were only moments away.

"You want to eat?" Rose asked. "Grab a platter!"

Dinner was a lively affair with everyone gorging himself on brisket, turkey, roast beef, an assortment of vegetables, and the inevitable pickles and rye bread. Jennifer sat between her niece and nephew, cutting meat, buttering bread, and enjoying the role of "Aunt Jennie."

David and Sarah entertained everyone with the more humorous side of their stay in Israel, telling story after story of their life in a far-off land. Jennifer wished she could tape the proceedings and play them back when her mind was clearer and her spirit lighter. Although she tried to participate, her usual wit had been dulled by Josh's presence. She felt like a prisoner forced to dine with her captors, careful not to arouse suspicion and instigate an interrogation. Throughout the meal, she avoided eye contact with everyone except the children.

After dinner, when the children had bivouacked in Rose's bedroom, Jennifer wound up seated next to Josh. Fortunately, he and David were discussing the political structure of the Middle East, and Sarah was explaining her job at the American Embassy to Marty, so no one noticed Jennifer shrink into a corner. No one, that is, except Rose. As she passed David's chair, she nodded her head in Jennifer's direction.

Rose's not-so-subtle cue was unnecessary. All evening, David had been aware of Jennifer's uncharacteristically sober mood. Times when he had expected her to laugh, she appeared hard-pressed to smile, and statements that normally would have produced rebuttal or argument had been greeted by passive silence. Her attitude had been brighter on the ride out, but now David realized that he had never once asked about Charles's health. What's more, during dinner, no one had mentioned Charles's name or inquired about his absence. It was possible that Jennifer felt slighted.

David faced the couch where Jennifer sat, so he could study his sister more closely. As he watched, he noticed how relaxed she seemed with Sarah, even with Marty and Rose, and when he spoke to her, she responded warmly. The longer he watched, the more apparent it became that it was Josh who triggered the dull gray that periodically clouded her eyes and caused her lips to freeze in a tight smile. Each time Josh looked at Jennifer or spoke to her, her face became rigid and her voice strained.

There was something else that concerned David. Her shoulders bore a stubborn tilt, and her wide, almond-shaped eyes sometimes blinked a millisecond too long. To the untrained, these actions might have been meaningless, but to David, they were signals. His eyes narrowed as he watched her hands. Sure enough, her fingers were curled into a fist. Not too tight, but every once in a while, her nails scratched the palms. She was experiencing spasms in her back, and he knew all too well that those spasms were the result of extreme stress. As a doctor, he wanted to prescribe a vacation from whatever had caused her pain.

As a brother, he longed to put his arms around her and soothe her distress. He couldn't demand an explanation, nor did he have the right to pry. But nothing said he couldn't observe.

Around midnight, Marty excused himself. Reunion or no reunion, in four hours the bakery ovens had to be turned on. His exit prompted Rose to finish the dishes and reminded Sarah and David to check on the children. Jennifer and Josh were suddenly alone, surrounded by an uncomfortable silence.

Josh, usually so at ease, struggled to find the right words. Everything that sprang to his mind stalled at his lips. He saw pain in Jennifer's eyes, and he sensed that he had put it there. He believed that it was he who had paled her face with disappointment and furrowed it with hurt. He didn't know about Charles.

"Jennie, please. Don't shut me out like this. Speak to me." His hand reached out and stroked her cheek, but she pulled back, retreating even further into the couch.

"There's nothing to say." Jennifer knew that wasn't true. She wanted to cry and be held. To confess and be absolved. To stumble and be caught. But she couldn't bring herself to do any of these.

"I've hurt you," Josh went on, wishing he had said, "I love you" instead.

"I'll handle it."

"Can I drive you home?"

"I'm taking David's car." She spoke softly, but she wanted to scream. *Why didn't you take me home last Friday night? Why didn't you take me with you and love me and protect me from ever learning the truth about Charles? Now I have to face the failure of my marriage and my own failures as a woman. I wanted us to share love and happiness, but you refused. I won't share shame and embarrassment with you.*

"I spoke to Elyse de Marco the other day about creating a new label." Jennifer's businesslike tone cut him short. "How serious were you about wanting to back Elyse in a new business?"

"I don't want to talk about Elyse or business."

"But I do." Her voice was cold, yet she longed to ask him how serious he was about Elyse. If he loved her. And why the rules were different for Elyse. "Do you want to back her?"

"I thought she didn't want to go wholesale. She always said she preferred doing single items for her boutique."

Jennifer's eyes bore into Josh's, telegraphing messages he was unable to decode.

"*Their* boutique. Elyse owns that shop with her husband."

Josh's face went white. Suddenly, he thought he understood Jennifer's chill distance. She felt betrayed. She thought he had lied to her.

"I didn't know. You must believe that, Jennie. I had no idea Elyse was married."

"It doesn't matter whether you did or didn't." Jennifer's voice was ice. "I'm only interested in whether or not you'll fund this new business."

There was no sign that she had believed him. Not a single trace of softness appeared around her mouth. She faced him with a brittle unforgiving look.

"I'll speak to my attorney and have the papers drawn up as soon as possible." Josh's voice was dull with defeat.

David stood in the elbow of the darkened staircase, listening. He felt like a teenager again, rooting for a relationship. But adolescents didn't speak with pain in their voices, and they didn't hide their feelings behind wooden soliloquies like the two people in his parents' living room. David, who ached for Josh and Jennifer, was dying to burst into the room and force them into an embrace, but he huddled in the shadows until he was certain that the conversation had ended, and then he rejoined his sister and his best friend. Sarah returned, as did Rose, but the party was over. And still, no one had mentioned Charles.

Twenty

American Airlines' Presidential flight number three was airborne, headed for California. As clouds billowed past her window like peaks of meringue, Jennifer felt at peace for the first time in weeks. Her anger was abating, but the hurt remained.

"Nickel for your thoughts."

Jennifer turned to Terk. He handed her a cup of black coffee. She wondered how long he had been watching her and what he had observed.

"Why a nickel?" she asked, blowing on the steaming liquid.

Terk looked aghast, his eyes wide with mock amusement.

"I'm surprised at you," he said, shaking his head in disbelief. "In coach, seatmates offer a penny for thoughts. This is first class. Or hadn't you noticed your spacious accommodations?"

His easy mood was infectious, and Jennifer forced herself to shelve her ghosts temporarily.

"Forgive me," she said, trying to look properly contrite. "I'm subject to memory lapses at thirty thousand feet."

"Well, get hold of yourself. You've been lost in the middle distance ever since Captain Marvel started taxiing this boat down the runway. Now how about telling me what's been going on inside that gorgeous head of yours?"

She was tempted to tell him, to share her confusion and seek support, but she was not a teenager. Jennifer held that adults did not burden their friends with emotional riddles.

"You won't believe this, but I was simply enjoying the view."

Terk emptied two Sweet n' Low packets into his coffee.

"You're right," he said. "I don't believe you. I'd bet a

swift hundred bucks that you were preoccupied with the fate of mother magazine."

Jennifer thought she detected a note of disapproval in his voice, and it sparked a flutter of defensiveness.

"I am not preoccupied. I merely want to get a job done. As a matter of fact, now is the perfect time to go over our strategy for the Neiman-Marcus meeting."

The tone was stilted. The eyes refused to look at him. The posture was stiff. Anxiety was written all over Jennifer. He recognized the symptoms. He was not certain of the cause, but he was willing to help effect a cure.

"I'd love to discuss business, but it's not allowed," he said.

"I beg your pardon?"

"While you were doing research on cloud formations, the cabin attendants went through their preflight song and dance, and since you weren't paying attention, you didn't hear them say that work was not permitted on board this aircraft."

"Really." Jennifer noted the glint in his eyes as he buttered his croissant.

"Absolutely. It's a strict FAA rule. Passengers are to relax and enjoy the flight. Besides, there'll be plenty of time for business after we land."

"But we have five hours until we hit L.A. If we're quiet, no one will know."

"You are a woman obsessed, and I, for one, would like to know where you get all this die-hard devotion."

"Bloomingdale's. Second floor. Next to the bathrobes."

"Well, they must be having a two-for-one sale, because you are almost passionate about this pineapple promotion, and for the life of me, I don't understand why."

Jennifer understood her compulsive attitude all too well. She was sublimating her personal disappointments onto *Jolie*, but she could not, and would not, explain that to Terk. It would be too embarrassing to tell him that *Jolie* had, by process of elimination, become the center of her life; that her husband had betrayed her; that a man whom she had assumed loved her had rejected her. The truth was that now she had nothing other than *Jolie* to be passionate about, but it was a truth that refused to be spoken.

"Pride, my dear Watson," she said. "It would offend me to sit back and let Fellows dump *Jolie* like so much excess baggage. If they want to sell us, fine, but let them do it because *Jolie* is valuable, not because it's useless!"

"But if someone wants to buy *Jolie*," Terk said, "they must think it's valuable. People don't cough up millions of dollars for white elephants."

"Maybe so, but I'm afraid a new owner might compromise the magazine. How often has it happened that new management alters the basic philosophy of the original publication?"

"What if the basic philosophy is counterproductive?"

Jennifer looked at Terk quizzically.

"Take that Towers guy," he said. "He felt that *Jolie* was hurting itself, as well as a large segment of the fashion industry, with its dedication to the almighty designer label. Maybe he's right and we're wrong."

There was a certain logic to what Terk said. Jennifer tried to remember the conversation with Eben Towers, but more than hearing his words, she visualized his face, with the tight lines around his mouth and the angry look in his eyes.

"I will admit that on the surface he made a lot of sense," she said. "But something about him turned me off. I didn't trust him. There was too much hostility in his attitude for me to take his opinions seriously."

This time Terk avoided Jennifer. He, more than anyone, knew how correct her instincts were.

"Towers or no Towers, I agree that *Jolie* needs to pull itself up out of the cellar, and if you think Brad's idea can do it, I'll go along with you. Besides," he said, winking at her, "if this project turns out well, we could come out of it looking like heroes."

"I suggest we worry about the bottom line first and the headlines later."

Terk suddenly stopped wrestling with his mushroom omelette, and folded his arms across his chest.

"Do you expect me to believe that if this promotion is a whopping success and lots of people jump up and down and hail you as the greatest thing since peanut butter, you won't love it?"

Jennifer smiled, but Terk had touched a nerve. She was not accustomed to being confronted with the superficial side of her dreams.

"You'd get off on it!" he said. "You'd wallow in the applause of your adoring fans, and don't try and tell me otherwise. You're prettier, of course, but you and I are very much alike, and we share something very basic."

"And what may I ask is that?"

"I'll give you one clue. It's almost as much of a turn-on as sex. You have thirty seconds to come up with the correct answer."

Jennifer pretended to ponder the question and then looked at Terk, her face bright with discovery.

"Gregorian chants. That's it, isn't it? We both love Gregorian chants. Now, do I win the refrigerator?"

"With a response like that, this is all you deserve." He tossed her a tin foil packet of guava jelly.

"I'd rather have the refrigerator."

"The correct answer, my pet, is ambition. We are both slaves to the bewitching force that motivates and controls two-thirds of the human race. You are a baker's daughter, and I am a bartender's son. Our backgrounds were less than spectacular, to say the least, and that makes us prime targets for the pull of ambition."

Although his voice was light and the words humorous, there was an undertone that did not escape Jennifer. In his own way, Terk was reaching out and establishing a connection between them.

"Your problem," he continued, "is that you equate ambition with evil things like greed and heartlessness. I don't. I define it in terms of filling in the blanks. Children of poverty want money. People who go unnoticed as children want recognition as adults. And the rich lust for power. It's a universal truth."

"Okay! Okay! I confess." Jennifer held both hands up in a gesture of surrender. "I'm an ambition-crazed female who won't rest until my black desk is sitting in the Oval Office. Are you satisfied?"

"Not quite," he said. "Lusty men are never satisfied. They always want more."

"And I take it you are an extremely lusty man."

"I am, and believe me, you can take it any time you want."

Jennifer looked away, hiding the blush that suddenly colored her face. Quickly, Terk changed the subject.

"In approximately three minutes, the movie goes on. If you want to watch it, fine, but I warn you, it's a stinker."

"What's the alternative?"

"You can play with the earphones, reread the New York Times, or talk to me."

And talk they did. Over the next few hours, Jennifer found herself telling Terk the story of her life, recreating the loneliness of her early years and the horror of her accident. Eventually, she even confessed that she and Charles were separated. It was not important to tell him why. It had been such a long time since she had opened herself up to anyone that his understanding felt seductive. She needed to give something of herself to a man, even if it were only words. Terk was, without question, a desirable man, and it was obvious that he viewed her as a desirable woman. Right now, that assurance meant more to Jennifer than anything else.

She began to relax, and Terk urged her to sleep, which she did. As he thought about their conversation, Terk found something very revealing about Jennifer's pose: the legs folded beneath the body, the hand delicately cupping her chin, a few wisps of hair brushing across her face. She appeared fragile and vulnerable, and he wondered if this was her true essence. Before today, he had known her as a strong and capable business woman with a fiery, irrepressible spirit. True, he had also seen another side that exuded humor and generosity, but until now, there had been no roundness to his perception of her. Jennifer had opened herself to him, and although he was glad that he had helped, in a way, he envied her. He wished he felt secure enough to shed his armor. But Terk was not a trusting man. He had been betrayed too often by people close to him to grant anyone the privilege of knowing him completely.

Jennifer stirred, and Terk retucked the blankets around her. Sleep had tinted her cheeks the same delicate pink as her sweater, and she looked like an innocent child. But she wasn't a child, he thought, and neither was he. They were adults and, knowing his own penchant for camouflage, he knew that adults were rarely innocent. Everyone harbored secrets. Everyone lived with some amount of guilt. It was all a matter of degree. Jennifer would triumph over hers. He wondered if he would be that lucky.

Devon Bovary, a member of *Jolie*'s merchandising department, pointed to each girl as if her index finger were a magic wand. To the hundreds of young women in the audience, it was. She was selecting the last of the volunteers who would be made over by the *Jolie* team of fashion and beauty experts handling the JOYEUX JOLIE show at The May Company. Each time Devon picked someone, the remaining hands stretched higher, accompanied by shrill voices pleading for a chance to come up on stage.

Jennifer, in a raw silk pant suit the color of just-ripe bananas, stood in the back of the Young Sophisticates Department where the show was being held and marveled at the enthusiasm of the five o'clock crowd. Young women ranging in age from seventeen to their midthirties, dressed in everything from beach gear to business suits sat crosslegged on the floor in front of the eight feet by four feet platforms that constituted the *Jolie* stage. Two huge Christmas trees adorned with miniature *Jolie* magazine covers and glittery gold balls framed the area. On one side, a hairdresser and his assistant were already working on a brunette with waist-length hair, while makeup artists blended foundations and applied a tawny base to the eager face of a young woman with a boyish haircut.

Up-tempo Christmas carols rocked in the background as Devon escorted several of the volunteers backstage where they would be dressed in holiday attire. The remaining girls settled near the two beauty experts. As Jennifer glanced at her watch, she realized that Devon was about to introduce the six women chosen to represent the Los Angeles branch of the *Jolie* Job Council, a network of women who fed information to the magazine on the working women in their area.

One by one, they strode across the platforms as if they did this sort of thing every day, wearing sequins, silks, satins, lightweight velvets, everyone spinning and preening in the spotlight, while Devon detailed the salient fashion points of their outfits. Then she interviewed each of them, inviting them to explain how they adapted the latest trends to their particular lifestyles.

Jennifer tuned out the question and answer segment and let her mind focus on Terk. He was squiring the Neiman-Marcus executives around The May Company in an effort to illustrate the many ways a *Jolie* promotion benefitted a store. Jennifer had offered to accompany them, but Terk said it wasn't necessary. He knew Jennifer preferred to check the details of promotions-in-progress, and besides, he was accustomed to working his salesman's act as a single. For Jennifer, these few minutes were an opportunity to rehash the disheartening phone calls she had been receiving from the *Jolie* offices in New York. For the three days she and Terk had been in Los Angeles, all she had heard from the East Coast had been gloom and doom.

Brad had been the first of many Cassandras. The sales team that had been sent to Boston had struck out. Although Jordan Marsh had not given an outright "no," they had expressed skepticism about a fee-paid promotion. Gwendolyn Stuart had met with Saks Fifth Avenue, and even her considerable clout had not been strong enough to persuade them to move off their wait-and-see attitude. Brooke Wheeler had sent one of her associates to Rich's in Atlanta, Hudson's in Detroit, and Woodward & Lothrop in Washington. The results were little more than "let us know who else is doing it." They were all waiting for the first domino to fall.

Brad had also informed her that advertising bookings were slow. Manufacturers appeared hesitant to hitch their wagons to the tropics, and several had stressed the importance of retail support. If the stores refused to go along with The Big Pineapple, Brad feared that many advertisers would cancel their space and leave *Jolie* with the biggest loss in their history.

The show had been on for an hour and was now entering its final phase. Anxiously, Jennifer searched the floor for Terk and his entourage. It was imperative that they watch the crowd's reaction as the makeovers were presented. This was the *coup de grace*, the moment when the "befores" became "afters." If this didn't sell the promotion, nothing would.

Devon led several young women to the front of the platform. No matter how they had been styled, the hairdos were soft and flattering. The makeup was delicate, yet dramatic. And the clothes were stunning. Each girl wore a basic outfit, some in pants, some in skirts, all in something designed for holiday partying, all wanting a touch of panache. Suddenly, Devon sprang into action. She covered a silky camisole with a feathered jacket and sashed a waist with satin. She offset the starkness of a black sweater with a lacy jabot. She knotted an openwork shawl on the shoulder of a straight-lined chemise. She rainbowed a three-piece ivory silk with multicolored beads; stuck a single feather into a chignon; added a sequined bag to leather pants and a silk fencer's shirt; and gave one woman with a Chinese jacket an elegant fan to use as a wrist ornament. The audience exploded, applauding their approval as each outfit emerged as something unique and as each of their peers left the world of denim and entered a stratum of glamour and elegance.

One after the other, the twelve volunteers were transformed and then lined up as the show's finale. Devon waited for the applause to slacken and walked center stage.

"I'm Devon Bovary, and on behalf of *Jolie* magazine and The May Company, I wish you a happy, healthy holiday season. *Joyeux noel.*"

The crowd dispersed, and Jennifer immediately checked to see how many went to the racks in the adjoining clothing departments. The main purpose of these shows was to sell store merchandise. Spreading good will for the magazine was a fringe benefit. Clusters of women gathered around the Job Council representatives to talk about jobs and clothes and ask for advice. The younger women hit the special JOYEUX JOLIE boutique that had been set up and scoured the racks and tables for the accessories that Devon had used. With a sigh of relief, Jennifer noted that long lines had already formed at the cash registers. But where was Terk?

While she waited, she reached into her purse to study a dummy ad she had received in the mail that morning. Before she left on this trip, the beauty department had informed her that one of the leading cosmetic houses had agreed to provide one of their new perfumes as a tie-in with the April issue. Jennifer had left instructions for an advertising campaign and a coordinating promotion package to be mocked up for her approval.

The proposed ad had Patrick Graham written all over it. The bottle was curved like a bulbous tree trunk with a stopper designed to resemble palm fronds. Next to the bottle was a silhouette of a naked woman with luxuriously straight hair hanging down her back and her arms upstretched in a languorous pose. The slogan read: "WRAP YOURSELF IN SARONG. A TOUCH OF PARADISE." So simple, yet so seductive.

Jennifer had called to congratulate Patrick, but her call had been intercepted by Brooke Wheeler. According to Brooke, she had stood over Patrick's shoulder, directing the design and, since Jennifer's copy staff was so overloaded with other work, had had to write the copy herself. She also said that because time was of the essence, she was going to bring the mock-ups to Cosmetique herself.

Jennifer was furious and told Brooke so. First of all, she knew that Brooke was lying. Patrick Graham didn't need anyone monitoring his work. Her copy staff knew how important this project was and would never turn it away. And who had given Brooke the authority to present a promotion project to a client? Immediately, she asked to speak to Mimi, but Brooke, in an obvious rush to get off the phone, hastily informed Jennifer that Mimi had been out for several days and hadn't even called in. Jennifer found the entire incident unsettling.

"I've seen you before. Now, I'd like to see you after."

Terk had walked up behind her and circled her waist with his arm. Jennifer turned to face him, but his arm continued to hold her.

"After what?"

"After anything you'd like," he said, squeezing her waist.

"Can we continue this verbal foreplay another time?" Jennifer looked around to see who, if anyone, was watching. "Where are the boys from Neiman's?"

Terk's hands dropped at his sides. "They left."

Jennifer's face turned dark.

"What did they say?"

"They said they're going to meet us at ten o'clock at The Pink Tulip, *the* hottest disco in town. So, let's change, grab dinner, and get our boogie shoes on."

"I'm not going anywhere until you tell me what they said about buying The Big Pineapple. Didn't they like the show? Didn't they watch the crowd?" Jennifer's voice was insistent.

"I had them off to the side, and they saw everything. My guess is that they loved it since they applauded along with the rest of the audience. But they didn't John Hancock anything."

Jennifer looked upset.

"Hey, darlin', I didn't expect them to commit today anyway." Terk draped his arm over Jennifer's shoulder. "Patience, my dear. Patience." Terk started to lead her toward the fashion coordinator's office. "Let's make nice to the folks here and check the register tapes. I want to be able to tell those cowpokes how much The May Company raked in thanks to *Jolie's* show-and-sell extravaganza. And then, my sweet, you and I are going to do the town!"

By the time Terk left Jennifer in her room it was three-thirty in the morning. She was a little high, her back ached, and she was certain that her feet had died hours ago. Although her body begged for a hot shower, she stripped off her clothes and lay down on the carpet to do her stretching exercises. As she did, she reviewed the evening and summed it up in a single word: ironic.

She and Terk had dined at Le Bistro, where the ambience encouraged champagne and suggestive compliments, both of which Terk supplied in great quantities. Jennifer had left the restaurant feeling beautiful and desirable. But then, the instant they entered The Pink Tulip, Jennifer had felt a surge of panic. All around her were gay men scantily clad in T-shirts and running shorts, or bare-chested with skin-tight jeans. They held each other and danced with a sensuousness that embarrassed her. Everywhere she looked, there were men with men, women with women. True, there were many straight couples there too, but they faded into insignificance as Jennifer surveyed the scene.

Rather than give in to the whirlpool of emotions eddying within her, she willed herself to dance and threw herself into her performance. She pretended that the men dancing around her didn't disturb her, that they didn't remind her of Charles, and that the sight of them wasn't painful. She wondered if Charles ever went to places like this, if he ever danced with such wanton abandon and displayed his lust so publicly. She couldn't imagine it, but then again, she had never suspected he was gay in the first place.

For a woman accustomed to admiring glances, Jennifer found it disconcerting to be in a group where she was treated like a shadow. She was wearing a lipstick red jumpsuit with harem legs and a one-shoulder top, and she knew she looked devastating, but she had no appeal here. She was out of place, a visitor in a foreign land where she didn't speak the language or understand the customs. For a moment, she wondered how gays felt when forced into a gathering of straights, and she felt a surprising swell of sympathy.

When the music slowed, she clung to Terk, trying to lose herself in the feel of his body and the strong male scent of his cologne. After a while, she began to relax and to feel less threatened. Oddly enough, then she found herself becoming aroused by the sexuality that surrounded them. Jennifer pressed closer to Terk.

When he left her at her room, without even asking to come in, she was disappointed. Now, she reasoned that although she was separated, he was not. Perhaps he felt it wiser not to start something neither of them could finish. Perhaps he just wasn't interested. Either way, Jennifer was alone. She headed for the bathroom.

She never heard the door open, so when Terk stepped into the shower with her, Jennifer was shocked. She started to protest, but the sight of him, completely naked, holding a bottle of champagne in one hand and two glasses in the other was so outlandish, all she could do was laugh.

"I thought you might want an after-dinner drink," he said.

His tone was so matter-of-fact that Jennifer forgot to feel self-conscious about her own nakedness.

He filled both glasses and handed her one, putting the bottle on the floor outside the shower.

"To Jennifer Cranshaw." He raised his glass to hers. "I'd ask for your autograph, but I don't think I have a pen on me."

Jennifer laughed again. The whole situation was absurd. Two people standing stark naked in a hotel shower carrying on a casual conversation. Terk smiled too, but his eyes remained fixed on hers, and she could see that his mood was anything but casual.

Water careened off their bodies and sluiced around them in rhythmic splashes, but they just stood there, staring at each other, drinking, not speaking, letting the air get thick with steam and desire. Terk took his glass and hers and placed them on the ledge, pulling the lever that allowed the water to stay in the tub. He fingered her hair, twisted it into corkscrew curls and then dropped the titian spirals onto her neck. Streams of water flowed down her shoulders, and he traced them, never straying past her back, never touching her where she wanted to be touched.

His lips grazed her cheek, moved under her ear, and nestled in the hollow of her neck. His kiss was tantalizing in its sweetness, and she surrendered to the joy of his mouth covering her body. Finally, his lips closed over hers, and he pulled her toward him. The water continued to wash over them with a seductive spray of warmth, gathering around their feet in gentle waves.

Slowly, his hands began to glide over her, sliding, slithering, slipping down her back and around to her breasts. There was a tender deference in his attitude that made her feel like a goddess, an icon being worshipped and adored. She exalted in the experience, relishing the sensations that swept over her.

Terk bent down and held her as he arched her back and sucked on her nipples. In a way, Jennifer felt strange watching him at her breasts and feeling him grow hard against her thighs. She felt like a voyeur, but it excited her, and she let her hands drop, eager to grasp his virility, wanting to touch and hold him. Her knees trembled as his mouth left her breasts and traveled down to her thighs. A deep groan escaped her lips as gently, Terk guided her down into the half-filled tub, straddled her and massaged her with a delicacy she would have thought incongruous with passion.

The water mingled with his touch and sent shivers up and down her legs. Terk moved closer, reunited their lips and placed himself near her, letting her feel his need throbbing against her. All control ebbed away. She needed Terk. She needed to feel a man's body hungering for her and filling her body. Terk thrust himself inside her until they were both oblivious to everything except the intense pleasure of two bodies melded into one.

Jennifer's head began to feel light, almost faint. Sharp prickles needled her breasts. It was coming. Soon. Her legs stiffened. Her breath caught in her throat. She wanted to prolong the excitement, but she felt dizzy. Transported. And then it came. The shudder. The thick wetness. The spasm of release. She felt him too. And she was glad.

"Your husband is a jerk!"

"I beg your pardon?"

They were lying in Jennifer's bed, drinking coffee and eating Danish. They were still naked, and in spite of a slight champagne hangover, Jennifer felt marvelous.

"If I were married to you, I'd never let you get out of bed."

"You're not so bad yourself, Mr. Conlon."

"I'm glad you think so. Then you won't object to my plans for the day."

Jennifer eyed him quizzically.

"Since the New York office will probably try to get in touch with us today and since there is a possibility we'll get a call with Neiman-Marcus' decision, I think our best bet is to stick close to a phone."

"And to which phone would you like to stick?"

Terk reached over her, took the telephone on her side of the bed, and placed it on her stomach.

"Just in case it rings." He leaned over and nuzzled his nose in between her breasts.

"I hate to be a spoilsport," Jennifer said, "but what if it rings and the caller happens to be your wife?"

"Hopefully, I'll be busy, and you can tell her that with a clear conscience."

Terk sat up and returned to his Danish.

"Terk, I know that last night and even now, whatever passes between us is really not serious. It's sex. Pure and simple and wonderful uncomplicated sex. That's okay with me, but I don't love the idea of being the other woman in someone else's life."

Terk refilled Jennifer's coffee cup.

"Jennifer, you are an incredibly sexy woman, and there is no question that I have wanted to ravage your body for a long time, but you are not breaking up a happy home or destroying my marriage. My wife did both of those things all by herself."

There was a sadness underneath Terk's words, and Jennifer urged him to talk about his marriage. Maybe it would help him. Maybe it would help her.

"Did you love Deirdre when you married her?"

Terk was quiet for a moment.

"Yes, I did. She's an exciting woman. Vibrant. Aggressive. Bright. Beautiful. Wild. . . . And terrific in the sack. She'd be every man's ideal if she didn't practice castration without a license. But I guess nobody's perfect."

"I guess not." It was Jennifer's turn to be silent.

Terk went on to describe his life with Deirdre. He told Jennifer how Deirdre's possessiveness and money had eroded whatever relationship they might have had. He even told her about Zena Welles, what she had meant to him then, and what he hoped she would be to him now.

"You know," Jennifer said. "You were right when you said that you and I are alike. We both married up, so to speak. We both attached ourselves to people who seemed to have what we lacked, thinking that their status and position would guarantee our happiness. But it didn't."

"That's because our pride made us piggy." Terk fluffed Jennifer's pillows and turned on his side to face her. "We weren't content to be rich by association. We had to do it ourselves. We had to prove our own worth, to create our own successes."

"And still, it wasn't enough," Jennifer said half to herself.

"At least you didn't fuck yourself trying, like I did."

"What are you talking about?"

"There must be something about the naked body of a woman that makes me want to confess my sins. Can you handle the story of my life?"

"The story, please."

Terk outlined his predicament. Although he told her the truth about his indebtedness and his skimming, he deliberately neglected to tell her Towers's name. He could see by Jennifer's reaction that the little he had said had frightened her.

"How are you repaying him?" she asked.

"A pound of flesh at a time."

"Terk, I'm serious. Where are you getting this money?"

"I have a little side venture that pays very well."

Jennifer had a thousand questions, but Terk's attitude told her he had said as much as he was going to say.

"I've never met this guy, but my instincts tell me that if you ever cross him again, he'll throw you to the wolves faster than you can say 'penitentiary.'"

"How right you are, but don't let it give you wrinkles. I'm being careful, and just as a matter of insurance, I have a few things on him that might prevent him from saying too much about me to anyone."

"I don't like the sound of the whole thing."

"I'm not too crazy about it myself, but I have Zena in my life and you in my corner, so how can I go wrong?"

"Let me count the ways."

"I also have you in my bed," Terk said, sliding next to her. "And I've never been a man who wastes an opportunity."

Twenty-One

E lyse's head slammed into the corner of her cocktail
table. A sticky warmth trickled down her neck,
and her hands went up to protect her from the
unrelenting fist that continued to pummel her body. She
held onto the table for support and pulled herself to her
feet. She wanted to run, but she ached. Her face felt bru-
talized. Blood dribbled out of her nose. Her lips felt thick
and fleshy. Her legs refused to respond. Then, a sharp,
punishing stab bolted through her, knocking the wind out
of her and bringing her to her knees. Her head reeled
from the pain, and she tried to crawl away, but the hand
kept coming at her.

A voice pleaded. Elyse recognized it as her own, and
even through the hollow echoes of her battered skull, the
intensity of her screams hurt her ears. But the hand refused to listen. It came at her again and again, striking,
slapping, insistent upon violating her. Curled into a tight,
violent knot, it attacked her abdomen and buckled her
flesh. Then there was another crackling noise and a terrible weakness. In the distance, she heard an agonized
howl. Brilliant spots flashed before her eyes. A staggering
pain overwhelmed her. And then there was nothing. Nothing but blackness.

When Elyse finally opened her eyes, she saw the
shadowy figure of a man standing at her side. She blinked
and rubbed her eyes, forcing herself to focus. The man allowed her time to adjust to her first few moments of
consciousness, not speaking, gently checked her pulse, and
then read something from a metal clipboard.

"Welcome back." The man's voice was deep and sooth-
ing. "I'm Dr. David Sheldon, and I claim all responsibility
for the unattractive girdle now holding your ribs together."

Tentatively, Elyse touched herself. Instead of warm, supple flesh, there was cool, stiff adhesive winding around her midriff. She pressed down, and the soreness made her wince.

"You're doing much better," David said as he lifted her hospital gown and examined her bandages. "The last time we poked at you, you almost leaped off the bed."

His fingers went to her face, and she watched his reassuring smile turn somber as he palpated her cheeks and the area around her eyes. As he probed, Elyse realized that her skin felt mushy, puffed, and wounded. Instinctively, she went to touch her face, but the doctor intercepted, took her hands, and placed them at her sides.

"From the looks of this, you went the full fifteen rounds." He tucked the blanket up under her arms.

Stark, brittle scenes flashed before her, a documentary in chilling black and white. Elyse trembled.

"I fell," she said, feeling pressed to explain.

Even though she had turned away from him, David had seen the terror that had invaded her eyes. They both knew she was lying, but David understood her response. He had treated too many assault victims not to sympathize.

"Elyse." His voice was calm and reassuring. "I'm not going to press you for details, but the fact is you were savagely beaten. If it were within my power, I'd probably relocate the guy's teeth, but my job is to mend your broken bones, and that's all I intend to do."

"Thank you," Elyse whispered. There was something so genuine about Dr. Sheldon's manner that Elyse felt her anxiety subside and trust begin to grow in its place. "How long have I been here?"

"Three days, four hours, and twenty-two minutes. Not that anyone's counting, you understand. And aside from jabbing you with needles every few hours, I want you to know that our crack nursing staff has taken wonderful care of your flower shop."

He waved his arm in the direction of a large rolling table opposite her bed that overflowed with huge floral arrangements. In addition, several large baskets filled each window sill, and in a big green vinyl chair, an enormous teddy bear held a basket of pink roses. David read that card first: "Thought you might need a friend. Love, Josh."

Elyse wanted to smile, but her lips refused. The other cards bore messages and homemade poems from friends, the boutique staff, and several suppliers. It was when David pointed to a spare glass vase on her bedside table that she felt tears well up in her swollen eyes. Standing in the vase was a single white rose, its petals still clasped together in an embryonic bud.

"There was no card with that one," David said. "But I can see that none was necessary." He stood beside her and dabbed at her eyes with the tip of a cotton towel. "He must be someone very special."

"He is."

David started to ask the identity of the man who sent the bud, but even in the short time he had spent with Elyse, it had become apparent that this woman was an extremely private person with doors she kept securely locked.

"How would you like a visitor?"

"Who is it?" David noticed the terror reappear in her eyes.

"A fellow by the name of Joshua Mandell." Elyse visibly relaxed. "Oddly enough, I happen to know Mr. Mandell, and I'm willing to approve his visit, if you're up to it."

"Did he bring me here?"

"No. A woman did. An Ardis Cohen?" Elyse nodded. "Evidently, Mrs. Cohen went to your apartment after work to drop off some fabric samples. When you didn't answer the doorbell, she got the superintendent to let her in. Fortunately, she had the good sense to call an ambulance immediately."

"How did Josh find out?"

"While Mrs. Cohen was waiting, she called Josh for the name of a doctor. Evidently, they're friends from way back. Josh gave my name, and I was waiting for you when the ambulance pulled in."

"I'm glad," Elyse said.

"Me too."

David patted her hand and brushed a few stray wisps of hair off her face. In spite of her bruises, David found

Elyse de Marco remarkable looking, a sensuous combination of untouchable beauty and inviting vulnerability, like a woman-child. She reminded him of his sister. He didn't know whether or not Elyse and Jennifer were friends, but he was aware that they knew each other. He had overheard Jennifer and Josh discussing Elyse de Marco that night in Bayonne, but what the relationship was between Josh and Elyse and Jennifer, he did not know. Something told him that inadvertently, Elyse was part of the tension between Josh and Jennifer. He only hoped that they were in no way responsible for what had happened to Elyse.

David went to the door and motioned to Josh, who had been standing just outside in the hall. As Josh neared her bedside, Elyse read both concern and relief in his eyes. She sensed that he was trying to smother any disgust or shock he might feel at the sight of her, but he was unable to stifle it completely. She felt his breath on her neck as he bent down to kiss her, and although she tried to give him a confident smile, she could do no better than a half-hearted grimace.

While Josh and Elyse talked, David deliberately busied himself with the IV tube. He watched the two of them carefully, searching for clues as to the extent of their involvement. David assumed that yes, they had been, or were still, lovers. What intrigued him was that he felt no vibrations of love. They touched each other and spoke in that personal way born of intimacy, but there was something missing, that almost imperceptible difference that separated affection from devotion.

David chided himself for being so nosy. After all, Jennifer was married, and if Josh were in love with this woman, he should wish him well. So why was he butting in where he didn't belong? Because David couldn't deny the signals he had picked up the other night in Bayonne. A current had passed between his sister and his friend. He saw it and felt it, not because of the positive way they had treated each other, but because of the negative. They had been afraid to touch each other, even accidentally, afraid to offend, watchful of every word and gesture. Something special existed between them, David was sure.

"Who did this to you?" Josh was on his feet, demanding

an answer, outraged at the sight of her bruises. "What bastard beat you this way?"

"Josh," David said, moving toward his friend and restraining him, "Elyse is my patient, and if you upset her, I'm going to have to throw you out."

Josh merely glowered at David. He stuffed his hands in his pockets and stormed over to a window. David checked Elyse's pulse.

"How do you two know each other?" Elyse asked, hoping to divert Josh's attention. He didn't answer.

"We grew up together," David said, pressing a button to summon a nurse. "I think you know my sister, Jennifer Cranshaw."

Elyse looked at David Sheldon as if for the first time. They had the same wide-set, almond-shaped eyes, she noticed, and the same full lips, but David's face was rounder than Jennifer's and his chin line stronger. Even with only a cursory analysis, Elyse decided they shared kindness and compassion as well.

"I'm sorry, David, but I have to know what happened!"

Josh's outburst startled Elyse. As he turned to face David, she could see by the rigid lines around his mouth that none of his anger had dissipated.

"If Elyse isn't up to talking, Josh, she doesn't have to. She's my patient and right now, her health takes precedence over your curiosity."

One of the floor nurses came in and handed David two white tablets that he gave to Elyse along with a cup of water. As she resettled herself, she tried to evaluate the tension level in the room. Josh had retreated once again to the window, his back stiff and his neck straight. David too seemed preoccupied, and she felt somehow responsible.

"My husband beat me up," she said after a few minutes' deliberation. "I don't think he could help himself."

"Bullshit!" Josh exclaimed. "In all the time we've known each other you never mentioned you were married, and now I see why. The guy is a pig!" He noticed a trace of fear dart across Elyse's face, and he forced himself to calm down. "Elyse," he said, more softly, "I might be able to accept the fact that in the midst of a really heated argument, anyone could throw a punch, but he knocked you around pretty good, and I'll bet this isn't the first time."

"It isn't. But this is the worst."

"Then why do you stay married to him?" *And why am I always telling women to leave their husbands?*

"I can't leave."

And why do those women always give me the same answer? he thought wryly.

"Why not?" David Sheldon's curiosity was aroused, but he couldn't decide whether it was because of Elyse or because of the strange look on Josh's face.

Elyse turned to David, sensing that she would feel easier explaining to him than to Josh.

"Loyalty, I suppose. Gratitude. Background. Mario is a man of tremendous pride. Years ago, I banished him from my home, but in his Italian mind, I'm still his woman. He accepts the fact that since that time there have been other men in my life, and he is far from celibate, but if I ever got a divorce, he would lose face, and he would never allow that to happen."

"You can't remain shackled to a nonexistent marriage for the rest of your life, Elyse. At some point, you may want to marry again. You may want to grab some happiness for yourself."

Josh listened to David and wondered how his friend would feel if he knew that Josh had argued the very same points with Jennifer.

"There are other reasons," Elyse said.

"Like what?" David didn't mean to press, but he could tell that the sedatives had relaxed her, and he honestly felt she needed to unburden herself.

"Like that single white rose." Elyse's eyes misted as she reached for the pristine bud and took it out of its vase. "This is my tie to Mario de Marco."

Slowly, and as articulately as her condition would allow, Elyse told her story.

The Lanzanas lived in Greenpoint, Brooklyn, a working class community with a predominantly Italian character. Elyse's father, Big Gianni, was a dock worker, as were most of the men in the neighborhood, and her mother, Anna, was a seamstress in one of the local dress factories. Within the confines of this modest circle, Big Gianni

considered himself a success. He and his wife and his two
children lived on the upper floor of one of the nicer two-
family houses in the area; he owned a barely used Chevy,
and he had been president of his lodge for two full terms.
For a fisherman's son from Naples, he was living well.

Big Gianni had come to the United States shortly after
he and Anna had married, and like many of his compatriots, he had remained very old world in most ways. He
spoke only Italian at home and believed that he, by virtue
of his maleness, was the unquestioned head of the house.
He also saw nothing archaic about arranging suitable
matches for his children. Before Elyse was even old
enough to appreciate the difference between the sexes, she
had been verbally pledged to Mario de Marco, the eldest
son of Big Gianni's best friend. To Gianni, it was a brilliant match, because Mario was a boy with an assured future. His father, Carmine, was a rigger, dispatching a
small fleet of trucks and cranes throughout the city to haul
heavy construction equipment. It was a solid business,
connected to an industry essential to the nation's economy
and therefore secure. Mario was also handsome, and
mated with his *multa bella*, Elyse, Big Gianni figured he
would have the most beautiful grandchildren in Greenpoint.

Anna worked in a small dress factory housed in a dilap-
idated building and run by a man permanently poised on
the brink of bankruptcy. The equipment was in a constant
state of disrepair, and the general working conditions
were just this side of abominable, but Vittorio Tierone
was one of their own. He allowed his employees extra sick
days when they needed them; always put something extra
in their Christmas envelopes, no matter how bad his year
had been; and he never docked anyone for taking off for a
special Saint's Day, so no one complained. One afternoon,
Anna was working on a sleeve when she dropped a spool
of thread on the floor. She bent down to pick it up and as
she did, her shoulder knocked the wooden slab that held
her sewing machine. The bolts that held the machine to
the table had loosened long ago, but no one had bothered
to fix them, thinking the weight of the machine would
keep it stable. As Anna went to get up, the lumbering

machine slipped and slid backwards, landed on her spine, and crippled her forever.

For months, doctors and physical therapists tried to restore mobility to Anna's lifeless legs. They tried exercise, medicine, whirlpool baths, even psychiatry, but her condition was hopeless. When she finally returned home, Anna was despondent. She would never walk again, and that knowledge filled her with a desperate sense of uselessness. True, she felt grateful to be alive, but she had a husband to care for, a daughter and small son who needed her attention. It was her job to clean the house and cook for her family. It was her responsibility to provide money for the children's Sunday shoes and weekends at the beach. Now, instead of being a helpmate, she was a burden. Weeks went by, and Anna sank deeper and deeper into depression. She had stopped crying. She had stopped speaking. All she did was stare at the empty space before her eyes. Big Gianni begged her not to worry. He told her over and over again that everything would be all right. He even told her how much he loved her in front of the children. He promised that the Lanzanas would make it, and much to Anna's surprise, they did.

Elyse was twelve at the time of her mother's accident, too young to comprehend the significance of what was happening, but skirting the periphery of her mind were questions: like how the hospital bills had been paid, and where the shiny wheelchair had come from, and how her father had managed to afford their new ground-floor apartment. Several times she asked Big Gianni where the money had come from and how he planned to repay the loans she assumed he had taken, but each time, he assured her that Giancarlo Lanzana owed no one and that he would rather die than take charity.

Elyse might have pursued the matter, but she hadn't the time. When her mother lost the use of her legs, Little Gianni was only seven, and, in effect, Elyse had become his mother. She fixed his lunch, helped with his homework, walked him to and from his friends' houses, bathed and fed him, and tucked him into his bed at night. In addition, she tended to both her parents' needs as well as her own schoolwork. But the biggest responsibility, Elyse felt, was to bolster her mother's spirits.

She began to treat her mother's mental rehabilitation like a crusade, throwing herself into it with a religious fervor. When Vittorio Tierone presented Anna with a special sewing machine that she could operate with her elbow, Elyse felt as if she had just discovered The Holy Grail. It seemed logical to Elyse that if Anna resumed sewing, she would regain some semblance of self-pride, but Anna refused to make Elyse or Little Gianni anything on the horrid machine. Elyse cried, stamped her feet, swore that she wouldn't go to another school dance if she didn't have a new dress, but Anna still refused, apologizing for her helplessness in a wooden voice.

It finally dawned on Elyse that the core of Anna's despair was the loss of income. Sewing had been the means to that end, and Elyse was determined to create a situation where it could be again. After a few days of constructive thinking, Elyse came up with a plan. Then all she had to do was pray that it would work. It had to. Her mother's life depended on it.

Unknown to Anna, Elyse hung signs in all the local shops, advertising expert seamstress services for reasonable prices. She waited anxiously for the first customer, but after two weeks when no one had called or come to the house, Elyse activated part two of her plan. The next day, Amalia de Marco, Mario's mother and Anna's closest friend, stopped over to ask Anna a favor. Carmine had two very important dinners that they had to attend, and since Amalia really couldn't afford new dresses, she wondered if Anna would remake two of her old ones.

Anna just stared at her friend. She tried to apologize politely, but Amalia drowned her out, insisting that Anna was the only one who could help her.

"How can I measure hems?" Anna said bitterly. "I can't bend. I can't stand to chalk seams. I can't reset shoulders."

Anna's voice was so filled with pain and remorse that Amalia almost weakened. She wanted to take her friend in her arms and hold her, but Elyse's demanding eyes forced her to continue.

"Elyse can do that for you." Amalia made it sound so casual, so spontaneous. "You tell her what to do, and I'm sure she can handle it."

At first Anna protested, but Amalia was so confident in the results that she decided to give it a try. Soon after, several other friends came, each with invented excuses as to why no one but Anna could help them, each demanding that she charge them for services rendered. Rather than insult them, Anna created a fee schedule, lowering her head as they handed her the money, but smiling inside. Within six months, Anna and Elyse had a thriving business. Elyse functioned as Anna's legs, and soon the Lanzana team mended, altered, and created dresses for most of the women in Greenpoint, as well as many from surrounding neighborhoods.

They bought a machine for Elyse with some of their profits, and each day, Anna taught her daughter another dressmaking trick. Elyse learned quickly, handstitching zippers and finishing seams so that the insides of the dresses were as neat and attractive as the outside. Anna showed her how to take a standard pattern and, by adding or subtracting inches and details, how to use one pattern for several sizes and designs. Because Anna was a traditionalist, she stuck to basics, but Elyse always added something special to her dresses. She slanted pockets when they should have been straight; used contrasting colors for collars and cuffs; added lace to heavy wools to soften the effect; cut skirts on a bias to accommodate fuller figures; anything that might help distinguish one dress from another. After a while, customers came to expect the unexpected from the Lanzanas.

When Elyse was twenty, she married Mario de Marco, to the surprise of no one. The first three years were spent in Greenpoint. Mario went to work for his father, and Elyse continued to work with her mother, but now she took her share of the profits home to her husband. Just as her mother had done, Elyse never mentioned her financial contribution to the marriage, and just as her father had done, Mario ignored it. Their apartment was small. They went out frequently with friends. They had managed to squirrel away a tidy sum as savings. And Elyse was happy. She had no reason not to be. Her life was simple and uncomplicated, and not only was her husband the handsomest man in Greenpoint, but he was an extraordinary lover. He was passionate and inventive and during those early years, Elyse loved him more than she had ever thought possible.

Mario too was happy for a while. If not for his job, he would have been completely content, but Mario had dreams that might never be realized if he remained a rigger. He saw himself as much more, as someone grand and respected, and each day as he rode about the city in one of his father's trucks, his discontent grew. He watched the rich and envied them. It was not merely the result of parentage. Many of those who incited his jealousy came from the same humble beginnings as he had. It was opportunity. Being in the right place at the right time with the right idea. He began to search for his opportunity. When the idea finally came to him, he wanted to kick himself for not seeing it sooner.

He was riding up Madison Avenue, as he had done hundreds of times, but that day he noticed the shops. Wealthy women strolled up and down the street, meandered into one shop or the other and exited with boxes that Mario knew represented large expenditures of money. Elyse was his salvation. She loved to sew, he reasoned, and everyone said she had a talent for it, a real genius in fact, for design. Then and there, Mario decided to open a store. Elyse would sew and he would sell. It all made such sense. Elyse was making money now by designing dresses, only she was sharing her talent with her family. Mario was her husband, and anything she earned rightfully belonged to him.

Mario kept his plans to himself until he had found a small store with rent he could afford just off Second Avenue. Despite Elyse's objections and her fears, they left Greenpoint and moved their few pieces of furniture into the back of the store. Mario placed the sewing machine right next to the bed. While Elyse tried to build up an inventory, Mario threw himself into the decoration of the shop. He wandered into every chic salon he could find and tried to get the feel of them. To his credit, with a small outlay of cash, Mario created an elegant backdrop for Elyse's designs. In his travels, he also scouted merchandise. He watched the women as they rifled through racks of chiffons and basic blacks. He noticed that they seemed disappointed much of the time, as if they were

searching for something that didn't exist. He instructed
Elyse to let her imagination fly, to create fantasy clothes
that the rich would find impossible to resist. Exclusivity
was key. Elyse complied, and within a short time, the first
de Marco Boutique was turning a profit.

Mario couldn't afford advertising, but his Latin charm
and dark good looks delivered many fancy invitations to
the de Marco mail box. Mario dragged Elyse from party
to party, exhibiting her like a prize heifer, never neglect-
ing to mention that her clothes were one-of-a-kind origi-
nals. In the process of building the business, Mario also
inflated his ego. He was propositioned constantly and soon
found he enjoyed courting the attention of elegant
women.

He never intended to hurt Elyse. In fact, he was astounded when she confronted him in a fit of rage over his
unfaithfulness. Hundreds of husbands philandered. That
didn't mean they loved their wives any the less. It was the
nature of the beast, a male privilege, the proper order of
things. Maybe so, but Elyse didn't see it that way. After
much arguing, Mario consented to a brief separation, certain that after a few months of no sex, Elyse would come
crawling back to him. He was wrong.

It was when Elyse told him that she wanted to quit the
boutique that Mario turned nasty. It was degrading
enough that she had left his bed, but if she left the
business, he would be ruined. He had put too much of
himself into the operation to allow her to tear it down just
because her pride was hurt. They were now in a class
neighborhood, on Seventy-second Street, catering to the
cream of society, and commanding outrageous prices for
their designs. Mario was a minor celebrity, and he was not
about to give that up. When Elyse insisted on a divorce
and a financial settlement from the sale of the business,
Mario felt it necessary to use his only weapon. He informed her that he knew about Little Gianni skimming
funds, and if Elyse left, he would make certain that the
big boys found out about Little Gianni's profiteering. He
didn't have to say another word. Elyse knew that if Mario
was true to his word, her brother was a dead man. She
never returned to Mario's bed, but she never missed a
day's work from that moment on.

"The temptation must have been too great for Gianni," Elyse said, noticing the sad look in Josh's eyes. "It only happened once, but with the mob, there are no second chances."

"How do you know Mario wasn't bluffing?" David Sheldon couldn't believe what he was hearing.

"I don't. I only know that once, Little Gianni disappeared for about two months, just after Mario and I had had another fight. Again, I had threatened to leave and again, Mario threatened to turn Gianni in. Until I heard from my brother and knew he was safe, my life was hell. I never told Gianni about Mario's threats, but I insisted that I know his whereabouts at all times. I also made him renew his promise to stay as clean as he could. Now, when he's out of town, he sends me a single white rose to assure me that he's all right and still clean. I love him too much ever to flirt with his life, and Mario knows it."

"What set Mario off this time?" Elyse wondered why David was doing most of the questioning. Josh was strangely silent.

"Your sister convinced me to create a special collection under a separate label. At first I thought I'd be able to figure a way out of all of this, but now I see I was wrong. Mario stopped by and caught me working on the designs for the new line. He went berserk, and for all I know ran straight to Greenpoint the minute he left me."

"Elyse, I know these sound like empty words, but your brother is a grown man now, and he, not you, is responsible for his life."

Josh listened to David and was tempted to agree, but he could feel Elyse's fear, and he knew that no matter what anyone said, she would always carry this burden. *But maybe she didn't have to,* he thought. Josh always believed that a snitch was a snitch because he wanted to get his dibs in first, before someone else squealed on him. Josh was willing to bet his entire fortune that Mario de Marco had his own secrets. And Josh was going to find out what they were.

Twenty-Two

"**W**hew! This one is hot!" Buzzy Stoller let loose with a raucous wolf whistle that rebounded off the darkroom walls.

Even in the dusky crimson light of the small, cramped space, Zena could see the lascivious leer in Buzzy's eyes.

"Man, I'd love to get lost in this chick's panties for a week or two. She is one foxy-looking broad."

Zena stood opposite Buzzy, her hands immersed in a tin pan filled with developing solution. As she seesawed the paper back and forth in the liquid, she watched Buzzy peruse a long strip of film.

"I know you're dying to tell me what you're working on, so go ahead and spit it out."

Buzzy held the celluloid strip in front of Zena.

"I hold here in my hands some of the classiest porno shit you've ever seen. Not only is it raw, unadulterated sex, but the girl who stars in these flicks is incredible!" He put the film up to the red light again as if to assure himself that the object of his adoration hadn't faded. "I think the reason she's such a turn-on is that she doesn't look like the type who has to fuck her way to stardom. Know what I mean?"

"I didn't think Harry handled stuff like this," Zena said. She had rented darkroom facilities from Harry Washor for years and had always thought the bulk of his business came from fashion photographers, catalogues, and freelancers like herself.

"He doesn't," Buzzy said, winding the film into a metal reel. "The guy in charge of this operation approached me on the sly. I make a few bucks, the guy I work for gets top-notch quality, and Harry knows from nothing. It's the perfect setup."

Zena had shared a darkroom with Buzzy often enough to know that he liked to chat while he worked, but she didn't feel up to it tonight. She had too much on her mind. Terk was on a business trip, and Zena had mixed feelings about his absence. She was grateful for the time to sort out her feelings, but there was no doubt that she missed him more than she had expected to, more than she wanted to.

On the surface, Terk had mellowed. He was reaching for stability and order. When she had first met him, he had been adventurous, daring, almost dangerously bold. Now, it seemed as if he looked both ways before crossing a street.

Zena had changed too. Once, she had let her heart rule her life. Now, she plotted her moves carefully. After Terk she had transferred her passion for him onto her career. She had set goals and worked toward achieving them, allowing nothing and no one to interfere.

Her picture was finished, and she snapped the photograph onto the drying rack so she could study it. It was a multi-image shot of a vulture suspended in flight. The bald, featherless head hung low, the neck extended like the shaft of a periscope searching for carrion. Usually, the vulture loomed as a hideously ugly creature, but here, with its wings poised and arched like the upper lip of a woman's mouth, it was transformed into something graceful and balletic.

"Want to see a blowup of Lady Belle?" Buzzy asked.

"Who?" Zena was so preoccupied that she had forgotten all about Buzzy and his film.

"Lady Belle. The porno star I've been telling you about."

Zena hesitated. Scanning pictures of sex goddesses was the last thing she wanted to do.

"Hey, nothing raunchy. Just some publicity stills." Buzzy leaped off his chair and went to his canvas briefcase. "I made a few extra to hang on my wall."

While Buzzy rifled through a stack of eight by ten glossies, Zena hung another photograph to dry. A huge, lumbering rhinoceros stared cross-eyed at a small bird perched on his snout. Swamp grass and a long, opaque string of saliva dribbled out of his mouth, his jaw twisted as if stalled in midchew.

"Here she is." Buzzy held up a picture for Zena's inspection. The girl was beautiful, with light silky hair decorously covering a naked shoulder. One hand clasped a piece of lace to her breasts, providing a modest, but inadequate shield. Through the openwork Zena could see the young woman's full, but firm breasts, the dark nipples poking through the creamy lace. What intrigued Zena more than the pose was the woman's face. Lady Belle confronted the camera and stared bold-faced at her audience, her tongue licking her upper lip. Her head was erect, enticing all viewers to fantasize about the various pleasures she had to offer, but the eyes were filled with an incongruous timidity. There was sadness lurking in those eyes, a veil that told of secrets and regret-filled decisions. Zena felt a swell of sympathy for this unknown woman. She too had made decisions in her life that had caused pain. She too had made hasty choices that had haunted her for years after. She wondered what had prompted this fine-looking girl to sell her body for the prurient satisfaction of others.

"I know this sounds silly," she said to Buzzy, who hovered over the picture like a proud father, "but I'm sure I've seen her somewhere. Has she ever been in a legitimate movie or modeled for some famous magazine?"

"Not a chance. The guy who runs this operation keeps it real tight. He only sells to private customers with big bucks. You know, horny executives who get off on entertaining their friends with hard core and convention guys who treat their special customers to a night of Simon Says."

"Simon Says?"

"Yeh. First they show these flicks, and then everyone grabs a hooker and does an instant replay."

"But the girl?"

"No way. I'm telling you this is kept real hush-hush. Mr. Big gets unknowns and pays them plenty to get off in front of a camera. And the thing that makes these films so special is that the backgrounds are always super posh, and the performers are real upper crust."

"Who's the guy behind it?" Zena couldn't take her eyes off Lady Belle.

"Who knows? My bet is that the name he gave me is a phony."

Zena looked at the picture again. Lady Belle, another body being picked apart by vultures. There was no doubt in Zena's mind that she had seen this woman before. She couldn't remember where, but something told her it was important to find out.

"Mario de Marco will never bother you again."

Jennifer and David stood by the windows in Elyse's hospital room and watched as Josh gently stroked Elyse's hand. Jennifer had been back from Los Angeles more than a week before David contacted her and told her what had happened. Most of the black and blue from the bruises had faded into a jaundiced yellow, but still, Jennifer could see remnants of violence spotting Elyse's face and arms.

"What makes you so sure?" David asked.

He felt extremely protective of the courageous woman with the bandaged ribs and the Nefertiti eyes, and he wasn't going to release her until he was certain she would be safe.

"I had a detective trail your loving husband," Josh said, directing his answer to Elyse. "I also ran a check on his business activities. Although he has a lot of friends in the Organization, he's never taken a dime from any of them."

Elyse paled. "I told you," she said with defeat in her voice. "He stays on their good side. He butters them up by giving their wives free dresses and things, and to them, he's just a good boy from Greenpoint. They trust him, and that's what scares me. All he'd have to do is drop one hint in the right place, and my brother is a dead man."

Jennifer had spent the last few hours listening to the details of Elyse's ordeal, and though she had been horrified, her response had been controlled compassion. Now, something in Elyse's tone stirred a boiling anger within Jennifer. Anxiety and concern were feelings she had experienced many times, feelings with which she could relate. But this was fear—gut-wrenching, life-threatening fear—and she despised the man who had caused it. No one had the right to instill this kind of terror. No one had the right to inflict this kind of pain.

"He's called her every day," Jennifer said, repeating what David had told her. "He even had the nerve to try and see her."

"I know all that," Josh said patiently. "But he won't do it again." He nodded to Jennifer and David, who responded by pulling chairs closer to Elyse's bed.

"According to my private investigator—and I assure you he's the best—Mario de Marco is an overzealous Romeo who decided to make doing pleasure a business."

"Don't tell me he's a pimp!" David's voice rang with distaste.

"Quite the contrary," Josh said. "Mario is self-employed. He provides a service for the bored, horny women who frequent this city's more affluent circles. Mario finds them at the many parties he attends and, in the course of conversation, extends a hand in friendship. He invites them to lunch while their husbands are off somewhere on business trips, and then they go shopping, at which time Mario gives them the benefit of his fashion expertise.

"While in the stores, he mentions in passing how much he loves lapis cufflinks or how he's always preferred cashmere sport jackets to wool. Then, he takes these more-than-willing women to bed. He strokes their egos and their bodies until they want nothing more than to spend their afternoons with the rakish Mr. de Marco. That's when Mario plays hard to get. He hems and haws about seeing them until the cufflinks or the jacket is delivered to his door. Once the item is his, he is theirs, for as long as they want."

"That's disgusting!" Jennifer was outraged.

"Unfortunately, Jennifer, Mario is not unique. There are plenty of men who prey upon frustrated women." David could have predicted Jennifer's reaction, but Elyse surprised him. Where he might have expected anger or even embarrassment, he was certain that a brief smile had touched her lips.

It had, but it was not the nervous response David had thought. As Elyse listened to Josh, she remembered what it was like to make love to Mario. She, more than anybody else, knew that any woman who had been to bed with him once would be eager for an encore.

"These flings usually don't last very long," Josh continued. "Eventually, the husbands come home, and the wives bid a fond adieu to Mario. He was doing pretty well with this scam, because he had been clever enough

not to tangle with women whose husbands might feel
compelled to break his legs. But then he screwed up. Liter-
ally."

Josh's voice became softer, and he leaned closer to
Elyse, who was fidgeting with the strings of her bed
jacket.

"About four months ago, Mario met an extremely beautiful woman who lived in a fancy duplex, limousined
around town, and dripped Harry Winston and Bulgari.
For quite a while, they had a thing going, but this lady
never picked up Mario's hints. A few weeks ago, he got
piggy. He told her the boutique had gone sour and he
needed a little money to tide him over. She refused, and I
guess that pissed Mario off, because he smacked her
around. That was his big mistake."

"Is she going to press charges?" Jennifer said, trying to
avoid the sight of Elyse's hand in Josh's.

"Even though I'd love to see that happen, that wouldn't
solve the problem of Gianni. However, my man put a tail
on this lady and found out that she is mistress to one of
the big dons in Greenpoint, of all places."

Elyse was too stunned to react.

"Did she tell her benefactor what happened?" David
still wasn't sure where all this was leading.

"No. She's petrified to admit that she betrayed him."

"So, Mario gets away with this too," Jennifer said.

"Not if I can help it." Josh turned to Elyse. "I decided
to play a hunch. I figured that Mario didn't know the real
identity of his newest conquest, so I took a chance and
paid him a little visit last night. When I mentioned the
young woman's name, I drew a blank, just as I had suspected I would. But then, I told him whose mistress she
was. I informed him that I had been in touch with this
woman and that she had said she probably wouldn't say
anything, but I made him aware of the fact that her decision didn't affect me at all. I suggested that he give Elyse
an uncontested divorce, split the business fifty-fifty, and
forget whatever he knows about Elyse's brother. When he
balked, I warned him that if he ever said word one about
Gianni, within twenty-four hours the same person would
be told about him and his free-flying fists."

Jennifer felt frightened for the first time that afternoon.

"What if he comes after you?"

"He wouldn't do that." Elyse's voice was almost inaudible. "He's afraid of powerful men. That's probably why he takes out all his aggression on women. It makes him feel important."

"I think I can safely say he won't come near you again." Josh bent down and kissed Elyse softly. "You can leave the boutique and concentrate on your new line without worrying about any interference from him."

It took Elyse several minutes to gather her thoughts. Until she did, the others remained silent.

"I've finished all the sketches, Jennifer, and when I get out of here, I'll put them into fabric samples." She sounded so shy and scared that Jennifer wanted to cradle her in her arms.

"Let's not worry about that now. You just get better."

"How did things go in Los Angeles?" David said, helping to shift the conversation away from Mario.

"The verdict still isn't in, but I'm holding positive thoughts."

"And I think we're holding Elyse back from getting some well-needed rest," Josh said as he stood up and looked at Jennifer. "Your brother has put his doctor's face on, and I think he'd like us to leave. We are on our way."

As Jennifer followed Josh out of the hospital, she tried to understand her feelings. Her emotions were bouncing off each other like bumper cars in an amusement park. As indignant as she was concerning Mario's behavior, and as impressed with Josh's courage, it didn't erase the picture of Elyse clinging to Josh before they left.

"I can't believe that guy actually thought he could get away with all this," Josh said as he helped Jennifer into his car. "He had to know that sooner or later he was going to trap himself."

Charles had trapped himself, and Jennifer wondered if he, too, had expected to continue his double life without being discovered. She had thought about Charles often during Elyse's recitation. Jennifer found herself comparing her situation to her friend's. True, Charles had battered her emotionally, but had it been intentional? Had he meant to hurt her the way Mario had meant to hurt Elyse? Somehow she thought not.

"I'm not defending him, but sometimes people do things in spite of themselves," she said. She was thinking of Charles . . . but also of Terk.

Ever since Los Angeles, Jennifer had harbored the feeling that Terk was up to his ears in something that could drown him if he weren't careful. Although their relationship had resumed its previous nonsexual nature, they were closer than they had been before. They had established a bond, and that bond permitted certain confidences. She knew, for instance, that he planned to tell Deirdre he was leaving. She also knew that he was about to make the last payment on his debt, but something else nagged at her. Something he didn't say. Questions he refused to answer. She wanted to help him, but she didn't know how. There were too many unknowns and unknowns frightened her.

"How's Charles?" Josh had stopped in front of her building.

"Fine," she said, fumbling for her keys.

"Jennie . . ."

"Josh, please."

He took her by the shoulders and forced her to face him.

"I love you Jennifer, and what's more, I think you love me."

I'm only beginning to realize how much, she thought, wishing she had the courage to tell him the truth. He lifted her chin, and as she looked into his eyes, she saw love and caring and the belief that she had been honest with him. Suddenly, every instinct she had told her to tell him what had happened and allow him to help her the way he had helped Elyse. Every instinct but one—pride.

It all seemed so ironic. She had rejected Josh to chase rainbows in her youth, because she had thought he didn't offer enough. Now, it appeared that he had it all, but she was coming to know that sometimes all was not enough. It seemed ironic, too, that in the eyes of Josh and perhaps the rest of the world, she projected the image of a self-assured woman, someone totally in control of her life. In truth, she had always relied upon her men for support. First her brother, then Josh, then Charles and, most recently, Terk. She couldn't afford to do that anymore. She had to be her own woman. She had to know herself completely, why she had failed as a wife and succeeded as a businesswoman, her assets as well as her liabilities. And she especially had to accept herself. Only then would she be able to commit herself to anyone, especially Josh. But until that time, she had to be alone.

"Jennie, I don't know what's going on inside that beautiful head of yours, but I hope you work it out. For both our sakes."

Jennifer opened the car door and turned to Josh, her face thoughtful and just a little scared.

"I hope so too," she said.

Twenty-Three

"I won't allow it!"

"Somehow, I don't remember asking you for permission," Terk said. "I'm leaving, and there's nothing you can do about it."

They stood at opposite ends of their bedroom, separated by more than space. While Terk tossed the last of his belongings in an open suitcase, Deirdre glowered at him, her ivory complexion blushed with rage.

"I'll fight you every step of the way. Do you hear me?"

Terk snapped his suitcase shut and started for the door, but Deirdre moved quickly to block his path.

"Why?" Terk stifled an urge to push her aside. It had been a difficult few hours, and he longed to be done with the whole scene. "Think about it," he said. "Without me in the picture, you can live happily ever after. I'm sure your father would be beside himself with joy. He might even buy you Ohio as a good riddance present."

"Don't do this to me." Deirdre grabbed his arm. Her voice tightroped between warning and despair. "I need you."

"For what? A punching bag?" Terk edged his way

closer to the door. "You've made my life a living hell. I'm burned to a crisp, chérie. There's nothing left to fry."

He opened the door and walked swiftly down the long hall that led to the circular staircase. Because he heard no footsteps behind him, he thought Deirdre had finally conceded defeat, but just as he placed his foot on the first step, she came running after him.

"I need you!" Her voice was shrill with panic. "Don't you believe me?"

"Frankly, no."

"But I do. I always have. Why do you think I married you? As you have said so often, I could have had anyone I wanted. You were right. I could have." She followed him down the steps, her voice rising as they went. "But I wanted a man. A man who would love me and let me love him in return. A man who would make me feel like a woman and not like a bank book."

"I tried," Terk said. "God knows, I tried."

"Did you?" Deirdre stood beneath the crystal chandelier that dominated the entrance hall. "You were so caught up in defending your pride and your manhood that you refused to allow yourself to love me. Instead, you competed with me."

"And you always won, didn't you?"

"You thought so." Her eyes began to water. "It does take two to make a marriage, Terk, and where I may have been emotionally absent much of the time, you were never really there."

Her words were like acid on a wound, and for an instant, he recognized truth in what she had said, but he had waited too long to leave her to debate the intricacies of their marriage now. He lifted his suitcases and, without looking at her, went toward the door.

"I love you." The words were strangled, but they stabbed at him enough to compel him to turn around.

She sat crumpled on the floor of the majestic foyer, her shoulders bent like a broken doll, her face buried in her hands. When she looked up, her cheeks were streaked with tears, and she reminded him of an exhausted child, a toddler eager to stop pretending to be a grown-up and return to the safety of being cared for.

"I love you," she said again, between sobs. "Don't you

see that? I've always loved you. You've been my strength and my support. I can't survive without you."

Terk had expected anger. He had even anticipated a few tears. But there was an honesty in her eyes that jarred him.

"You have a strange way of expressing love, Deirdre."

"I'll change. Or at least I promise to try. Just don't leave me. Help me. I don't know any other way."

Terk stared at her as if she were a stranger. At that moment, so pathetically vulnerable, she was.

"No, I don't think you know any other way. That's why I don't think it'll ever work for us."

"It can work. I know it can." Her eyes pleaded with him, but he made no move. "You always came on so rough and gruff. I thought you wanted a woman who matched your strength. I didn't want you to discard me or ignore me the way my father ignored my mother. She was weak and submissive, and he walked all over her. I swore I'd never be treated like that."

"Maybe you overplayed your part," Terk said, astounded. "It's too late, Deirdre." He walked to the door, his suitcase unexpectedly heavy.

"You're making a mistake. You'll see that."

Terk tried to close his ears, but her voice rebounded off the walls. Oddly enough, it projected warning, not hostility. He stared at the woman who had been his wife. Her blonde hair was disheveled, and her satin robe wrinkled around her legs. She appeared fragile and wanting, needy even here, fortressed by her wealth. The picture startled Terk, and for a moment, he felt as if a magnet were pulling him back against his will. Quickly, he twisted the brass doorknob that led to the outside. Closing the door behind him was one of the hardest things he would ever have to do.

Deirdre wasn't sure how long she remained sprawled on the foyer floor, but when she finally picked herself up and went to the library, her legs wobbled and her body felt chilled. She poured herself a brandy and added a few logs to the fire, until they spit and crackled, relieving the silence. She wondered if Terk was with Zena. She wondered if he was holding her in his arms and making love to her. Deirdre saw him stroking the other woman's body and felt her own insides ache with desire. She saw him caressing Zena and pulled her robe tighter, pressing the cool fabric against her skin. She envisioned him kissing Zena, and soon, hot tears washed away the unsettling mirage.

She hadn't meant for it to turn out this way, but perhaps Terk was right. It was too late now.

He was gone, and, yes, her father would be thrilled. But her father's bed wouldn't seem empty and cold because of Terk's absence. And her father's life wouldn't suddenly turn stale and meaningless. Deirdre refilled her brandy glass and paced the library, trying to clear her head. She loved Terk, and she wanted him back. She concocted one scheme after another and discarded each one. That was how she had lost him. And then, Deirdre contacted the one person she knew could help her; the one person who would understand the hollow pain she was feeling and the insidious desperation that had invaded her soul. Deirdre called her mother.

Twenty-Four

J ennifer's calendar was as crowded as a rush-hour bus. She had meetings all day, both in and out of the office. As she watched the snow fall outside her window, she hoped that the storm would hold off until later that evening. With even the slightest bit of precipitation, traffic snarled, and pedestrians with oversized umbrellas turned sidewalks into obstacle courses. She wished she could rearrange her schedule, but the only possible sacrifices appeared to be lunch with Elyse and a five-thirty squash date.

She was about to call Elyse when Hilary West strode into her office dressed in corduroy jodhpurs, high boots, and a fringed cowboy shirt.

"Take a good look," Hilary said, pushing her glasses on

top of her head. "The next time you see me, I shall be garbed in one of those snappy white jackets with the sleeves that tie around the back."

Hilary slumped down in the chair facing Jennifer's desk, dropping her clipboard on her lap.

"Before you order padded Levelors for your cell, would you like a cup of coffee?" Hilary nodded, and Jennifer poured two cups of hot coffee from the ceramic pot she kept next to her desk.

"Thanks to Bradford Helms and Gwendolyn Stuart, there isn't a judge in this country who, at this very minute, wouldn't find me terminally insane!" Hilary gulped her coffee and then continued. "They've turned this April cover girl project into a major competition. Each one has sent at least twenty perfect-for-the-pineapple girls up to see me, and not one of them has ever been within a thousand miles of Hawaii. I can now state, with full confidence, that I have interviewed every Oriental model in the city of New York!"

"There are no Hawaiian girls registered with the agencies?"

"Not a one, but I think I've solved our problem."

"We can't send a crew to Hawaii, Hilary. There's no time."

"And no need. I called Columbia and asked them for the names of any Hawaiian students registered at the university. I also called NYU. Standing outside your office are five authentic aloha girls."

"Well, don't just sit there feeling smug. Let's have a look."

Hilary left Jennifer's office and returned with five bewildered-looking young women in tow. Jennifer smiled to herself, The halls of *Jolie* were certainly a far cry from the halls of ivy. Two advertising department secretaries were trying out iridescent roller skates, and Brooke was holding a loud impromptu meeting with Patrick Graham.

Brooke had become a problem, behaving like a pesky mosquito, buzzing around Jennifer's office as if she knew something Jennifer didn't. Often Jennifer would walk by Brad's office only to find Brooke leaning over his desk, whispering to the publisher in a most conspiratorial way. If she walked into Brad's office, all conversation stopped.

Jennifer couldn't help but suspect that Brooke was plotting something, but she had no clue as to what it might be.

She turned her attention to the five nervous young women, trying to put them at ease. While she chatted about schools and vacations, Hilary went to work with a Polaroid camera, taking shots of each cover girl candidate. Now she spread the Polaroids on Jennifer's desk. As Jennifer studied them, she could see that three of the young women were completely wrong. The camera either flattened their features or sharpened angles, making them look hard and unattractive. The other two—Nina Kahala and Loki Pouna—were promising. Both were tall and model-thin. The more she looked at Loki's high cheekbones and clear, toffee-colored skin, the more she wanted to use her for the beauty story.

But Nina Kahala was Jennifer's cover girl. There was a delicate sensuality in her large, sloe eyes and blue-black hair. Her skin was a soft, milky tan that reminded Jennifer of cappuccino, and would make a stunning base for the bright makeup tones expected for spring. Jennifer could just picture her with a red hibiscus, Hawaii's state flower, poking out from behind an ear, with bare shoulders necklaced in a tiny floral lei.

Jennifer interviewed each girl and asked each to sign release forms. Then, Hilary ushered them out to the reception room. In a few minutes, she returned for Jennifer's verdict.

"Bring Loki and Nina to Gwen, Brad, Bettina, and Marnie," Jennifer said. "I don't think we can use the other three photographically, but I'm going to speak to the features editor about using them for an article on how Hawaiians feel about the mainland. As for you, you can congratulate yourself on a stroke of genius. Nina and Loki are perfect, with just that unknown innocence we need for an issue like this. Well done, Ms. West."

"Thank you, Ms. Cranshaw." Hilary nodded. She was beaming. "I have one more item on my agenda. I understand there's a mysterious new collection being featured in April. If you need models, you're running late."

Jennifer smiled at Hilary. She was good at her job; efficient, dedicated, and enthusiastic.

"I've got the model, but thanks for the reminder about time. I'll get on it immediately. In fact, on your way out, would you ask Patrick if he can come in here?"

While she waited, Jennifer checked her calendar again. Her days were filled with meetings and most nights she brought work home. Her few off hours were taken up with exercise classes, an occasional theater outing with Sarah whenever David was tied up, or dinner with Elyse.

With Charles there had been the concert series at the Philharmonic, ballet at the New York State Theater, and command performances at every Broadway opening, but those were prescribed weeknight activities. What did they do on weekends? Did they do anything spontaneously? Somehow, Jennifer couldn't remember very much. They both worked late a great deal, and they both traveled. Jennifer played squash and tennis. Charles played handball and swam. Occasionally, Charles worked on his stamp collection while Jennifer did needlepoint. They watched television and read—different programs and different books. In many ways, life without Charles was the same as life with Charles. The thought disturbed her.

"You wanted to see me?" Patrick stood before her desk, his manner distracted and uncomfortable.

"I need you to handle a special shooting for me," she said, asking him to take a seat, wondering why he kept looking back toward the hall. "As you know, a special line of clothes has been designed for the April issue. I'd like to have the designer, Elyse de Marco, photographed in her own designs, and I'd like you to oversee the sitting."

"Okay." He lit one cigarette from the other. "Do you have any thoughts on the way you'd like the layouts to look? Any specific design elements?"

He appeared nervous and uncharacteristically unsure of himself.

"The concept is native New York," she said, keeping a careful eye on Patrick. "Paradise comes to the big city. That sort of thing. Slick and slightly offbeat, I think. Use your imagination. You'll find Elyse a pleasure to work with, but her identity must be kept a secret." She was certain she saw him cringe. "I don't want any press leaks before we're ready to launch the publicity campaign."

"Jennifer. I don't like to get involved in political power plays."

"What are you talking about?"

"Brooke Wheeler just told me that whenever you scheduled this shoot, I was to tell her so that she could supervise it."

Jennifer was stunned. She was also angry. Brooke had overstepped her bounds once too often.

"What else did Brooke say?" Jennifer knew Patrick's loyalties were with her.

"She told me that Brad had authorized her to do this. Plus, she wants to know the name of the designer *before* I go ahead and hire a photographer. You're telling me this whole thing is top secret. What's going on?"

"Nothing I can't handle," Jennifer said, seething underneath her calm. "This project is to remain secret. When I first conceived this idea, I spoke to Brad about it. He agreed that I was to find the designer, arrange the shooting, and attend to all the publicity details. Until he tells me that has changed, I am still in charge of this project."

"What should I tell Brooke when she asks me about it?"

"Tell her to see me," Jennifer said. "You take care of hiring the photographer. I'll take care of Brooke Wheeler."

The snow was thicker. Huge flakes clung together, coming down in big white clusters that turned to brown slush the instant they hit the street. Jennifer left the General Motors Building where she had spent two hours negotiating a sizeable advertising package with Revlon and decided to walk part of the way home. People all around her were crowding onto buses or jousting for taxicabs. Mindful of the slippery sidewalks, Jennifer weaved her way through the crush of commuters and Christmas shoppers. It was the second week in December, and the Christmas countdown had begun.

The city looked festive with stores dressed up in tinsel and lights and brimming with holiday goodies. As Jennifer trudged up Madison Avenue, window-shopping along the way, she wished she could capture some of the spirit for herself. Jennifer always suffered from holiday depression, a real sadness that overcame her each year. It was a lonely time for her, a time that brought back memories of school vacations spent alone in an empty house and then, later, nights working in the bakery when other girls her age were out having fun. The bakery was open six-and-a-half days a week beginning before Thanksgiving, ending the day after New Year's; for Jennifer, the holidays were a test of physical endurance.

For the past eight years, thanks to Charles, Jennifer's annual melancholy had faded in a whirl of tree-trimming and party-going. This year, there would be no tree to trim, no parties to go to or give.

There would also be no Christmas dinner at the Cranshaws, at least not for Jennifer, and she would miss it. Usually, it was a wonderful day with a fire blazing, an apartment full of people, mulled apple cider and lots of caroling. She wondered if Charles were going and, if so, what he would tell his family about their situation. One thing was certain. He would attend Christmas Eve services with Celeste and Wyatt. That was another Cranshaw tradition, but one in which Jennifer had never participated. There, her presence would not be missed. As she thought about it now, browsing in a gift shop, she realized that the small exclusion had always triggered a recurrence of her holiday blues. She spent the evening alone waiting for Charles, and although she always managed to find something to keep her busy—last-minute gift wrapping or an old movie on TV—that night made it clear that Christmas didn't belong to her and she didn't belong with the Cranshaws.

Jennifer suddenly felt concern for Charles. He always had such mixed feelings about Christmas with his parents. He loved the traditions, the tree, the dining room bursting with food. But Wyatt had been so stingy with his affection and so miserly with his praise for Charles, that to see his brothers' children receiving the love he felt he had been denied affected him deeply. He rarely said anything about it, but Jennifer knew how much it hurt him. Now it seemed strange to realize that she had known when he was hurting, when he was upset, and when he was angry. How could she have been so sensitive to his shadings and so blind to his essence?

By the time Jennifer had reached Seventy-seventh Street, she had accumulated several bulky bundles. She had found Hanukah presents for Asa and Lia, a beautiful handmade robe for Elyse, and a glass pig filled with popcorn for Mimi, which she had had sent to the office. Just then, Jennifer remembered that Mimi lived on that block. On impulse, she pushed the buzzer with *Holden* printed next to it and waited for Mimi to respond. She was turning to leave, when Mimi finally answered.

When Jennifer reached the fourth floor of the brownstone, she was exhausted. She hadn't realized how tiring her trek uptown had been, and the steep flights of stairs hadn't helped. But when the door opened, Jennifer forgot all about her tiredness. Mimi looked dreadful. Her hair was pulled up in a scraggly ponytail, her face was pale.

"I was in the neighborhood, and I thought I'd look in on you," Jennifer said, leaning her umbrella against the wall and shaking the snow off her coat. "If you wouldn't mind a visit from Nanook of the North, I'd love to come in."

Jennifer couldn't tell from Mimi's smile whether she was glad to see her or merely being polite. She led Jennifer into the apartment, picking up stray newspapers as she went. She took Jennifer's coat while Jennifer removed her boots and blew warm breath into her hands.

"I was just about to make some soup," Mimi said. "Would you care to join me?"

Jennifer offered to help, but Mimi declined, pointing to a chair where Jennifer placed herself and studied the disarray around her. Mimi had been sick off and on for several weeks, and each time Jennifer had asked what was wrong, Mimi had concocted another illness. She'd claim to have the flu or a virus or a lingering cold, but there was never a runny nose or raspy cough to substantiate her story. Even now, Jennifer could find no signs of medication, only dirty coffee cups and empty cookie boxes.

Mimi's apartment was on the top floor with a huge skylight directly above the open sofa-bed. There were two plump armchairs covered in a small country print, an oak table with four Windsor chairs, and a desk against the long far wall. Despite the mess, Jennifer noted that the furniture was good and the knickknacks on the wrought iron étagère were expensive pieces of American folk art. Over the desk were three crib-size quilts, each in a differ-

ent pattern, each handmade. Mimi had a fire going in the
fireplace, but it seemed to do little to warm the room; Jennifer felt a draft.

"How are you feeling?" she asked.

"Much better, thanks." Mimi kept her back to the room
and stirred the canned soup as if its flavor depended on
perfectly timed revolutions of the spoon.

Jennifer could see that Mimi was in no mood for small
talk, so she picked up one of the newspapers near her
chair. It was from Houston and open to the society page.
Jennifer's eye immediately caught the wedding announcement of Mary-Beth Holden. The face in the photo bore a
strong resemblance to Mimi. Mary-Beth had the same
blonde hair, cut slightly shorter, the same aristocratic
neck, and the same smile, although from a smaller, less
seductive mouth. Jennifer quickly skimmed the article.
Miss Holden was attended by her two younger sisters,
the paper reported, at her marriage to Marcus Canfield
Egan, a vice-president of Holden Enterprises. The reception was held at the estate of Gresham and Patricia
Holden.

Mimi put the soup on the table, along with a loaf of
French bread and a crock of butter. Jennifer was so absorbed in the details of Mary-Beth's wedding that Mimi
had to call her twice to come to the table.

"I see your sister got married," Jennifer said, hoping to
brighten Mimi's somber mood. "Do you know the young
man?"

"I should. I almost married him myself."

Mimi's voice was bitter, but held no jealousy. "Daddy
couldn't palm that yo-yo off on me, so he gave poor
Mary-Beth my hand-me-downs."

"Maybe it was your sister's choice?"

Mimi buttered a thick slice of French bread. There was
something hard, almost brittle in her attitude.

"Doubtful. My sisters saw what happens to a child who
doesn't obey their Daddy. They're afraid to take the
chance of being disowned."

Jennifer's napkin slipped off her lap, and as she bent
down to pick it up, she noticed a large purple mark on
Mimi's leg. She had seen those welts before and had al-

ways wanted to ask about them, but never quite dared. Maybe tonight.

"Were you invited to the wedding?"

"Hardly. I'm not allowed inside the front gate, let alone in the parlor."

Jennifer felt chilled by the anger and resentment in her voice. She wanted to soothe Mimi, but she didn't know how.

They had finished dinner. Jennifer cleared the table. Mimi remained withdrawn and silent. As she pushed her bathrobe sleeves up to wash the soup bowls, Jennifer spied a gash on Mimi's forearm.

"Did you love this Marcus Egan?"

"No."

"Then why did you get engaged? Why did you let it go so long?"

Mimi handed Jennifer the clean dishes, and Jennifer dried them, putting them in the small cabinet above the sink. Mimi took her time answering Jennifer's question. When she did, she sounded as if she were talking more to herself than anyone else.

"I always tried to please my parents," she said with a shrug. "I suppose that dating Mark was the same as trying to get good grades in school. I tried to tell my father that I didn't love Mark and that I didn't think we'd be happy together, but Daddy wouldn't listen. Marcus Egan was his mogul-in-training, and in order to insure his loyalty to Holden Enterprises, he needed to marry into the family. I was the first in line."

"What happened to make you leave?"

Mimi wiped her hands on a dish towel and poured coffee into large mugs. When they had settled on the couch, Mimi leaned forward and looked directly into Jennifer's eyes.

"Do you like sex?"

The question startled Jennifer.

"Yes, I do."

"Me too. That's why I couldn't marry Mark. He wasn't the first man I'd ever slept with, but he was undoubtedly the worst. There was no way I could stand before God and swear to remain faithful to a man who left me completely cold. I would've had an affair on my honeymoon, and to me, that would've been worse than defying my father."

"So you ran away?"

"As far and fast as I could. I never told my father the real reason, because I'm sure he thought all his precious daughters were still virgins. I know I don't have to explain all this, but believe me, it wasn't as if I had slept with half of Texas." She stared down at her lap, her fingers rolling the hem of her robe. "I did tell my mother. Of all people, I had expected her to understand. She has an affair a year, but I guess she was afraid if she sided with me, Daddy might throw her out too."

"You're still terribly hurt, aren't you?"

When Mimi looked up, Jennifer thought she saw moisture in her eyes, but Mimi's mouth was tight. Defensiveness had wrapped itself around her like a cobra.

"I will admit that I had hoped he would be more concerned with my happiness than with securing an heir to his dynasty. I was wrong."

"He followed you here, didn't he?"

"That he did." Mimi rose from the couch and added a log to the fire, poking and jabbing at it until it caught fire. "We got into a terrible fight, and finally, I told him why I had jilted the man of his dreams. I told him that his wonderful, brilliant, up-and-coming protegé was a terrible fuck."

Mimi kept her back to Jennifer, but she could see by the stiff shoulders that the pain of the confrontation had returned.

"You know what he did?" Mimi swiveled around. Her face strained against the tears welling up in her eyes. "He called me a slut and told me he was glad to be rid of me."

Jennifer felt as if someone had just punched her. She felt anger and pity and sadness. Mimi was fighting to retain her dignity, but when she returned to the couch, she began to cry. Jennifer went to her and wiped her eyes with a handkerchief.

"Mimi. I've noticed that every once in a while, you have bruises on your arms and legs. You've also been out sick. Does any of this have anything to do with your father?"

"In a roundabout way."

"Do you want to tell me about it?"

"I don't think you want to know."

"People don't get bruises doing pretty things."

Mimi searched the cushions of the sofa for her cigarettes. She lit one and watched the smoke rise toward the skylight.

"Have you ever heard of Lady Belle?" she asked.

"I can't say that I have. Should I know her?"

"Not really. Lady Belle is a porno star. She does top-of-the-sheets tricks with hired men, and in certain circles, she's quite famous."

Jennifer stared at Mimi.

"And you're Lady Belle." She said it softly, hoping Mimi would say no, knowing that she wouldn't.

"Lady Belle. Star of the triple-X movies. Queen of the convention circuit. That's me!"

"Why?"

Mimi puffed on her cigarette, sorting her thoughts.

"Money. Revenge. Spite. Maybe all three. I'm not sure."

"How did it start?"

"Not innocently. I came on to a man I thought was something special. I thought he would make a wonderful lover, and I was very brazen about it. Then he told me I ought to be in pictures. Dirty pictures. I don't know what possessed me, but I agreed."

"And the bruises?"

"They're recent. When it first started, things went okay. This guy, my agent, was never on the set. He had some other dude acting as the director, and it was just me and some good-looking stud who could keep it up long enough to make things interesting." Then, Mimi laughed, but it was a sound that rang with hurt and self-disgust. "We were all in it for the money, even the guys. Most of them were putting themselves through school."

Suddenly, Mimi looked shy. "Believe it or not, I'm seeing one of them rather steadily. You'd like him, Jennifer. I know it sounds funny, but he's really very fine. It's just that people do strange things when they're desperate."

Jennifer couldn't remember ever seeing a porno movie, let alone meeting someone who starred in them. She felt as if she had been living in a cave. She was shocked and maybe even a bit repelled, but Mimi was in pain, and right now, that was all that mattered.

"The bruises?"

"Right. Things were pretty straight for a while, but then, Herr Director developed some strange tastes. The nice guys were out, and in their place were sleazy creatures who got their rocks off by beating women. Jennifer, I know you're trying to help, but it would only embarrass both of us if I continued."

Jennifer put her arm around Mimi and lifted the girl's chin so that Mimi faced her. There was such regret and humiliation in Mimi's eyes that all Jennifer's thoughts of approval or disapproval faded.

"You don't have to say anything else, unless you'd like to tell me the name of the creep who got you into all of this?"

Mimi backed away. "I can't do that."

"Why are you protecting him?"

"Because he's really a nice guy. He was desperate, too. He never wanted to be involved in something this seamy, but he had a debt to pay."

A shudder ran through Jennifer. A thought began to incubate. Whenever Terk spoke to Mimi, she appeared tense and up-tight. Terk had a debt to pay. He was a wonderful lover. It was not inconceivable that Mimi might have come on to him. But no. It was inconceivable that Terk would resort to something like this. Jennifer shook her head. The thoughts and the pictures were there, but she refused to put them together. Concentrate on Mimi, she told herself. Forget that Terk said he had a side venture that paid very well.

"What does all this have to do with your father?"

Mimi was crying. "He called me a slut. A part of me wanted to prove him right." She looked at Jennifer, unable to stop herself from sobbing. "Do you want to hear my fantasy? It's sick. I know it's sick, but I used to pray that my father and his fine, upstanding friends who get together at least once a month to watch porno flicks, would rent one of mine. All I wanted was for him to see me up there, doing those things he imagined I did. It would serve him right. It would humiliate him the way he humiliated me."

"Maybe you hurt him enough when you ran away. He may be one of those men who loves but can't express it properly. He was angry. He said whatever came into his head, but I'll bet that deep down, he wanted to bundle you up and take you home."

"Then why didn't he?" She sounded like a little girl.

"Because any man who's achieved what your father has is burdened with an overdose of pride, and believe me, pride can prevent a person from doing things that just might make them the happiest."

"Are you saying I should go home?"

"Not necessarily."

"Then what should I do? I'm so ashamed."

"Learn from it. Don't waste the experience. Find something positive."

"I found Michael."

"Now find yourself."

"You make it sound so easy."

Jennifer looked at Mimi. There was no way for Mimi to know that Jennifer, too, was involved in a search for self, that Jennifer, too, was struggling with the strangling grip of pride.

"It's not easy, Mimi, but you can do it."

"You're very strong, Jennifer."

Only for others, Jennifer thought. *But I'm getting there.*

Twenty-Five

The door to Jennifer's office was closed, but nothing short of cement blocks could have muffled the noise in the hall. Loudspeakers had been turned on at four o'clock, and the air vibrated with bouncy Christmas carols. Typewriters clattered at a hurried-up pace. Telephones jangled. Excited voices called out to borrow a lipstick or a splash of cologne. And every once in a while, someone walked by and bellowed, "Ho! Ho! Ho!"

Upstairs, in the showroom, the annual *Jolie* Christmas party was about to begin. Jennifer's day had been hectic, and though she, too, was anxious to join the festivities, she still had copy to review and calls to return. Quickly, she read the copy, penciling changes on one piece, approving another, and reminding Brooke to include page rates on a third.

Then, she picked up her telephone messages. Deciphering Mimi's handwriting was like decoding the Rosetta Stone, but from what Jennifer could see, nothing was urgent. One struck her as odd, however. Her mother had called early that morning. "No message. Just wanted to chat." Rose never called her in the office and certainly not this time of year. She knew the bakery would be jammed with customers, but she picked up the phone anyway. She had dialed half the number when Mimi poked her head in.

"Jennifer, you have a visitor."

Before she had a chance to object, Mimi ushered in Celeste Cranshaw.

"I hope I'm not disturbing you." Mimi had gone, but Celeste remained by the door, waiting to be invited in.

Jennifer put down the phone and stared at her mother-in-law. No matter how uneasy Celeste looked, in no way did her discomfort equal Jennifer's. Under normal circumstances, Charles's family made her nervous with their rigid formality and prissy affectations, but now she felt positively skittish. There could be only one reason for this visit, and she was not prepared to discuss Charles. Especially not with his mother.

"Don't be silly. What a pleasant surprise." Jennifer got up and walked around her desk, hoping her mouth had obeyed and formed a smile, not a grimace. "I was just finishing up some last-minute chores."

"Your secretary mentioned something about a party. Perhaps this isn't a good time."

Jennifer wanted desperately to agree with her. "It's just an office gathering," she said. "It'll be going on for hours. I have plenty of time."

She helped Celeste out of her coat and led her to a chair. As she pulled up another chair for herself, she realized that in all the years she had been married, this was the first time she had ever been alone with Celeste. Her stomach somersaulted, and she grabbed a cigarette.

"I would ask how you are, but I can see that you're fine. You look lovely," Jennifer said. Actually, she thought Celeste looked pale and drawn. Her eyes were tired and her skin sallow.

"Thank you, dear. So do you. I don't think I've ever seen that outfit before."

Celeste's voice was pleasant, but tinged with mild disapproval. At first, Jennifer didn't understand. Then, she remembered that she was wearing one of Elyse's outfits. Celeste had never seen Jennifer in pants, let alone something as highly styled as these. They were pleated and full at the hips, tapering to just above the ankle where they ended in a narrow cuff. A raspberry angora sweater with full, blousy sleeves complemented the nubby tweed of the slacks, but the broad, dimpled shoulders must have put Celeste off.

"I found a wonderful new designer, Elyse de Marco. Everyone at the magazine thinks she's an up-and-comer." Why was she being so defensive? "I see you've been shopping too."

Jennifer pointed to the Saks Fifth Avenue bags sitting beside Celeste. For a hopeful second, she prayed that she had misinterpreted the purpose of this visit. Maybe it was nothing more than a spur-of-the-moment impulse.

"Have you been to Bloomingdale's?" she asked in a chatty, girl-to-girl voice. "They have the most fabulous boutique on the fifth floor. It's stocked with the best—"

"I spoke to Charles this morning." Celeste cut Jennifer short. "He called to tell me you won't be having Christmas dinner with us. May I ask why?"

Jennifer didn't know whether Celeste's imperious tone was born of anger or distress, but something inside her seethed. A rage Jennifer thought had calmed rekindled itself. How dare Charles put her in this position? How dare he leave the explanations to her?

"What did Charles say?"

"He told me you've decided to separate. Is that true?"

Jennifer's first instinct was to laugh. Celeste made it sound as if the separation had resulted from a rational discussion between two rational adults. *That's not the way it happened,* she wanted to scream. *I found him in bed with a man!*

"Yes, it's true." Jennifer swallowed her thoughts, wincing from the aftertaste they left in her mouth.

Celeste didn't respond. If she noticed Jennifer's agitation, she pretended not to. She sat quietly, not moving, her eyes focused on something beyond Jennifer's desk. Her hands were folded on her lap, and in spite of her thick woolen suit and fur hat, she looked as if she were in her living room, entertaining her bridge club.

"Was it something Charles did?"

Jennifer's breath caught in her throat. Was it possible she knew about Charles? No. Even if she suspected something, she would have repressed it. Anger bubbled inside Jennifer. She hated the idea of defending Charles. She thought about smashing Celeste's illusions about her precious son, of telling her what he was, of forcing Charles to defend himself. But she couldn't.

"It was no one's fault," she said, looking away.

Again, there was silence.

"Was it something I did?"

The question shocked Jennifer. For weeks, she had been obsessed with the subject of blame. She felt that the greatest portion of guilt rested with Charles. Yet, in a way, she did feel that Celeste was responsible, just as she felt that Wyatt had contributed to Charles's homosexuality. The one question she couldn't resolve was how big a role she herself had played.

"You've always been wonderful to me, Celeste. This has nothing to do with you." Jennifer's back began to throb, and as she reached for another cigarette, her spine twinged with pain.

"That's kind of you to say, but I know it hasn't been easy being a Cranshaw. Wyatt was not always as gracious as he might have been, and I know my other sons hurt you terribly. I can't help but feel that I should have done something about it."

For the first time since she had known Celeste, Jennifer

took the woman's hand. She was surprised at how small it was and how warm.

"Charles and I just weren't making each other happy anymore." Had they ever really been happy with each other?

"Is there another man?"

The irony rocked Jennifer.

"No." She saw Charles in their bed. She heard Josh's rejection. "There's no one else."

"Maybe if there were children," Celeste said half to herself.

"Children don't keep people together."

"Sometimes they do."

Jennifer was extremely uncomfortable. Celeste seemed determined to find reasons and answers. Jennifer could have supplied them, but she would continue to hold her tongue. She would continue to hide the truth. Not to protect Charles or herself, but to protect Celeste. The truth would punish her most of all.

"Maybe," she said gently, "but in our case, it's irrelevant. There are no children."

Celeste nodded and fidgeted with her purse. Jennifer shifted in her seat, trying to find a position that would take some of the pressure off her back.

"Wouldn't it be better to try and work it out? Charles is a reasonable man. You're an intelligent woman. There must be some common ground."

"I don't think so."

Again, Celeste played with her purse, opening it, pretending to look for something, closing it. When she spoke, her eyes remained on the lizard bag.

"But then you'll be alone," she said in a whisper. "Nothing is as bad as being alone."

It was then that Jennifer knew Celeste had been speaking in code, using a between-the-lines language to talk about herself. She wasn't happy with Wyatt, but rather than own up to a mistake, she had elected to compromise. She didn't act. She reacted. She didn't think. She responded. Just to keep peace. Just so she wouldn't be alone. The thought made Jennifer shudder.

"I'll be all right," she said. "I have my work, and for now, that's enough."

"Is it?" Celeste's eyes were kind and caring as she reached out to her daughter-in-law. "I know it's rewarding, and certainly, at a time like this work can be a blessing, but don't make it your whole life, Jennifer."

"You sound like my mother." And Josh. And David. And even, Charles.

Celeste laughed and patted Jennifer's hand.

"Then you should definitely listen to your mother."

She rose from her chair and went over to one of the shopping bags, took out a package and handed it to Jennifer.

"I had planned to give you this on Christmas Day." A shy smile crossed her lips. "I ordered this quite a while ago. I hope it's not totally inappropriate."

Jennifer opened the box. In it was a large Christmas tree ornament, flattened on one side to hold a picture of her and Charles. They were sitting on the floor in front of the Cranshaws' tree, gift ribbons festooned around their necks, their faces bright and cheerful. Jennifer felt her hands tremble.

"It's lovely." She had tears in her eyes.

"You're very special to me, Jennifer. I don't want to lose you."

Celeste's voice broke, and something inside Jennifer hurt for the both of them. Today they had touched each other, and Jennifer regretted all the years they had spent standing at arm's length. In the past, she had viewed Celeste as a caricature, a sketch without substance, but she had been wrong. Before her was a woman fully painted, with shadings and shadows, colors and tones.

Jennifer hugged her mother-in-law, wondering why she had never hugged her before. As Celeste's arms returned the embrace, Jennifer allowed her tears to fall. She didn't know if she'd ever see Celeste again.

The showroom was brimming with holiday spirit. Pine garlands strung with tiny white lights scalloped the walls. Jennifer's neon pineapple hung in front of the projection screen, dripping with tinsel. A huge Christmas tree stood to one side, decorated with ornaments donated by everyone on the staff, each ornament meant to symbolize another aspect of the magazine—snapshots of staff members, miniature *Jolie* covers, and Christmas balls painted with the slogan of each *Jolie* promotion.

Most of the guests were laughing and singing along with the carols being piped in, shaking hands and wishing each other well. Only Brad looked out of synch. He stood by the bar, his face set in a bah-humbug scowl. He had just spent an hour sitting outside Selwyn Fellows's office. For two days Brad had been asking for an appointment, but Fellows's secretary had been unusually evasive, almost curt. Today, knowing that Fellows was about to depart for Christmas in the Bahamas, Brad had decided to take matters into his own hands, but Fellows must have slipped out his back door.

It was a full month before the closing date for the April issue, and already the figures were ahead of even the most liberal expectations. They were seventy pages over their usual April bookings, and the salesmen were still getting calls. Just last week, a medium-priced sportswear firm, Morceaux, which had been a *Jolie* advertiser until two years before, had called Brad about a six-page insert. In fact, the last month had marked a dramatic upswing. Neiman-Marcus had called Jennifer with a yes on the fee-paid promotion, signing on for several of their stores in key cities. Other retailers had followed. In all four major sales regions, top-flight stores had committed to The Big Pineapple. Even the secondary promotion was going well. More than seven hundred smaller stores had applied for the Pineapple paper promotion.

Brad should have been ecstatic, but instead, he was consumed with panic. First, it was too much of a coincidence. It looked as if the same hand that had pushed *Jolie* down was now lifting it up. Second, none of this was worth anything if he couldn't convince the Fellows board of the upswing. He had gone to the chief executive's office with a sheaf of papers and a speech he hoped would help forestall a sale. There was no reason for Fellows to go to such lengths to avoid him, unless the sale were already a *fait accompli.*

"Did you get the present I left you?" Brooke Wheeler's voice startled him.

"Yes, I did. It was lovely, Brooke. A bit extravagant, but greatly appreciated." He didn't tell her that he had returned the Cartier lighter the very same day he found it on his desk.

"I have another present for you, but this one you have to collect in person."

Brad had been expecting this. As he sipped his scotch, he felt his pulse quicken. Even over the din he heard Brooke invite him to her apartment after the party. And he heard himself decline.

It was a triumph in control. Brooke looked sensational. Her thick honey-colored mane flew wild about her face. Her voluptuous body was encased in a pair of suede pants and a sweater. He knew that if he looked at her too long he might weaken. He felt her hips touch his, and her musky scent filled his nostrils. They had already spent one incredible night together, a night to be regretted.

Brad wished the episode had been less exotic, less spectacular, because now he knew that Brooke was using his delight in her sexual expertise as a weapon. She had placed him on a tightrope, and he had to work at keeping his balance. She seemed to think that their single intimacy entitled her to favors. She had stepped up her complaints about Jennifer, become quite brazen with her demands. She wanted Jennifer's job, and she had said as much. While Brad still questioned Jennifer's overzealous dedication, he had refused to give Brooke a definite answer. In response, he noticed that she began to question him about his divorce, the trial date, the name of his lawyer, the names of his children. There was no question that, if scorned, Brooke would go to any length to extract revenge. He had made a mistake with Brooke. He only hoped it wasn't fatal.

"Merry Christmas, darling." Brad had never been so glad to see Gwendolyn Stuart in his life. She swooped over to him and kissed him on both cheeks. She acknowledged Brooke with a peck on the cheek and a brief nod.

"I've just seen the proofs on that Nina Kahala, and they are divine! We're going to do it. This April issue is going to be simply smashing!"

Gwen's excitement was infectious, and for the first time in days, Brad felt hopeful. Gwen rambled on about the success of the cover shooting, singing Jennifer's praises.

Brad sensed Brooke's displeasure, but he made no effort to bring her into the conversation. When Gwen began to detail Marnie Dobbs's report from Hawaii, Brooke excused herself and wandered off. Brad watched her over Gwen's shoulder. He shuddered as he saw the vindictive look in her eye.

"You just missed the comedy routine of the year." Terk greeted Jennifer at the door, handed her a glass of white wine, and led her into the room. "The Brooke and Brad Show."

"I didn't know they were scheduled to perform."

"Actually, it was a private showing, limited to those with the good sense to keep an eye on them. You should have seen it. She nuzzles next to him and whispers whatevers in his ear. He reconnoiters the room and then looks at Brooke with lust in his eyes. Her hips press against his. His hips linger and then prudently pull away. They chat. Gwen enters stage right. Brooke exits stage left. It was a howl!"

Jennifer didn't find Terk's anecdote amusing. It only confirmed her suspicion about Brooke.

"You are certainly worth waiting for, but what the hell took you so long?" Terk looked at Jennifer with an appreciative eye. "I was beginning to think you weren't going to make it."

"I had a visitor." The meeting with Celeste had clouded her mood, and as she sipped her wine, she tried to generate some enthusiasm.

"Was it a tall, dark and handsome stranger?" Terk asked.

"Hardly. It was my soon to be ex-mother-in-law."

"There must be a full moon. My mother-in-law took me to lunch today."

"How was it?"

"Interesting."

"How's Deirdre doing?" she said, realizing that she had never asked Celeste the same question about Charles.

"Not too well according to Winnie. Since she's not the buttinsky type, I tend to believe her."

Deirdre had closeted herself in their Westchester home, refusing to see anyone but her mother. Even the great

Parker Walling had been denied an audience, and that, Terk found more revealing than anything else Winnie had said. Lately, Terk had begun to wonder how different their lives might have been if he had challenged Deirdre's father head on. Even if he had lost, he might have won Deirdre.

"How are things going with Zena?" Jennifer spotted Mimi and her boyfriend Michael at one of the buffet tables.

"She works too damned much! Night after night, she's holed up in some darkroom. I hardly get to see her."

"You sound jealous." Jennifer wondered if Charles had ever felt that way.

"It's tough competing with a telephoto lens. Although, I will confess, I've been working on my zoom technique. It's almost perfect, but I could use a little more practice. Interested?"

"Fascinated, but no thanks."

There was a nervous edge to Terk's voice that worried Jennifer. In Los Angeles, Terk had spoken of Zena with reverence, as if she were an angel, complete with halo and wings. Absence and time had woven a cloak of fantasy around her. But now Terk sounded disillusioned. Had he fallen in love with a memory?

"Did you meet Mimi's friend?" Jennifer pointed toward the buffet table and then turned back to Terk to watch his reaction. There was none. His face was expressionless.

"No, should I have?"

"I thought you and Mimi were friends." Jennifer disliked testing Terk, but so many separate thoughts were begging to be put together.

"Mimi's my friend. Brad's secretary's my friend. That doesn't mean they come to me for boyfriend approval." He obliged Jennifer by looking over in Mimi's direction. "He looks nice enough, but why are you playing mother hen?"

"Because I like Mimi, and she's had a tough time lately."

"What kind of tough time?"

Jennifer felt her stomach flutter.

"She let herself get involved in something that wasn't quite kosher." Jennifer didn't know how far to take this conversation. After all, she was merely playing a hunch. If she were wrong, she would have betrayed Mimi's confidence. And if she were right? She didn't know what she would do if she were right.

Suddenly, it didn't matter. From the other side of the room, someone called her name. Her brother, David, was pushing his way through the crowd, and the look on his face was frightening. Jennifer remembered her mother's call. Why hadn't she called her back? Maybe Marty had burned himself the way he had a few years ago. Maybe he was sick. Or Sarah was sick. No. David wouldn't be here if it were Sarah or the kids. It was Josh. Something had happened to Josh.

"Jennifer, come with me!" David grabbed her arm and steered them out of the showroom as fast as he could.

"What is it? What's wrong?" Jennifer's heart palpitated, and she felt cold.

David brought her over to a couch and sat her down.

"I've been trying to reach you," he said. "Sarah's already called Charles at his office."

Why would anyone call Charles about Josh? Jennifer's mind was racing. Names. Faces. Situations. Each one more terrifying than the last.

"Did something happen to Celeste?" If he said yes, she'd feel terrible. If he said no, would she have the courage to face the alternatives? "She was just here. Was it an accident?"

David shook his head. "It's not Celeste. It's Mom."

Jennifer began to tremble. Questions formed on her lips, but the words wouldn't come.

"She had a heart attack."

"Oh, God!" Jennifer felt as if she couldn't breathe. Her mouth went dry, and her body shook uncontrollably. "But she called me this morning."

"It happened an hour ago."

"I never got back to her." Jennifer's voice was strangled, almost incoherent. "I was busy. And then Celeste came. I started to call, but . . . I was busy."

David heard the guilt. He felt her pain. He took her in his arms and cradled her like a child, stroking her back, wishing he could prescribe something that would soothe the "should-haves."

"But she's going to be okay, isn't she?" Jennifer pulled away, her eyes pleading with him. "You saw her. You're going to make her better, aren't you, David?"

On her face was the same bewildered desperation he had seen when she was thirteen, wrapped in bandages, hooked up to machines. He had felt helpless then. He felt helpless now.

"Jennifer. She's dead."

Twenty-Six

The funeral director's office was too hot and too bright. Jennifer tried to concentrate, but her head felt fuzzy. Thoughts drifted in and out, surfacing and then retreating, refusing to link together in any logical sequence. She heard Celeste saying, "I don't want to lose you." She pictured Rose having a heart attack in the bakery. She heard David telling her that Sarah had called Charles. She imagined Marty's face when he got the call about Rose.

"Is the plot in Mr. Sheldon's name?"

Jennifer wasn't sure how her father had gotten to the hospital, but a doctor had taken him home and sedated him. Sarah was at the house now, making calls and tending to Marty. David and Jennifer had come straight from New York to the mortuary so that they could attend to the business of burying their mother.

A large man with thick black hair and pasty white skin sat behind a mammoth desk. His face was appropriately sober, his voice deep and monotonous.

"Does your father wish the casket opened or closed?"

Jennifer wasn't really paying attention, but she knew he was asking questions and filling out forms, diligently recording the facts of Rose's life in triplicate. David responded to each inquiry with nonemotional precision. If Jennifer hadn't been seated next to him, she, like the mortician across from them, might have thought he was in complete control. But every so often, she felt him shiver, and there were tiny beads of sweat dotting his palms.

"Would you like a notice to appear in the newspaper? We use a standard form that lists family members as well as the time and place of the service."

The room was deliberately muted. Everything was pale blue with subtle stripes and nondescript patterns. Paintings depicting the tranquility of the heavens and the peacefulness of mountaintops hung on the walls. And each table bore a lacquered plaque with Biblical quotations intent on explaining the meaning of death and the necessity of acceptance.

"Mrs. Cranshaw?" The man was speaking to her. "I need you to select something for your mother to wear."

Jennifer stared at him, unable to respond. Then, her eyes wandered to a paper bag sitting on the floor next to the desk. In it were Rose's uniform and her shoes.

"And if you could, would you tell me how she wore her hair and her makeup? We want to prepare her properly."

Jennifer shook her head as she felt a wave of nausea wash over her.

"I know this is difficult, Mrs. Cranshaw, but I need your assistance. Perhaps if you had a recent photograph?"

"Maybe at home, I'm not sure." How did he expect her to think? He was speaking about her mother in the past tense. He was using words like "the deceased" and "the body." He wanted to "prepare her" and arrange for her "eternal resting place."

David reached into his jacket, took out his wallet and handed the man a snapshot.

"Pulled back," she said quickly, hoping the embarrassment she felt hadn't translated itself into a blush. "She wore it pulled back with barrettes." Tears gathered, and her throat tightened. "It never stayed, though. She was always pushing it off her face. And she loved pink lipstick. It didn't go with her hair, but that's all she wore. Pink. The brighter, the better."

Hot, puffy droplets trickled down her face. How many times had she tried to get Rose to change her hairstyle? How many lipsticks had she brought her? It never seemed to matter to anyone else. Right now, she couldn't imagine why it had mattered to her.

"Thank you, Mrs. Cranshaw." The man was smiling at her, "She'll look lovely, I assure you." He rose from his chair and walked to the door. "If you'll both excuse me, I have some things to check on."

Jennifer stared at the empty chair for a moment and then turned to David.

"Did I ever tell her she looked lovely?"

Her brother kissed her softly on the cheek, tasting the salt of her tears. He wiped her eyes with his handkerchief and then dabbed at his own. Damp tresses stuck to Jennifer's skin. Gently, he brushed them aside. "She thought you were beautiful."

Jennifer nodded. There were pictures of her all over her parents' house and newspaper clippings tacked up behind the cash register in the bakery. Why didn't she have a picture of Rose?

"I still have so much I want to say to her," she said. "I'm not ready for her to die."

"We'd never be ready," he said, trying to blink away faces of patients he had lost and families he had consoled.

"But we were just beginning to understand each other."

David remembered all the fights he had refereed, all the anger that had passed between Jennifer and Rose. At the time, he had dismissed it as part of a process, but now, seeing the caul of sadness that enveloped Jennifer, he knew that she was remembering and suffering from regret.

"She understood you better than you think she did."

He took her in his arms, and they both wept, holding onto each other like toddlers in a thunderstorm.

"David?" She had broken from his embrace. She was trembling, and all color had drained from her face. "Was I a good daughter?"

Before he could answer, the funeral director returned with a sheaf of papers in his hand and a key.

"Dr. Sheldon. Mrs. Cranshaw. Would you follow me?"

"Where are we going?" Jennifer was frightened. Rose was there, in that building. He had said so. Was he taking them to see her? Jennifer didn't want to go.

"We must pick out a casket for your mother."

He led them out of the office, across the hall, and into a dimly lit room. It was cooler in here, and Jennifer felt a chill run through her. Standing on carpeted pedestals were sample caskets, different sizes, different materials, each one softly illuminated by its own spotlight. The carpeting was dark, creating the illusion that the coffins were hovering in midair.

Jennifer felt faint. The mortician was talking, explaining each item, leading David from one to the other. His voice droned and soon became a noisome echo. Jennifer stood by the door, staring at the coffins, her vision blurred. For a moment, she imagined that she had slipped beneath the earth into an ebony cavern. Hoarse whispers welcomed her to the netherworld of the dead. She couldn't see anyone, but she heard them. They were pounding on the boxes, trying to get out, pleading with her to help them.

"I can't," she yelled. "I can't do it!"

David ran to her and tucked his arm around her waist for support. The funeral director's head snapped sharply in her direction. The ghostly mirage faded, and as it did, her voice broke into loud, mournful sobs.

"I don't want to pick out anything. I don't want my mother in a box. I don't want my mother dead!"

It was bitter cold, and harsh, blustery winds howled through the streets, shattering the fragile silence of the large chapel. A bay of stained glass windows glowed at the insistence of a strong winter sun and brilliant rainbows surrounded the altar like a gossamer cloak. Rose Sheldon lay in an open casket just below the pulpit, her body pillowed and bumpered with white satin, her sepulchre guarded by two large baskets of white flowers.

Marty Sheldon stood by his wife's side, his body swaying to the uneven rhythm of his keening, his anguish ricocheting off high-vaulted walls and empty pews. He prayed. He wept. He beseeched God to help him. But most of all, he told Rose how much he loved her; how desolate his life would be without her. David stood next to his father, his strong face lined with grief, his tears flowing unchecked. Sarah tried to comfort her husband, and as Jennifer watched from the back of the chapel, her sense of isolation increased. Her father was with Rose. David was with Sarah. And her only companion was a throbbing, unrelenting sorrow.

Last night, her companions had been girlish toys and childhood memories. She had stayed in her old room, and despite the tranquilizer David had given her, she hadn't slept. Images of Rose had danced in the darkness. Happy times, sad times, one by one, the past had paraded before her like scenes in the play that was her life. The visions taunted her until she begged for an encore, a second chance at being a daughter. There were so many things she might have done differently. So many words she might never have spoken.

"Jennifer?"

Charles's voice hit her like a slap. Her body stiffened, and when she turned to him, her face flushed.

"I came to be with you," he said. Gray shadows rimmed his eyes, and she noticed an uncommon sallowness in his skin. He moved to touch her arm, but she backed away. "I also wanted to pay my respects to your mother."

Jennifer lowered her eyes. Often, in recent weeks, she had tried to summon up the courage to confront him, but each time her resolve had buckled. She had left his messages unanswered, his calls unreturned.

"Is there anything I can do to help?"

"You've done enough!" She heard the sharpness and immediately regretted it. "I'm sorry. I didn't mean it that way," she stammered. "I meant it was very thoughtful of you to bring me the clothes."

Charles had come to Marty's while she and David had been at the mortuary. He was gone by the time they arrived, but he had left a suitcase packed with everything she might need for a week's stay, including the outfit she wore today.

"You always did have marvelous taste," she said, fingering the black silk dress. "But you didn't have to buy all this for me."

A veil shaded Charles's eyes. When he spoke, his words were measured.

"You changed the locks. I didn't want to embarrass you by asking for a key."

She was embarrassed. Her cheeks reddened, and she looked away. If he had gone to their apartment, he would have known how completely she had banished him from her life. She had trashed even the smallest memento, voiding his presence as if he had never existed.

Surprisingly, she began to feel a quiet admiration for Charles. In a way, coming here had been quite daring. There was no way for him to predict her response to his appearance. She might have screamed at him and told him to leave. She might have snubbed or humiliated him. Yet he had come anyway.

"I also want to thank you for spending time with my father last night," she said with deliberate softness. "Sarah said you were a great help in settling him down."

"He was fighting the sedative. He needed to talk, and I was available to listen."

"Don't be so modest. Sarah said you were wonderful with him." In fact, she had raved about Charles, about how caring and compassionate he had been, how gentle and understanding.

"It wasn't a chore, Jennifer." He looked down the aisle at Marty. "Your father is suffering. I wanted to help."

"I know," she said, following Charles's gaze. "He looks so frail."

"He's lost his wife. It's very painful."

His words rocketed through Jennifer like bullets, hitting her insides with explosive force.

"I can't talk to you about this!" Her voice cracked, and her hands jittered.

"I'll leave." He started to go, but she grabbed his arm.

"I don't want anyone to know. Not today."

Fear insinuated itself on her face, darkening her eyes, and tightening her lips. Charles sympathized with her. He knew what it was to hide behind a lie, to keep a truth from one's family, perhaps even from one's self.

"I won't give away any secrets," he said. "I'll do whatever is expected, and I'll do it well. I'm very adept at playing roles."

"Charles, I . . ." She heard the bitter melancholy in his voice. He was angry and hurt, and she didn't blame him.

"This isn't the time!"

He broke free of her grasp and started down the aisle. She watched as he spoke to her family. She was about to join them when the rabbi summoned them into another room. Slowly, she collected herself. With tentative steps, she approached her mother's coffin. Her hands gripped the side, and for an instant, she felt her knees go weak. Gold barrettes clasped Rose's auburn hair, and bright pink lipstick rouged her mouth. A shaky smile of approval crossed Jennifer's lips as she smoothed the chiffon gown Rose had worn to David's wedding.

"We're alone now," she whispered. "I waited because I have something very important to tell you."

She bent down and rested her head on Rose's chest.

"I love you. I didn't tell you often enough, Mom, but I do love you." She paused, pressing her head against her mother, wishing for a response. "I tried to be a good daughter. Really, I did. I tried to do what you wanted, to be what you wanted me to be." Her mouth quivered, and her throat felt parched. "But I had so many dreams, so many fantasies. I thought I knew what would make me happy, but you know what, Mom? I'm not happy."

Tears sprinkled down her face. She lifted her head and stared at Rose.

"I feel so lost. I need you to help me. I need you to tell me what to do!"

The silence crushed her, and her sobs grew deeper and more soulful.

"Jennie." A hand touched her shoulder. "Why don't you come with me?"

Josh lifted her to her feet, and when she turned toward him, he was struck with how hauntingly beautiful she looked. Her hair was pulled back in a severe bun, and although her face was stark white, her eyes shone and her skin glistened. It was all he could do to keep from holding her and caressing away her pain. Instead, he wiped her eyes and for a few moments just stood with her alongside the coffin.

"I was such a disappointment to her."

"Jennie, please." He put his arm around her and softly kissed her hair. He could smell the delicate floral of her perfume, its scent tinged with the salty tang of drying tears. "She thought you were brilliant and beautiful and just shy of being God's most perfect creation."

Jennifer shook her head in a gesture of denial.

"I gave her expensive gifts, newspaper clippings, titles

to impress her friends. She couldn't have cared less about any of it!"

"That's not true. She was very proud of you."

"No." Her voice was faint, almost distant. "She wanted grandchildren from me. A family to sit around her table and eat and laugh."

With shaky fingers, she touched her mother's hair. She didn't want to touch her face.

"We have to go," Josh said, gently trying to steer her away.

She stepped back and turned to him. Her eyes appeared vacant, as if her grief had washed away all emotion.

"She wanted you as a son-in-law. I didn't give her that either."

He took her in his arms and held her to him.

"She had me as a friend."

Jennifer nodded her head and burrowed further into his embrace.

"She loved you, Josh," she whispered.

"I loved her too."

The polished mahogany casket inched its way into the frozen earth. The brass dolly stumbled, and its cargo rattled, hitting the sides of the freshly dug grave. The mechanism stopped and started, hesitating, as if reluctant to carry on with the rite of burial. Clumps of dirt fell on the coffin in hollow thuds, splattering into a thousand beads that skittered across the gleaming wood.

Jennifer and her family surrounded the grave, huddled together against the biting cold, listening to the rabbi. He had known Rose for years, and he spoke eloquently, reminding the mourners of the fullness of her life. She had taken great pleasure in her children and grandchildren. She had been a devoted wife and an active, responsive woman in the community and the temple. She would not be forgotten, he said, because she had touched many lives with her warmth and her charity. Jennifer took little comfort from his words. Her mother was dead, and she felt numb, as if a part of her had been amputated.

Her eyes scanned the large crowd that had gathered at the cemetery. Elyse was there. Terk. Celeste and Wyatt.

David and Sarah's children. Aunts, uncles, cousins, neighbors, old-time customers of the bakery, and most of the Jolie staff. Elegant members of the fashion community, swathed in funereal splendor, stood shoulder to shoulder with Jennifer's relatives. The contrast was striking and, for Jennifer, symbolic. Her family was a far humbler group.

Jennifer pulled her fur coat closer and hugged her body. Once again, she turned her attention to the broken earth. The reality of the event seemed almost unfathomable. The person in that box had been her mother, the woman who had given her life; who had cared for her and watched over her; loving her no matter how many obstacles Jennifer had put in her way. Now Rose was dead. Her body was still and soon would be sealed off from humanity forever. Jennifer bowed her head.

She was a daughter. A mourner. One who would weep for the departed. Yet she didn't weep. She wanted to, but the longer she stood there, the more apparent it became that fear inhibited her grief. For a frightening instant, Jennifer envisioned herself in that casket. Who would mourn her passing? What would they say about her? She had been a wife, but one who had failed her husband. She had no children, but not because she was barren. She had many acquaintances, but few good friends. Yes, she had been a success, but in what way? Suddenly, Jennifer felt separated from something universal. She looked over at David and Sarah holding their children and each other, and it became painfully clear. She had made no connections. She had created no ties.

Charles stood next to her, as he had throughout the chapel services and the ride to the cemetery, but his attention was based on pretense and deception. Her arm was linked through her father's, and she appeared caring and supportive, but how often had she really thought about her parents? How often had she asked about their health or taken an interest in their problems? She claimed to love her brother, but hadn't she alienated him also? Hadn't her needs and wants taken precedence over his? How much of herself had she given to any of them? Josh had once told her that she had made no circles, that she had denied her family. She had been angry then, and insulted. Now, she wondered if his words had been a warning.

Suddenly, she heard the rabbi ask the family to join him in the Kaddish, the traditional Jewish prayer for the dead.

"Yisgodol . . . v,yiskodosh . . . sh,nei . . . rabah."

Jennifer repeated the age-old phrases after the rabbi. Her father's voice was firm and believing. So was her brother's. Her voice was low and unsure, stumbling over the Hebrew. She bowed her head and closed her eyes, whispering the "amen" that concluded the prayer.

When she opened her eyes, she saw that her father had walked to the front of the grave. He was a religious man, and she should have guessed that he would request that he, David and Rose's brothers honor the tradition that required the men of the family to cover the grave. Marty's large hands shook as someone handed him a shovel. He refused it, bending down and scooping up several handfuls of dirt with his bare hands. He threw the dirt into the grave and winced as it hit the casket.

Rose's two brothers joined Marty, but they too seemed hesitant to hold a shovel. They just stood there, immobilized. David leaned down, spoke to his children and walked forward. His face was smudged, and he cried openly, unashamedly. Then, Jennifer saw his shoulders straighten. Tears continued to streak his cheeks, but he shoveled the dirt on top of the grave swiftly and expertly. He was doing what he felt his mother would have wanted. Ending it. Closing the sore that was hurting all who were present.

Jennifer felt her knees buckle. If Charles hadn't caught her, she would have collapsed. He held her to him, and she didn't resist. Her strength was gone. Her eyes stared at the dirt. A voice spoke to her. It was Celeste. Jennifer nodded, but she hadn't heard a thing. Others came over and offered condolences. Jennifer's eyes remained fixed.

As the crowd began to disperse, Charles and Josh tried to ease her toward the cars that would take them back to Marty's house. She walked, but she wasn't conscious of the effort. Her sensations had been dulled, her sight blurred by tears. A car door opened, and someone went to help her into the car.

"No!"

She jerked free of their grasp and ran back to the gravesite, bumping into people, tripping on the uneven lawn. Several stragglers milled about in small clusters, chatting, talking about their plans for the day, but when they saw Jennifer, they stepped aside to allow her some privacy.

Jennifer stared into the hole where her mother lay. She was vaguely aware of eyes studying her, and she tried valiantly to maintain her dignity, but tears flowed from her eyes, and her body trembled as she looked into the hollowed ground. For a long time, she just stood there letting the sharp coldness sting her face and her hands. Then, she noticed something. The men had missed a spot. Part of the casket was still visible.

Slowly, she bent down and grabbed a fistful of dirt.

"I love you, Rose Sheldon," she said. "And I'll miss you."

Her hand released the dirt. It was done. Her mother was at peace.

Twenty-Seven

"Man! I could use a short snort. How about if we hit the local watering hole after we clean up here?" Buzzy Stoller wrapped three reels of film in a traveling case and plunked them on a table in a gesture of finality.

"I don't know when I'll be through. Besides, I really have to get home." Zena had been working in the darkroom since early that morning. Her neck felt stiff, and her legs were cramped.

"You're letting this new guy of yours cramp your style," Buzzy said. "What's the big deal if you stop off for a little brew?"

As Zena leaned over the developing tins, a bubble of resentment caught in her throat. Terk was inhibiting her.

If not for him, she might have been finished with this assignment days ago. Ever since he walked out on Deirdre, he had become so possessive that she had begun to feel like a hostage in her own home. At this very minute, she imagined him sitting in her living room watching the clock and listening for her key in the door. Thank goodness she had never given him the name of this studio. If she had, he'd be parked outside the door like an angry parent clicking off the minutes past curfew.

"If you can wait about half an hour, I'll be ready." Zena suddenly decided Buzzy was right. She needed a drink, and Terk would just have to wait.

"Take your time. I've got to hang around until Mr. Big gets here anyway. He's picking up the last of the films tonight."

"Has Lady Belle retired?" Zena still hadn't shaken the notion that she had met the infamous Lady Belle, but obviously the meeting, if indeed there had ever been one, had been too brief for her to remember.

"They've all retired. No more skin flicks for Mr. Big. No more paychecks for me. Too bad. I was becoming one hell of a lover watching those things."

"I'd love to meet your Mr. Big," Zena said, half seriously. "I've never met a real, true-to-life sleaze."

"First of all, he's not what you think, and secondly, I can't introduce you. He's heavy into privacy."

"I'll bet he is."

Buzzy's benefactor repulsed Zena. To her, he was a vulture who preyed on the innocent. Yet each time she denigrated him, Buzzy rose to his defense. He painted Mr. Big as a decent, personable man who just happened to latch onto pornography as a way of making a quick buck. Zena might have dismissed Buzzy's loyalty as something bought by a series of large checks, but she could tell that Buzzy genuinely liked this man, and that fascinated her.

The harsh sound of the doorbell interrupted Zena's thoughts. Buzzy leaped off his stool, grabbed the case with the film, and headed for the front. Zena motioned that she was finished developing and that he could open the door without disturbing her. While Buzzy conducted his business, Zena went about the task of straightening up the darkroom. She emptied the tins into the sink and rinsed them out, using a damp cloth to mop up the table where she had been working. Every few minutes, she checked her prints to see if they were dry. When they were, she placed them in special envelopes that would protect them until she got home. As she snapped her briefcase shut, she heard Buzzy's high-pitched laugh.

She had almost forgotten about Buzzy's friend, and suddenly she realized that Buzzy had left the door ajar. She knew she shouldn't eavesdrop, but she couldn't resist. What kind of man made his living from smut? Zena decided that he was probably short and skinny with a shiny sharkskin suit and pointed-toe boots. She pictured a long, narrow face with small, hooded eyes, pockmarked skin, a thin nose with a slight break, and no lips. Proving or disproving her theories about Mr. Big had turned into a game for Zena. She had set up her bets, and now she wanted to see how well she had done.

On tiptoe, she eased her way to the door, opening it just a bit further so she could see more clearly. Two men stood in the shadows by the receptionist's desk. The outer offices were dim, so she had to strain to see them. Buzzy was easy. His yellow sweater was like a marker. The other man was almost completely hidden, but she could tell that she had already lost her wagers. The man was tall, and his suit didn't shine, and his camel-colored coat was probably cashmere. Zena was concentrating so hard on her mental scorecard that she never really paid attention to their voices. Then she did. Mr. Big's voice was deep and resonant. His laugh was bawdy, just as she might have expected, but there was something unexpected. The voice sounded familiar.

Quietly, she nudged the door so that she could slide out without being discovered. Hugging the wall, she crept nearer the front, searching for a spot where she could see them, but they wouldn't readily see her. The room directly behind the front desk housed filing cabinets where Harry Washor kept copies of every print he had ever made. Zena kneeled down and hid between two of them. At first, she merely listened. Something inside her prevented her from looking up.

"You've done a class job, Stoller, and I appreciate it."

"Thanks. I can't say I didn't enjoy it. If you ever need my services again, just give me a call."

"I don't think so. I've shut the operation down, and I don't plan on starting it up again."

Zena couldn't breathe. She knew that voice as well as she knew her own, but still she refused to look up.

"Whatever happened to Lady Belle?"

"She's met the man of her dreams, and I would assume that very soon, she'll be getting married."

"Shit! And I always thought I was the man of her dreams."

Zena couldn't stand the suspense a moment longer. Slowly, she lifted her eyes and stared in the direction of the voice. When she looked at Terk, her hands shook, but she didn't know if it was from shock or rage. She tried to control herself, but as she heard Terk say goodbye and watched him turn toward the door, she rushed forward, stumbling over her own feet as she went.

"You're disgusting!" Zena's voice had elevated an octave above her normal pitch, and it reverberated with hostility.

"Hey, Zena!" Buzzy started for her the instant he saw the look on Terk's face. "I asked you not to come out here."

Zena ignored him. She shook his hand off her and continued toward Terk. who looked surprised. but in control. When she reached him, she just stood there, clenching her fists and glaring.

"Buzzy, get lost." Terk never took his eyes from Zena while they waited for Stoller to leave.

"I needed the money," Terk said when they were alone. He knew how weak that sounded, how inadequate it was, but judging Zena's mood, he decided that bluntness was the best approach.

"Lots of people need money, but they don't stoop to flesh peddling to get it."

"True. But I needed a lot of money, and I needed it fast." The look on her face frightened him. Her eyes were glossy, as if a high fever had taken possession of her. "I'll explain it all when we get home. Let me get your coat."

Zena didn't budge.

"Where did you get your stars? Did you audition each and every one of them? And who is Lady Belle?"

"It's not important."

"It is to me."

He tried to lead Zena to a chair, but she pushed him away, as if he were a leper.

"Lady Belle works for *Jolie*. Her real name is Mimi Holden. Are you satisfied?"

"Jennifer Cranshaw's secretary." Zena had met her at the *Jolie* party at Cloud 9. She remembered now. Mimi's fresh, dewy look had set her apart from the rest of the slick, highly polished crowd, and Zena had been impressed with her. She listened numbly as Terk told her that he had recruited several Fellows employees, young women who needed extra cash to meet their monthly expenses. Most of them had come to New York from out of town and had been unprepared for the high cost of living.

"I'm not proud of what I've done, but it's over now. All of it. It's finished." Terk was being as gentle as he could.

"And so are we." Zena started for the darkroom, but Terk caught her by the arm.

"Why won't you even listen?" he said, pleading with her. "I know it's seedy, but I didn't mean to hurt anyone."

Zena spun around and glowered at him. Her entire being was shivering with outrage and disappointment.

"You're a gutter rat. You always have been, and you always will be. Now get out of my life. I can't even stand the sight of you!"

Terk stepped back and stared at her. He understood her shock as well as her anger, but something didn't sit right with him. Thoughts bumped against each other, thoughts that suddenly came together in a startling reality.

"I've given you an out, haven't I? You've finally found your escape."

"What are you talking about?"

"I'm talking about you. Us. The way you've managed to avoid the subject of marriage." As he spoke, his eyes bore through Zena like a laser. "I thought you were waiting for me to be free, but that wasn't it at all, was it? You've just been biding your time and hoping I would do or say something that would let you out. Just like the last time."

"How dare you!" Zena's eyes were wild with contempt.

"How dare you try and turn this around to where you're right and I'm wrong!"

"I'll tell you how I dare. Because there's something that's making you shake, and it's not my porno films. What happened eight years ago that made you leave?"

"It's none of your business. My life is my own, and all my decisions have been made by me, for me, and for no one else!"

The play of the game had shifted. Suddenly, Terk was taking the offensive, and Zena was forced to defend herself. She ran toward the darkroom, but Terk moved faster, cutting in front of her and blocking her entrance.

"I don't even want to be in the same room with you. You're filth!"

"You're right," Terk said, alert to her every response. "What I did was ugly. I made dirty movies and took advantage of girls like Mimi Holden who needed money and probably something else I don't even understand, but what you're doing is just as ugly. You're unwilling to listen, and frankly, that surprises me. Even Deirdre with all her faults would listen."

"And since when is Deirdre so wonderful?" Zena was crying. Her voice was a mixture of anger and fear, which only served to pique Terk's curiosity.

"Since I see that she, at least, is willing to honor commitments and take risks." Terk continued to prowl around Zena, hunting. He had picked up a scent, and he was determined to track it. "You've been in the jungle long enough to know how animals work. They scratch and claw and spit and rip the guts out of anything that threatens them. You've seen it a thousand times. You've glorified it in your work, but when it comes to people, you look away."

Terk's words hit Zena like a whip. She snarled at him and dodged his hulking presence.

"Don't make yourself sound so brave. You're a coward and you're scum and you'll never change!"

Zena turned away from him, but before she did, something in her eyes drew Terk toward her. He grabbed her arms and held her firmly. He was certain that she was hiding something.

"If I'm so slimy, why did you come back to me? And

come back you did, honey. You crawled into bed with me the first chance you got. What's more, you loved it! It feels good to get dirty once in a while, doesn't it?"

"I hate you!" Zena screamed at him, her face flushed with rage. "I loathe and despise you!"

"You hate the fact that you love me and that you're afraid I won't stay with you."

Zena practically growled at him.

"I could have made you stay with me the last time."

"Really? And what power is it that you think you could have used?"

Zena stood across from him, her hands gripping her arms, her fingers white and bony. An eerie smile crossed her lips, a half circle that gave Terk chills.

"A son," she said. "Is that powerful enough? I had your son, and if I had wanted you, I could have had you."

Terk felt as if a cement block had been thrown against his chest.

"What are you talking about?"

"When I left you eight years ago I was three months pregnant. I went to Switzerland, had the baby, and put him up for adoption. I gave away your son."

Zena watched the color drain from Terk's face. He looked stricken, and for the moment, she worried what he might do to her.

"How could you? I had a right to know."

"You gave up those rights when you told me you couldn't leave your wife."

"You never said you were pregnant."

"That baby was mine to do with as I pleased, and I gave him away."

Terk's voice was weak, as if all energy had been siphoned out of him.

"No. It wasn't because I wouldn't leave Deirdre. I see it quite clearly now. At first, the idea of a baby intrigued you. You toyed with it, played with it, mulled it over until it was too late to have an abortion. But then it struck you. The baby was a trap. If you had told me you were pregnant, you knew that I would have moved heaven and earth to be with you, but that's not what you wanted. You didn't want a husband and a child. You wanted to be freewheeling, independent Zena Welles."

Zena collapsed in the nearest chair. She buried her face in her hands and cried as she hadn't since she was a child and her dog had died. Something had died now too. Not a pet or a person, but something deeper, something more spiritual. She heard it in his voice, as the tempo slowed and the timbre dropped, as his love evaporated and loathing took its place.

"I'm not what you think, Zena. I'm a man who wants roots and ties, and I'm going to find that baby. It would have been wonderful to have a child with you, but now I'll have him without you."

Without even looking at her, he turned and walked out of the studio. Zena heard the door slam, and for a while, it echoed in her ears. He meant what he said. She knew that. Somehow, he would find the boy who was their son. And what would she find? Nothing. Instantly, she knew what had died in that room. Her chance at happiness had suffered a fatal blow, and the horror of it all was that it had been done by her own hand. Once again, she had made a decision by herself and for herself. And once again, she experienced an overwhelming sense of regret.

She stared at the door, feeling an oppressive cloak of emptiness wrap around her. A mournful sob escaped her lips as the face of that tiny infant merged with the face of the only man who had ever really loved her.

"Come back," she screamed. "I don't want to be alone!"

Twenty-Eight

Jennifer picked her father up at the house, and the two of them drove quietly to the center of town. It was after five, and traffic was heavy. Parking places were at a premium. Aside from the normal late-day crush, it was the start of the annual January Sidewalk Sale, and Bayonne had been transformed into a giant carnival. Balloons bobbed from streetlamps and fire hydrants. Crepe paper streamers decorated awnings and doorways. Enor-

mous white banners announcing the week-long extravaganza stretched across the busy roadway. And outside
every store, long tables sat piled high with odds and ends
from the winter season.

Broadway was jammed with after-work shoppers eager
to get first crack at the sale-priced merchandise, so Jennifer and Marty strolled leisurely up the avenue, jockeying
around the crowds as best they could. Occasionally, they
stopped to chat with neighbors or to wave to passersby,
but most of their energies were spent trying to avoid being
jostled and bumped. Anxious bargain hunters combed
through cartons or fluttered around clothing racks. Store
owners hawked their wares like barkers at a flea market.
And every few blocks, a phonograph blasted thumping
rock music to attract free-spending teenagers who didn't
look to barter about price.

During the walk from the parking lot, Jennifer had allowed herself to be distracted by the noise and color that
enlivened the street, but her mood changed drastically
when she reached the bakery. The space where the
SHELDON'S BAKE SHOP sign used to hang was blank.
The window that once groaned with an overabundance of
nut-crusted cakes and plump, fruit-filled pies was empty.
Metal display racks meant to hold trays of cupcakes and
baskets of rolls sat naked, except for a few pink doilies,
which had been faded by the sun, their scalloped edges
curled up like pointed-toe Turkish slippers.

Jennifer followed Marty into the store and for a few
minutes, the two of them stood silently by the door. Everything was there. The slicer sat next to the cash register;
the waxed paper dispenser was still in position next to the
scale; the string winder held its place at the far end of the
counter, and the glass cases were polished and shiny. But
every bin and every shelf was bare.

She walked behind the counter and ran her hand along
the bins where Rose had housed the cookies. Crumbs
stuck to her fingers, and she was tempted to lick them, to
taste again those happy times when she used to fill her
pockets with chocolate cigarettes and buttery rounds
topped by multicolored sprinkles. Instead, she brushed the
crumbs away and wandered into the back, past the big
mixing machines and rolling racks. When she opened the

freezer, she expected to be greeted by a cold draft and mounds of fresh whipped cream. A puff of warm, stale air filled her nose with a sour smell. Quickly, she slammed the door.

"Why did you sell?" she asked as Marty picked an apron up off the floor and hung it on a hook.

"Without your mother, the bakery has no meaning for me."

"But this was your whole life," Jennifer said, fascinated by her own response. For years, all she had wanted was for her parents to sell the bakery, and now that it was done, she was protesting the loudest.

"My life was with your mother," Marty said. "This was a job."

He turned and went to the wall cabinets where he kept his recipes. He took them down and began to sort them out into piles. Jennifer lifted herself up onto the long wooden bench that occupied the center of the room. It was strange to see the bench so clean. Strange, too, was the silence.

"How do you know you're going to like living in Florida?"

Marty stopped packing his books and turned to his daughter.

"What could be bad?" he said, trying to reassure both himself and her. "There's lots of sunshine. My brothers and sisters are there. So are the Mandells and other friends from Bayonne. I might even take up golf. Who knows?"

Jennifer heard the doubt in his voice and wanted to leap on it. She wanted to use it to convince him to stay; to keep the bakery and the house; to keep her past intact. But she couldn't. Those were her needs, not his.

"I'll miss you," she said.

"They have planes. You'll come and visit." He smiled at her. She tried to smile back, but her lips merely quivered. "It's time you started planning a new life too."

Jennifer looked away. Weeks ago, she had told Marty about her and Charles, editing the part about Charles's homosexuality, and swearing her father to secrecy with the vow that she would tell David and Sarah herself, in time. Marty had been disappointed, but not as upset as she had imagined he'd be. Somehow, she sensed that he had expected her marriage to fail, and that embarrassed her.

She reached up to the shelf over her head and took down an old cigar box. In it, she found a few wrinkled cloth bags, icing tips, and the metal circle Marty had used to make roses. She put the box back, but kept the little disk, holding it firmly in her hand.

"Trying to save a bit of your childhood?"

Jennifer stared at her father. She had never thought he was aware of her feelings. Then again, she had taken Rose's insights for granted too.

"I guess." She spun the circle around in her fingers. "Funny, isn't it? When I was small, I loved the bakery. Then, everything changed, and all I wanted to do was get away from this place."

"I hated it too." Marty twirled a huge mixing bowl on its stand, and the old mechanism creaked. "But it was all I knew how to do. Besides, your mother loved it. She said she didn't, but all you had to do was watch her behind that counter and you knew."

"But Mom had dreams," Jennifer said with a defiance she didn't understand. "She told me she did."

Marty went to where Jennifer was sitting. He took her hand in his and patted it gently.

"Of course she had dreams. Everyone does. She and I just couldn't afford to chase them."

"Because you were too busy trying to make enough money for David and me."

Suddenly, she wondered about her father's dreams. What had he wanted out of life? Why hadn't she ever asked him?

"Don't sound so guilty." Marty lifted her chin and looked into her eyes. "Seeing our children fulfill themselves was fulfillment enough."

Jennifer didn't know if he was salving her conscience or telling the truth, but her face brightened.

"Was it? I mean, did you and Mom really approve of me?"

Marty laughed, but she saw a drop of moisture wet his cheek.

"You were your mother's pride and joy, Jennie. She got great pleasure out of your success."

"But she never seemed to think my career was important. All she talked about were David and Sarah's children."

"Asa and Lia were her grandchildren," Marty said. "And yes, she would have liked you to have children too, but she knew you weren't happy with Charles."

"I couldn't tell her. I couldn't tell anyone," she said, knowing that it was pride and not lack of listeners that had forced her to keep silent.

"That's all over now. You and I have to start new lives!"

She looked at him perched next to her on the wooden bench and marveled at his spirit and his resolve. His words were hopeful, but she knew that beneath them lay uncertainty and no small amount of loneliness.

"You're a brave man, Dad."

"Not really. I'm not happy here, so I'm going to try and find peace somewhere else."

It was getting dark, and Jennifer thought about turning on a light, but she didn't want to move. This moment of sharing was too special to disturb.

"You have a lot of wonderful memories to bring with you," she said, moving closer to him. "I don't have that comfort."

Marty put his arm around her, and she nestled her head on his shoulder.

"You're young, Jennie. You can create new memories."

"I'm not finished with the old ones yet."

"Again, we're in the same boat." He kissed her hair and hugged her. "We both have to learn to let go. Your mother's gone, and I'm here. So I have to keep the past where it belongs and use it as a stepping stone to the future."

Jennifer sat up and looked at him, a shy smile curling her lips.

"You're giving me a very subtle lecture, aren't you?"

He nodded. "Not so subtle. Let your hurts and disappointments teach you. Don't let them keep you a prisoner."

"Mom's gone. The bakery is closed, and now you're moving away. I feel abandoned."

The sadness in her voice touched him, forcing his mind back in time. Instead of the sophisticated woman Jennifer was now, he saw a small redhead in fluffy pigtails and flannel pajamas clutching a teddy bear.

"No one has abandoned you, Jennie. This is all part of life's cycle. We have to move on."

"I don't know if I can handle it," she whispered mostly to herself.

Marty took her by the shoulders and demanded that she look him squarely in the eye.

"You are Rose and Marty Sheldon's daughter," he said. "You come from sturdy stock, my girl, and whether you want to own up to it or not, you are a survivor!"

"Am I?"

Marty kissed her forehead and smiled.

"You bet you are! You just have to give yourself a chance."

She put her head down on his shoulder again, feeling the safety of her father's embrace.

"Give Josh a chance, too," Marty said. "He may have been part of your past, but it's possible that he's part of your future too."

Jennifer's eyes grew moist as the two of them huddled together on the hard bench, holding each other in the darkness. In a few hours, the new owners were scheduled to arrive. A little girl's voice begged Jennifer to stop them, to lock the door and make them go away. But tomorrow the shelves would be filled; the oven would be hot; and whipped cream would return to the freezer. A new name would hang outside, and new faces would smile from behind Rose's counter.

Jennifer felt Marty slide down off the bench, and she jumped to her feet. Carefully, she followed him through the shadows and out to the front. Her pace was slow, and she knew it was because she didn't want to leave. Her entire life was tied up in this store. When she had loved it, it was a haven and a shelter. When she had hated it, it was the focal point around which she molded her existence. Whoever she was, whatever she became, it had all started here.

Marty opened the door to let them out and then closed it.

"Well," he said. "This is it. Say good-bye, Jennifer."

He turned the key in the lock, and the sound echoed in her ears.

"Good-bye, Jennifer," she said.

Twenty-Nine

"She needs medical attention, not a suntan. When she said she and Charles were going away for a long weekend, that was fine, but this is turning into the longest weekend in history!"

David Sheldon had been grumbling all afternoon. He and Sarah had brought the children to Josh's for Scotty Mandell's birthday party, but instead of singing and celebration, they were mired in debate and conjecture. Jennifer had been gone for more than three weeks.

"Take it easy," Josh said. "Everyone handles loss in his own way. Maybe your mother's death and the sale of the bakery affected Jennifer more than you know."

"I know all too well how deeply she was affected," David said. "Why do you think I'm so concerned? Her back is getting worse, and if I were to hazard an educated guess, I'd say she's in terrible pain. Didn't you notice how bent her posture was? How she held onto things when she walked? How slow her steps were?"

Sarah had noticed all that, and more. She had followed Jennifer back to Rose's grave the day of the funeral. She had witnessed her sister-in-law's grief, but what had disturbed her most was the aura of despair that surrounded Jennifer then and had deepened in the weeks that followed.

"Other things were gnawing at her," Sarah said, seeing again the strain on Jennifer's face and the agitated gestures she had used to punctuate her speech.

"It's the magazine," Josh said, almost too quickly. "*Jolie* is in the midst of a crisis, and Jennifer has taken its salvation on as her own personal crusade."

"I disagree." David was pacing, his hands stuffed into his pockets. "I think that whatever is bothering Jennifer is intensely personal."

Sarah was fiddling with her napkin, so she didn't see the way David stared at Josh or the way Josh avoided his friend's eyes.

"If it is, she didn't tell me." Josh was suddenly very uncomfortable. "We used to be close. We're not close anymore."

David nodded, but he couldn't get the conversation he had overheard in Bayonne out of his mind. Something about it didn't sit right with him. The tension between Josh and Jennifer. The unspoken words. The charged atmosphere. David was certain that Josh knew more than he was saying.

Just then, the doorbell rang, and Josh jumped to answer it. As he went to the foyer, he considered telling David about the night he and Jennifer had spent together, as well as their abortive rendezvous the following evening. Would it be helpful? Or would it be a betrayal? It had happened months ago, and Jennifer had kept him at arm's length ever since. Also, it appeared as if she and Charles had reconciled their differences. They were inseparable at Rose's funeral. They were away together now. Whatever had happened between himself and Jennifer had obviously been nothing more than an interlude.

"I'm sorry I'm late." Elyse smiled apologetically. "Where's the birthday boy?"

Josh helped her off with her coat and relieved her of her packages.

"All the kids are in Scotty's room, being entertained by Jimbo the Clown. The adults are trying to entertain themselves in the dining room and doing a lousy job."

Sarah greeted Elyse with a warm embrace. David gave her a quick buss on the cheek.

"What's with *herr* doctor?" Elyse asked. "He seems preoccupied. Am I interrupting something?"

"He's on a search and destroy mission." Josh's voice was light, but pointed. "No one has heard from Jennifer, and big brother is having a fit."

"I expected her back over two weeks ago," Elyse said

as she took her seat. "Does anyone know why she extended her trip?"

"We thought you knew something." David sounded disappointed and more than a little worried. "I'd call her, but she never said where she was staying."

"Maybe we're all overreacting." Josh took his place at the head of the table. "It's freezing here, and she probably went someplace warm. Why not stay?"

"What happened to the crisis at the magazine?" David didn't even bother to mask the suspicion in his eyes. "Two minutes ago, *Jolie* was terminal, and you had Jennifer holding its hand until the bitter end. Now you're telling me that the patient suddenly recovered enough for her to stay away indefinitely?"

"I'm not telling you anything," Josh said impatiently. "I'm just offering a possible explanation."

"And one which makes a lot of sense." Sarah didn't understand David's hostility, or Josh's defensiveness, but she didn't like either. "Use your surgical skills on the coffee cake. I want to know what's happening with Elyse." Sarah gave her husband a knife and a look.

Elyse couldn't help smiling at the two of them. Since her stay in the hospital, the Sheldons had practically adopted her. At first, she had been bewildered by all their attention, attributing their interest to her relationship with Jennifer, but Sarah and David had bombarded her with such genuine affection that she had come to think of them as family.

"I'm fine," she said. "A little fuzzy today, but fine."

"You're not overworking, are you?" David sounded almost parental.

"No. I just had a late night."

"Were you out with Kevin?" Josh said casually, and then counted the seconds before Sarah spoke.

"Who's Kevin?"

Elyse blushed.

"He's one of Josh's vice-presidents."

"Kevin Wagner is also the new man in Elyse's life." A self-satisfied grin brightened Josh's face.

"He's helping me with the business, and yes, we see each other occasionally."

"Four times a week and sometimes for lunch," Josh said in a loud stage whisper.

"Forget all that. Tell me about the man." Sarah was eager for details.

Again, Elyse blushed and again, Josh answered for her.

"He's four feet tall, bald, has a barely noticeable lisp and a penchant for wide-lapeled plaid suits."

Sarah gave Josh a playful frown. "Stop teasing," she said as she turned to Elyse. "Judging by the flush on your cheeks, I assume this Mr. Kevin Wagner is fairly fabulous. Am I right?"

"He's very nice." Elyse was afraid to admit to herself how wonderful he was.

"Well done, Mandell." David lifted his coffee cup in a salute. Then, his face turned serious. "Have you heard from Mario?"

"A couple of times, but not since I moved and unlisted my phone number."

"What did he say?"

Elyse shifted in her seat and the others immediately tensed.

"He's not happy about this new venture. He's even more upset that I refuse to see him."

"Has he threatened you?" Sarah asked.

"No. I think Josh put the fear of God into him." Elyse didn't tell them about the mysterious phone calls in the middle of the night or the strange unsigned notes that had prompted her move.

"Have you heard from your brother?" Sarah knew all about Gianni and why Elyse was so hesitant to turn Mario over to the police.

"He's fine. At least *he's* thrilled about the new company."

"Is there any way Mario could sabotage all this?" David directed his question to Josh.

"No. She's part of JM Industries now. There's no way he can interfere without my knowing it."

Josh's tone told David that extreme precautions had been taken to protect Elyse, both personally and financially, but Elyse's manner told him that she knew if Mario wanted to get to her, he could.

"I can't wait to see the new line!" Sarah wanted to get

off the subject of Mario de Marco. "When will it be in the stores?"

"The first collection is scheduled to launch in April. I just finished designing the winter collection, and it should go into production within the next few weeks, but really, the success of this whole operation hinges on the success of *Jolie*'s April issue."

"And that brings us right back to Jennifer," David said.

Silence descended on the table like an uninvited guest. Everyone stared at his plate and pushed food around, searching for something to say. Finally, Elyse spoke.

"Don't be angry, David. Jennifer needs this time away."

"I'm not angry," he said, his voice low and heavy. "I'm frustrated. She's hurting, and I don't know how to help her."

Elyse reached across the table and took his hand.

"You can't help her," she said. "She has to do this by herself."

Thirty

It was after eleven when Jennifer awakened, and for the time it took to blink away the filmy residue of sleep, she felt disoriented. Slowly, the shapes and colors of her bedroom came into focus. A strong winter sun had edged its way through the slatted blinds and dappled the walls with scattered streaks of light. She felt something hot touch her hand and remembered that she had slept with a heating pad, hoping that its controlled warmth would ease the grinding pain in her back. The long hours traveling and the stiff mattresses in Celeste's villa had taken their toll on her weakened spine, but the trip to Acapulco had been more than worth it.

She reached over to the night table and swallowed a muscle relaxant, giving it a few minutes to seep into her system before easing her way out of bed and padding off to the kitchen. As she waited for her coffee to perk, she called the office. She was anxious to know what had happened during her absence, and Mimi was eager to fill her in. The good news was that April was already being touted as the most successful issue *Jolie* had ever put together and that May's bookings indicated that the upward trend would continue. The bad news was that Brad had been acting strangely, snapping at staffers for no apparent reason and closeting himself in his office for hours at a time, allowing no one entrance.

"Is there any mail I should get to immediately, or can everything wait until Monday?"

"The only must-do is a party," Mimi said.

"What party?"

"Cocktails and dinner at the apartment of Claiborne and Amanda Stark. The invitation was hand delivered. I believe it's a command performance. Everyone whose name graces the masthead was invited."

Jennifer knew instantly that this gathering had to do with the future of *Jolie*. Surprisingly, the prospect of hearing that the magazine might have been sold didn't bother her as much as it would have a month ago. While in Mexico, she had done a lot of soul-searching, and in the process, she had reorganized her priorities. She had come to view *Jolie* as a part of her life, rather than her reason for being. She still cared, still felt committed, but not at the expense of everything else. No, it wasn't the party that upset her, it was that she knew she had to get in touch with Charles immediately. She didn't want to run into him at his partner's home with things unresolved between them.

"When is this gala?" she asked.

"Don't faint, but it's tonight. Seven o'clock and the attire is black tie. I don't know if I did the right thing, but I RSVP'd for you. In case you're interested, you'd be delighted to attend."

"I don't know if delighted is precisely how I feel, but I shall attend."

Jennifer hung up and carried her coffee into the bathroom, sipping it thoughtfully as she prepared to shower. She had planned to call Charles sometime over the weekend, but now it was imperative that she reach him today. As far as she knew, he had never been involved in any transactions concerning *Jolie*, but at the closing of any major deal, everyone in the firm joined the celebration, and unless this was a highly unusual circumstance, Charles was sure to be there. Jennifer struggled with herself, annoyed at the way this party had interfered with her schedule. Not only did it force her to act before she was ready, but also it raised some touchy details she hadn't wanted to contend with. How did they handle their appearance? Did they go together? Separately? Would they even be speaking to each other? On the plane back to New York, she had thought of little else other than what she would say when she saw Charles. She went over lines in her head, practiced approaches, tried to anticipate scenes and responses, but now that their meeting was imminent, she wondered how well-rehearsed she really was.

Jennifer stepped into the shower and luxuriated in the hot water that splashed against her body. After all the barely tepid baths she had endured in Mexico, she vowed to steam and suds herself until her skin puckered.

After, with a bath towel saronged around her torso, she sat down and began to massage her limbs with moisturizer, half expecting to feel the stiff inflexibility that accompanied tension. But her muscles felt relaxed, and she knew that the suppleness was more than just the result of a shower or a pill—it was an inner resiliency. As she glanced up into the mirror, she smiled at her unmade face. A loud silence pervaded the apartment, but for the first time since Charles had left, the quiet didn't frighten her.

At some undocumented moment, Jennifer had shed the weighty mantle of shame and faced her situation for what it was—something beyond either her control or Charles's. What's more, she felt that some good had come out of all this difficulty. Her intense involvement with success had prevented her from looking at herself with honest clarity. Inadvertently, Charles had forced her to stand back, to look at Jennifer Cranshaw in the raw, without the opulent wardrobe, without the veneer of social prestige, without the protection of a title or a busy appointment book.

Before she had time to dwell on the matter, she heard the doorbell ring. Forgetting that she wore nothing more than a towel, she ran to the foyer.

"Where the hell have you been?" David brushed past her as if he expected her to slam the door in his face.

"Atlantic City," she said, delighted to see him.

"I didn't know they had a boardwalk in Acapulco."

"You're such a tease," she said, amused by his behavior. "You knew all along where I was."

"Only because I gave your secretary a trumped-up story about a family emergency."

She had no defense, but neither did she feel like offering one.

"David, darling. I don't want to shock you or anything," she said, following him into the living room, "but take a good look at the person standing before you. This is a grown-up person, an adult, a woman well past twenty-one and capable of taking care of herself."

He paused to look at her. She didn't look very grown-up then, standing there with no shoes, no makeup, and a skimpy towel barely covering her bronzed body.

"I'm not asking you to punch a time clock, Jennifer, but I got slightly nervous."

"There was nothing to be nervous about."

"Maybe, but caring is a habit I find hard to break."

Jennifer walked toward him, blanketed by his concern, and flung her arms around his neck, hugging him the way she used to when they were children.

"I love you too, really I do, but I just needed to get away. And, in case you're interested, I had a very nice time. I'll throw on a robe and tell you all about it."

David sat in the bedroom so Jennifer could unpack while they talked. As she rummaged through her luggage, separating presents from laundry, she rambled on about the Cranshaws' villa, the weather, some day trips she had taken, and the recuperative powers of the sun. David sat on the edge of her bed and listened quietly. It wasn't that he had no interest in her travelogue, but something felt strange. When Jennifer went to her dressing room to unpack her cosmetic bag, he surveyed the room. His eyes wandered from the bed to the closets to the drawers and then back to the bed. While Jennifer chatted, he opened several dresser drawers.

By the time Jennifer returned to the bedroom, David had investigated the living room and the den.

"Were you listening to me?" she said.

He stood soldier-straight, staring at her as if she were speaking in code.

"What's wrong?"

"You tell me."

Jennifer was confused. The look on her brother's face alternated between anger and hurt, and she couldn't imagine why.

"I don't know what you're talking about, David. I had a wonderful time, got a gorgeous tan, and I feel better than I have in a long while. What could be wrong?"

"Did Charles have a good time too?"

He had caught her off guard. She had completely forgotten that she had lied to David.

"Charles didn't go with me," she answered quietly.

"Could it be that Charles didn't go with you because Charles doesn't live here anymore?"

Jennifer needed time to gather her thoughts. She had never been deliberately dishonest with David before, and she knew that her subterfuge had offended him. There had always been a bond between them, an unspoken pledge to be open and forthright. Even during their more difficult times, neither had lied to the other.

David had known she was hiding something from him, but he had sensed her need to work it out by herself, and so he had let her be. Now, he wondered if his decision had been wise. David cautioned himself not to push.

"Charles and I have been separated since October," she said finally.

"Why didn't you tell me?"

"I didn't tell anyone," she said. "I couldn't."

"Why not?" David could have listed several reasons for Jennifer leaving her husband, but something warned him to keep still.

"I was embarrassed."

"Lots of marriages fail, Jen. That's nothing to be ashamed of. It didn't work, that's all."

"There's more to it than that." Jennifer lit a cigarette, looked away, and then looked directly at her brother. "One night I came home and found Charles in bed with a man." She said it so softly that it took a few seconds for David to react.

"Oh, my God!" In quick flashes, he pictured the incident, recoiling at the trauma to which his sister had been subjected.

"I never guessed he was gay." Jennifer was practically whispering. "I don't know whether I was deliberately blind or just too self-absorbed, but finding him like that really pulled the boards out from under me."

David was having trouble keeping tabs on his emotions. He was angry. He was horrified. And yet, he felt compassion for Charles and sympathy for both of them. "What did he say?"

"I don't even know," Jennifer sighed. "I didn't listen. I just threw him out."

"What surprises me," David said, "is that someone like Charles would be so indiscreet."

"He never meant for me to find out. I came home unexpectedly."

"But you live here."

"Here's where the story gets complicated," Jennifer said. "For a long time, on some subconscious level, I think I suspected that Charles was having an affair. Too many business trips. Too many late meetings. That sort of thing. Anyway, I ran a big party for *Jolie*, and that night, he left with a woman I know. He said he was going to drop her off and go back to his office. I called over there twice. When there was no answer, I went home with Josh."

"Josh?" David's head was reeling. The night in Bayonne. The electricity between them. The strain. Josh's uneasiness the day of Scotty's party.

"We made love, and it was as if there had never been a Laura or a Charles." Jennifer was so involved in what she was saying, she didn't see that David was lost in thought. "It was just Josh and me, and nothing else seemed to matter. The next day, I was euphoric, and like some silly teenager, I plotted to spend the weekend with him. Only Josh turned me down. I went home alone, and that's when I found Charles."

Her eyes were damp with the pain of remembrance. Suddenly, she pulled her fingers through her hair and tossed her head back like a proud filly. She laughed, but the sound was hollow and without mirth.

"See this fabulous woman?" she said. "This sexy, irresistible creature? In one night, two of the most important men in my life rejected me."

"I haven't rejected you," David said, moving nearer to her and holding her hand. "And they haven't either. In all fairness, I don't think Charles could help what happened. As for Josh, that man adores the polish on your toenails, and you know it. Why didn't you go to him?"

Jennifer wiped her eyes and breathed deeply, trying to regain control.

"I couldn't. Josh has this idealistic view of those he loves," she said. "I failed at a marriage."

"What makes you think Josh is perfect?"

Jennifer had not expected such a question, least of all from David, but it prompted her to think before she answered. She had never analyzed this particular feeling about Josh before, but she had no need to. Wherever she turned, others offered unsolicited confirmation of her assessment. Men respected his business acumen and hailed him as a leader. Women battled for him. Even when Jennifer had been younger, she had rejected his proposal because everyone claimed he was perfect for her. It was just that perfection she had sought to escape. Now, she admired it, but it made her shy and insecure about telling him the truth about herself.

"I can't believe I'm putting Josh on a pedestal and you're taking the opposite stand."

"That's because I know where his weaknesses are. I accept them, just as he accepts mine, but Joshua Mandell would be the first one to understand. He's had a few failures of his own."

"Business failures don't count."

"Personal failures."

David proceeded to tell Jennifer about the night Josh's wife died. He told her about Josh's affair with Coral Trent and his garment center carousing. Jennifer was shocked and confused.

"Why didn't he tell me all this?" she asked. "Why didn't he follow me that night?"

"Probably for the same reason you didn't go to him. Pride. Fear of looking less perfect in your eyes. Plus," David said, "he could never allow himself to be an instrument of marital destruction. He could never deal with the guilt. Especially with you."

Jennifer was struggling. Part of her was bursting with understanding and apology. Another part was angry and hurt.

"Want some brotherly advice?" David sensed her ambivalence. He knew that she needed time to see her problems with Charles through to their conclusion. He also knew that she feared time was her enemy where Josh was concerned. "Josh isn't going anywhere. Take it slowly. When you're ready, you'll tell Josh what happened, how you feel, what you think about your future. But don't rush it. You're coming to a new understanding about yourself. Strengthen it. Solidify it. And then, if you and he still feel destined to be together, I personally will handle the wedding. Sound reasonable?"

Jennifer kissed him softly on the cheek.

"If you came into my life and you weren't my sibling, I'd grab you up in a minute!" she said.

"Not if I grabbed you first!"

Jennifer and David spent most of the day together, and by the time he left, she felt positively buoyant, but the warmth that cloaked her quickly chilled when she realized that she had not yet spoken to Charles. In less than three hours, she was expected at the Starks'. She called Charles's office, but he was out at a client's and was not expected back. She was about to dial another number when suddenly and sadly, she realized that she had no number to call. She didn't know if he was at a friend's or a hotel or his parents' apartment. She tried to recall whether he had ever left an address or a number on her tape, but even if he had, she had never memorized it, and now it would have been erased. She debated calling Celeste and then dismissed it as too embarrassing for all concerned. Clearly, her choices had narrowed to one: going to the party, confronting him calmly, making the best of a difficult situation, and arranging to speak to him afterwards.

As she dressed, Jennifer sensed a nervousness rooting in the pit of her stomach. So much about this evening was uncertain. Had the magazine been sold? Who had bought it, and what was Jolie's future? Would Charles be there? She felt blindfolded, incapable of focus. She had just clasped a hammered gold, rose-petaled choker around her neck when the doorbell rang.

The minute she heard Charles's voice, she experienced a flutter of panic. Suddenly, she felt unprepared for a face-to-face meeting with him. How would she feel when she saw him? How would he react to her? Would there be anger? Tears? Or nothing more than a throbbing silence? She opened the door slowly, almost suspiciously. When she looked at him, she felt a knot form in her throat. He was extremely wan, his normally pale face grayed and shadowed with stress, his eyes lifeless, a diluted blue without light or sparkle.

She invited him in and fixed him a drink as they exchanged halting cordialities. They waltzed around each other as if they were partners in a verbal gavotte, stepping in toward each other, bowing gracefully, and then retreating, all with the utmost courtesy. For reasons she couldn't understand, she felt compelled to turn on all the lights, and the living room reverberated with an icy brightness. Charles sat stiffly on one end of the couch, his back erect, sipping his drink with the precision of a military plebe. Jennifer sat at the other end, no more relaxed than he, scrunched into a corner, using the stiff cushions to fortify her.

"I'm sorry to barge in like this, but I know you're going to Claiborne and Amanda's, and I thought it best to see you beforehand."

He didn't look at her when he spoke. Instead, his eyes focused on a spot somewhere in the carpet in front of his seat. As Jennifer looked at him, she was reminded instantly of what a truly elegant man he was. Aside from obvious signs of strain, Charles wore his tuxedo with ease, as if it were everyday attire, not like most men who felt confined and restricted by formal clothes. Charles enhanced his clothes, bringing to them a patrician grace that Jennifer had always admired, just as she did now.

"Actually, I'm glad you stopped by. I tried calling you, but when you didn't answer at the office, I was stymied. I don't know where you live."

He turned to her, just for a moment, and then looked away again.

"I've been staying at the Algonquin, but at the end of the month, I'm moving into a new apartment."

His voice was lackluster, his speech almost mechanical, and Jennifer felt her heart ache. For all this time, she had believed herself to be the tortured one, the suffering, last-to-know wife betrayed by a villainous husband. Never once had she given any thought to his pain, his torment. The man sitting beside her hurt, and she could see the pain in the stiffness of his posture and the tilt of his head.

"Charles, please look at me." She reached for his hand, but he retracted it. "There's so much that needs to be said."

His eyes met hers, and in them she saw a veil of melancholy and the muted gaze of resignation. She took his hand and held it, feeling the moisture that had collected in his palm.

"I never meant to hurt you," he said.

His words rang with sincerity, and she knew that her response had to be gentle, yet honest. There had been too many lies already.

"I've spent a lot of time and energy hating you, Charles. Even more time wanting revenge. I felt you betrayed me, you insulted me, and, worst of all, you rejected me."

His head lowered, his eyes once again returning to the floor.

"But," she continued, "I've come to realize that you didn't mean to do this to me or to yourself. I may not have all the pieces in their proper slots, but I don't hate you anymore."

He looked up, studying her. She was magnificent, like a mythical bird plumaged in gold, and he still thought her to be one of the most beautiful women he had ever known. Suddenly, their years together flashed before him, vivid but edited, with the bad obliterated, the good highlighted. He felt no need to stop the scenes, no desire to dwell on one particular moment. He had done that already. For the past few months, he had used his after-work hours as a retreat, a time for isolation and reflection. He had taken moments from all stages of his life, microscoped them, dissected them, and finally replaced them in his memory. He had viewed them as objectively as he was able, and his examination had forced him to conclude that their marriage would have aborted no matter what his sexual preferences had been. Their relationship had been a parentheses, a propitious interlude. Jennifer had needed an oasis where she could cultivate her ambition and plant the seeds of a new identity. He had needed a harbor, a safe place to moor while he decided on a destination. They had found each other and used each other, and the result was that both had benefited and both had lost.

"It wasn't so bad, all those years, was it?" he said at last.

Jennifer moved closer to him, sensing his need for assurance.

"No, it wàsn't. We shared a great deal. We gave to each other and supported each other, and I'm grateful for that. You introduced me to worlds I didn't know before you. You taught me style. And you taught me class."

"You were an able student."

"And I taught you to laugh."

"That you did," he said, a weak smile straining his lips.

"The best part was that you never laughed at me, only with me. You didn't laugh at me, did you Charles?"

It was his turn to comfort, to reassure, and he stroked her hand tenderly.

"You were always a delight, like a carbonated drink that bubbled and fizzed around me. No, I never laughed at you. I cried for you sometimes though, knowing that eventually I'd have to hurt you."

Jennifer felt herself relaxing, easing into the security of fond remembrances. The immediate past had been shelved, at least for the moment, while they eulogized their time together.

"Do you remember the day I took you roller skating? And that Halloween when we made jelly apples and you cracked a tooth? The best was that Sunday when we picnicked in Central Park and got sloshed on champagne. Do you remember how I made you play Fred Astaire to my Ginger Rogers tap-dancing around the fountain?"

He laughed and nodded his head.

"People thought we were insane," he said.

"But we had fun."

"That we did."

He sipped his drink, and once again his face became serious, as if it was important to relive the good times and expunge the bad. When he looked at her again, she was relieved to see a softness returning to his eyes.

"You know," he said, "I think the thing I loved about you most is that I could run through the park with you and laugh. Laughing and rejoicing were not rewarded at my father's home."

Much as his words pleased her, deep down Jennifer felt a stinging need to expose thoughts she had kept secret, to bare feelings she had repressed for so long that they had become sores ulcerating her insides.

"That night, when I found you with that man, I was so humiliated, so hurt, I shook for days after."

Charles moved toward her and then 'stopped. He wanted to put his arms around her, to comfort her, to apologize, but he wasn't sure she would accept him and feared rejection as much as she did. Jennifer had noticed his movement. She understood his hesitation.

"It's taken me a while, but I've come to realize that we were both at fault, both hiding, both denying who and what we were."

Charles' eyes filled with questions, but he sensed her need to soliloquize.

"When I married you, I loved you in my head, not in my heart. I wanted what you represented. Social acceptance. Class. Status. I saw you as another pane in the glass house I was constructing for myself, a house so illusory and fragile that if you hadn't knocked it down, someone else would have. I wanted to be someone I wasn't. I wanted my girlish dreams to become reality."

"There's nothing wrong with dreams, Jennifer."

"Jennie."

"What?" Charles was puzzled, especially by the shy look on Jennifer's face.

"Did you ever know that Jennie is my real name?"

"No, I didn't."

"Well, it is. Jennie Kay Sheldon. That's how it reads in the hospital records. I became Jennifer when I was in college, when I thought that by changing my name, I could transform my destiny. I've spent years trying to be Jennifer, and it hasn't made me or anyone close to me happy. So I've decided to try being Jennie."

"It suits you," he said, as if seeing her for the first time. "It's warm and real."

He smiled at her and squeezed her hand. It was the first genuine smile she had seen on his face all evening, and it pleased her.

"That's the point," she said. "I wasn't real before. I wasn't honest with you or me or anyone else. I was as deceptive in my way as you were in yours. We were living a play, acting out roles we had created for ourselves. We surrounded ourselves with props and spoke on cue without ever allowing our real selves to surface. Then, you left me. You walked out because for you, the play had ended. I hated you for it then, but now I applaud you. It was very courageous. You declared yourself free to be who you are. It's taking me longer, but I think I'm getting there."

Charles tried to absorb all that she had said, as well as some she hadn't. He had not expected such strength or honesty, but he was grateful for both. Then, he looked at her, with her red hair shimmering in the light and her tanned skin making her eyes darker and deeper. She was a beautiful woman, inside and out, and he didn't regret a moment he had spent with her.

"Even though I knew we could never last 'til death do us part,' I did love you, Jennie Kay Sheldon Cranshaw. And I still do in my own way. My only regret is that we never had children. You'd make a wonderful mother," he said.

Soft, puffy tears rolled silently down Jennifer's cheeks, catching on a shaky smile.

"And you make a wonderful friend."

Silence came again, but this time it was a reflective quiet, blanketing them with cottony comfort as they sat holding hands and sharing more than they had ever shared before.

"Charles, do you have a lover now?"

The question startled him, and he looked at her, hesitating.

"Does it bother you to discuss this with me?"

"It feels a bit strange, but no, it doesn't bother me," he said. Then: "Are you disgusted? Do you think I'm sick and depraved?"

"I think you're a dear man," she said, leaning over to kiss his cheek. "I know you to be caring and intelligent and sensitive. I could never think of you as anything else."

Charles stood, took Jennifer by the hand, and lifted her to her feet. They stood very close to each other, and she felt his breath on her face. Then he kissed her, gently and dearly.

"You know how I hate to be late," he said. "And we do have a dinner party to attend. May I escort you, fair lady?"

"I'd be delighted, kind sir." Jennifer curtsied. Her entire being felt refreshed and revitalized. She had overcome so many things—hurt, loss of pride, prejudice perhaps, and most of all her own weaknesses. Knowing that Charles had waged a similar battle and that he too had triumphed was a wonderful reward.

"Maybe afterwards, I'll treat us both to an eggnog," Charles said.

Thirty-One

Brad Helms rarely drank martinis. He only opted for the volatile mixture during times of extreme stress—and this was one of them. Tonight, the *Jolie* ordeal would come to an end. Inside, his emotions seesawed. Although he prayed for a favorable conclusion, there was a part of him that didn't care, as long as it was finally over.

Brad had driven himself to a state of nervous exhaustion. His brooding, handsome face had grown harsh, lined with worry and suspicion. He had had little sleep during the past few weeks, and no matter how often people presented him with a positive view, he countered with a negative. The April issue had been a resounding advertising success. Bookings had exceeded even the most outlandish expectations. That should have tranquilized him; instead, it unnerved him. He saw it as a coup for whoever was behind the move to buy *Jolie*, a lucky break that would allow the purchaser to reap an instant profit.

Ever since the invitation to the Starks' had been delivered to his office, he had been obsessed with uncovering the truth. Again and again, he burrowed through records and folders and ledger sheets, some for the third and fourth times, digging for the one clue that would give him what he wanted most, proof that *Jolie* had been the innocent victim of an audacious plot, rather than the victim of inept management. The Starks' invitation might have signaled a *fait accompli*, but Brad was determined to continue his detective work until he unearthed the name of the one person who had provoked this crisis, that one inside man. Or woman.

During some of Brad's more desperate moments, he had come to agree with Brooke and, in his own mind, had started to build a case against Jennifer. Although his evidence was scant and circumstantial, it was convincing. His original idea, dedicating an entire issue to one state, was risky. He knew it and so did the others in his office that day, yet one person had leaped up in support of the idea. Maybe because that person knew she was not at risk? Then there was the fact that Claiborne Stark was her husband's partner. Why was the sale being announced at his apartment instead of at the office? Was her husband backing a consortium that was about to present *Jolie* to Jennifer as a token of his love and devotion?

Brad sat at his dining room table arguing with himself. Though he couldn't believe that Jennifer would be involved in something so underhanded, Brooke constantly reminded him about Jennifer's secrecy and her ambition; the way she seemed to be taking this project so personally, insisting on overseeing every last detail. Then again, there was Brooke's ambition, her insistence, her lightly veiled threats.

Suddenly, Brad stopped shifting papers. His eyes riveted on one pink sheet. He had found his culprit.

"Conlon!" Brad's eyes were glazed.

It all fit. When he had first heard of Morceaux, Brad had thought the name sounded familiar, but he couldn't remember why. Now he knew. Terk Conlon had worked for Morceaux before he came to *Jolie*. Terk had joined the staff, and within six months, Morceaux wouldn't spit on *Jolie*. And neither would a dozen other companies about the same size. Brad rifled through some other files. Every manufacturer who had deserted *Jolie* within the first year after Terk's arrival was part of the same conglomerate—Towers Industries. And the other advertisers who had jumped ship? All middle-priced manufacturers who had obviously followed the leader. It was too big a coincidence.

"And will it be a coincidence when they announce that *Jolie* has been sold and in the next breath name Terk Conlon publisher?"

Brad left the table and went to the mirror, absently checking his bow tie, trying to sort out his thoughts. When Terk had first come to *Jolie*, every magazine had been in tough shape. The market had gone soft, and budgets all over town were being sliced in half. Whoever had backed Conlon must have decided to make certain that *Jolie* never recovered. Once the other magazines staged a comeback and *Jolie* continued to lag, they must have made an offer. The more *Jolie* slid, the better that offer must have looked.

Brad took another sip of his martini, went to the closet, and took out his coat. He had his proof, but he had found it too late. There was nothing he could do except comfort himself with the thought that he had not been responsible for *Jolie*'s downward slide. He had not failed. He simply had been beaten by someone who played the game better than he.

Thirty-Two

The far corner of the Starks' massive living room served as Eben Towers's command post. From there, he could remain relatively inconspicuous, listen politely to Selwyn Fellows and the Fellows attorneys discuss the financial ramifications of their deal, and still keep his eyes trained on the door. It was early, and in keeping with cocktail hour protocol, no one sat, but grouped in small bunches, trading places every few minutes as if on a timer, mixing and mingling, seeing and being seen. Only Towers held his position. To the casual observer, he appeared relaxed, but mentally, he was crouched down on his haunches, waiting for that glorious moment when he would pounce like a fox on a chicken coop.

Before this evening, Towers had held the scepter of power, his name known and respected by many industry strongmen, but that dominance had resulted from the vast accumulation of wealth. In a few hours, his realm would increase when he was crowned with influence. He would be a force, a man of consequence, whose favor would be courted and curried. On some, he would bestow favors; others, who had deigned to dismiss him in the past, would be denied even the most minor request. It was they who had prompted him to vie for control of *Jolie,* and now that he had it, they would pay dearly for their insults.

As he surveyed the site of his victory, he felt his excitement grow, and he congratulated himself on his choice. Selwyn Fellows had wanted to make the announcement at the *Jolie* offices. Claiborne Stark had suggested taking over the top floor of "21," but Towers wanted to flaunt his importance and his connections by having this party in the home of one of the most prominent couples in New York.

The atmosphere was positively exhilarating. Beautiful people milled about, casting a glittery aura benefiting a

308

gathering of celebrities. One hundred and fifty people had been invited, some more famous than others, but each one select. There were Fellows Publications executives, partners in Stark's law firm, titled staffers from every Fellows magazine, a number of major ladies-wear manufacturers, and a fair assortment of high-priced designers. To add to the sparkle were columnists from *Women's Wear Daily*, the New York *Times*, and *Fashion Report*, and Albert di Salvo, the photographer, circulated, recording the gala evening for the public and the trade.

This was the inner circle of the fashion world, an assembly dusted with glamour and luxe, but it was the subtle undercurrents that invigorated Eben Towers. His small eyes, pale and hooded, prowled the crowd, studying faces so he could assess the collective mood. Expectancy filled the air, scenting the room. Most people sensed that this was more than just a casual party, especially those associated with *Jolie*. Towers watched each of them attempt to hide his apprehension, but he was attuned to camouflage, and the tremulous vibrations Towers felt heightened his pleasure, affecting him like an aphrodisiac. Their anxiety stimulated him, only because it increased the drama of his surprise. The fate of the *Jolie* staff was going to rest on the shoulders of one of their own, one who still had not arrived.

Many of the guests had expressed a mild curiosity about the diminutive man closeted with Selwyn Fellows, but Brooke Wheeler was not one of them. During her many years in New York, she had attended enough penthouse suppers and Southampton clambakes to mingle easily with the well-to-do, but nothing had prepared her for the staggering opulence of the Starks' River House triplex. Her eyes widened the instant she stepped into the palatial marble foyer, and she had barely blinked since, for fear that she might miss some small, but exquisite, detail. If it weren't so horribly déclassé, she would have asked to be shown around upstairs, but rather than appear gauche, she restricted herself to the main floor where she wandered from room to room, awestruck by the splendor of her surroundings.

Like a child at Disneyland, she traveled from room to room on the pretext of greeting colleagues, but in truth, Brooke was sightseeing. Though she rarely indulged in envy, by the time she settled in the living room, she was besieged by definite twinges. Black lacquered walls backdropped enormous canvases by Frankenthaler, Stella, and de Kooning, drawn into proportion by the extra-high ceilings for which the River House was famous. Huge white couches also fell into scale, arranged on deep-toned Oriental rugs, banked by marble end tables decorated with museum-quality objets d'art. Even the guests seemed kissed by the magic wand of affluence, gliding instead of walking, whispering instead of shouting, tittering instead of laughing. The ambience was regal, and Brooke drank it in until she felt lightheaded and giddy.

Amanda Stark intrigued her. She watched as Amanda moved among her guests with shoulders-back elegance. This silver-haired woman gowned by Galanos and jeweled by Bulgari had a noble bearing, a majestic carriage that marked her as a member of the elite. She was moneyed, above everyday considerations, a person privileged to live out Brooke's fantasy of selecting whatever she wanted without ever looking at a price tag.

Brooke had never seriously considered marriage, but she had to admit, she wouldn't mind leading Amanda Stark's life. Brooke smiled to herself and looked around for Brad. Though he had been avoiding her so far this evening, she knew it was because he was petrified that someone in that room might know Ivy Helms. His trial was scheduled to start within the month. When it was over, Brooke had every intention of being there to console him.

Amanda stopped to chat with Gwendolyn and Frank Stuart, and Brooke headed straight toward her editor-in-chief. Gwen made the appropriate introductions, and the four of them exchanged cocktail party informalities. Brooke turned to look at Gwen. She was smashing in a one-shouldered silk georgette dress tiered in navy and pink, her dark hair swept back to reveal delicate pink coral earrings dropped from diamond studs.

Though she looked completely at ease, Gwen was so edgy that the rustle of a taffeta skirt was enough to

unhinge her. Frank had given her a Valium shortly before
they left their apartment, but it had done little to soothe
her jitters. Each time a new face appeared at the door,
Gwen shuddered, wondering if that man or that woman
was about to make an announcement that would drastically alter her life. Much as she loved parties—and no one
loved them more than Gwen—she couldn't erase the
thought that they were being wined and dined before facing a firing squad.

While Frank and Brooke talked, Gwen's mind raced in
all directions, some more logical than others. She would
have liked nothing better than to believe that this evening
had nothing to do with her, that she was a name on a
guest list, a place card at a table, but her instincts warned
her otherwise.

" . . . and the president of Plutarch Fashions has been
trying to corner me all night. Wherever I go, he's no more
than two steps behind. I've been expending so much energy avoiding his grabby hands, I'll probably fall asleep
over dinner!"

Brooke had been reporting the party goings-on with
sportscaster enthusiasm, and though Frank appeared
amused, Gwen had no patience for idle gossip.

"Brooke! Stop blithering! There's a guillotine hanging
over our heads, and you're prattling on about nonsense."

Brooke felt her face flush. She hated when Gwen struck
an imperious tone. "We really don't know what's happening tonight," she said in her own defense. "Maybe Joseph
Fellows is stepping down, and we're all gathered to crown
Selwyn Fellows Chairman of the Board."

"And maybe they'll serve peanut butter and jelly for
dinner." Gwen's sarcasm earned her a stern look of repri-
mand from her husband.

"Brooke's right," he said. "No one knows for sure that
Jolie has been sold, so I suggest we keep our tempers intact." Frank had tried everything to distract his wife, but
unfortunately he agreed with her. The best he could hope
for was to keep her calm and to offer support if, and
when, it was needed.

"And what does Jennifer think?" Brooke asked, a decided edge to her voice.

"Jennifer isn't even here yet, and she's usually right on time."

Gwen turned to the door, hoping that the promotion director would pick up her cue and make an entrance. What Gwen didn't know is that she was not the only one watching and waiting for Jennifer's arrival.

Brad had cloistered himself in the drawing room where creamy white walls and dusky black couches provided a striking counterpoint to the design of the living room. Turkish-tucked silk pillows color-keyed to the palettes of Hans Hofmann and Barnett Newman stood on their corners forming a diamond-shaped line, like soldiers in formation, sparking the couches with splashes of parrot green, marigold orange, lipstick red, and sultry purples. Windows swept one entire wall, and several of the guests had gathered there to savor the view.

Brad feigned occasional interest, but he was struggling with the temptation to buttonhole Selwyn Fellows. One minute his pride urged him to tell Fellows what he knew, based on the notion that he had nothing to lose, but then the next minute, his instincts warned him to be still because he had nothing to gain. If Fellows had been involved in a conspiracy, he wouldn't appreciate being confronted with his role in the contrivance. If he wasn't, he would be grossly offended by Brad's accusations. Either way, it seemed to serve no desirable purpose, and Brad was hesitant to burn any unnecessary bridges.

A cocktail waitress brought him another martini, and he sipped it thoughtfully. Mentally, he patted himself on the back because he was more relaxed than he had ever imagined he would be under circumstances such as these. He had resigned himself to the sale of *Jolie* and, ultimately, to the loss of his job. Business was politics, he reasoned, and politics was very much a game. He had been bested by a man he had never considered better than he, and that hurt, but he had vowed to conduct himself with dignity. He would accept his dismissal graciously, and though he might choke on the words, he would come forth and offer his congratulations to *Jolie's* new publisher—Terkel Michael Conlon.

He was lost in thought when Selwyn Fellows approached and asked to speak to Brad in private.

"Is that him?"

Terk stole a quick glance at Eben Towers, then turned to the woman clinging to his arm. Although she had lost weight and was a shade too thin, Deirdre looked extraordinary in a Saint Laurent evening suit.

Several weeks ago, just days after his clash with Zena, Winifred Walling had come to ask if he would reconsider his decision to leave her daughter. She begged Terk to see Deirdre, to talk to her, to try and find some way to make their marriage work. Terk had agreed, but not only as a favor to Winnie. His disillusionment with Zena, the pressure created by his debt to Towers, and the crisis at the magazine had left him battered. Motives, consequences, facts, fantasies—he analyzed them all. Throughout, Deirdre insinuated herself on his thoughts, and he found that as his self-awareness increased, his hostility toward her diminished.

"That's him," Terk said, looking again at Towers. "Take away the velvet tuxedo, the silk shirt, and the patent leather party shoes, and you have a modern-day Marquis de Sade. He must have left his whip with the butler."

Deirdre squinted at the small man on the other side of the room. "He looks like the sort who always carries a spare. I don't like him," she said.

"I told you the other night, my relationship with Mr. Towers was not based on mutual admiration and affection."

"The idea of your being that man's toady is repulsive!" Deirdre snapped.

Terk slid his arm around her waist and began to steer her out of the living room, into the foyer. "Forget it," he said. "It's over."

Deirdre stopped and faced him. "Is it?" she asked.

"Absolutely. I'm paid up, the debt is cleared, and Eben Towers is now part of the past." Terk tried to maneuver her into the library, but she refused to move.

"He used you, Terk," she whispered. "And at the risk of upsetting the delicate balance of our détente, may I remind you that you tend to bear grudges?"

Terk laughed, but his eyes grew dark. "True. I don't like being pushed into corners."

An apologetic smile curled Deirdre's lips. "No one knows that better than I," she said.

Terk took her hand, squeezed it, and led her toward the bar, where he got them fresh drinks. As they stood there silently, he studied his wife. He couldn't get used to how frail she looked, nor to how soft she had become. He didn't delude himself into thinking that she had totally abandoned her penchant for power, but she was making an obvious effort to control her aggressiveness—thinking before speaking, asking, not demanding. Even her sense of pride had mellowed. Just the other night, she had asked him to come home. When he said he wasn't ready to do that, he had expected her to have a temper tantrum, but instead, she greeted his decision with quiet acceptance.

"What are you thinking about?" Terk asked.

"I wish you had told me all this before. I could have helped." Her voice was small, almost shy, and Terk bent down to kiss her cheek.

"Thanks," he said, "but Towers wanted more than money. He wanted revenge."

"Don't you?"

"I'm too tired for revenge. Too much has happened, and besides, I pushed myself into this corner. Towers just made sure I stayed there."

Deirdre nodded, but she wasn't convinced. She was certain that Terk hadn't told her everything. He had confided his involvement with Towers, even some of the things he had done to extricate himself, but Deirdre's instincts told her the story had been carefully edited. Deirdre could read more into a brief look than most people read in a paragraph, and Terk wasn't as calm as he wanted her to believe. He appeared too cautious, too forgiving. The Terk she knew was neither of those things.

Over the past few weeks, they had seen each other a great deal, and though they tip-toed around with tentative cordiality, Deirdre had felt them inching closer together. They had discussed things they never had before—her father, his father, their past, their future, even some of their dreams—and where she had always recognized Terk's enormous sensitivity, the depth of it surprised her. She found that he harbored resentments over simple slights. Comments and incidents someone else might have viewed as innocent, Terk interpreted as insults. No. Eben Towers's enslavement was not something Terk could dismiss this easily.

"Deirdre, don't dwell on this." Terk tapped her shoulder to get her attention. "It's really not worth it."

Deirdre smiled and followed him over to another group of people, but indescribable feelings nibbled at her. She tried to ignore them, but she had a weird premonition about this evening. Something wasn't right. Maybe it was the fact that the one person Terk didn't speak to was his boss, Brad Helms. Maybe it was the fact that Jennifer Cranshaw, the woman so inextricably involved with *Jolie*, had yet to arrive. Or maybe it was simply that she didn't trust a weasel like Eben Towers.

Brad stood in the library, dumb struck, mindless of the stares of those who had observed his meeting with Selwyn Fellows. He felt the heat of their curiosity, but he needed time to absorb the brief, but enlightening conversation. He had listened carefully, alert to any nuances that might have confirmed Fellows's participation in the conspiracy, but he had found none. As far as the head of Fellows Publications was concerned, the sale of *Jolie*—and he had admitted the conclusion of such a deal—had been business, nothing more, nothing less. But then Fellows said something that confirmed Brad's long-held belief that few things were ever as simple as they seemed. He had come here tonight believing it would be a one-act play with an uncomplicated plot. The climax would come when Selwyn Fellows handed the reins of the magazine over to its new owner. The audience would applaud, and the play would be over. Now he felt as if he had just been cast in a Hitchcock thriller. There were pages of dialogue between now and the finale, but when it came, an unsuspecting audience would be brought to its feet. Brad could hardly wait.

Jennifer and Charles were the last to arrive, and as Amanda Stark came to greet them, most heads rubbernecked toward the door. Jennifer embraced Amanda, momentarily unaware of the stir she had created. While a few cultivated tongues tsk-tsked at their tardiness, inquisitive eyes gave her and Charles the once-over. Even the most blasé of the fashionable assembly admired the striking redhead spotlighted by the foyer's crystal chandelier, her tanned skin making her look like a glimmering nugget of precious gold. Although they offered the expected apologies, secretly Jennifer was glad they were late. Tension hung over the crowd like a cloud of gray-green smog, and as she and Charles made their way into the living room, she sniffed at it. Wherever she looked, smiles appeared strained, conversations sounded stilted, postures were plastic and stiff.

"I think they've got the covered wagons in a circle," Charles said.

"Did Claiborne tell you anything?" Jennifer whispered.

"Not a thing. Obviously this deal, if there is a deal, was kept very hush-hush. I don't think security was this close on the Manhattan Project."

"According to the rumor mill, *Jolie* is the odds-on favorite for a sale," Jennifer said, studying faces, "but I guess everyone fears a dark horse."

"I suggest we take off in separate directions and scout the territory." Charles squeezed Jennifer's hand as he turned toward the drawing room. "Call if you need me," he said.

After all this time, it felt strange to be comforted by Charles's presence, but comforted she was, and for the first time in her life, Jennifer wished to see into the future, to know if she and Charles would remain friends or if they would drift apart like balloons in the wind. She watched him disappear down the hall, struck by a sudden pang of loss. Part of her longed to run after him, to cling to the familiar and to hide from the unknown, but that was fantasy, unreal and impossible. Charles was now part of her past. Tonight was reality, tomorrow was the future, and she would have to handle it as best she could.

She was about to look for a waiter when a waving hand brought her to Gwen and Frank Stuart. As Jennifer gave them a brief synopsis of her trip, she noticed how often Gwen jiggled her bracelets and knew that beneath this glamorous façade was a frightened woman. Gwen sat high on the masthead and, therefore, suffered the rattling insecurity of leadership. Jennifer could almost hear Gwen's inner voice chastizing her, punishing her with the notion that if she had done a better job, Fellows would never have entertained even a thought of selling *Jolie*. She had done her best, but now she faced the possibility of being told publicly that her best was not good enough.

Jennifer sympathized because no matter what the reason, dismissal telegraphed cruel messages. Nothing softened the impact, and no position provided immunity. Why me? Why not someone else?

"You have a lot of catching up to do."

Jennifer turned to the friendly voice behind her. Patrick Graham handed her a glass of white wine, his boyish face flushed with a shy smile.

"How fortified do you think I'll have to be?" she asked.

"The natives are extremely restless," he said, "but no one has been able to find anything out."

Jennifer followed his gaze into a corner where the usually unflappable Marnie Dobbs stood huddled with her husband. He appeared to be counseling her, and even from a distance, Jennifer could see how unsettled they were. At the opposite end of the room stood several members of the sales staff. From the looks on their faces and the tinny sound of their laughter, Jennifer knew that they had pulled out every tired joke in their repertoire as a means of distraction. Suddenly Jennifer looked away, afraid to catch the vibrations.

"Judging by the lecherous stares you're generating, I'm not the only one in this room who thinks you look exceptionally gorgeous this evening," Pat said. "If asked, I'd say you're hovering at about a twelve."

"Had I known that," Jennifer said, pleased by the compliment, "I would have worn this outfit more often. I always thought of it as an eleven."

Pat wanted to tell her that it wasn't the outfit, spectacular though it was, but rather her inner electricity. Jennifer was a vivacious woman, and her vibrant charm had always been her most attractive feature, the singular quality that had distinguished her from other women who were merely beautiful.

"You also look incredibly calm," he said.

"It's the tan. Beneath this Acapulco bronze is a bilious green."

"You're doing a superlative job of hiding it, but I must tell you, you're running second to Terk. He's so cool you'd think this whole shebang was nothing more than a belated New Year's Eve party."

Jennifer turned toward the foyer where Terk was glad-handing his way through the crowd, smiling and backslapping and working the room. Jennifer couldn't decide if Terk had costumed himself in self-defensive bravura or if he had truly adopted a laissez-faire approach to the proceedings, but he did appear unusually buoyant. He was minus the nervous twitches that afflicted the rest of the staff, and she watched with intense interest as he squired his brilliantly plumed wife from cluster to cluster. Strange, she thought. He pointedly avoided her. For months, Jennifer had suspected that Terk knew more than he was letting on, but whenever she had questioned him, he had accused her of having an overactive imagination. Jennifer knew him to be a complex man. She tried to quell the uneasiness she felt about his behavior, but her instincts told her to keep an eye on him. She couldn't help but wonder what he was doing with Deirdre, but then again, she reasoned, he must have been just as curious about Charles. Maybe that was why he had sidestepped her. Maybe he felt there would be some awkwardness in their conversation. And maybe he was hiding something.

"I think that bell is the signal for us to find our places in the dining room," Pat said, taking her arm to escort her in.

"I think it's the signal for the fourth round," Jennifer said, unable to take her eyes off Terk.

"Do you think it'll go the full fifteen?" Pat asked.

"No. I think the fix is in, and someone's going to take a dive in the fifth."

This had been a very taxing day, starting with David's surprise visit, his revelation about Josh, her bittersweet, but draining, meeting with Charles, and then the grinding tension of the party. Throughout it all, Jennifer had forced herself to remain calm and in control, but as they exited the dining room and she saw Claiborne Stark mount the first step of the winding marble staircase, her reserve began to falter. Voices lowered and soon an expectant hush settled over the crowd. Charles slipped a reassuring arm around Jennifer's waist. When she heard Claiborne's clear baritone introduce Selwyn Fellows, she was grateful. She would be alone tonight after all of this was over, but she wasn't alone now.

Selwyn Fellows was a man of medium height, balding and bespectacled, but he carried himself with the dignity of a general. Jennifer had always found him to be rather wooden and impersonal, and as he smiled at his audience, she wondered if he had given any thought to the emotion involved in what he was about to do, if his world included human feeling or merely revolved around a profit and loss statement.

"On behalf of everyone assembled," he started, loud enough for even those in the back to hear, "let me thank Claiborne and Amanda Stark for hosting such a stellar evening."

Just as Jennifer expected, the applause was polite, but hurried. Everyone, Jennifer included, felt tortured by the passage of time, a process that tonight had seemed to elongate seconds into minutes and minutes into hours. She felt as if she had been held captive for days and was about to hear the terms of her release.

"As you all know, those of us who run Fellows Publications think of it as a family, a group of people united by a sincere love of fashion and a desire to beautify the world in which we live. Like most families, there comes a time when the structure of the basic unit must undergo change. For a long while, we have sought to add to our family tree, and now we have. I am proud to announce the acquisition of the finest men's-wear periodical in the country today, *Epicure!*"

Gwen's face visibly brightened at Fellows's announcement, and she joined her companions in enthusiastic applause. Jennifer knew how desperate Gwen was to accept this purchase as the *raison d'être* for the evening's festivities, but Jennifer had discerned a comma in Fellows's speech, not a period. She saw Frank Stuart whisper something in Gwen's ear. Jennifer presumed it was an "I-told-you-so." It took a while for her to locate Brad in the mass

of people, and when she did, the look on his face startled
her. It was circumspect, without remorse, touched with a
bit of expectancy, and Jennifer congratulated him on his
inner fortitude, a quality she had never attributed to him
before. He was behaving admirably, and she was proud of
him.

"Naturally," Fellows continued, "we wish to put our
stamp on *Epicure* immediately, and to do so, we have
selected a new publisher. He is a man born to a world of
style, a man with his own personal sense of refinement
and taste, a man whom we trust will lend some of his own
sartorial dash to the pages of our newest addition. It is
with great pleasure that I announce the new publisher of
Epicure, Mr. Bradford Helms!"

Brooke felt faint. Brad had barely spoken to her all evening. Obviously he had known about this. She applauded
loudly, watching Brad walk up the landing and shake the
hand of Selwyn Fellows.

Jennifer smiled. She was pleased for Brad and thrilled
that Fellows had made such a wise choice for its new venture. It surprised her, but only because it was so logical.
Brad loved men's wear. It showed in the way he dressed,
the way he carried himself, and when she thought about
it, she realized that he had never been completely at ease
at *Jolie*. He had never fully assimilated into the world of
fads and trends and chiffons and silks. Husky tweeds and
velvety flannels were more his forte, and she had no doubt
that he would make *Epicure* a stunning success.

Then her hands paused midclap, and her breath caught
in her throat. She was struck by the sudden realization
that Brad's exit left the top spot at *Jolie* vacant. Quickly,
she scanned the crowd looking for a face, an attitude, a
posture, anything that would reveal who was about to accept the mantle of *Jolie* leadership. Something on Brad's
face had said that he knew.

"Needless to say, it is with great pleasure that I accept
this new post." Brad's voice reverberated with satisfaction, his handsome, patrician visage softened by the bash-
fulness that comes to those singled out for praise. "Along
with the pleasure, however, comes regret. I've made many
friends at *Jolie*, and I shall miss them terribly. I shall miss
their creativity, their incredible optimism, their verve, and

even their temper tantrums, but I take with me a sense of pride that I was able to be associated with such a noble group of people. I only hope they'll miss me too."

Patrick Graham didn't know where to look first. He was immensely pleased for Brad and wanted to witness his moment of glory, but he couldn't take his eyes off Brooke Wheeler. She appeared stricken, almost as if she had just learned of the death of someone close. In all people, no matter how saintly, an evil gremlin exists that derives pleasure from revenge, and Pat's gremlin was ecstatic. Throughout dinner—and he had been unfortunate enough to share her table—she had acted like a helium balloon, buoyant and floating from one conversation to another. Now she was deflated, and he saw panic and anger blotch her face. Everyone was concerned about *Jolie*'s new master, but Brooke had courted only one possibility, and her card had been trumped.

As Brad stepped down and returned to his place, the crowd buzzed while the *Jolie* sales staff besieged their former boss with congratulatory handshakes. Gwen could barely move. Her initial flush of excitement had faded, and she felt pale with suspense. She fretted that her worst fears were about to be realized, that the new publisher of *Jolie* would bring someone in from the outside to fill her position. It was not uncommon for publishers to bring with them editors known to be compatible with their philosophies. Frank grasped her hand and tried to speak to her, but she fixed her gaze on Selwyn Fellows and waited.

"Again assuming the role of parent," Fellows said, speaking slowly, waiting for the noise to abate, "I have another announcement. A gentleman has asked for the hand of one of our young women, and we have granted permission for their union."

Jennifer was so nervous that she thought if he didn't drop his pater-familias similes, she would scream. Marnie Dobbs and Bettina Kharkovsky had closed ranks around her, and she could hear them mumbling to each other.

"*Jolie* is about to leave the folds of Fellows Publications, but she is being given into the capable hands of a man intimately familiar with the young woman's apparel market. He is a gentleman of profound reputation in the industry, and although he is a neophyte where publishing is concerned, we have no doubt that his leadership capabilities and his financial genius will provide *Jolie* with a bright and prosperous future. May I present the new owner of *Jolie*, Mr. Eben Towers!"

Jennifer felt dizzy. She looked to Charles for an explanation, but he too appeared shocked. She watched Towers take charge of the makeshift dais and steeled herself for his inaugural address. She supposed that in a way, she was luckier than most of her compatriots. At least she knew who he was. Marnie, Brooke, Gwen, most of the salesmen, Pat, were all turning to their neighbors with questions. They were about to get answers.

Eben Towers stalked up to the landing like an exiled king about to reclaim his throne. He shook hands with Selwyn Fellows and then waited for him to find his seat. All around, tongues clacked and heads bobbed. They were shocked, just as he knew they would be. They were smiling, jerky, nervous smiles and inside, Towers smiled too, but for very different reasons.

"As I stand here and gaze upon this extraordinary assembly, I see many friends and acquaintances, business associates and colleagues, but to some of you, I am a stranger, perhaps even an interloper. For almost thirty years, I have been involved with fashion, and without hesitation, I can tell you that the idea of owning one of this nation's most influential magazines is indeed a heady experience. This glorious evening marks the culmination of years of wishful thinking and months of strenuous negotiation. To those who have endured the rumors, the endless speculation, and the agonizing secrecy, let me assure you that the worst is over, and the best is yet to come!"

Towers dismissed the look of skepticism in the eyes of many front row occupants. It was the look of bewilderment and concern etched on the faces of his adversaries that interested him.

"As a manufacturer, I've been a fan of *Jolie* for as long as I can remember, mainly because *Jolie* represented the voice of America's up-and-coming young women, those ambitious females daring enough to stretch for independence. For most of its forty year history, *Jolie* remained loyal to these women, transmitting a consistent message that encouraged individual interpretation of fashion trends as well as personal expression in all areas of their lives. *Jolie* was the leader of the leaders.

"Over the past few years, however, that focus blurred, and *Jolie* began to shepherd sheep. Why? Because they, like so many others, found themselves caught up in the rising tide of something known as the designer phenomenon. Suddenly, labels became essential, appearing outside garments instead of inside where they rightfully belonged. Initials began to be stamped on everything from pantyhose to sunglasses, and the slogan most frequently trumpeted by the trade press, advertising agencies and magazine editorials was, 'You are *who* you wear.'

"I can remember a time when young career women shopped constantly, always on the lookout for something new to wear. Spontaneous purchases were commonplace, and buying new wardrobes for each season was part of the normal order of things. They shopped without guilt because a single jacket didn't cost the equivalent of a month's rent. Everything is different today. Now, young women are encouraged to buy 'investment clothes,' single pieces that are supposed to satisfy their yen for fashion. They're told to be satisfied with less because less is more. In my view, that message has created consumer insecurity, put hundreds of manufacturers out of business, and changed the structure of an entire industry. Names have become symbols of acceptance, and price tags have become barometers of self-image. My purpose in buying *Jolie* is to reverse that trend. Not by campaigning against designers, but by campaigning *for* fashion over celebrity, style over signature."

A complete range of facial expressions greeted his speech, starting with outrage and working its way down to smirks of approval. Feet shuffled uncomfortably, and heads weaved as comments were passed from one to the other. Only two faces registered anything approaching neutrality: Terk Conlon appeared amused, and Jennifer Cranshaw was obviously reserving judgment.

"My goal is to see *Jolie* return to her rightful place as leader of the young women's magazine field. We're going to dust the cobwebs off an old philosophy and revitalize an entire market. *Jolie's* editorial pages will sing with new freedom, bursting with the artistry of the young shown in clothing for the young. From now on, only two names will be important: the name of the consumer and the name of the magazine she reads. And that magazine will be *Jolie!*"

He paused for a breath, grateful for the loud applause started by his manufacturing colleagues who would greatly benefit from his promises. He noticed that even the staff of *Jolie* clapped their hands, almost fervently in fact, and he felt rewarded. They believed he was right, but as he scanned the room, he saw those who just as fervently opposed his theories. They were the men he had set out to best, the men whom he had befriended when they all attended design school. For years, after he had entered manufacturing, he fed them, nurtured them, housed them whenever they were in need. He even financed some of their businesses. They had been his protegés, until they became celebrities. Suddenly, they forgot to return his calls. His name was left off guest lists. Luncheons became rare, soon nonexistent. Overnight, he became nothing but a rag merchant, and they wanted no part of him. He had bided his time, and now as he saw them stand in startled silence and felt their fear, he was warmed by the flames of vengeance.

"I'm sure that those people whose job it is to put *Jolie* on the newsstand each month are anxious to hear whether I am Attila the Hun out for a blood bath, or Casper the Friendly Ghost, an interested, but nonintrusive presence," he went on. "I've studied the *Jolie* masthead carefully, and I have only two personnel changes to make. Any others will have to come from the new leadership. The first change is that of Advertising Sales Manager. There is a gentleman at *Jolie* who has proven himself to be a tremendous asset over the years, overcoming what can sometimes be the scourge of past celebrity to grow into a fine and creative salesman. Mr. William Zorn!"

Jennifer's eyes darted across the room to Terk. Her breath caught in her throat as she heard him replaced without so much as a thank you or an explanation, but Terk was smiling, applauding his cohort with football stadium abandon, whistling his approval. Jennifer was totally confused. She liked Billy Zorn and yes, she thought he would make a competent Advertising Sales Manager, but

Terk was just not the type to take something like this so lightly.

Brad watched Terk also, but he was not confused. He felt Brooke's fingers pinch his arm, but he was not about to remove his eyes from Terk's face.

Deirdre had released Terk's arm so he could congratulate his successor, but as the crowd settled once again, she grabbed onto him for support. Inside, she felt volcanic rumblings, as if steaming black lava were about to pour down from the ceiling in a suffocating torrent. She disliked Towers for what he had done to Terk, but more than that, she didn't trust him. If her father had taught her anything, it was that to some, revenge was addictive. Her husband's face glowed with anticipation, and, for his sake, she hoped she was wrong. Position was important to Terk, and he had sacrificed more than his share to arrive at this evening. She prayed that in the next few minutes, Terk didn't feel heaven's gate slam in his face.

Towers continued, "Since Brad Helms has been awarded the captain's chair at *Epicure,* the publisher's chair at *Jolie* has been vacated. Since I am seeking to forge ahead in new directions, I have searched for someone capable of leading pioneers. *Jolie*'s new publisher is a person with an aggressive commitment toward the best, someone who will accept nothing less than complete success, someone who personifies the gutsy independence of *Jolie*'s readership. It is with great pleasure that I present one who has earned the right to be publisher of *Jolie,* Jennifer Sheldon Cranshaw!"

For several seconds, there was no applause, merely stunned silence. Jennifer was thunderstruck, her heart pounded in her chest, and she felt as if she had just hit a skid on an icy road. She was momentarily out of control. She felt Charles hug her and heard congratulations offered from those near her, but she heard them through a fog. She wanted to laugh and cry and shout and scream, all at the same time, but most of all, she wanted a minute to think.

Jennifer was not a religious woman. She relished certain traditions and customs and, when pressed, admitted to a belief in God. She was, however, extremely spiritual. Many things appeared to her as tests. This was one of

those tests. She had just been named publisher of one of
America's foremost magazines, a magazine she herself had
helped place on top. More than that, she was the first
woman publisher of a fashion magazine. Women were editors-in-chief and held many other key positions, but the
office of publisher had remained a male stronghold. Was
this a sign? Was she being told that to suppress her talents in search of emotional fulfillment was wrong? Jennifer struggled with herself, seeking a response from
whatever spirits had touched her. She felt Charles nudge
her toward the front of the room and knew she had no
time for conundrums.

Her first steps were hesitant, then steady and secure.
She walked through the crowd slowly, accompanied by
the explosive roar of sincere applause. The room reverberated with an ovation worthy of her newly bestowed
honor. She had accomplished what no other woman ever
had; she had been given a title no other woman had ever
held. The *Jolie* staff hooted for her, forgetting all protocol,
cheering loudly as she stepped onto the landing and shook
hands with Eben Towers. Marnie Dobbs dropped her
usual reserve and shouted, "Brava! Brava!" Bettina
Kharkovsky echoed her friend's cry, clapping her hands
and grinning with approval. They were stunned, yet overwhelmed with relief. Jennifer was a known commodity, and
they felt safe and secure. Brooke Wheeler, however, felt
anything but safe. She didn't know whether Jennifer knew
of her double-dealing, but she knew better than to underestimate the object of all this raucous attention. She
felt several pairs of eyes staring at her, and for a minute,
she thought she heard a malicious giggle or two, but instead of shrinking back in defeat, Brooke edged her way
toward the front, clapping and cheering like a second in a
champion's corner. Gwen Stuart was too elated to applaud. She simply stood and smiled at Jennifer, her eyes
misty, the tension in her body easing. She was thrilled by
the announcement, both as a colleague and as a woman,
and her face beamed with happiness and respect.

"You knew, didn't you?" Brooke hissed into Brad's ear,
hoping he heard her over the din.

Brad nodded, catching Jennifer's attention and raising
his glass in her honor.

"Why didn't you tell me?" Brooke whispered.

Brad turned to her.

"I'm very pleased," he said evenly. "Jennifer is a talent, and she deserves this kind of tribute. As for myself, this whole nightmare has worked out rather well. I'm excited about heading up *Epicure*. And Jennifer will do a bang-up job with *Jolie*."

Terk never even noticed the embarrassed glances of those around him. He never felt Deirdre clutch his arm. He stood in horrified silence, glaring at the two people silhouetted against the circular staircase. His body was rigid and taut, like the cord on a crossbow, and his eyes flamed with such fury that he half expected Towers to topple over from the ferocity of his anger, but Towers deliberately avoided Terk, showering his attention on Jennifer, the new publisher of *Jolie*.

"For the first time in my life," Jennifer said, suddenly overcome with shyness, "I think I'm at a loss for words."

She breathed deeply, trying to silence the fluttering in her chest. The crowd had quieted, and as she looked out at her audience, she directed her gaze at Charles. They might have decided not to share the rest of their lives together, but she was grateful that they were able to share this moment.

"I accept this appointment with a great deal of humility," she said. "It is truly an honor and one which I share with all my friends at *Jolie*, because putting out a magazine is like conducting a symphony orchestra; one person waves a baton, but without talented, responsive musicians, the baton is nothing but a skinny piece of wood. Those of us who've been with *Jolie* for a long time have experienced the delicate sweetness of success, as well as the bitter aftertaste of failure, and you don't have to be a baker's daughter like I am to know that sweet is a whole lot better! I thank Mr. Towers for this incredible opportunity, and I promise to do my best to be worthy of his confidence."

Jennifer extended her hand to her benefactor who led her down off the landing and into the crush of well-wishers. As Towers graciously accepted the congratulations of his friends, Jennifer basked in the generous outpouring of hers. People she didn't even know wormed their way to her side to offer their support. It seemed as if everyone wanted to shake her hand or kiss her cheek. Everyone but Terk Conlon.

"You won't get away with this!" Terk snarled at her, and for the first time since she had known him, Jennifer felt afraid, afraid for both of them.

The party had begun to break up, and many of the guests had already taken their leave. She had been saying good-night to Brad when Terk had grabbed her elbow and spirited her into the pantry.

"I don't know what you're talking about," she said, stepping away from him. Violence glinted in his eyes, and she wondered if he were really capable of hurting her.

"I was supposed to get that job. I was supposed to be the publisher." Terk came toward her, pushing her back up against a wall. "I earned it doing that Napoleonic fuck's dirty work, and I'm going to get it."

"Terk, I never knew anything about it. Believe me, please. This came as a shock to me too."

"Well, don't get used to the title, lady, because you're not going to have it for very long!"

Jennifer couldn't even respond. She was trembling, and her mind clogged with thoughts she wished she could erase. Terk was overwrought, and he paced nervously, as if something inside him had snapped and he had no control over his movement. Suddenly, he stood over her and spoke in a harsh whisper.

"You should be grateful for what I'm going to do," he said. She didn't answer. She was afraid to speak for fear of tipping him off the emotional tightrope he was on. "He did this as a publicity trick," Terk said. "Don't you see that? First woman publisher. It's worth more newspaper ink than the sale itself."

He turned away from her, and she heard him laugh, a hard-bitten cackle that echoed with a hollow sound.

"Who would give a shit about a magazine changing hands?" he ranted. "No one! So that worm found a way to exploit the press. You, my sweet, are the bait. Do you think for one insane minute that he's going to let you run *Jolie*? Not a chance. He's going to run it and you!"

Now that she knew Terk's connection to Towers, she

understood his anger, but he was attacking her, and she
didn't deserve it.

"Nobody runs me," she said, "and you know it! I am
qualified for this job, and whether you like it or not, I'm
going to take it on. What's more, I'm going to do a hell of
a job, so stop making a fool of yourself!"

"A fool? You think I'm making a fool out of myself?"
His voice had risen, and she could see his hands shaking.
"I'll tell you when I made a fool out of myself. When I
trusted you, that's when. You made a deal with him,
didn't you? He came to you with some wonderful offer,
and you sold me out?"

"I did not! I didn't even know about your relationship
with Towers until just now." Jennifer glared back at Terk,
indignant at his accusations. "And even if he did make me
an offer, which he didn't, how could you even think that I
would sell you out? For what reason?"

"You've been sleuthing around for weeks trying to find
out if I was the nasty ogre who pushed your sweet little
Mimi in front of those porno cameras, haven't you? Well,
I did!"

Jennifer wanted to cover her ears with her hands. She
didn't want to hear this. He was hurting, she could see
that, and she suffered for him, but some truths were best
left hidden.

"And I'll tell you what else I did with those cameras,
sweetheart. I figured that bastard might double-cross me,
and so I took out a little insurance policy, and now I'm
going to collect on it."

"Terk, please." Jennifer grabbed his arm and held onto
him. "You did what you had to do. I understand that. He
had you in a bind. You owed him an outrageous sum of
money, but don't do something now you'll regret for the
rest of your life. Obviously, he wouldn't hesitate to ruin
you. Don't push him. Let it go."

Terk's face clouded over. He appeared to be in a
trance, hypnotized by desperation. Jennifer shuddered at
the sight of him, feeling his hostility prick at her like tiny
acupuncture needles.

"I took a few pictures of the distinguished Mr. Towers,"
he said, his voice seething with revenge. "He's a flaming
faggot. It was easy to get him to go with the young stud I

hired. He followed this guy to a special apartment I had rigged up, and now all Towers's kinky little habits are locked in my safe at home. I'm going to invite that doddering old queen to a private showing, and when he's finished, you're finished."

"Terk, don't!" Jennifer tried to follow him, but he had broken free of her grasp and stormed out of the room. "He'll throw you in jail," she murmured to the empty space. "You don't have to do this. I'll help you," she mumbled. "I don't know how, but I'll help you."

Jennifer hugged herself, trying to stop the tremors that shook her body. She refused to let him sink back into the abyss he had struggled so hard to escape, but standing there, in the dim light of the pantry, she wondered what, if anything, she could do.

Jennifer didn't know that she was not alone, that someone else had overheard the entire conversation. Jennifer might have been searching for a way out, but the eavesdropper was not. That someone knew precisely what to do.

Thirty-Three

April first was an historic day in the annals of *Jolie* magazine. Newsstands all across the country carried the revolutionary issue, and as quickly as sellers stacked them up, buyers snatched them off the racks. For weeks after, circulation experts would be kept busy analyzing whether it was the enormous advance publicity, the tantalizing picture of Nina Kahala on the cover, or the vivid magenta headlines heralding page after page of paradisical pleasures that had prompted such heavy consumer response. In anticipation of a favorable reaction, Jennifer had ordered hundreds of thousands of extra copies printed, and by the middle of the month every last one of them would be sold. There would be no returns on April *Jolie*.

Naturally, the publicity about the sale of *Jolie* and Jennifer's appointment as publisher didn't hurt the cause. Newspapers feasted on her. She had become a national celebrity, and the press loved her, writing articles tracing her rise and quoting her on everything from her favorite recipe to foreign policy. She was the first woman to wear the mantle of publisher of a fashion magazine, and until the notoriety wore off, whatever she said was newsworthy.

Jennifer attempted to maintain perspective, turning down more talk-show interviews than she accepted and keeping the focus on the magazine and its objectives instead of on her personal life. The constant attention was fun some of the time, tedious much of the time, and more often than not, complicated her life. She and Charles had discussed divorce, but rather than attract negative publicity with a quickie settlement, their attorneys filed quietly in New York.

Everyone on the staff eagerly awaited the appearance of the April issue, but no one was more anxious than Jennifer. She had had her taste of fame and notoriety, and now she wanted the spotlight shifted onto the magazine. As she sat in her new office and leafed through her copy, her mouth formed a satisfied smile. April *Jolie* was spectacular.

The cover, subject of much controversy, was glorious. Nina Kahala's milky tan skin glowed with clear and dewy perfection; her pitch black hair glistened with blue-white highlights; her eyes sparkled beneath subtle shadings of purple and pink. A hot orange hibiscus peeked out from behind her ear, and she stared out at her audience with captivating shyness. Jennifer had viewed many covers in her years at the magazine, but this one was truly unique. Nina projected a sultry innocence professional models might have been hard pressed to produce. To Nina, posing was a new experience, a thrilling event in her life, and her excitement had filtered through the lens and onto the glossy cover.

The editorial section was a triumph. Each page encouraged the reader to move on to the next, promising surprises. The first portfolio focused on active sportswear photographed on the fabulous grounds of the Mauna Kea

Hotel on the Big Island of Hawaii. Gwen had exercised her powers as editor-in-chief to override objections to her decision to use a sports photographer for the shoot instead of one of their habitual fashion photogs. These twelve pages, each one a marvel, proved her right. There was a reality to these pages Jennifer had never seen before. Usually, celebrities posed, and clothes were shown *sans* wrinkles. Here, they were shown as they were meant to be worn, on athletes playing their game. Nancy Lopez and Jan Stephenson had consented to a one-on-one golf match so they could be captured in action, surrounded by a crowd of enthusiastic spectators, some of whom were *Jolie* models outfitted by the fashion department. Chris Evert Lloyd and Tracy Austin staged a singles match before a delighted group of Mauna Kea guests. Young women training for the summer Olympics track and gymnastic teams worked out in jogging clothes and brilliantly colored leotards, caught in stop-action pictures that were lyrical, balletic and real.

The mood shifted abruptly to one of sleek sophistication with the "Native New Yorker" section that featured Elyse de Marco's designs, some of the most enthralling fashion photographs she had ever seen. Once Patrick had met Elyse, he hired Francesco Scavullo for the shoot, convinced that only Scavullo could do justice to Elyse's steaming sensuality. Elyse stood barefooted on a sheet of white no-seam paper, its enormous roll clearly visible at the top of the page. The visual was stark and harshly simplistic, punctuated only by the addition of ingenious neon sculpture.

In one shot, a tubular palm tree with a purple trunk and hot pink fronds intensified the high-heat colors of Elyse's printed silk harem pants and bandeau top. In another, royal blue cloud shapes hovered over her as she posed in a one-shouldered white bodysuit, hip-wrapped with a blue and white print pareo. Neon flowers sprung up from an imaginary garden to complement the delicate lehua flowers woven into a headband and lei for Elyse. The tiny red blossoms softened the sexiness of one of Elyse's famous sarong dresses, this one draped in slinky red fabric laced with golden threads. Elyse was magnificent, her raven-black hair wind-blown to wildness, her eyes kohled in navy to accentuate their mysterious character. She was a temptress, gowned in seduction, exuding an Eve-like sinfulness that blended innocence and desire into a potent portrait.

Bettina's beauty pages exploded with color. Four pages of full-face models told the cosmetics and hair stories, displaying both the newest palettes for spring and summer makeup and the floral genius of Vincent Matteo. Tiny orange blossoms plaited into one model's silver-white hair created an image of an island virgin, her pale face kissed with the coral shadings that spoke of warm-weather days and balmy nights. Unconscious glamor was the message communicated by a striking brunette whose tawny skin had been brightened by lush pinks and royal purples. Baby's breath and azalea had been tucked into a sophisticated twist, resting gently on a roll of thick, black-brown hair. Loki Pouna's toffee-colored skin provided the perfect canvas for artists taken with murky teals and sea-water greens. Her panther-black hair hung straight to her shoulders, topped by a crown of miniature gardenias that spoke of purity and innocence. All the pictures had been taken through a vaseline-coated lens, and they looked like oil paintings, each one a visual definition of beauty.

Interspersed among the pictorial stories were feature articles dealing with life in an island culture. A quiz tested readers' color preferences as a way of determining personality. Interviews with islanders presently living on the mainland gave their perspective of life outside the tropics. "The Eye of the Beholder" delved into the question of what was beautiful to whom, charting the opinions of Polynesian wahines, transplanted mainlanders, Chinese, and kamaainas, those who had lived in Hawaii for a long time. "Adam and Evedom" discussed the effects of paradise on sexual behavior. The Career Department zeroed in on Hawaii's generous support of women with a piece entitled "Grass Skirts and Attaché Cases," and Environments detailed two houses that typified the open-air decorating philosophy of the islands.

The section on evening clothes pitted fantasy against reality, and where the idea had been accidental, the result was visually arresting. While Marnie had been in Hawaii, a group of local boys took to following the crew, whistling at the models, and interrupting the shoot. As a way of appeasing the basically harmless gang, Marnie asked them to pose with a tall blonde dressed in shimmering white lace. The contrast was so striking that Marnie searched for other ways to blend posh with punk. A willowy chiffon dress meant for lawn parties looked even more feminine draped over a stool in a truck stop diner. Silk pyjamas billowed in the wind as the model worked alongside pickers in a pineapple grove. And a pale peach tunic and skirt took on new elegance riding in a rickshaw.

The entire issue pulsated with electricity. Jennifer adored each and every page, but one stood out as her favorite. The masthead, the first since the change in management, had been reset to accommodate personnel shifts. The only disconcerting note was the absence of Terk's name. Aside from the fact that Eben Towers had never gotten back to her about rehiring Terk, Jennifer had neither seen nor heard from Terk since the Stark party. She had called his hotel, his house, and several of his favorite hangouts, but to no avail. Out of desperation, she called Winnie Walling. After explaining who she was and her relationship to Terk, Jennifer asked if there was any way she could get in touch with him. If he were here, maybe Towers would change his mind. Winnie was polite, but of little help. She told Jennifer that Deirdre and Terk had flown to Europe less than a week after the party, but she was not at liberty to give out their address, and she had no idea when they were expected back.

Jennifer was convinced that they were never coming back; that Terk had made good his threat to blackmail Towers with those salacious films and now was forced to hide in order to escape Towers's bloodhounds. The situation upset Jennifer terribly. Professionally, she missed Terk's creative zest and his incisive sales technique. Personally, she missed the man and fretted about his wellbeing. His anger had been frightening, and even though she knew she wasn't, Jennifer felt partly responsible. She had to know what happened, but it was becoming painfully clear that her only source of information was Towers himself. Somehow, she had to get him to tell her whether or not Terk had used his insurance policy.

As she debated strategy, her eyes lingered on the masthead. There, in bold capital letters was a line of type that gave her immense satisfaction: PUBLISHER . . . JENNIE SHELDON.

Thirty-Four

E ben Towers stared at Jennifer and wriggled in his seat as if he had an itch he couldn't scratch. She was positioned squarely in front of him, her face set in a dare, her posture rigid and unyielding. He had been examining figures and studying projections for more than an hour, and throughout, Jennifer's narration had sounded like a voice-over on a commercial for Terk Conlon. Bookings had slowed. Inserts, one of the most profitable of all advertising packages, had dropped off, and if something was not done, and soon, April would be viewed as a flash-in-the-pan issue, and *Jolie*'s upward trend would be reversed. Without resorting to pot shots at Billy Zorn, Jennifer had managed to present an excellent case, displaying evidence that pointed toward nothing greater than a mediocre future for *Jolie* under Zorn's management. She portrayed him as charming, efficient, and modestly effective, but without the creative aggressiveness required of a leader. Disaster was not in the offing, she said, but then again, neither was stunning success. In her quiet, yet forceful way, she had pushed Towers into a corner: did he sacrifice *Jolie* on the altar of his revenge, or did he set aside his personal grudge in the interest of all concerned?

"When you appointed me publisher," Jennifer was saying, her voice crisp and tight, "you stated publicly that you would not interfere with the management of the magazine. It was on that basis that I accepted the job."

"I have been true to my word," he said, leaning back in his chair like a school principal faced with a recalcitrant student.

"Not quite."

"And in what way have I stepped on your toes?"

He was patronizing her, but in a strange way, she welcomed the offense. It was easier to argue with a declared opponent than to try and deal with someone who expressed concern and interest on the surface, but harbored opposition and resentment underneath.

"You are making it impossible for me to insure that every issue will equal this one." She tossed a copy of April *Jolie* onto his desk, scattering several papers and overturning a stainless steel pencil holder. He scrambled to collect the debris as she continued. "If certain changes aren't made now, this will be a one-of-a-kind issue, and you will have made a terrible investment."

Those who knew Towers as a man sophisticated in the ways of business and skilled in adversary situations would have been astonished to know how uneasy he felt in Jennifer's presence.

"I don't want Conlon working for me," he said in a way he hoped would discourage argument. "He worked for me once, and it proved to be an unpleasant experience for us both."

Jennifer appeared unmoved by his tone and his explanation. She leaned forward and met his gaze with a directness that startled him.

"I don't want him working for you either. I want him working for me!"

"Even if I agreed," Towers said, "there is no place for Mr. Conlon on staff. Mr. Zorn has done nothing deserving of dismissal, and I feel that demoting him would be detrimental to the esprit de corps."

"I've already taken that into account," Jennifer said with the calmness of one well-rehearsed. "Terk could come in under another title, overseeing both the sales effort and coordinating advertising and editorial. Call him executive sales manager or whatever you like, but get him back!"

"What if I refuse?" Towers said, his mouth becoming tight and dry.

"Then I'll be forced to resign!"

"That's ludicrous," he snapped, angry that she would challenge him in this way, surprised that she would go this far.

"I don't think so. You haven't presented one salient reason for not reinstating Terk. If you insist on clinging to a personal bias in the face of all the facts I've given you, then I'll be compelled to quit and to believe the rumors I've heard about you."

Eben shoved his chair away from his desk, stood, and walked toward the windows, sweat beading up inside his clenched palms. Jennifer's smug confidence unnerved him, so he turned his back on her, gazing instead at the crisp spring sky. After a few minutes, he faced Jennifer.

"And what were these rumors?" he asked.

Jennifer leaned back in her chair. His attitude had changed. She sensed disquietude, agitation, and yet her instincts told her that her threat of resignation was not the sole cause.

"The story that's making the rounds," she said, "is that you promoted me for publicity reasons only. That you never had any intention of allowing me to run Jolie. That you were exploiting me in order to endear yourself and Jolie to the young women who make up our audience."

"That's ridiculous!" He was angry. His mouth screwed into a snarl, and his eyes turned menacing. "It's also extremely egotistical. What makes you think that you're important enough for me to use you as a PR ploy?"

Jennifer rose from her chair, matching his anger. "I don't overestimate my importance, but don't you dare underestimate me either. We both know that the fashion industry is totally dependent on the whims of women. They buy the clothes, and they buy the magazines. Making me the first woman publisher of a fashion book brought you tremendous press coverage. This was a landmark appointment, and there's no way you can tell me it was an accident. It was a clever move, and you deserve congratulations. You've gotten a lot of mileage out of me."

"And you got a title out of me. I'd say we're even!"

His words hit their mark. For years Jennifer had telegraphed her desire for power and influence. He had accused her of being a climber, and she was guilty. She had painted her own portrait, and if she was displeased with the image, she had no one to blame but herself. Forget it, she told herself. Whatever impression he had of her, he had. She was not here to defend past motivations or explain present objectives. She was here to find out what had happened to Terk.

"If you think a single line of bold type on a masthead is enough for me, Mr. Towers, you're dead wrong. I want complete control, not figurehead status. Now either you promise to follow a hands-off policy, or I'll go to the press with tales of exploitation and duplicity."

"That sounds like a threat, dear lady."

"Consider it a bargaining wedge. I don't need this job, nor do I care about the prestige attached to the title, no matter what you think. I care about doing the best job possible, and I can't do it without Terk Conlon!"

Towers strolled back to his desk, his face set in a contemplative pose. He knew Jennifer expected an immediate answer, but he was determined to make her wait, thereby affording himself a small victory. He sat in his chair, stroked his chin, and stared at her in frank admiration. He hadn't expected a grandstand play like this, but he should have. From the first, he had been impressed with her fierce sense of loyalty, and each time he had seen it displayed, his respect for her had increased. He had come to view her as a woman with principles and honor, a woman who did not capitulate for the sake of expediency. She did not renege on a promise, and she did not betray those within her inner circle. She had piloted the magazine to a successful landing, and what was more, Towers knew she would have done it without being rewarded with the publisher's job. So why did it surprise him to hear her defend Conlon? Her strong friendship with Terk was common knowledge, and given her crusader's zeal, it was only natural that she would try to rectify what she considered to be a grievous error. What surprised him, he supposed, was that she would be willing to put her job on the line. For too many years, Towers had concentrated on Terk's faults. It was difficult to believe that someone else was able to find in him virtues worth defending. But Jennifer had, and at that moment, Towers wished he were able to inspire such fealty.

Jennifer too, was beginning to wonder why she had gone to such extremes. Though she managed to appear calm and confident, inside she bubbled like a hot cauldron. So many different thoughts were running through her mind that she felt as if her brain had been chosen as the site of a national marathon. Here, she had gone and demanded that Towers return Terk's job, and she had no way of knowing whether or not Terk would accept it. She didn't even know where Terk was. Maybe he wouldn't want to work for Towers—or with her. Maybe he held her responsible for losing the publisher's chair and bore a grudge. And maybe he was in Europe because he had gone too far. Jennifer was starting to question her own rationality. If Towers did agree to rehire Terk, she figured she could safely assume that he hadn't made good his threat. But she'd have to find him and get him back here before Towers changed his mind. Easy. She'd beg Winnie Walling, bribe her if she had to, to help get him home. Then she'd have to convince him that this job was a good one, one with power and prestige. Not so easy. He had been promised the publisher's seat. This was second best. She knew it, and he'd know it. If she downplayed her position, it might sound patronizing, and if she exaggerated his position, it might sound phony. She was a "have." He was a "have not." And she had what he wanted. She'd work it out, she told herself. She'd work it all out, if only Towers would stop playing games and give her his decision.

"You have my permission to rehire Terk Conlon in whatever capacity you wish." Towers said it simply and quietly. Almost too simply, Jennifer thought. "I admire your loyalty, Jennifer, even though, personally, I think it's misplaced."

He hadn't done it. Terk hadn't shown those films to Towers. Jennifer felt so relieved that she wanted to flop down in the nearest chair and laugh. This whole charade had been worthwhile.

But Jennifer was only partly right. Terk Conlon hadn't shown Towers the tapes. Deirdre Conlon had. And as Eben Towers watched Jennifer leave his office, so triumphant and pleased with herself, he hadn't had the heart to snatch this victory from her. Jennifer had proved herself a fighter, and he admired that, but, thinking back on the first skirmish, he realized that Jennifer lacked something Deirdre Conlon had been born with—the killer instinct.

Deirdre had marched into Towers' office with all the bravura of a leading lady accepting her fourth curtain call. Towers had been expecting Terk. He had anticipated him bursting through the door, and he had been prepared for that confrontation. He hadn't been prepared for Deirdre.

"What can I do for you, Mrs. Conlon?" He led her to a seat opposite his desk and then sat primly in his gray leather chair. Once settled, he leaned back and assumed an executive attitude: distant, distracted, and just shy of patronizing.

Deirdre was unfazed. Slowly, she dropped her lavish fur onto the back of the chair, and surveyed the room. She took her time, crossing her legs and smoothing her skirt, milking the moment long enough to set Towers's teeth on edge.

"I think you know exactly what I want, Mr. Towers. I want you to make good on your obligation to my husband." Her voice was as soft as a purr.

"Excuse me, please?" Towers felt the need to stall. He was at a disadvantage. "I was unaware of the fact that I had any obligation to your husband," he said, stuffing a pencil-slim cigar into an ivory cigarette holder.

"Don't play with me, Towers. My husband embezzled funds from you. You caught him, he confessed, and you set out the terms of his penance."

"That is all true, Mrs. Conlon, but I believe that that implies an obligation on Terk's part, not mine." He puffed on his cigar and then curled his lips into a patient smile. "Let me assure you though, that I've been repaid and have erased Terk's debt from my ledgers."

"That's very kind of you, but I think you're omitting a slight detail. The original agreement called for Terk to repay whatever monies he stole from you, which he did. It was not part of the deal to play lackey. You coerced him into doing dirty tricks for you, Towers, and in return, you promised him the publisher's job at *Jolie*. Feel free to correct me if I'm wrong."

Up to this point, Towers had been wary, but unconcerned. Deirdre was defending her mate, acting out the role of the devoted wife. Perfectly natural. Nothing to worry about. Except that Deirdre Conlon had never been a devoted wife, and she was not known for being natural and conventional. She sat before him, still and stunning, yet he knew not to be seduced by the portrait.

"At one time, I might have considered that possibility," Towers said, "but it seemed unwise to continue the anxiety produced by such an unsettling relationship."

Deirdre leaned forward, rested her chin on her hand, and glared at him. Her blue eyes had turned granite gray, and her coral-tinted lips had stiffened.

"You fucked him!" The voice was kitten soft, but the tone was cold as steel.

Towers was visibly rattled. Suddenly, he suspected that she had not entered this room unarmed. Like a soldier tip-toeing through a mine field, he held his breath while he waited for her to unleash her assault.

"You're not a very honorable man, Eben Towers."

"Neither is your husband."

"True and false."

"Excuse me, please?"

Deirdre smelled his fear; she heard the quiver in his voice, and it delighted her. She wanted him to sweat, to suffer the way Terk was suffering. She had an urge to lash out at him, to punish him for humiliating her husband, but she held back. She was an experienced warrior, and she would wait it out.

"Embezzlement is dishonorable. That much is true. But Terk made good on his debt and at great personal cost. You welshed on your end of the deal, and in any circle, that stinks!"

Towers didn't like the tenor of this conversation. If she

had a weapon, he was going to make her use it. If she didn't, he was going to throw her out of his office.

"Mrs. Conlon, I'm beginning to find this discussion tedious. As far as I'm concerned, I don't owe Terk a thing. He's a crook and God knows what else, so please don't insult either of us by nominating him for sainthood. Your darling mate is a rogue with grandiose dreams."

"That may have been true once," Deirdre said, painfully aware of her role in the construction and destruction of those dreams. "But it's not true anymore. Terk has reassessed his priorities. Titles are secondary; power is a state of mind, and besides, he has all the money he could ever want."

"And that money, my dear, is yours."

"Ours," she corrected. "But since you put it that way, I think Terk should receive certain remuneration for seven years of services rendered. Even though it's grossly inadequate, I'd venture to say that ten thousand a year would do nicely."

"You must be kidding," Towers snapped, crushing his cigar in the nearest ashtray.

"I've never been known for my sense of humor, Mr. Towers."

"You mean to tell me that you want me to pay that thief seventy thousand dollars? You're mad!"

"Not yet, but don't push me." Her voice had hardened, increasing Towers's agitation. He rose and paced around the office while she remained gracefully seated, staring at him like a dignitary from a reviewing stand.

"I want seventy thousand in reparations, and I want Terk to be given an important job at *Jolie*, second in command to Jennifer Cranshaw."

"She would never agree to that and neither would Terk. He seems to feel that anything lower than first place is beneath him."

"Jennifer would be delighted. So would Terk, and so would I."

"I won't hear of it," he said, punctuating his sentence by crossing his arms across his chest in a gesture of defiance. "It's blackmail!"

"You should know. You're an expert at it."

"I resent that. I only demanded that Terk repay what he stole."

"And you extracted a pound of flesh for every dollar. You held an ax over his head for seven years. You made his life miserable, Towers, and mine too. And you're going to pay!"

"I will not! And there's nothing you can do about it."

"That's where you're wrong."

Suddenly, she slid from her chair, went to the door, and locked it. Then, she reached into her handbag and removed a cartridge of video tape. Without uttering so much as a word, she went to his television, turned on the video machine, and slipped in the tape. Towers stood in petrified silence, waiting for a picture to come on the screen. He was so startled at the turn of events that he didn't grasp the significance of what he was witnessing. The picture was dark, the figures were in the distance, and the room was momentarily unfamiliar. Then the camera zoomed closer, and Towers froze. There he was, spread-eagled on a bed, his face pinched in ecstasy as a young blonde boy coated his skin with honey. The hired stud rubbed him, massaged him, and then feasted on him. He heard his own voice begging and pleading, saw his hands grasping at the nubile young man, but the stud ignored him, doing his trick, earning his money. The camera came closer, framing Towers's face, leaving no doubt as to who was in that bed. Towers covered his face with his hands, shuddering because he knew all too well what was next. Another boy, thin and ebony black, climbed onto the bed, his waist girdled in leather, his wrists bound with rope. He sandwiched Towers in between himself and the blonde. Ehen couldn't watch another second of this. He ran to the machine and clicked it off, his body coated in sweat, his clothes sticking to him with a clammy coldness.

"Where did you get this!" he demanded.

"That doesn't matter," Deirdre said. "The fact is that I have it."

"Give me the tape!"

"I don't give gifts," she said, waving it in front of him.

"Then I'll buy it from you." He sounded defeated, beaten, yet Deirdre felt no pity.

"Somehow I thought you'd say that. It'll cost you seventy thousand, and a position at *Jolie* for Terk. That's as good as you're going to get and better than you deserve."

Towers struggled to maintain some semblance of dignity as he walked to his desk and took out his checkbook. His hands shook as he wrote out a check and gave it to Deirdre. She never even looked at it. She simply folded it and slipped it into her purse as if it were nothing more than a shopping list.

"We're leaving for Europe tomorrow, and when we return, you'll make good on the second part of your promise."

Towers nodded vaguely, images of himself and those two young men flashing before his eyes.

"By the way," she called over her shoulder as she neared the door. "Don't mention our little visit to Terk. I want him to think that all this was your idea. Understand?"

He looked at her, consumed with hatred, enflamed with rage. He could have killed her then, strangled her without so much as an afterthought, but he was too weak to move. The door slammed, and his body jolted at the sound. Suddenly he was surrounded by the numbing silence of failure. He had always considered himself a master manipulator, a skillful schemer, but he had been outwitted. Perhaps he had underestimated Terk. Certainly, he had underestimated Deirdre. He stared at the tape, almost afraid to touch it at first. Then he picked it up and as he held it, he wondered if perhaps the problem was that he had overestimated himself.

Thirty-Five

J ennifer's life had become a waiting game—waiting to
see the figures on an upcoming issue, waiting to hear
from Terk, waiting for the next meeting, the next appointment. Her days had evolved into a scheduled same-
ness, her nights a calendar with vacant squares. Soon, she
found herself walking around in a somnambulant state,
fighting off the hollow echoes that seemed determined to
follow her. Where was the exaltation she had expected to
find at the top? Where was the excitement of a constant
challenge? The thrill of achievement? She was publisher
of *Jolie,* yet something was missing. Her existence had
narrowed to a straight line, no ups, no downs, no meaning.

Fits of loneliness attacked her with increasing fre-
quency. Thoughts she managed to fend off during the day
asserted themselves under the cover of darkness. Half-
dreams that merged fantasy with reality battered her
consciousness, disturbing her when she was awake, haunting her when she tried to sleep. One dream repeated itself
with unsettling regularity. She was sitting behind a desk
with hordes of people seated around her. The desk started
to grow, getting larger and larger until it was impossible
to see over it. Frantically, she climbed up onto it, looking
down, straining to see. She crawled out to the edge, calling for her father, Josh, her mother. She bent over,
flailing her arms, screaming into the void. Suddenly, she
fell. No one was there to catch her.

Each time the dream occurred, it jarred Jennifer, and
again, she tried to understand what she had done with her
life and why. How many times had her mother reached
out to her, and she had smacked Rose's hands away with
sharp comments and disapproving stares? How many
times had David tried to guide her, Sarah tried to comfort
her? Even her coworkers had offered their hands in

friendship, and she had politely, yet firmly kept them at arm's length. She had pushed them all away, just as she had pushed Josh. Isolation had become a habit, her career an excuse for distance.

Night after night, the dream taunted her, dragging her deeper and deeper into herself. Yet each morning, the burden seemed lighter, and that encouraged her to continue. This morning, she finally faced her dream and all its implications. She had created a vacuum, and now she had to fill it. What had she been so afraid of? That people might get too close? That they might get to know her? Or that they might discover she didn't really know herself.

But I am getting to know myself. She propped herself up in bed and reviewed her list of assets and liabilities, successes and failures. Assets: bright, able, pretty, hardworking. Liabilities: stubborn, demanding, prideful, reserved. Successes: job. Failures: personal life. She repeated the list again and again, adding, subtracting, analyzing, judging. *I am who I am,* she thought, *and what's more, I like me!*

For the first time in ages, Jennifer allowed herself to smile, and it felt wonderful. She felt buoyed by self-confidence, elated by self-discovery. Even her back, which had grown tortuously tight, felt looser and less painful. As she eased her way out of bed, she decided to do something special that night. The stores were open late. Maybe she'd go shopping. Maybe she'd call Elyse, and the two of them would go to a movie. Maybe she'd call David and Sarah and have dinner with them. Or maybe she'd call Josh.

Jennifer rearranged the flowers in the centerpiece, realigned the wine glasses, and fussed with the silverware, nudging a fork closer to the edge of the table, then pushing it back toward the plate. Three times she lit the candles, and three times she blew them out. She checked her watch and then checked herself in the mirror. Nothing had changed since the last time she had looked. Her hair was full and lustrous, her makeup soft and subtle, her white cashmere sweater and silk pants a perfect blend of sultry sophistication. She could smell the veal roasting in the kitchen and reminded herself that the wine was chilling in an ice bucket on the bar. It had taken all day to decide what to cook and what to wear. Now, she had second thoughts on both.

The doorbell rang, and Jennifer ran to the mirror again, licking her lips, fluffing her hair, smoothing her slacks, and taking a deep breath. Her hand felt moist as she turned the doorknob. The minute she saw him, she knew she had done the right thing.

"Hi." Josh handed her a bouquet of flowers and walked past her into the foyer. She could tell by his unsteady smile that he was as nervous as she was.

"I'm glad you could make it," she said, closing the door and following him into the living room.

"Everything looks lovely," he said, noticing the soft lighting and the delicate fragrance that perfumed the air, noticing too the absence of a third place setting on the table. "You didn't have to go to any trouble just for me."

"I felt like it," she said brightly, ignoring his unspoken question, for now allowing him to come to his own conclusions about Charles. "It's spring. The weather is glorious. And we haven't seen each other in a very long time." She waited for a response, but there was none. "Why don't you fix yourself a drink while I put these flowers in water."

When she returned, Josh was seated on the couch. He had poured a glass of white wine for her, Scotch for himself. Jennifer hesitated for a second, and then seated herself across from him.

"I understand that Jolie is a rousing success under your leadership. Congratulations." He raised his glass to her and then gulped his drink.

"Thank you," she said, feeling the strain between them. "And congratulations on your partnership with Elyse. She tells me her designs are walking out of the stores."

He nodded. Jennifer picked up a tray of canapés and held it out to him.

"How's your father doing?" he asked, biting into a cheese puff.

"Great. He's getting settled in, meeting new people. I hear he's seen a lot of your parents." He nodded again. "How are the children?" Jennifer hated the awkward silences.

"Great. They send you their love."

They were running out of conversation, and Jennifer was getting anxious. They were like strangers going through their social paces, asking the expected questions, responding with the expected answers.

"How do you like working with Eben Towers? Industry scuttlebutt pegs him as a real taskmaster."

Jennifer had hoped to steer the conversation in another direction, but because she couldn't think of anything else to talk about and because she valued his advice, she told Josh all about her recent meeting with Towers, recounting the details of Towers's abortive relationship with Terk and Terk's threat of blackmail.

"The whole situation scares me," she said. "Towers is manipulative and vengeful, and I can't believe he would have cared whether I walked out or not. He could have replaced me in a minute. Why did he give in? And why so easily?"

Josh sensed that Jennifer was genuinely troubled, and it bothered him that she had been prepared to sacrifice her job for Terk. It was something she never would have done for him.

"Maybe Towers's mind had been made up long before you ever walked into his office," Josh said. "Maybe he had extracted his revenge the night of the Starks' party. From what you tell me, Terk was properly humiliated."

"Possible, but somehow I can't get those films out of my mind. They make a powerful weapon," she said.

"Your friend Conlon has done some shady things in the past, Jennie, but I don't think he's suicidal. He spoke out of anger. People say a lot of things they don't mean when they're angry."

The sudden clang of the telephone jolted them both. Jennifer jumped to answer it, and the instant she said hello, Josh knew who was on the other end.

"You can't imagine how relieved I am to hear your voice." Jennifer scrambled back onto the couch, put the phone on her lap, and tucked her legs underneath her. "I've been calling you all over Europe. Where the hell are you?"

Josh sipped his drink and watched Jennifer. Terk Conlon's whereabouts were of no concern to him. Obviously they were very important to Jennifer.

"When are you coming back?"

Jennifer's thick mane of auburn hair was tousled, her eyes suddenly bright and alive. Josh marveled at how, after all these years, her beauty still affected him. Her sweater had dipped down off her shoulder and the sight of her flesh was extremely inviting. She was a sensuous woman. It was difficult for him to be with her without wanting her.

"Terk, don't be vague. I have to know when you're coming back. . . . You do have a reason. I went to Towers. He's agreed to offer you the executive sales manager slot. . . . I know how you feel about him, but I need you. . . . Don't be funny."

Josh winced. He felt jealous and immediately chided himself for being juvenile. Their paths had taken them in separate directions, into other beds and the arms of other lovers, but somehow, he hated the thought of another man knowing the softness of her flesh and the warmth of her embrace. Even her husband.

"We're a good team, Conlon, and you know it, but if you wait too long, Towers will find a way to finagle his way out of this, and I will personally break both your legs! . . . Second honeymoon? Great. I'm happy for you both, but do me a favor. Don't extend this little honeymoon until your golden anniversary."

Though her tone was light, Josh could see how tense she was. Her fingers curled the telephone wire until it was tight as a spring. Jennifer needed Terk on her team, and Josh understood that. No matter how talented a leader, the more qualified the staff, the greater the success.

"Don't tell me you can't come back just yet. . . . Why? Because it makes me nervous, like you're waiting out some statute of limitations. . . . But I am serious. Terk, did you show Towers those films?"

Josh watched a brief smile flick across Jennifer's lips.

"I thought you had. I thought . . . well, never mind what I thought. But if you're not playing Butch Cassidy, why can't you come home?"

Jennifer's eyes widened and then narrowed. Josh saw the glimmer of moisture, and his curiosity piqued. Whatever Terk was saying had greatly affected Jennifer. Josh wanted to cross over to the other couch, take the phone away, and cradle her in his arms. But there was something protective about her attitude, the way she stared into the phone and held the receiver with both hands, caressing it as if to soothe away Terk's distress via long distance. Josh remained in his seat, hurting for her, hurting for himself.

He had known Jennifer since adolescence, and now, observing her, he pondered the changes he had been witness to over the years. From the first, Jennifer had been an amalgam of insecurities and derring-do, bold determination and perishable vulnerability. He had seen her suffer great physical pain and endure it stoically, but then again, he had seen her sob over the trauma of being deserted and forgotten by her friends. Those years had rewritten her reality, creating a chasm that demanded to be filled. Jennifer had filled it with fantasy. What hurt was that her fantasies hadn't included him.

Josh was so engrossed in his own reverie that it took him a few seconds to realize that Jennifer had put down the phone. A veil of sadness had draped itself over her eyes, broken only by the tears which dropped unchecked down her cheeks. Josh moved to her side, holding her, feeling her tremble against him.

"Do you want to talk about it?" he asked gently.

He felt her shoulders shrug against his chest.

"Is Terk coming back?"

She didn't answer. He handed her a handkerchief, which she used to wipe her eyes. He felt her breathe deeply and knew she was trying to regain her control.

"Does this have anything to do with Towers?"

Jennifer lifted herself up and leaned back into the couch, away from him, as if she needed privacy. She stared at him, but he could tell she didn't see him. She was regrouping, absorbing what she had been told, digesting it before she shared it. When she did speak, her voice was low, her phrasing measured.

"Terk has a child," she said. "A son, by Zena Welles. When she left him, eight years ago, she was pregnant, only she never told him. She gave the child away, and now Terk and Deirdre are searching for him." The tears began again, and her lips trembled as she attempted to halt them. "How could she?"

Josh heard the disgust and the disapproval, but clinging to her words was a whisper of envy. He took her hand and stroked it, knowing that her response had just as much to do with her as it did with Zena.

"Zena and Terk had a fight several months ago," she continued, suddenly speaking faster, as if to cleanse herself of the story. "She told him about the child, but refused to tell him anything more. The only clue he had to go on was that she had had the baby in Switzerland."

She picked up her wine glass and swirled the liquid around, looking for answers and motives.

"Deirdre has turned out to be a terrific lady," she said. "When Terk told her, she insisted that they go to Europe immediately. They found the hospital, and they've even unearthed the name of the adoptive parents, but they've moved around quite a bit, and Terk and Deirdre have had trouble tracking them down."

"Maybe that's for the best," Josh said quietly.

"How can you say that? Terk has a child he's never seen."

"And that child probably doesn't know anything about Terk. For eight years, this little boy has been loved and cared for by two people he considers his parents. What happens to him if and when Terk barges in to claim him? Is it fair to take the boy away from the only home he's ever known? I feel for Terk, but I also feel for the child."

"I wasn't thinking about the boy. I was thinking about Zena Welles and wondering how she could have given her own baby away just because Terk wouldn't marry her."

Josh left the couch, refreshed his drink, and debated with himself. If he were honest, he would have to say things that might upset Jennifer further, and that was the last thing he wanted to do. The phone call had rattled her, and she looked like a fragile gardenia, all white and pale, crushed in the corner of the white sofa.

"Maybe putting the child up for adoption had nothing to do with her relationship with Terk," he said.

"What does that mean?" She sounded defensive, and she regretted it, but her antennae had tuned in to his thoughts and picked up an approaching criticism.

"From what you've told me and from what I know about Zena Welles and her rise to celebrity, I'd guess that she might have toyed with the idea of having the child and Terk, but then came to view them both as encumbrances, burdens that might have weighed her down on her climb up the ladder of success."

"And people in glass houses shouldn't throw stones. Is that what you're saying?" She felt her composure slipping away, but she was helpless to stop it.

"What I'm saying is that sometimes things are not always clear-cut. I'm sure Zena loved Terk at the time and held onto illusions of marriage and white picket fences and chocolate chip cookies. Everyone has illusions, but when her bubble burst and Terk didn't leave Deirdre, she had to cling to what she knew best, and that was her work. She made a choice, and you shouldn't be so quick to condemn her."

"Because I'm no better than Zena Welles? Because you think I used ambition as a method of contraception? Because deep down you think I would have done the same thing?"

Jennifer was shaking, reeling at the thrust of her own words.

"No, as a matter of fact, I don't," Josh said, maintaining the distance between them, sad that it was there to begin with. "But, if you're honest with yourself, you'll admit that you're glad you were never faced with the decision."

Jennifer rose from the couch and walked over to the windows. The blinds were pulled up, and she could see the rippling waters of the East River stretched out before her. A tugboat chugged along, fighting the tide. Jennifer, too, felt conflicting currents pulling at her. Once again, Josh had confronted her with a truth she had fought to avoid, but instead of agreeing with him, something inside her rebelled.

"How dare you speak to me about honesty?" she said, practically spitting the words at him. "Why didn't you tell me about Coral Trent and the night Laura died?"

Her question knocked the wind out of him. Only one person could have told Jennifer that story, and it was unlikely that David would have betrayed a confidence in the course of casual conversation. When did he tell her? And why?

"I want an answer," she snapped. Tension had become anger, and he sensed that it had been building for a long time.

"It didn't have anything to do with you," he said.

"It had everything to do with me." Her voice lowered to a cold whisper, and her eyes glared at him. "I threw myself at you, and you rejected me without ever telling me why."

"But I did tell you. I said I wanted an honest commitment, not a back-street affair." Although it was the truth, it suddenly sounded lame, even to him.

Months of repressed hurt bubbled to the surface. Jennifer hadn't intended to attack him this way, but the deep insult she had suffered hit her all over again.

"You sat in that restaurant preaching to me about pretense and image while all the time you were keeping secrets so you could protect your own precious image. That's known as a double standard, my friend."

Her words stabbed at Josh like tiny knives. For an odd instant, it wasn't Jennifer confronting him. It was Laura, accusing him of infidelity, demanding an explanation. He wouldn't have had any answers for Laura. He wasn't sure he had any for Jennifer.

"How much did David tell you?"

"Enough."

"Then can't you understand that I couldn't interfere? That I couldn't handle the responsibility of breaking up your marriage?"

"I used to think you could handle anything." Her voice rang with disappointment.

"I'm not perfect, Jen, and if that's what you thought, I'm sorry."

"Sorry's not good enough!" She began to pace like an animal that had just picked up the scent of an enemy. Her mind raced and her back throbbed, forcing her to grab onto a chair for support. "Dump Charles, you said. Do it now, you said. And when I didn't dance to your tune, you punished me. You tossed me over like so much excess baggage. Is that how you treated your wife?"

Jennifer heard her own words, and for the first time that night, she really looked at Josh. A terrible pain lined his face.

"Now it's my turn to be sorry," she said. "I went too far."

"Yes, you did." Josh turned his back on her, and a hostile chill filled the air.

For a long time, they both were silent, as if waiting for a blackboard to be erased so they could start over again.

"I shouldn't have taken you on like that. I haven't been totally honest either." Jennifer's voice was hushed, uncertain. "My marriage ended that night we met in the restaurant. Charles hasn't lived here in months."

Josh didn't know whether to laugh or scream. The entire evening was bizarre. He hadn't seen or spoken to her in so long that when she called, he had been hesitant, but hopeful. Instead of a reconciliation, he was being assaulted by one horrible surprise after another.

"Why didn't you tell me sooner?" he asked.

She inched her way back to the window, keeping her back to him, as if it were easier to speak to the darkness. "Pride. Anger. A sense of failure I couldn't deal with."

"Were you afraid I'd pass judgment? Obviously, I'm in no position to do that." He made no attempt to hide his sarcasm.

Jennifer turned around, remaining by the window. "Charles is a homosexual." Josh's expression never changed. His jaw was set, his cheekbones rigid. "After I left you that night, I wandered around for a few hours. I had told Charles I was going to spend the weekend in Bayonne. When I went home, he was in bed with another man."

Josh winced, shaking his head in disbelief.

"For a long time, I was furious. I was hurt and confused and probably ten other things that I can't name right now. I spent hours blaming first Charles and then myself. I began to believe it was my fault. That I hadn't been enough of a woman."

"Nothing could be further from the truth," Josh said gently. He wanted to comfort her, but clearly, she was embarrassed. Her eyes were lowered, and her shoulders were stooped. "Is that why you went away? To try and make sense out of what happened with Charles?"

"I had to make sense out of a lot of things," she said, lifting her eyes and looking at him. "Charles. My mother's death. Me. Us."

"Did you come to any conclusions?"

"I thought so. When I came back, I thought I was ready to settle down. With you, if you'd have me. But then I was made publisher of Jolie."

"So what!" The rage he had been controlling began to break out of its leash. "What does one thing have to do with another?"

"It's a big responsibility." She was insistent, defensive.

"So is running JM Industries, but it doesn't have any bearing on the rest of my life."

Tears of frustration welled up in her eyes, but she refused to let them fall. Words formed in her mouth, but she refused to let them out.

"Why did you invite me here tonight, Jennie? To ask me to wait while you made up your mind whether or not you love me? Forget it. I'm finished playing games with you."

Without saying another word, Josh put his drink down on the bar and started for the door. Jennifer remained by the windows, transfixed, unable to move. She heard the door close, and suddenly, the fragile façade she had maintained over all these months shattered, smashing her emotions into tiny, tearful fragments.

"Don't go!" she shouted. She started to run after him. A sharp pain pierced her spine, causing her to trip and fall. In a panic, she willed herself to her feet, catching up to Josh just as he reached the elevator.

"I planned such a beautiful evening. I'm sorry. I didn't mean to . . ." Her voice broke. "I love you," she cried. "Love me back. Please. Don't leave."

Her words bounced off the walls of the hallway, ringing

in Josh's ears like an alarm clock jostling him out of a deep sleep. He had waited so long to hear her say that she loved him, that he couldn't react. He just stood there, staring at her.

The elevator door opened, and the elevator man poked his head out. "Anyone going down?" Jennifer's heart pounded in her chest. Each second felt like an eternity.

"No," Josh said. "Thanks anyway."

Jennifer felt weak with relief. "Come back inside. We'll talk." She reached for his hand, but still, he didn't move.

"We've talked enough." His eyes were dark and serious. "I've loved you for a very long time, Jennie, and I love you now, but this is a one-time offer. You can take it or leave it, but if you turn me down this time, you'll never get another shot." Slowly, a sly smile curled his lips. "You have sixty seconds."

Jennifer flung her arms around him. "I don't need sixty seconds," she said, loving him more than she ever had before.

A huge smile lit Josh's face as he pulled her to him and kissed her.

"I'm so lucky to have you. I should have married you years ago," she said as he lifted her off the floor and into his arms.

"Yes, you are, and yes, you should have." His lips nuzzled the soft flesh of her neck as he walked back into her apartment, heading straight for the bedroom.

She wrapped her arms around his neck and kissed him, luxuriating in the familiar feel of his mouth, the familiar taste of his tongue. As he set her down, he lifted off her sweater, his hands pressing against her back. His touch affected her like an electric charge, sending needlelike prickles coursing through her body. She slipped off her clothes and lay down on the bed, waiting for him, allowing her own excitement to build. The minute he was next to her, something ignited, and she clutched at him with a passion she had never felt before.

She felt different, eager, anxious to fuse herself to him in such a way that they'd never be separated again. As his fingers stroked her, she knew why. She had committed herself to him, not only with her body, but with her heart and her mind as well.

Jennifer drew Josh to her, wanting all of him, needing to give him all of her. His love surrounded her, wrapping her with voluptuous contentment. As she continued to hold him, she felt the faint trickle of happy tears. At last, she had reached out and made her connection. At last, she had formed her circle.

ABOUT THE AUTHOR

Circles is DORIS MORTMAN's first novel. A former fashion editor at a magazine very much like *Jolie*, she is an avid golfer and a fanatic Yankee fan. She lives in New Jersey with her two children and her husband, an attorney.

"AN ENORMOUS, ENGROSSING FEAST"
—The New York Times Book Review

THE MADNESS
OF A
SEDUCED WOMAN

by Susan Fromberg Schaeffer
author of ANYA

Agnes Dempster is a mysteriously beautiful woman who has shielded her heart against anything but a perfect love. Not until she meets one dynamic man does she experience the first awakenings of all-consuming passion. To him she gives herself completely, joyously, desperately. Until betrayal demands from her a terrible and unforgiving vengeance....

"A remarkable book.... A riveting, intricate and altogether astonishing novel."
—Alice Walker, author of THE COLOR PURPLE

Read THE MADNESS OF A SEDUCED WOMAN, on sale August 1, 1984, wherever Bantam paperbacks are sold or use the handy coupon below for ordering: